The Beehive Cluster

A Novel for all Ages

Rosemary Pavey

The Midnight Oil Artisan Press
2013

Published by The Midnight Oil Artisan Press 2013

Cover illustration and design by Rosemary Pavey

The Midnight Oil Artisan Press
www.paveypenandpaint.com

Printed by CreateSpace

ISBN: 987-0-9927463-0-8

To K,

who never gives up!

Acknowledgement

My grateful thanks to all who have helped me in the creation of this book and without whose patience and goodwill nothing could have been accomplished.

Quotations are from 'Day Hours' pub. A.R. Mowbray 1959
Chapter 36: At Compline p.233 Responses and p.233 Hymn
ll.5-7
Chapter 39: At Vespers p.216 Psalm 144 v.5 and v.7.

The Author

Rosemary Pavey was born in 1960 and works as a writer and painter in Sussex, dividing her time between her studio at the Turner Dumbrell Workshops, Ditchling, and Stoneywish, a local Nature Reserve.

Other forthcoming Books by Rosemary Pavey include:

The Magpie's Nest – a novel
Painting and Chaos
Christmas Ghosties – Tales for a Winter Night

To find out more about any of these or exhibitions, talks and other events please visit: www.paveypenandpaint.com

Contents

Part One: Introit. Christmas

Part Two: Processional. Easter

Part Three: Octave Simples and Doubles. Half Term

Contents Cont'd.

Part Four: Antiphon. Midsummer

Part Five: Vigil. Feast of St. John

Part One

Introit. Christmas

Chapter One

On the Boat

Trudi leant forward into the icy darkness, resting her chin on the rail of the ferry and searched for the lights that would signal land ahead.

The sea was calm, silvered a little against the side of the boat. Overhead, a scattering of stars. Behind her, she could hear the noise of passengers on board - some drunken youths singing in the bar, a baby crying, excited children scampering up and down the deck. They were all going to the Christmas Market in Vargsberg. They were going to see the real reindeer and Swedish snow and breathe in the hot, spicy aroma of glogg, Sweden's festive punch.

Behind her, too, just on a little bench by the stern, she could hear her parents talking and a cosy sense of excitement crystallised inside her. *Remember this*, she told herself, taking another gulp of frozen air and tucking the end of her plait into her mouth. *Later, when I'm grown up - remember this. I'm eleven years old - just at the beginning of everything and I'm going back to my family's homeland to start a new adventure. This is the beginning of everything that really matters - not going to the Christmas market, though of course we will do that too - but stepping out of the everyday life of school and home and all the routine, boring things that have to be done in England - to be somewhere utterly different. We are on our way to visit my own Swedish grandfather and where Grandfather Larsson lives, there is nothing boring. There are bears and wolves and wild cloudberries. Danger and magic.*

Trudi remembered Per's house from her earliest visit, with all the vividness of a dream. And she remembered the man who had then appeared so unbelievably old, whose voice rumbled deep in his boots and whose dazzling blue eyes had filled her with wonder. Jurgen, her younger brother, said you couldn't remember what you saw when you were three. He had heard the grown-ups say so. But when Grandfather Larsson came to stay in the summer, his voice was just as she recalled it - a little feebler, perhaps, because he had been ill - but his eyes could still blaze with an arctic severity.

From the moment he entered the house, a disquieting draught of northern air seemed to blow in with him. It got into the cupboards and under the beds and it whistled through the leaves in the garden. It brought whispers of far off times and places, and scattered the household's careful arrangements. But to Trudi it was a breath of enchantment. Everything about the old man confirmed that memory from eight years ago and convinced her she had been right all along: Grandfather Larsson was a very exceptional person. And, curious and fascinated, she tried every way she knew to worm her way into his confidence. Per had led a harsh life as a forester and a hunter in Sweden. That much she knew. And he had travelled. His experiences were etched in the rugged lines of his face, and in his huge, sensitive hands that could fashion things with such dexterity. He had seen the Northern Lights in Samiland and talked with shamans. He had weathered blizzards and battles and encounters with wolves. Deep inside him stretched a hidden world, so vast, Trudi could only peep from the edge and hold her breath. And within that vastness, she stood convinced, lay secrets beyond imagining.

Nothing from that unfenced, uncharted place fitted into the bite-sized existence where normal people like the Larssons lived. Life in their world was a timetable, conveniently parcelled and labelled, to be taken, like medicine, throughout the day. Two p.m: double chemistry. Three p.m: piano lesson. Three-thirty: check text messages. Five p.m: t.v. Seven p.m: homework - a download or an upload - a programme, a game on the computer. But time for Per had neither beginning nor end. And once Trudi had glimpsed the scale of it, she could not get it out of her mind. When her grandfather returned to Sweden, Trudi felt that part of her went with him. Suddenly it no longer mattered whether she was captain at hockey or not. She dawdled and was late for choir. She forgot to complete her homework. She even felt bored by the deluge of information in class. And people noticed and began to worry.

Miss Protheroe put her finger on it at the school parents' evening: "Trudi promised to be such an outgoing girl. So lively and keen to participate. We wonder if everything is all right at home?"

Trudi's mother inwardly writhed. Her children had never been doubted before. Nonetheless, she put on her best face: "Well, you know, she did have that terrible experience last summer. And it's bound to take time for the wounds to heal."

"Oh quite. We do understand. Being attacked by a dog is a dreadful thing for anyone. Thank goodness her grandfather was there to step in."

Kirsten's reluctant smile showed that, for her, the blessing came at a price. Of course she was grateful. She would remain forever indebted to the man who had saved her daughter and during the days that followed the affair she had come to tolerate, no, even indulge his eccentricities. But the draught that Per let in from Sweden brought her only shivers of anxiety. Life had been so simple before: just the four of them and their studies and their hobbies - everything going so well. Now there was this subversive *something* in their midst, and it boded no good for any of them.

Trudi refused to have anything to do with the school psychiatrist. She insisted that she was not at all bothered about the dog bite. She bore the scar on her arm as a trophy in class and assured everyone that, if anything, she now liked dogs better than before. She simply had lots to think about and she enjoyed being alone with her thoughts.

This trip, for instance, was rich food for thought. They were going to spend Christmas with Per in his little wooden house in the forest. It was incredible to think that they would soon be sitting by his stove and listening to the ice snapping in the trees outside. Trudi let the idea expand like a leaf unfolding. There would be stars and candles and pickled herring and something wonderful was sure to happen. She felt so certain. Per would see to it. He had as good as promised her so on the telephone. "Trudi," he confided, only days before they left. "Bring with you the Sami belt I gave you. Something bad is happening here and I think we may need it." The Sami belt was a shaman's belt Per had picked up in the Arctic. And a shaman's belt meant magic.

She did not hear her father come up behind.

"Dreaming, Trudi?" he murmured, putting his arms around her and gripping the rail in front. She felt his cheek, warm against her own as he stooped and scanned the horizon. His curly beard tickled. "What can you see?"

3

She gave him an evasive smile.

"Nothing." She could not share her thoughts with a grown-up, not even with Sven. Marvellous as he was, she knew her father would not understand.

He had a boyish, uncomplicated view of life. Oh, he was clever, all right. He gave lectures all over the world about plants and the forests they lived in. That was his job. His study at home bulged with crumpled specimens, lovingly labelled and numbered. But the knowledge was in his head. He didn't talk to his plants. He didn't hear what their dark hearts were saying, as Per did, and as she sometimes thought she did. No, dearly as she loved him, Trudi felt he was too innocent to understand such matters.

Sven winked and tapped his nose. "Secrets - eh!" he laughed. "Now look, over there. That is Vargsberg harbour."

Trudi turned to her left. She had mistakenly assumed that the lights would be straight ahead, but here they were now, red and green and pricks of apricot, strung out in a line.

"Come and eat something. It won't be long before we're there." And he bundled her away from the side.

Her mother sat on the bench with Jurgen unpacking the last of the food. She looked so slim, so elegant in her soft woollen cowl and winter coat.

"Trudi, have some of this now. We may not have time later. And *do* stop sucking your hair, darling - it looks so awful." She gave a reproving smile and handed her a paper package. Jurgen had already plundered his. There was soup in an insulated beaker and miniature pasties and seedy rolls stuffed with egg and dill. In a separate twist of paper, star-shaped gingerbreads and little golden buns with curly, raisin-studded tails. Kirsten surveyed the feast in dismay:

"Dear heavens! *Look* at this! Whatever has the woman put in here?"

Trudi knew exactly what her mother was thinking. She was thinking that it was unhealthy to eat so much pastry, but Trudi's mouth began to water at the sight of the food so lovingly prepared and something tickled beneath her ribs, as if her heart had moved, or skipped a beat.

4

Auntie Barbara had made the picnic back home in Newbridge. She had arrived all hot and flustered as they were loading up the car and hugged them in her fat arms and kissed them goodbye.

"These are for you to eat on the journey," she said in her broad American accent. "You mustn't starve them, Kirsten! These are for the car, and these are for the ferry. And these are for when you get there - and don't squash *those*. They are pepper biscuits for Grandpa to put on his tree!"

Kirsten took a deep breath and grimaced. "Barbara, you don't need to do this." Barbara was her oldest and dearest friend, but she always overstepped the mark. "We can get food on the boat. And in Sweden, at the Christmas Market, there will be more pepparkakor than you can possibly imagine."

Barbara, unstoppable, waved all objections aside. "Oh, Kirsten, don't be so antiseptic!" Trudi knew that Barbara would overrule her mother. Somehow she always did. Her blunt good-humour simply flattened opposition. She went on scolding and wagging her head till her brown topknot wobbled and her eyes shone. "These are from *me* to Grandpa, for *Christmas!* *I* mixed 'em up. *I* rolled 'em out. *I* put on the icing. *You* may not understand but *he* will! Mine will also be better than anything you can buy!" she added, which was almost certainly true. Then she folded her arms, so that was *that!*

Kirsten could only sigh and give a suffering smile of thanks. You couldn't argue with Barbara.

But Trudi was glad that Barbara broke the rules. It was comforting now to think that her chubby fingers had arranged the biscuits so; Trudi traced their sugar patterns affectionately with her own, then sat beside Jurgen and laid them on her lap.

"I'll bet you those two buns that Chelsea lost their game this afternoon," Jurgen began.

Trudi, absorbed in her thoughts, had no intention of playing. "I'm not betting."

"You're scared you'll lose."

"I don't care about football!"

"It's not about football - it's about buns." Jurgen cared about both. He was feeling sore that he had missed the match. It seemed a bore to be away from his friends and his home at this time of year.

"Well eat your own. I'm not interested."

How he hated it when Trudi was so superior. He made a grab at one of her cookie-stars, just for fun, to stir her up a bit. But she hit back and the biscuits bounced onto the deck and crumbled.

"That's it!" Kirsten began to fold the bags away. "No fighting. Pass the things back you two. It's almost time to find the car anyway. And you've been so good till now. You don't need to show us up here. Can't you see? People are looking."

"Yes, yes. When we get to the hotel - then you can poke each other's eyes out as much as you want!" Sven confided, with a wink.

At that moment, the ferry loudspeakers played a little tune: *"Attention please. Attention. Would passengers from non-EU countries please proceed to Passport Control. Thank you."*

Chastened, they handed back their papers. Jurgen gave one final kick and Trudi one look of disdain and they made a temporary truce. The prospect of arriving was too interesting for other diversions and now that the passengers were crowding the exits, they would need all their wits just to stay together.

"Bet you the rest of your biscuits that you fall over before I do on the ice," Trudi hissed as they shuffled along. Her spirits were rising.

Jurgen considered it and decided the odds were good for him. First, he was a boy and they had better balance than girls. And secondly, Trudi was impulsive about snow and more likely to take a risk. "What will you give me if I win?" he countered.

A pause.

"Give me your amulet," he teased, knowing she would not agree.

Trudi brushed him off. "No way!"

"Give me your amulet."

"I'll give you a thump! You can have my silver-gel pen."

"What would I want a girlie thing like that for?"

"All right. You can have what's left of my chocolate reindeer."

"Done!"

Trudi put her hand instinctively to her throat. The wooden amulet that Grandfather Larsson had made her in the summer was still there on its string, an exact replica of the good-luck charm his own mother had given him when he was a baby. It had the shape of

6

a Sami hunting bow - good against bears and fevers and the cruelty of the north wind. She would never be without it now. It was her courage and Per had confided to her that she would need a deal of that in the life that lay before her. This 'something that was happening', for instance, would it be as dangerous and exciting as Per's last adventure with the dog?

As a rule he never used the telephone. But when he asked for her the other evening he sounded like a conspirator. "No need to tell the others, eh?"

"What did he say?" asked Jurgen, straightaway sensing something was up.

And Trudi lied without hesitation. "He said don't forget to bring gloves and ear-muffs. It will be very cold."

But her heart had slipped and was adding an odd beat now and then. There *was* a secret, just as she thought, and it was going to be her secret very soon.

Chapter Two

The Christmas Market

The impulsive Trudi wanted her adventure *right away*, but first there were delays and disappointments, for time moves in different ways for adults and for children.

Children live in an eternal now, but grown-ups... grown-ups need *plans*. They love nothing better than devising lists of tasks for themselves so that their time is sliced up into strings of appointments and phone calls and shopping trips... interminable preparations. Children spend frustrated hours, waiting for these lists to end. But as soon as they slip away to their own secret world and find something absorbing to do, something really important, like digging a hole or talking to a worm, why then the parents protest: *"Come along darling! Stop dreaming! No time for that now. Don't you want an ice cream?"*

An eleven-year-old, who is not yet indentured to the future, drifts through life like a hostage on a boat. They have a foot in either world. They want to get on, but they want to savour life too. When they grow up, they think, they will steer a different course - do away with chores and duties. How different things will be! How free! But of course that never happens. Before they know it, they find they have become list-makers too! They are already in a hurry. *'Where did time go?'* they wonder, feeling suddenly old. It has slipped away while they were busy and the long days of childhood are gone forever.

On that first day in Sweden, the Larssons went to the Botanic Gardens in Vargsberg so that Sven could deliver a tree. It didn't look much of a tree to Trudi, just a stick in a pot, but her father insisted it was very rare and precious - a bristle-cone pine, whose great-great grandparents were the oldest living things on earth. And if we didn't look after them, they could simply disappear.

Well, if anybody knew about these things, then Sven did. While he talked to important people, Kirsten and the children wandered round the exhibits, past seemingly endless specimens of things that were endangered in the wild, but, though Trudi knew that it was all very important, and that something must be done to save the disappearing forests, it was hard to get a feel for the plants in their hot-houses. After that, Kirsten wanted to see the shops and they trailed behind her through the Salutorg, the city's market place. Somehow, despite its impressiveness, Vargsberg did not feel a suitable place to begin a tale of mystery and danger - too bright, too modern with its cosmopolitan department stores and blocks of municipal buildings. The gardens looked so neat, the canal so confined. Perhaps Trudi was tired. Perhaps she was dreaming of something which could not really exist. In the afternoon, they made their way to Isandeland.

And there was no denying that Isandeland was different. If magic could be parcelled and sold by the metre, then the Christmas Market had all you could ever wish to buy. Sights, sounds, scents, nothing had been forgotten. In the blue, fading afternoon, the trees sparkled with millions of lights, and the air rang with happy voices. There were little wooden stalls beneath the trees, fragrant with seasonal food and choirs in embroidered costumes, singing carols. The music floated out - past a café carved in ice, where the drinks, decanted from a crystal swan, were served in ice-mould glasses - past gangs of pantomime elves distributing presents, and on up to the treetops and the winter stars. Yet still something still did not feel right. The magic *almost* took off. Trudi so wanted it to. But then she could not help noticing that the snow was not real snow - it was made in a vast refrigerator - and the reindeer in 'Lappland' looked lost and bored.

"Want to stroke one?" asked the reindeer man. Trudi really did. The animals were smaller than she had imagined, but exquisite in every detail, with soft dark eyes and splayed feet. Their breath steamed hot. The one standing nearest shook her head and her bell jangled. Trudi remembered what her grandfather had told her about the great herds that ran in the Arctic. They lived on lichen and they were as wise as the wolves that once tracked them. When they pulled a Sami sledge, their bells clapped out a tune like the wind in yacht riggings. But the solitary bell here sounded sad. "They need to be in real snow," said Trudi.

Sven laughed at her. "Well, there won't be real snow *here*, you goose! We are too near the coast. Wait till we get inland. You'll see what you want all right! Let's find the ice rink!" Irrepressible,

9

he strode off with his family in tow, his shoulders and curly mop of hair bobbing above the crowd.

Kirsten kept them all together. She liked the bustle and the elegance of the place. Even the clothes of the visitors were stylish. She bought things for the house back in England and presents for friends. She belonged with these sophisticated people and their bright Scandinavian designs and, luckily for her, Sven was too busy exploring to notice how much money she spent. At the ice rink she ordered a coffee and sat with her bags while the others hired their skates.

"Ready?" They had hardly tied their laces before Sven caught Trudi and Jurgen by the hands and set off with a whoop and the rush of cold air knocked the breath out of their lungs. Trudi stopped thinking and gave herself up to the moment. They were flying now, laughing, rosy-cheeked, dodging the other skaters, skimming faster and faster to the music. People of every description had been drawn onto the rink: young, old, even novices, who clung to the sides or to the arms of the official assistants.

There were solitary, pensive skaters, with hands clasped behind their backs, lost in the rhythm of their stride; then groups of giggling teenagers, and one little fellow in a striped vest, plump as a bee, who ran at the ice, clomping his feet in a desperate dash. How he survived, careering from one side to the other remained a wonder, but he did. At times the space became crowded, then, spontaneously emptied, as the skaters came and went.

During one of these intervals, a young helper, ingloriously dressed as a rabbit, and bored with dawdling about, seized his chance to show off. His long legs suddenly creased at the knees and he carved a lightning figure of eight, spinning on his heels and flying backwards, delighting in his speed. From where she sat, Kirsten saw the scene unfold before her, but there was nothing she could do. The rabbit ploughed straight into Sven and the children and they all collapsed in a heap.

"Quits!" said Trudi to Jurgen. "You can keep your biscuits!"

The rabbit slunk off for a reprimand and the Larssons dusted themselves down, laughing.

This was how Kirsten liked to see them, busy, active, cheerful, how they were *meant* to be, and if Miss Protheroe had only been

10

able to glimpse them now she would hardly have dared to suggest that anything was wrong. But coming to Sweden posed a risk.

True, the fun just now on the ice had successfully revived the old, arch, bossy Trudi who had always dazzled her teachers in the past. Staying with Per, however, might be another matter, for Grandpa Larsson was not like his Swedish neighbours, and Christmas at his house - remote, chilly, perhaps not very clean – would be a far cry from the comfortable celebrations they were famed for. The whole experience might simply fill Trudi's head with more absurd distractions. Already, the long, expensive journey had put a strain on the family's nerves. In a moment of regret, Kirsten allowed herself to blame her husband. Sven, after all, had insisted that they took up the Swedish invitation. Otherwise they could have gone skiing in Austria and seen all the snow they wanted from a cosy chalet. Well, it was too late now to nurse such thoughts.

She took a deep breath and, swallowing the last of her coffee, mastered her frustration. When the others returned, shining-eyed, they would find no trace of anxiety in her. She had done a course on staying calm.

That night they set off for the country. Driving at night was quicker and easier and, in any case, the next day would be Christmas Eve, an important day. They must arrive early to help Grandpa with his preparations. The children tucked up their feet in their sleeping bags and lolled, stupefied, as the oncoming traffic flashed by. Jurgen played a game on his phone. Trudi wound down her window a little to feel the breeze on her face. The cold air came from places she did not know – from the ice fields of the Arctic...

"Who's fiddling with the windows?" asked Kirsten almost immediately. "Is it you, Trudi? You'll mess up the air conditioning darling - and it makes it too noisy in here. Put your side up, there's a good girl. It's freezing out there."

Trudi reluctantly did as she was told and closed her eyes, imagining the draught instead. Her head still spun from the excitement of skating and soon she was fast asleep.

When she woke the car had stopped and they were surrounded by darkness. Sven got out and paced about, stretching his arms and legs. A light appeared some way off and a greeting rang out.

"Hej! Halla!" called Sven. Though Trudi could understand no more than a few words, she loved to hear him talk in Swedish. The cadence and pitch of his voice would change entirely as if a different person, who rented lodgings inside him, suddenly appeared and stuck his face out of the window. It was a mystery and a delight. Kirsten had been born in England and she stumbled in the language like a foreigner, but now she got out of the car and added a phrase or two.

As her eyes adjusted, Trudi saw that the light came from an open doorway and carved a path towards them through a pattern of dark trunks. Indigo shadows pressed on every side, but the path shone pale and she realized with a surge of pleasure that the paleness signified a ribbon of lamp-lit snow.

Sven was stamping in it and Kirsten's fur-topped boots were sunk deep in it. And there stood Grandfather Larsson, bareheaded, ragged-bearded, in a shapeless sheepskin coat, clapping their hands in his, his breath steaming.

"And the children?" he asked in English.

"Sleeping in there."

Trudi battled with the child locks and rapped her window. "Not asleep!" she protested. "Let me out!" And she threw herself into Per Larsson's arms. She had been practising so hard: "Godjul!" she cried. "Happy Christmas!"

"Come in, come in! Bring little Jurgen. Where is Jurgen, my friend? You must be tired. We can unpack later."

"*I* can unpack," said Sven, shouldering a bag or two anyway. And they trooped along the snow-path towards the light. Trudi glanced up at the towering, midnight trees with a thrill of awe. Here was everything she could possibly hope for: Christmas and real snow and Barbara's little ginger biscuits and the emptiness of the forest that they would explore tomorrow...

Though it was impossible to see it now, she had a mental picture still of Per's house, clear as a photo. There was the front door where a wolf once got in. And there, the little window where she had sat when she was three. It was a single-storey cabin in a clearing, just like the pictures in her fairy books, with walls made of whole tree trunks and a roof that came almost to the ground. In her mind she could see grass on the roof, which seemed odd, but modern 'green' buildings were often designed that way. Inside, one

12

big room, with a cast iron stove and a heady, intoxicating smell that came from a mixture of wet moss and tar and fish and new-baked bread. By the window, a great slab of a table and the chair where Grandpa sat, padded out with coats and old rugs. The floor - she struggled now to recall it - the floor was dark and crumbly. She had knelt on it briefly before being swept up in her mother's arms. It must have been bare earth. They didn't stay long. Only time enough for Per and Trudi to memorise one another's faces and decide they could be friends, before life whirled them apart.

She stumbled across the threshold, dazed and sleepy, ("Shoes off here!" ordered Kirsten) surprised to feel smooth boards beneath her feet. For a moment she thought there must be some mistake. Then she scolded herself for a fool. Of course, Jurgen was right. You couldn't remember what you saw when you were three. Her memory and fairy book pictures had become muddled in her head. Grandpa couldn't really have an earth floor. But the room was magical all the same. A soft light issued from a couple of lamps. And she could still smell fish and paraffin - Per had got it on his clothes - and the air had a fresh, piney tang which came from fir branches nailed above the door. By the stove - there *was* a stove - a tray of crisp bread with herrings and mustard and a bottle of clear spirit, plus gherkins, which Jurgen surveyed with disfavour. "No crisps?" he muttered darkly.

"Come, - ja, come!" Per ushered them in, all smiles. "Sit! Sit. Now you are the guests and I show you the Swedish way we make Christmas!" He had piled cushions and covers on his hard, wooden chairs and Trudi found a touching naïvety in his preparations. Pasted on the smoke-stained wall above the stove, were cut up Christmas cards from previous years. Paper Tomtes, Swedish house gnomes in their red, pointed hats, leaned drunkenly against the plates on the dresser, in company with a polar bear and a rather hideous Santa. A green-painted long-case clock, which she did not remember, ticked in one corner.

The family fussed and chattered, bringing in more cases, handing over gifts of food and flowers, which must be stored in the cool, relaying messages from old friends. Finally they settled and Kirsten began to pass round the plates and slivers of fish, while Sven poured aquavit into tiny glasses. Ignoring his wife's cautionary signals, he gave a glass to all. "Just pretend!" he

13

whispered blithely to the children. "You won't like it, but you can say 'Skål!' all the same."

"We *will* like it!" thought Trudi and Jurgen with one mind. But they couldn't drink even a sip of it. The fumes made them cough and in the warmth of the room they suddenly felt sleepy and confused.

Per saw all this from the corner of his eye, keeping up an excited banter the while, hopping about with fresh logs for the fire and busying himself over the sleeping arrangements. "Hep!" he nodded. "Sven and you, Kirsten, you will sleep in my room upstairs - and then Trudi can have the little room next door and Jurgen can stay down here by the stove with me."

As it happened, Trudi fell asleep on the settle where she sat and no one had the heart to move her. They put a pillow under her head and tucked a goose-down quilt around her and when she woke in the morning, the unfamiliar room looked ghostly in the half-light. Per was up already, clattering pans in the kitchen, and it took her some time to get her bearings. She put her hands behind her head and wriggled down under the covers.

How delightful it was, this sense of limbo. She felt weightless, disembodied, task free. Miss Protheroe could not possibly reach her here. And Christmas would be natural - no dusting and cleaning, no being polite to visitors. Barbara had made most of their preparations for them and Per would see to the rest. But she could not stay in bed for long. There was the house to explore - the upstairs that she had forgotten and the little scullery where Per did his washing, not to mention the log-store and sheds outside.

Throughout breakfast she kept an impatient eye on the window and as soon as it was light, ventured out into the snow. While Jurgen amused himself with hurling snowballs, Trudi tiptoed round the house. Now she had to revise her impressions. This house was charming, and rustic, but it was not built of trees. The walls, fashioned from red weatherboarding, had a peeling, neglected air yet stood centuries away from the earth-floored cabin in her mind. And Per himself, pottering about with his coffee-pot, he seemed different too. This cheerful, faintly doddery, domestic figure, hardly resembled the shape-shifter who had last summer enthralled her with legends of the Northern Lights. He seemed to have forgotten all about his telephone call and the shaman belt.

14

When she tried to catch his eye, or lean against his arm, he brightly fobbed her off. "Christmas Eve today, Trudi. So much to do. And we are going to keep it the old way. You'll see."

"But Grandpa…"

"Later, my Trudi. No time for 'buts' at Christmas. We have to get the tree. We have to cook the ham. And we must set up a *ney* for the birds!"

Trudi felt a stab of disappointment. The sunlight glittering on the frosted snow, the wood smoke, the little jug of juniper on her bedroom window-sill, even the aroma of the coffee, were perfect, nicer than she could possibly have hoped. Sven showed her fox-prints by the log-shed. Kirsten let her unpack Barbara's gingerbreads and tie on their red ribbons. When Sven and Per set out across the meadow behind the house, Trudi and Jurgen followed, carrying the axe that would fell their Christmas tree. And when they had chosen the tree and Sven had lopped off the lowest branches, they stood by, hugging themselves against the cold that stung their cheeks and crept into their boots, while the men finished the job and roped the trunk.

"Now we all pull together. This is a good way to get warm!" And they lugged the victim home, like hunters who had killed a bear. And Trudi felt sad for the tree and excited to take part, but she did not feel completely happy. At Isandeland, and now here, she found herself still looking for something more. She hung up the pepparkakor and the straw-plait stars that Kirsten had bought at the market. She ground the mustard seeds to glaze the ham. And all the time she was tormented by a jealous impatience. *When* would Per drop this public pretence and give her a signal? The secret that he had for her might not wait too long.

Perhaps in the evening, she thought, when they gave their presents and sliced the ham. Then, while the others dozed or amused themselves with their gifts, there would be time to talk.

But Per had made other plans.

Quite at the last moment he casually announced: "Oh, ja. And I have invited Mincke, my neighbour to dinner. He lives behind the hill here and he is all alone. And it's a good custom to welcome others at Christmas. Besides, I think you will like to meet him - you especially, Trudi. He is an interesting man. A writer and painter. And he keeps bees. Could tell your friend Corky a thing or two about bees."

Mincke arrived fantastically, like a scarecrow on skis, bareheaded and ungloved in the early dusk and Trudi instantly set her heart against him.

He looks like a scarecrow, she thought, *so tall and gaunt with that strange way of looking at you down his nose. And he's not even Swedish. Who knows what he is?* She had the grace to be ashamed of this judgement, for heaven knew, Per was not really Swedish. But for the moment it suited her uncharitable mood. The stranger's visit had come like a door between her and her desires and it would be a while yet before she realized that a door is a powerful mystery all by itself.

Chapter Three

Mincke

Mincke brushed the snow off his skis and propped them inside the door just as if he were at home, then hung his short jacket on Per's own coat-hook, jerked his head to each in turn and held out a red, raw-boned hand. Trudi shrank back. He had a permanently startled expression and his conversation, a sequence of angular phrases, came from a throat so hoarse you would think he had been shouting for a week. While his eyes nervously avoided all others, he kept one ear cocked, as though listening for someone who was not in the room. Altogether, he was a most unnerving person.

Per and Sven, as true, hospitable Scandinavians, welcomed him in and invited him to sit by the stove with something warming to drink and Trudi and Jurgen retreated to the kitchen, where their mother was slicing cheese. Kirsten closed the door behind them and put her finger on her lips. Though she shared their consternation, she was not altogether surprised. In fact, this was just the sort of annoyance she had expected in her gloomier moments.

Trudi, however, seemed beside herself. "Can't you tell him to go home? I don't *want* him here!"

Her mother glanced at her scowling face and secretly sympathised. But she could not wish their problems away. Mincke was here and they were here and politeness dictated that they must make the best of it.

This is what came of leaving 'progress' behind. For Kirsten, forests had always meant friends and laughter and wine and lanterns - all the pleasures of summer camping, with the comforts of civilization close at hand. Deep forests and their stranger inhabitants were not for her. Not in mid-winter. And certainly not for Christmas!

After her own immaculately modern home, she had expected to find Per's house a trial and sure enough, she did. The kitchen alone was enough to depress her spirits, for it was tiny and cramped, more like a larder-cupboard for tins than a place to create a harmonious meal. Nevertheless, as a dutiful wife, she had done her best. At some point in the past an enamel cooker and a fridge, both of which ran dimly on bottled gas, had found their way there and Barbara's Christmas ham now bubbled perilously on the hob, filling the room with steam while the gas hissed and popped and gave off ominous smells.

Yet despite her best intentions, Kirsten still felt aggrieved. She was angry that Sven stayed in the parlour chatting in Swedish and leaving her to do all the work, and indignant that Per had invited such a difficult character amongst them just when they were hoping to spend a cosy evening together. And though she put a lid on her discontent, it went on bubbling away in secret, just as vigorously as the ham.

Now she faced mutiny from the children. She must rise above it all - set an example - so she gave an impenetrable smile. And Trudi and Jurgen took note. Better be careful. They knew from experience that in the Larsson house, the weather was changeable. And that their mother was most formidable when she was trying to be good. Sometimes she could carry it off. Sometimes she brewed up a terrible storm. Whatever happened, she was always superb.

She had collected together all the bowls she could find and begun to fill them with the dozens of dishes that made up a Julbord or traditional Christmas feast. Thank heaven for the delicatessens at Isandeland! Kirsten had an artist's eye for arranging a pretty table but she didn't really cook, so at last she was grateful that they had brought the car and crammed it with Barbara's food.

"You have to remember, Trudi love," she reasoned, handing her a plate of meatballs. "*Put that over there and bring me the potato salad.* You have to remember that they do things differently in Sweden." She could hear herself speaking with two voices: one audible, cool and rational, the other tight-lipped, sarcastic, secret. "They like to take care of everyone at Christmas time. That's why you and Grandpa put up the *ney* this afternoon, so that the birds could fill their tummies at their own funny bird table." *And why I am here in this ridiculous apron.* The aside, though silent, gave a satisfying poke at life's vexations, and made her feel a little better.

"I don't mind feeding the birds," objected Trudi.

But Kirsten hadn't finished: "If the birds are happy, they say you will have a good harvest next year." *It can't be helped if they are funny birds that make life uncomfortable!*

"I don't *mind* feeding the birds."

"And it's not just make-believe. The Swedes are very practical. If the birds die in winter, then the bugs will eat the crops in spring. *These tomato slices go on there. And Jurgen, I can see you stealing those prawns!* Then in Sweden you have to feed the Tomte, too." There was no end to such traditions. That was why Kirsten lived a life averse from folklore. But at least Trudi was now talking and her scowl had lifted a little. Perhaps, if they could vent their ill-humour by laughing at people in general, they would find it easier to forgive one another. With any luck they might run out of grudges before dinner, for no one can digest their food when they are feeling cross.

"That's a story for babies," Trudi retorted, momentarily unsympathetic.

Kirsten pulled a 'just so' face. "A hundred years ago, the grown-ups believed it too. If you didn't leave the Tomte a bowl of porridge on Christmas Eve, well, you would have no end of misfortune."

"Superstition!" Jurgen pronounced.

Kirsten smiled in approval. True. Those old Swedes would look pretty foolish today and none but the smallest children would believe their tales. Luck did not come from elves and fairies. Modern people were masters of their own fate and would tolerate Christmas porridge now only as a game, like leaving a mince pie for Santa. Thank heaven those dark days were over for good.

"…Then you had to look after the poor and the homeless…"

"And the *dead!*" added Jurgen with relish.

"Never mind that."

Jurgen, however, was not to be stopped: "Grandfather told me. The country people used to sleep on straw on Christmas Eve so that the ghosts could have their beds and be comfortable!"

"What I mean," continued Kirsten, ignoring him, and preaching with such conviction she all but persuaded herself, "is that Grandfather is doing something generous and kind and very Swedish, by inviting this strange man to have dinner with us. He is all alone and it's too bad to be alone at Christmas. We must be friendly and make him feel at home. Right? Trudi? No sour faces! You looked at him as if he was a scarecrow when he arrived!"

Trudi winced. She watched her mother placing little dabs of caviar on the eggs in silent admiration. How marvellous she was, always rising to the occasion with the right word, the reassuring gesture. Without her, life would be a maelstrom. How she wished she had her poise! But her own mind churned in an endless stew, and already it had found something new to worry over.

That story of the Christmas ghosts, for instance. It was easy to laugh at fairy tales in daylight. But if Grandpa said something about the dead, it would be because he knew. He was not a man to make fun of the solemn things in life. Did he have a heap of straw somewhere, and if so, who would sleep on it, and which bed would the ghosts choose for themselves when they arrived? Who *were* they? Would they be slipping into *her* sheets that night and why had Grandfather told *Jurgen* and not her?

Her mother guessed what she was thinking and suppressed a sigh, for Trudi never missed a grisly tale. Of all things, she loved an enigma. The darker the mystery, the greater her appetite, while all sensible matters, like her studies at school, slipped neatly out of mind. Kirsten bit her lip. Of course, Per's stories would only encourage such waywardness. Per hardly lived in this world! She should have trusted her instincts weeks ago and insisted on Christmas in Austria. Now, already it was too late. Trudi would be imagining all sorts of unsuitable things and neither Miss Protheroe nor the school therapist would be able to talk her out of it.

"Come on," she said brightly. "Let's go in and be sociable. We can do it!"

Trudi returned her smile, but however much she wanted to be beautiful and rational, like her mother, her polarised little soul rejected Mincke and wished him back where he came from.

And he didn't exactly help himself.

Without consulting anyone, he had pulled out a stub of a pipe and blown into it before filling it with sour-smelling tobacco. Just when they were about the serve supper! And then his manners at table were a shock. He utterly refused the Christmas ham. He ran his fingers through his wisps of hair and stuck them into the winter salad. And he ate with his mouth open as though he hadn't been fed for a month. Jurgen smirked and nudged Trudi, but she wouldn't play. Gazing steadfastly at her plate she felt a sudden longing for home. At least in England she had her own room to escape to, and life was more comfortable. You could have a proper shower when you wanted, not a sauna with spiders, and the toilet didn't fill you with dread! This must be the only place in Sweden with such antiquated plumbing...

Later, she would see a ghastly comedy in that Christmas feast. They all wanted things to be perfect but their anxious feelings filled the room, electrifying the air with invisible sparks. And the more they tried to be festive and jolly the more this dark energy bounced back and forth, making their skins prickle and their nerves jangle. An idea flying up into that static would have been like a like a kite in a storm. Just a careless gesture, a chance remark and boom! Contact! Lightning would bring the whole charge down. Any one of them might have triggered it off quite by accident. Nobody *meant* any harm, least of all poor Mincke. Mischief had simply got into the air, setting them at sixes and sevens and they were all equally helpless to prevent it.

Time and again Trudi found herself wondering. Suppose... Suppose Jurgen had not felt quite so naughty, or her father half so desperate... Suppose she had not sat at table with a face like toothache... If Per had stopped his foolish grinning, or Mincke had smiled just once... would it have made a difference? The answer was probably no.

Young as she was, she knew that a tale, once begun, must follow on to its end. An innocent handful of snow could start an avalanche large enough to sweep all obstacles aside, for snow is sticky and binds to things. Just so, some moments are magnets for good or bad luck and Trudi concluded that that evening was marked for mischance - simply doomed from the start.

Almost at once poor Sven knew he was in trouble. He naturally suffered more than most, feeling his loyalties torn between young and old, for Per and his neighbour were clearly out of touch with the fast, smart world his English family knew. The children looked glum and Kirsten had a brittle gaiety that suggested she was secretly put out. He must try to bring them all together, so he regaled the company with jokes. These met with dutiful applause and when the first course was cleared away and he ran out of jokes, he tried a different ploy. Out came a red hat, which he crammed on his head.

"I'm the Christmas Tomte!" he announced, "and I *think* there are some presents behind the door." Crouching and grimacing, he lurched from the room and returned with a bulging sack. "Ah yes. This must be..." he squinted at the label, "...something very strange for Grandfather Larsson. A spoon, perhaps? Or an ear trumpet? Hand this over, Trudi."

Jurgen, bless his heart, gave an honest laugh. His turn came next.

"And here is one - oh yes - it's a spelling-test book for Jurgen. Lucky boy! And for Trudi, something very small. It's a box of matches! No. Doesn't rattle. Ah, a sponge for washing up!" The tension momentarily eased.

Grandpa unwrapped a pair of slippers, Kirsten, a beautiful bag. Even Mincke had a hastily labelled jar of cranberries. There were gifts from England: books from Barbara, honey from Corky and crystals and incense from Kirsten's holistic friends. Trudi had bought bubble-bath for all. Soon the room lay full of discarded paper and ribbons and by the time the pudding arrived spirits were rising. Chocolate brownie and peaches in brandy! But Per had also ordered rice porridge, because it was traditional and he thought the children might enjoy hunting for the almond hidden in it. Jurgen made a face.

"Taste a little," coaxed Kirsten, giving him a steely look. "You have to have this at Christmas!"

Silent, he watched the helping reach his plate. Then, waiting until he thought no one was looking, held his nose and gagged, while kicking Trudi under the table.

"Stop it!" she hissed. "Just eat it. It won't kill you!"

"It *will!*"

"Well then, *I'll* have your new skis and you won't have to do that solo for Beery after Christmas!"

This was scant sympathy. Jurgen pushed his spoon round the cinnamon-scented mash and fished out something small and hard.

"Ugh! Pooh! Is this it? The almond whatever thingy? Have I won the pig?"

"He has! Jurgen's got it!" Sven's party hat weighed heavily on his head. He felt that he was wading through porridge - they were all drowning in it. Perhaps the marzipan pig in its Isandeland wrapping seemed too small a prize for a modern child. Years ago, when he was a boy, he remembered, the pig had been a treasure worth coveting, yet Jurgen feigned disgust. It wasn't that he meant to be ungrateful. He simply didn't understand. But Kirsten, you could see Kirsten was furious. Mincke surveyed the scene with a frozen eye. And Per, who knows what he thought? He hid behind a wall of empty smiles.

"Trudi, open your present!" Sven played his last card. "It's from us."

The little 'matchbox' turned out to be her biggest gift - a mobile phone that was also a proper digital camera, sleek and pretty, in a pearly, pink finish. The device could do other things too, acting as calculator, calendar, clock, dictionary and atlas all in one. You could even play music on it and you could measure distances with a laser.

"I thought it might help you with your homework," said Kirsten encouragingly. "Do you like it?"

Trudi turned it over in her hand. This was a covetable prize and she felt suddenly overwhelmed.

"Use it!" cried Jurgen, perking up. "Use it! Ring someone up. Ring Barbara and Corky and wish them 'Happy Christmas'! Tell Corky to play his saxophone down it!"

"I don't suppose it will work here," laughed Sven. "We're a long way from a signal ..."

"No - no," Per interrupted, suddenly straight-faced. "Not so far. You can try. We have a new mast just up the hill there." He shot a look at Mincke, who was drumming his fingers on the cloth and breathing hard.

"Shall I?" Trudi turned to Sven. "You have to set it up."

"Jurgen's the man for that," he replied. "He's the wizard with anything technical."

Jurgen took the phone and weighed it, casting a critical eye. "Except that it's *pink*," he said, "it looks quite cool." Sven and Kirsten exchanged thankful glances. That meant that though he approved in principal, he wouldn't be seen dead using it, so their gamble had paid off. There would be no family squabbles over something that was pink. "It's almost like a Laser Wag."

"A *what?*" jeered Trudi.

"A Waggle Phone! Don't say you don't know what *that* is, Miss Know-it-all?" Jurgen ran his thumb over the keypad. "It's the next big thing. I mean, don't get me wrong, this is *nice*, but a Laser Wag can do all this and much more." He neatly deflated the moment. "My friend Angus has got a Laser Wag. But his Dad is mega-rich. Waggle means something to do with bees – Angus says it's a kind of dance they do to communicate. With a phone like that we can be cleverer than bees. We'll be able to communicate everything even without talking. Because of the lasers."

Blithely unaware of the blank faces round him, Jurgen ploughed on. As a self-appointed expert, he had launched himself into a subject he really loved and his eyes shone.

"Waggle Phones have the internet, of course. But they also have personal satellite navigation. You can find your way anywhere with one. And other people can find *you*. It's brilliant – you get your own personal guru to watch over you and help you. You know how scientists can read worms these days, with lasers and make them do anything they want? Well, a Laser Wag phone will be able to read your brain, so if you are feeling anxious, it can tell and give you advice without you having to ask. It will know if your blood pressure is too high. It can write down what you are saying, so you need never take notes in class. And it can read and copy documents too... Even MI5 use Laser Wag stuff... for spying. In the future you won't have to have a memory any more, because your phone will remember everything for you – you know, file everything properly, so it can't get lost..."

The sound of a chair scraping on the floor brought him up short. Mincke had risen to his feet and was clutching the table, swaying and staring wildly about him. His eyes flashed fire.

"Such a thing would be an abomination! An *abomination!* I go!" he gasped. "Excuse. I must go!" Leaving the company open-mouthed, he pushed roughly past them, grabbed his skis and flung out into the night. Per hurried after.

"Go well, Mincke," he called into the darkness. "Godjul!"

A stunned pause followed.

"Well!" Kirsten managed at last. "Whatever was *that* about? How extraordinarily rude!"

"Poor fellow must be mad!"

"*I* didn't like him anyway - I'm glad he's gone!"

"Did you see the scar on his arm?"

To leave in the middle of a meal - and without a word of thanks... No, Mincke certainly could not be Swedish!

But Per returned without comment and resumed his pudding. Last summer he had been a stickler for politeness and punctuality, but now he seemed to have lost interest in such things. Perhaps he was too busy with other thoughts. Perhaps he had forgotten.

"Let's see if you can make that call," he said.

Trudi felt desperate to know what had upset Mincke so, but she could not ask it now. The family fell silent as if they had been caught doing something naughty at school. They stole guilty looks at one another and they glanced anxiously at Per. *Had* they driven Mincke away? They could not tell. Per helped himself to the last of the porridge and left them to their own conclusions. So, in a new spirit of cooperation, they programmed the phone and called England and soon Barbara's vibrant, comforting voice came crackling through:

"Hey, we're fine! We're *fine!* How are you guys?"

"Good! Good, ja!" rumbled Per in reply. "Good pepparkakor! Tak! The best ever!"

"Told you so!" yelled Barbara immodestly. "How's the snow!"

Trudi grabbed the phone. "The snow is wonderful! We've got so much to tell you..." By a miracle the atmosphere cleared and they were all smiling again.

But Barbara cut in. She could not wait to listen to stories about snow: "We have awesome news for you, too! Corky's blind boy, Pedro, is coming over from Peru. They've booked him an op. at the Kingsbury hospital and the surgeon there reckons they'll be able to make him see!"

Chapter Four

Christmas Ghosts

Snow fell again that night. From her bedroom window Trudi could see the glimmer of the trees under their heavy, white blankets. The air was thick with flakes; a steady whirl that buried the world under a quilt of silence, too. Only where the crystals pattered against the pane was there any sound in the stillness. She put out her lamp and, by the light that crept under her door, studied her reflection in the glass. Sooner or later the Christmas ghosts would arrive and she must be awake to fend them off.

She wasn't alone for long. Very soon she began puzzling over the day's events and entered into animated conversation with herself just as though the face she could see before her was another person. This way, she could confide all the things she longed to say aloud but didn't quite dare, in case the grown-ups overheard.

"I'm not mad. Really," she whispered, her eyes pleading, innocent and large. *"I'm sure I'm not. I just see things differently. It's Christmas and we should be happy, but everyone is jumpy and cross. I watch Mummy and Daddy sometimes when they think no one is looking, and they are so solemn, you'd believe something terrible had happened. But then it turns out that they are just talking about money. They never used to care about silly things like that. I can't tell Jurgen. He's only eight and anyway he's a boy.*

"I thought I could tell Grandfather, but here in Sweden, he is different. He doesn't seem to want to talk to me. I don't believe he thinks I'm special any more. And I don't know whether that is because he has changed or because I got things all wrong in the first place. Either way, it means something horrid.

"Grandfather Larsson was my biggest hope. I felt so sure he would do something – make life special again. Until now, I could have sworn that I understood him better than anyone. After all, not even Daddy knows as much about him as I do – I mean, about his not really being Swedish and all that. Daddy left here when he was

26

too young to understand. But Grandfather trusted me. He told me last summer. He's not like other people...

"*For a start, he was born way, far-away in the north, near the Arctic Circle – half-Finnish, half-Sami and he came here long ago when he was just a boy, a refugee in the war. And I know other things about him too. Things he hasn't even told me. I can feel them in my bones. Deep down I am sure he still doesn't really belong here. That's why his cottage feels only half lived-in. He belongs to the forest and the wild places that other people can't see. He knows what the wind is saying, and where the wild birds go. He can slip out of his skin like the old Sami sorcerers, who knew all the secrets of life and death. But just now he is hiding that other self - playing tricks on me - pretending to be ordinary, as though he wants me to forget everything I learnt from him. Everything that is interesting and true.*

"*What should I do? I can't prove it now, but he did magic last summer and I saw it! That would be impossible if he was just another ordinary person, fussing about the news, and wondering where he had put his glasses...*" Seeing her own woebegone expression, her eyes filled with sympathetic tears.

She knew what the grown-ups would say. They would say that they were fine and that everybody had to worry about practicalities sometimes. She didn't accept that. Life was too precious to waste on dull, boring things. As for Per, they said, he was old and when you got old it was natural to slow down and want a quiet life... Old people couldn't hear properly and they couldn't see properly either, so they often got confused. One had to make special allowances for them... But Trudi threw out this argument too. She could picture her grandfather now, quite clearly beside her in the window pane. He looked spritely - in fact, bright as a button. Much fitter than he had been before. And he didn't seem at all deaf, just deliberately blank.

So a darker idea sowed itself like a seed of doubt inside her and sprouted a sheaf of bright, poisonous leaves: Suppose there never was a Grandfather who told her to bring the shaman's belt? If so, were Mummy's friends right when they said that Trudi made things up? That she simply wanted to be special? She had been mummy's girl, daddy's girl, teacher's girl, now Grandpa's... Was the fearless shape-shifter, stone-charmer, spirit-conjuror who had slain the mad dog, Beor, nothing but an imaginary dream?

Which man was real? This one, who avoided her eye and hid himself beneath a mask of mindless cheer? Or that other who had confided such thrilling stories before, and shown her glimpses of an ecstatic other-world? She was still under the spell of those tales: how he escaped from the Russians in Finland, how he lost his beautiful wife and Sven, his little son. How he searched for his mother amongst the Sami people of the North. Once heard, they became her tales and they would never leave her. But just now it seemed Per's spirit had taken off into the air, leaving only a shadow-self behind. *"He shows more feeling for that strange man Mincke than he does for me!"* Trudi lamented.

As if by magic, the likeness of Mincke joined them. Whoever, whatever was he? And why had he behaved so outrageously? In just a few days time, the trip to Sweden would be over and the chance of a Christmas adventure gone. Mincke - there he was with his hectic cheeks - had spoilt it all. Trudi glared at him in the glass. Life would go back to its tedious old timetable... Except, of course, that Pedro was coming!

Though space in the window was now getting crowded, she made room for *him* too. Pedro, she knew, was a crumpled photograph in Corky's wallet; a blind Peruvian boy he had rescued and placed in care while making a trip through the Andes. Pedro was a bundle of letters, dictated to the nuns at his orphanage and translated, in their neat handwriting, on pale blue airmail paper: *"Dear Uncle Tristram, I hope you are well..."* It was impossible to tell what he was really like. His face, heart-shaped, brown, with high, flat, Indian cheekbones, and a mop of dark hair, looked out from the photograph...

But then that was the thing about Pedro. Of course he couldn't look out. His eyes were silvered with the cataracts which had afflicted him from birth. Nonetheless, or perhaps because of that strangeness, Pedro was beautiful. In spare moments when Trudi was dreaming at school, or thinking alone, she would imagine that he was her friend. She knew he was clever. He had told the sisters that he would grow up to study law. He was a year older than her. And he lived safely thousands of miles away in Peru. Now he was coming to England, a real boy who might not be at all as she

28

imagined. Perhaps he would prove a disappointment, like Per this Christmas - a failure. She almost wished he would stay away. And then she felt ashamed. Of course it would be marvellous really. Wonderful for Corky, who was so kind and generous and needed to be loved. Even better for Pedro, himelf.

The lanky figure of Corky, with his crooked back and jester's face appeared out of the air and squeezed in beside her. Poor Corky had broken his shoulder in Peru, so far from help that the bones had set all wrong, which made it all the more extraordinary that he had devoted himself to Pedro. But that was Corky all over, thinking of others first. Barbara had made him put on a jacket tonight. There would be frost on the pane in the morning...

But surely there wasn't room for Barbara as well? Barbara dabbed a deprecating hand from the door. *"Don't be ridiculous child. Do you know what time it is? Just get some sleep, okay?"*

Trudi decided she could wait up no longer for the Christmas ghosts - clearly they were not coming - and crept, half-frozen to bed. She rolled herself into a ball, toes tucked into the end of her nightie, head buried beneath the covers, arms crossed like a winter dormouse, and as her shivering body thawed, tried to still her thoughts. Per had told her time and again last summer: *'Be patient'*, and here she was, just the same as ever, rushing ahead, grabbing, trying to read the end before the beginning. *'Be patient'*. It was too hard. Tomorrow they would have to clear the snow...

Strange, though, that Pedro should have such haunting eyes, silver, just like her grandfather...

Chapter Five

The Sneevelings

In the morning she woke deliciously warm. Though it was still dark, you could tell that the snow had stopped. Someone was outside already, chopping wood. She allowed herself to lie and listen, taking in breaths of cold air and savouring the thought, like a sweet in her mouth: "It's Christmas Day!" Somehow, she felt, it would make a difference.

Two hours later, with breakfast over, there were decisions to be made. Kirsten wanted to go to church. Down in the valley was the little white chapel with its grey, helmeted tower, where, long ago, Sven had accompanied his mother, as a boy. Today all the locals would be there, wearing their new gloves and scarves - greeting friends.

"I want to see the pew where you sat!" said Kirsten smiling.

Sven rubbed his head with his hand. "I can't remember! I was barely five when I left. And Grandfather would not know." He winked at Per. "He never came to church. All he ever said was "don't arrive too early in case you meet a ghost!" *(Those ghosts again! Did they sleep in the church as well?)*

"We could go into Litven afterwards and see the Christmas tree in the square. Get a hot chocolate maybe at the big hotel?" Kirsten shot an encouraging look at Jurgen. He would come if there was chocolate to be had. And she felt a desperate need to see civilization again. "Can you get the car going?"

"With the chains on the wheels, I don't see why not. We might have to dig ourselves out here, but on the bigger road we'll be fine. What about Grandpa, though? Maybe ..."

Grandpa was smiling, rubbing his hands. "You go, you go, my boy! I have something to do. And it will be good for you to get out. Must be quite boring here, especially for the children, eh?"

Trudi saw her chance.

"I don't want to go to church. I want to stay and read my book," she declared.

"On Christmas Day? We should all be together!"

"But I don't want to go! We never do normally." Trudi began to pout.

"Well, we shan't be long." Sven stepped in, ever the diplomat. "Trudi can keep Grandpa company – oh, and help get lunch!" he winked. *No wars, please God, on Christmas Day!*

Kirsten shook her head but did not protest. They would have to hurry to catch the start of the service. As daylight dawned, they trooped out to inspect the road and found encouraging signs. The fresh snow lay lightly on the old, easy to shovel aside. A new moon, just setting, dangled in the tree tops. There would be sun today, and that meant icicles.

As she waved them off, Trudi wanted to clap her hands. At last she was free! She felt so tired of them watching her, worrying over her, looking for signs of this and that, as the experts at school had advised. Well, she didn't need experts! She needed time to think and here was a perfect morning for it.

She was still standing, gazing, when Per appeared, buckling on his coat. "Trudi, get your hat and gloves. We're going for a walk." He clutched a stout walking stick, almost as tall as himself and his feet floundered in big snow boots. There was a new determination in his voice. "Hurry now!"

"Why? Where are we going?" she asked.

"We are going to Mincke's house. To see that all is well."

"Oh, *Mincke!*" she could not hide her disgust.

"Yes," said Per with a touch of severity. "And you will see why when we get there. Besides, one always visits friends here on Christmas Day. It is a custom."

Trudi was beginning to tire of Swedish customs, but she did not dare to show it. Something of the old intensity burned in her grandfather's eye and she remembered, with a frisson, that he could be terrible in anger. Secretly, she was overjoyed to see this side of him again and hastily throwing on her things, she presented herself outside.

Per gave her a critical look, then shook his head. "You are not going in a car, Trudi. Get another hat and put a belt around your coat. If we stop in the wood, it will be cold."

"Is it far?"

"Not far, but you should be ready. Maybe the weather can change. Hep!" He caught his breath. "And Trudi, better leave that phone at home. It won't be welcome where we're going."

Trudi thought of wearing the shaman's belt, but then decided against it. Mincke might ask about it and she didn't want *him* to know. She put her phone reluctantly on the table, but then after a moment's hesitation, changed her mind about that too. In spite of her respect for Per, she simply could not ditch a lifelong habit of knowing best.

Why should Mincke be allowed to ruin everything? she reasoned. *It would be nice to take photographs of the snow! And the phone-camera was her special present. She should be allowed to use it on Christmas Day! Grandfather need never know - she was so much quicker than him and, as Kirsten said, old people couldn't see so well. She could lag behind and snap something while he wasn't looking.* In a gesture of defiance, she slipped the device back in her pocket.

"Ready, Trudi?"

They settled into a halting pace. Per could not go fast because of his heart, and the snow hampered their walking, so there were frequent pauses and she soon became glad of his advice to wrap up. But the rests gave her time to look about her. *This,* this stepping into the unknown, was what she had come for, after all!

They had left the road behind and now ascended a path through the trees, the sunlight lying sharply between blue shadows and striking diamond points at every step. The whole world lay breathless, crystalline, beautiful beyond belief. As their feet sank into last night's snow, icier layers crunched and creaked beneath them. Their breath curled away in little eddies of steam.

Mincke's tracks from the night before had disappeared without trace, but his presence lingered on.

Finally, Trudi could keep quiet no longer. She slipped her hand through her grandfather's arm. "Why do you care so much about Mincke?" she asked.

Per cast her a sidelong look.

"You can understand when you know more."

"Tell me about him, then. He seems so… so fierce!"

"Hmm." Per nodded.

"Where is he from? He's not Swedish, is he?"

"Mincke is Dutch. But like me, a bit of a stranger - almost not from anywhere. Listen, Trudi. He is a poor old man, not easy to like, ja? But inside, something special. You will see!"

"Was he a refugee? Like you? In the war?"

Per looked at her again and this time there was a light in his eyes.

"My Trudi is clever! She remembers things well." He brushed the snow off a stump by the pathside and perched himself on it, breathing long and slow. Trudi sat the other side so they propped one another up, back to back. Eventually he felt ready to talk.

"I had some adventures before I arrived in Sweden. But while I was being fed and cared for here, poor Mincke had a struggle even to survive. He and his family were Jewish. His father sold pianos on the Kinkerstraat, in Amsterdam and as a very young child, Mincke lived in a house full of music and good talk and laughter. He had brothers and sisters to play with, and cousins and aunts, calling in for meals and arguing and singing all the day long. But then, you know, there came the war and the German soldiers arrived in their steel tanks and after that, Holland became a terrible place for Jews. Hup! They hunted them down just as if they were criminals."

Per wavered and stopped as if he saw the tanks rolling up before his eyes. Then he took another breath: "Mincke's family closed their shop and when others were ordered to the Jewish Quarter, they went into hiding, avoiding the troops as long as they could, but one day his father went out for bread and did not return. The next day, disaster! A raid. The old couple, who owned the house and those they were protecting, were arrested. Mincke escaped only because he was the smallest and because at the last moment, his brother pushed him through a rat hole into the neighbour's attic. Mincke was just nine years old, skinny as a bean, and wise enough to know that he must now fend for himself. The soldiers would be back. So he waited till nightfall, took a shirt and a couple of family photos and ran away.

"Down by the canal, a kindly bargeman took pity on him and smuggled him out of the city. So he began to run and for two years he kept on running, living wild in the woods, stealing from rubbish bins, afraid to speak to a living soul. Many times he nearly starved or died of cold. Once he was captured and only escaped because someone attacked his guard. Once he was left for dead, but somehow he kept going. Always, he thought, he must survive to be able to tell what he had seen. He was all that remained of his big family and he carried their spirit with him.

"Following the railway, he stumbled through enemy country until, somewhere west of Lubeck, he was picked up by a farmer who locked him in a stable and went for help. Now there would be more terrifying dogs and soldiers in uniforms! Mincke already decided that he would die rather than go with them. But he was lucky. The people who came next were quiet and grave and gave him food.

"'What is your name?' they said.

"Mincke sealed his lips.

"Then they looked at one another. 'What shall we do?' they whispered, in their incomprehensible accents.

"'Get him to Denmark. The Danes have sent their Jews to Sweden. Perhaps they will do the same for him.'

"So he was passed secretly from hand to hand, mostly at night, understanding nothing, till a fishing boat landed him on the Swedish coast.

"'Wait here,' said the fisherman. 'Someone is coming to collect you. I daren't stay any longer.' But Mincke could only think of running away, back to his woods.

"In Sweden, he lived wild once more, dirty, hungry, covered in cuts and bruises. He did not realize he could be safe here until one Christmas, the pastor at Pohlsberg found him hiding in his barn. So many strangers roamed the country in those days, the old man was not particularly surprised. And the local people had been complaining that things were going missing - eggs here, bread there. When you have nothing, you learn to become a good thief. But the pastor was a gentle-hearted man. He sat the runaway down in his kitchen and gave him bread and soup. Almost immediately, Mincke collapsed and fell into a fever that lasted for several weeks. When he regained consciousness, he had forgotten how to speak.

"It took much time and patience for the old man to help him find his tongue, but eventually the pair discovered they both knew a little German and, bit by bit, Mincke stammered out his tale. Now he had a friend - someone to defend him against the authorities. Father Anders got him papers, so he could stay in

34

Sweden and he let him live in his house, gave him an education. And Mincke was bright - always learning. After the war he taught at the school here, but he never forgot what happened to him and his people. Forever looking over his shoulder. Now he is an old man - recluse. Still alone. His wife died last year. No children. He takes fright easily."

"But he is safe now, isn't he?" urged Trudi.

Per pulled a face.

"Is that what you wanted to tell me," Trudi went on, "on the telephone?"

She had lost him now.

"So, we go and see if he is all right," he said brightly. "Christmas time, you see!" He rose to his feet, stamped them to drive out the cold and, with Trudi's arm tucked under his, set off once more into the snow.

At top of the hill, the woods fell away towards a lake.

"Oh, but it's wonderful!" cried Trudi.

"You like it? Mincke's house is down there, past the funny tree with the short branches." Taller than the others, this bizarre, mutilated specimen stood out alone on the ridge. It was like no other tree she had seen, not even the bristle cone pine.

Per followed her thoughts. "Not a real tree!" he laughed. "It is the mast I told about yesterday. But *very* lovely. Everybody wants one!"

Trudi shrugged and laughed back. There was something dark about this joke that she did not understand, but Per had moved on. "Eh, Mincke, put on the coffee," he murmured, as if his friend could hear: "We are knocking on your door nearly and quite tired!"

The door of Mincke's house stood ajar, despite the cold, but the place seemed deserted. No smoke from the chimney. No answer when Per called out. The snow lay scuffed on the path however, and grabbing Trudi's hand, Per followed the footprints round the side of the house to the garden. Even in its winter disguise, you could tell that this was a well-ordered plot, divided neatly between what looked like fruit trees, and squares of lawn. A figure was moving about at the end.

"Hej! Mincke!" called Per in greeting and the figure shot to attention.

"Per Larsson here, okay? Just a visit. We brought some biscuits - all the way from England!"

Mincke squinted at his intruders. In the low sunlight their silhouettes made them easy to recognize but he did not return the greeting. Instead he gestured with his hands, throwing them out sideways so that Trudi thought he resembled a scarecrow more than ever. Per kept walking though his smile had vanished.

"Mincke?"

"The bees," rasped the old man. And now they understood what he meant. "See what has happened?"

Trudi made out six or seven hives, tucked behind a low hedge. They looked homely and familiar under their snow bonnets. Corky kept bees on his nursery in Sussex and sometimes she helped him with them. She knew that they rested in the winter. You could feed them a little sugar perhaps, and that was all they needed till spring. But something here was wrong. Dark specks, like drifts of tea leaves, littered the ground as far as the eye could see. It seemed that the bees had abandoned their hives and were dying in the snow.

"Can't we put them back?" she cried, crouching down to look.

Mincke snorted dismissively: "Clearly you do not know about bees!"

"*Why,* Mincke?" asked Per. "All was well yesterday?"

"Of course."

"It's not the weather. Not warm enough today to tempt them out, despite the sun." He looked up at the strange mast on the hill. "Nothing new there?"

Mincke struck a blow in the air.

"Someone was *here*," he said bluntly. "Someone was here early. See, there are footprints round the hives and it stopped snowing, perhaps at three in the morning – I know because something woke me up."

"But the hives themselves have not been disturbed?"

"The snow on top is untouched."

"Not an animal. A bear perhaps?"

"Per Larsson! When did bears go hunting in winter! I can show you - human footprints - size forty eight perhaps - a man!"

"And all the hives?"

"As you see."

"These were not ordinary bees," Per explained as Trudi straightened up. "These were Mincke's special strain bred from European black bees. Very gentle. No stinging. And the best honey in the world. They were – how can you say - unique."

Trudi looked at Mincke with a surge of compassion. Tragic and ridiculous, he made a perfect clown, his pinched face blotched with cold, his eyes, windows onto an abyss.

"Come inside," coaxed Per, taking his neighbour's arm. "We make some coffee and think, ja?"

The old man allowed himself to be led.

"Can't we save *any?*" asked Trudi, hanging back.

"Not now." Per jerked his head towards the house. "We look tomorrow. See what is left."

"Not even these? We could warm them up again!" The dark, furry bodies had melted little pits in the snow where they had fallen and shed the last of their strength. She could not bear to abandon them so long as some still moved. And moreover, it was bad luck, really bad luck to lose your bees. A terrible omen. She knew that. Perhaps Mincke had forgotten the Tomte's porridge…

Once inside the house, Mincke roused himself, relit the fire and set some coffee on the stove. He made no reference to his sudden departure the day before. Perhaps he never accounted for himself. He seemed to have lost that part of himself that dealt with making pleasantries. Trudi wondered what kind of a woman could have married him. Her photograph stood on the dresser, smiling in black and white - she had a soft, round, kindly face and pale hair, permed into waves. She would have made him more comfortable, no doubt, softened some of his edges - the embroidered mats and ornaments in the room must have been hers. Did they have an understanding of one another, or did he bark as rudely at her as he did at the rest of the world?

Trudi knew such questions were private and no business of a polite person, but that only made them the more intriguing to her magpie mind. Hearing mention of her name, she slipped back into the present.

"I brought Trudi with me and see your work, Hans. She also draws. I thought you could show her the Sneevelings!"

Mincke turned to Trudi as if noticing her for the first time.

"You like stories?"

The phrase grated accusingly and for a moment Trudi glimpsed how terrifying he might have been in the classroom. *"You, Larsson! You have no homework?"* By comparison Miss Protheroe appeared positively cuddly. She could not then have known the affection and respect Mincke won from his pupils. But Trudi was not easily cowed.

Her parents had an ever-expanding galaxy of friends at home and loved nothing better than giving parties for them all, so the Larsson house was constantly full of strangers and from her earliest years Trudi felt quite at ease amongst them. As soon as she could walk, she had toddled round with plates of crisps and cookies, receiving kindly pats on the head and admiring compliments. And later, when she went to school, she had confidently faced up to all the extra tutors and coaches her mother thought would do her good. She found it easy to win them over - a dimple, a quip, a flash of impudence were generally all it took – so why should her charms fail now? She swallowed her alarm, put on a smile and gushed: "I *love* them!"

Mincke ignored her.

"Perhaps this will turn out to be a strange one!" he gave a savage snort that might have been intended as a laugh. "Remember my bees!" he rapped out instead. "Remember me. Because I am forgetting everything!"

"Hans!" cautioned Per.

"Everything!" Mincke shouted, in defiance. Then he launched himself out of his chair. "Come, I'll show you."

The room he led them to was a strangely cheerless affair, lacking even a fireplace. A desk stood in the window, commanding a view of the lake, but Sonja's homely influence, her photographs, ornaments and pretty painted plates had no place here. The shelf-lined walls were crammed instead, from floor to ceiling, with manuscripts in greaseproof paper bags. "This," Mincke pointed with a trembling finger. "This is my work."

"Your stories?" prompted Trudi.

"Yes. Stories, yes!"

"Are they about you?" she ventured, thinking of his escape.

Mincke's eyes rested on her briefly.

"No!" he leant suddenly towards her. "They are about YOU!"

Seeing her jump, he nodded, satisfied and then went on. "They are about the world. Innocence, courage, truth. And evil!" He was rummaging now among the packets. "So which are you? Are you a good person? Or are you weak and stupid? That's the thing, you see. Until you are tested, you don't know. You can't begin to know."

"Hans likes to tease," soothed Per. "He writes fairy tales - legends, and he paints the pictures for them too."

"Fifty years of my life is here," Mincke waved his hand. "And I cannot remember what I have done! Is that not comical?"

"Tell Trudi," urged Per. "She will remember. She is young. She can remember everything."

Mincke took down a bag at random, opened it and spread the papers on the desk. The pages had been taken from a square-ruled exercise book and were covered in close manuscript, a neat, upright, continental hand. Blue ink. Trudi made out a title: "Ny Saga". All the writing was in Swedish. "New Tales," he said, tracing the words with his finger. Per looked on.

"All the old stories you know already, no doubt." Mincke dropped some of his hostility. "They are about giants and witches and dragons and gold. Little elves in red hats. These are new tales. Today the trolls have combed their hair and put on tidy clothes. They are hard to see. But they are still there." He pulled out a different sheet, decorated in watercolour, and scrutinized it to reacquaint himself with the subject.

"Ja, here," his finger moved again. "Once you learn to recognize them, you will find them everywhere. I have called them the Sneevelings. Trolls in disguise. *Very* dangerous!" He made a grimace, but this time a smile had got into it. "They get up to all sorts of things. They are clever and they can sneak their way into any house. I spent my life trying to outwit them, and wrote down all their antics. But now," the smile faded, "now I am not sure of anything any more."

"Who is this?" Trudi pointed to a shiny figure in a tight blue suit, holding an inspector's clipboard under his arm. She wanted to keep him to the point, and he seemed happy now to comply:

"He's a Fluga. A Fly to you. He spends his day annoying people. Ringing them up for nothing at all. Sending them questionnaires in the post." Indeed, there were life-like, line and wash bluebottles perched along the margin, putting out their tongues, as flies do, to see what the paper tasted like. "And this," Mincke picked up speed as the memory came back. "This is a Geting, a wasp, who arrives just when you are about to have your dinner and always wants the best bit for himself. Somewhere here, ah yes - one of the Myras, an ant who is forever manufacturing useless things… cakes to make people hungry, and toys to make them bored."

"Don't you mean cakes to *stop* people being hungry? And toys to *stop* them being bored?"

Mincke laughed and almost choked on his spittle.

"No, no. That's the whole point! The Sneevelings have turned everything upside down. The sleeping pills in this world keep you awake and the policemen are burglars. The sensible people live in asylums. And the children are more clever than the grown-ups."

Mincke became more animated. His hand trembled as he leafed through his papers. His eye almost twinkled. Trudi could not help laughing. The drawings were witty, full of incongruous details: smiling cats, eavesdropping goldfish and the Sneevelings themselves, with their pointy insect faces, which blended so neatly into background you had to look hard to find them. The lines of Mincke's ink pen wriggled in and out of the layers of wash, with virtuosic skill.

Here sat the mouth-watering buns that made people hungry, their pink icing glistening. She thought of Auntie Barbara's baking and wondered what that literary glutton would think of these tales. *Would she sell them in her bookshop in England?* There was a doctor with a thermometer. The little boy in bed must be in mortal danger, for if this was an upside-down world, the doctor would almost certainly make him ill. But this boy had a canny look in his eye. He had poured his medicine into his hot water bottle when the doctor wasn't looking. Perhaps he was one of those clever children who could stand on their heads to see the world the right way up!

"Can you buy these stories in a book?" Trudi asked. She was sure Barbara would sell it, and hundreds of other booksellers besides.

Mincke shook his head. "No. Writing is one thing. Selling quite another. And publishers are tricky. Nothing ever pleases them. I got bored with addressing envelopes only to have them come straight back. Wrong paper. Wrong layout. Wrong type. I went back to writing, thinking someone can read it all when I am dead. But now, now I think they must be printed or they will be lost. Then I shall have lived and struggled for nothing."

"Oh no! You must print them! They are funny, crazy characters. People will love them! And you must do them in English too so we can all read them. What happens - do the children manage to outwit the Sneevelings and turn the world round again?"

Mincke rounded on her: "That *you* must tell *me*," he said. "I do not know any more."

"My friend, you are tired. And we must not keep you." Per patted him on the shoulder. "I think we can help you find a publisher, eh Trudi?"

"Daddy will know one," she said confidently. "Daddy knows everyone! He can do anything!"

"Eh - eh." Mincke pulled a face. "There may not be time. And I will not let the originals out of my sight. If the Sneevelings can get hold of anything they will steal it!"

"There will be time enough, God willing," Per concluded. "And now we must be going. The service at church will be finished I think, Trudi, and we promised to prepare some lunch. Take heart, Mincke. Let us speak to our friends and see what can be done. The papers are safe where they are just now and tomorrow I will come back and help you with the bees. Meanwhile, stay home. Keep warm. Eat your Christmas biscuits! Oh, and just one thing before we go." He paused at the door. "Perhaps you should show me what the television man did."

As the pair shuffled from the room Trudi took a daring decision. She recognized in Per's advice that reassuring tone that parents adopt when they mean to make children forget all about something. She knew it so well ...*tomorrow, darling... when you are better... when you grow up...* and she knew that it usually meant a fobbing off. But Mincke needed to print his stories *now*. Only children and old people know that you cannot rely on tomorrow. Anything can happen before tomorrow. So Trudi resolved to act straightaway. She would *show* Barbara how beautiful these drawings were and once she had seen them, Barbara would feel as passionate about them as she did herself. It seemed utterly wrong for them to be wrapped up and hidden in such an out of the way place, especially

41

when she thought of all that Mincke had been through. She would take a photograph of them with her new camera and show them when she got back to England. It wasn't stealing - just helping. But Trudi knew she must act quickly and secretly.

In moments she had snapped a handful of paintings and for good measure she also copied the title page and part of a chapter headed 'Snigel Strimma', which had little snails climbing round the margin. In fact, the snails had written the heading with the trails they left behind them. They were dear little humbug snails with spiral bandings just like the ones Trudi used to find amongst the garden weeds at home. She started, hearing voices in the hall. The old men had come back.

"Trudi we're leaving!" called Per and then *più piano:* "Listen, Hans. Don't use that television. Lock your door and do not open it to strangers. Huh? We will be back before you know it." Mincke seemed hardly to hear their farewells, but as they let themselves out he hurried after them and clasped their hands in his.

"God bless you!" he faltered, "for your kindness!"

There were tears in his eyes.

Chapter Six

The Problem with Being Disobedient

They walked for some time in silence before Trudi found her tongue.

"Grandfather, why did you look at the television?"

Per nodded. He was expecting the question.

"Six weeks ago, we had this new tree planted here." He pointed once more to the satellite mast on the hill. "Almost immediately, Mincke's television went wrong. It's not a big problem. He hardly watches it. But he telephoned the company and they sent an engineer. This engineer, he's very friendly and he seems to know right away what is wrong. Mincke gives him coffee and they begin to chat. In no time at all they are talking about bees. This television man collects beetles. They are, as you might say, birds of a feather. Mad about insects! Mincke shows him a beetle drawing he is making and the man is entranced. He promises to come the next day with a filter to cut out the interference and as soon as he plugs it in – magic! - the television works again. Everything fine!" Per trudged on a few paces and then sighed.

"Everything *not* fine?" prompted Trudi.

"No sooner has he gone than Mincke falls into a deep sleep and it is several days before he wakes up. The house is cold. The milk has gone off. But what really worries him is that he cannot remember the television man's name. This is most unusual. His mind is always so sharp. By the end of the day Mincke has discovered other things he can't remember. He is sure he bought a new cheese. He can't have eaten it. Where did he put it? And did he agree to visit his wife's cousin for Christmas? And what was the cousin's name? And what was his wife's name? Now he thinks he must be ill. But the doctor checks his blood pressure and says there is nothing wrong. He has been working too hard. Relax. Enjoy the holidays and come back in a couple of weeks if he is still worried. At the crossroads, Mincke is not sure of the way home. By the time he arrives at my door he is truly frightened.

"'Larsson, I'm going mad!' he cries. 'No, no,' I say. 'I'll see you home. The Sneevelings have hidden the cheese, no doubt!' I meant it as a joke, but as the days passed I could see that there was little to laugh about. Mincke next found that he could not remember his own work. He had to read the Sagas to remind himself of what he had written. And he no longer knew how the tales would end. The plot had simply vanished from his head. That was when he decided he must find a publisher. He wrote again to the literary agents in Stockholm, but without success. And by then he was not sure even whether he had posted the letters or not."

"He must go back to the doctor!" said Trudi.

"Yes, but now he trusts no one. It is too bad that he has lost his bees!"

"Perhaps the bees lost their memory too," Trudi was half listening, half watching the patterns of snow on the fir needles. She had heard Corky say that that could happen. "Maybe they forgot that it was winter."

"That's it! That's it, my Trudi." Per stopped and took her suddenly by the shoulders, his eyes blazing. "I *knew* you would be the one to understand!" Then he recovered himself and dropped his hands. "Hep! We must hurry now, or your parents will be worried. We have no lunch ready and whatever will they think of us - on Christmas Day too!" After a moment's reflection, he added in an undertone: "Perhaps better not to say where we have been just now, ja?" Then he tramped on, silent, thumping his stick into the snow.

Good King Wenceslas, thought Trudi. It was easier to walk, if she trod in the holes of her grandfather's footprints. So *that* was why the king in the carol told his page to walk behind him when he was tired. Dropping back she had time to look around her. How beautiful the forest was! Here hung a whole bunch of icicles, suspended from a branch. She pulled off her gloves and felt for her camera. She must have just one picture of the icicles - as a memento. And one of Per stomping on ahead. One of the blue hill behind them. One of black tree trunks... Per stopped to look round for her and she ducked and picked up her gloves.

"Coming!" she called, racing to catch up.

They arrived home in time to lay the table and find the remains of the ham. Trudi smiled when she saw it. Now she understood why Mincke had refused to eat it the night before. Not because he was rude, but because he was Jewish. Per should have warned them. But then sometimes he seemed forgetful too. The table looked pretty with the Christmas flowers and the last of the eggs and caviar. Trudi thought she would take a snap of it to show to Barbara along with her other pictures when she returned to England, but to her dismay she found her jacket pocket empty.

In a quiet frenzy, she went through all her pockets, checked her jeans, her rucksack, the rumple of clothes on her bed... No camera. She must have dropped it in the forest, somewhere near those icicles and how could she ever find it again or begin to explain what had happened, when Per had expressly told her to leave the thing at home? Even supposing it was found, it would be useless now for it would have been lying in the snow for hours. What a disaster! A fitting punishment for being so disobedient - stealing copies of Mincke's work, and secretly photographing her grandfather. Scarp wouldn't let anybody take a photograph of him. Scarp was a gypsy who lived in the woods at the bottom of the garden at home. He said that photographs were soul-snatchers. Per didn't like them either.

Poor Trudi was in trouble now. Such big trouble! And there was no one she could even tell. She had lost her best present and her naughtiness would be the final ruin of Christmas. Kirsten, she knew, would be furious. Sven hurt. Grandpa disappointed. Mincke outraged. And Jurgen would merely gloat and stir things up some more. She sank into paralysed despair.

When the churchgoers returned, laughing, from their hot chocolate and a swim in the hotel spa, they found her a very subdued girl indeed, and no amount of teasing would coax her into a smile. She and Per stuck to their story. They had been for a walk in the woods. It was very lovely. Then they came home and made lunch. No mention of Mincke, or the television man, or the Sneevelings, or the bees. But when Jurgen suggested that Trudi should take a photo of them all together, her nerve finally snapped and she fled upstairs in tears.

It took Sven twenty minutes to extract a confession from her. Holding her in a kindly bear hug, he smoothed her hair and made the kind of gentle noises only a father can, while offering her his own distinctly grubby tissue to blow on.

"You lost the phone," he repeated gently. "Well, it's not the end of everything, you know."

"But it *is!*" sobbed Trudi.

"There are other phones in the world."

"No. No you don't understand. I took some special pictures... And I *shouldn't* have..." Carried away by the tragedy of the moment, her voice wobbled, sounding so absurd, she teetered on the brink of a smile.

"Well," Sven sat her up and chucked her under the chin. "We'll have to find it then, won't we?"

This was the marvellous thing about Sven. No matter how foolish and impractical the challenge, he always set out with conviction and hope. You could almost believe he would succeed.

Trudi stopped crying and stared. He talked as if life could go on quite normally. "Will you help me?" she sniffled, incredulous.

"It's too late to do anything today. The light is already failing and we don't want to get lost in the dark. You and I - we'll have a walk tomorrow - before it snows again! Now," he tapped her this time on the nose: "was that a ray of sunshine I saw through the clouds?"

His mocking tone prompted another outburst of tears, but these were tears of gratitude and relief and signalled the end of the crisis. If only it could be possible to keep her misdemeanours from Kirsten, and above all from Per, then perhaps, Trudi believed, she would survive to tell the tale.

Sven himself felt glad to have her confidence. Something had been bothering him since his last days in England, a secret that had gnawed away all along at the party mood of Christmas, and he would be glad himself to spend an hour in the quiet company of the trees.

"She's overwrought," he fibbed to his wife. "Worrying about school I think. I've promised to go tracking with her tomorrow in the forest. She's happy now."

The day, nevertheless, seemed long. At four o'clock, a knock at the door roused them all from lethargy.

"Mr. Larsson? I'm looking for a Mr. Per Larsson." The visitor's voice sounded unfamiliar, high-pitched for a man, and marked, despite perfect English, by a giveaway Swedish lilt.

Sven blocked the doorway. "He's here. But I'm his son. Can I help you?"

"Stromberg." The stranger held out a black-gloved hand. "Olaf Stromberg. I'm working here, staying nearby. I have some news, bad news I'm afraid. There's been a fire."

Chapter Seven

Bad News

With that, Sven stepped back and the messenger came in, carefully removing his shoes. He had pale, floppy hair and weak, swimming eyes, a blur of blue behind gold-rimmed lenses. *Medium in height,* Trudi thought. *Slight build. Thirties perhaps?* His sensitive hands trembled as he sat down. *Weasel face. Don't like him,* thought Trudi. But he was all earnestness and sympathy. He took his mission very seriously. Per, from his corner, watched without speaking and left the role of host to his son.

"Yes, it's the house over the way. The fire broke out just after dark. Neighbours saw it. An old man lives there on his own. I feel terrible. I had met him only a short while before. A very interesting man, you know."

"Hans Mincke!" said Sven. "Is he hurt?"

"No, no, he got out. He's shaken of course. They've taken him away to be treated for shock. But the house, alas, is completely destroyed. A wooden house like that – well, it's just a matter of minutes once fire takes hold."

"But his work!" gasped Trudi, speaking out of turn. "What about his stories?"

Stromberg turned to look at her: "Did he have a library? I'm afraid it's all gone. The fire brigade are there now. They'll do an investigation, of course, but it looks as if the old boy left something on the gas. The neighbours said he was getting forgetful. What a tragedy. I'm so sorry. I think he was a friend of yours."

"A friend, yes." Per rose to his feet, cutting the visit short. "Very kind of you to come."

"He's at the Litven hospital. Social services will take care of him, but I thought you might like to know." Olaf's eyes wandered round the room, taking in the lie of things, perhaps looking for something. "If I can be of any help, here's my card. Please don't hesitate to call me."

Sven nodded. "We're off back to England after tomorrow, but listen, this is where you can find us." He hastily scribbled his address. "If there are any more problems here, perhaps you could let me know?"

"A pleasure!" smiled the visitor. "Goodnight Mr. Larsson, goodnight, goodnight."

As the door closed, Trudi flew into a passion. "But that's terrible!" she cried. "Poor Mincke! To lose everything again - his plates, his clocks, even the photo of his wife!"

"He is safe, darling. That's what matters," said Kirsten, wondering why Trudi had taken the trouble to invent such things.

"*I* thought you didn't like him," Jurgen observed.

"I didn't." Trudi made a swift recovery. "But - but I can be sorry for him, can't I?" She looked at Per, aware that she had been indiscreet, but Per seemed lost in his own thoughts. He had taken the stranger's news quite without surprise or emotion. Did he actually understand what had happened? Once more Trudi suffered a qualm of doubt. Did he *remember* that they had visited Mincke only that morning?

Sven tapped Stromberg's card on the back of his hand. Here was another crisis and it fell to him once again to save the day. At all costs they must stay cheerful. "Tomorrow I'll go into Litven and see that everything is all right. Will you come with me, Pappa? I'm sure your friend would be glad to see you."

Per shook his head. "No, no. It is a long way. Tell him - tell him he can come here if he wants. He must have a roof over his head."

Trudi turned to Sven. What about their walk in the forest? Would that be abandoned now? "*I'll* come!" she said.

Kirsten promptly rose to the occasion. "We can send him the Christmas flowers. And I'll make up some food. I wonder where his family are? Do you think that man Stromberg will find them? He seemed very genuine – very well-meaning."

Sven flashed Trudi a smile and pocketed the card. "We'll sort it all out tomorrow."

That evening they were especially nice to one another. Kindness eases the discomfort of guilt and each of them felt somehow responsible for the upsets that had so marred their time together. They had all been hiding their true feelings, after all, wishing for things they could not share. They had made rather a mess of their

49

Christmas and now they wondered if they had somehow brought misfortune on Mincke, too. Even Jurgen stopped teasing. He did not like to see Trudi actually wretched. What pleasure could there be in deflating someone who was already flat? Tomorrow the family would pack their things and in a day or two they would resume their English life as if nothing had happened. For Jurgen that meant football, which was fun, and cello practice, which was not, and all the excitement of being back with his friends. He still felt impatient to go home but he no longer wanted to show it and hurt people's feelings.

Kirsten, seeing the end of her ordeal in sight, made peace with Per's kitchen and threw herself into her chores with more of a will. She even hazarded some tactful improvements - arranging cups on shelves and replacing the worn out rug with one she had bought for home. As for old Per, he busied himself with his logs, innocently dropping bark and ash where Kirsten had just swept and trotting out old rhymes and sayings as though he had freshly coined them. He did not disclose the more sombre thoughts that sometimes threw a shadow on his face but Sven suspected he might be glad to have his home back to himself.

And Sven? Well, now that he no longer had to play the jester, he began to doubt the wisdom of bringing his family to Sweden, after all. They had clearly endured rather than enjoyed it. Perhaps he had been selfish, insisting on the trip. And that other matter was bothering him too. He had not had the courage to confess it to his wife before, but soon he would have to come clean. Yes, he would have to be especially nice to Kirsten...

The thaw that had begun that day continued all night, with warm air blowing in from the south. Per shook his head. Strange weather. You wouldn't expect a thaw till April. But every now and then you could hear the icicles crashing down, or a slow rumbling as the snow shifted on the roof. From the ground beneath Trudi's window came the gurgle of melt water, playing amongst the firs. She lay in the dark till late, listening and fretting about her phone. It would be sitting in a puddle. It would be ruined completely. Despite Sven's optimism, she felt frustrated and depressed. Even if they rescued the mobile, there were still Mincke's pictures... all wasted in the fire. And the poor bees... Who now would save the bees? The Larssons could not help. They were going back to

England. And what could Per do on his own? Even walking up the hill tired him.

In her mind she considered again the stranger who had brought the news. Something nagged her about him - something that was not quite right. His shoes? He wore tight, elastic sided boots with long toes. No. Not that. His hands? So clean and pink... Or that business card that he had given her father? As Sven put it in his pocket, she thought she recognized the rainbow pattern of the logo printed there. But where had she seen it before? A twisted ribbon, looped sideways in a figure-of-eight. Jurgen had one scribbled on his rough-book at school. He and his friend Angus were always drawing them... Was that what Angus had on his Waggle Phone?

Trudi felt she could bear the worry of it all no longer. She would tell her father all she knew tomorrow. If she didn't, she would burst!

Chapter Eight

The Celestial Hunt

In the end Sven made the journey to Litven alone, promising to be back before lunch. The melted snow had frozen during the night and thawed again and now lay in glassy puddles making the ground treacherous underfoot and Trudi and Jurgen took Per Larsson's little sledge, built themselves a slide in the meadow and played on it till their trousers were wet and their faces ruddy.

Per shook his head. "They should have done it when the snow was dry. But then they didn't want to play! Hep! Children!"

Standing at the window, he looked suddenly bereft and Kirsten felt a pang of pity. Suppose this was the last time they saw him? He had changed greatly since the summer. Now he was quiet and biddable, showing no sign of that primordial energy which had so unnerved her only months before. After what had happened to Mincke she wanted to be kind. But Per did not want to talk about Mincke. He repeated his offer to take him in, and that was all he would say. No one knew if the old curmudgeon would come. It seemed more likely that he would stay in the care of the State.

Mincke was sitting, glassy eyed, in a hospital dressing gown, when Sven found him and did not even answer to his name. The nurses said he was still in shock. That nice Mr. Stromberg had called by again. Nothing more could be done at present and Sven patted him on the hand and left.

With the snow beginning to melt, he thought it might be hard to find good animal tracks today, but he kept his promise to the children and set off with them into the woods while Kirsten packed for home. Actually, he needn't have worried, for the thaw had barely reached the forest floor. In the shade, there were ring patterns where branches had dripped overnight and fresh rabbit trail scampered in and out, but otherwise the snow looked fresh as ever. They found fox spoor and the remains of some red berries which had passed through a bird. Then more impressions – a whole web of comings and goings. Deer slot. Ghost feet. Every mark telling a tale... Out on the open path, however, things looked different. The sunshine had slipped in and puddled about in yesterday's tracks till they gaped like yeti prints. You could see where Trudi and Per had paused and turned about to get their bearings. Clusters of icicles hung everywhere. Looking for a particular spot was going to be difficult.

"Perhaps I stood here," said Trudi, peering amongst the branches. "Grandfather was down the hill ... Oh, all the trees look the same!"

Sven poked about nearby with a stick, while Jurgen ran on ahead. He had come in on the secret about the phone and thrown himself enthusiastically into the hunt.

"It's hopeless!" Scuffing the path with her foot, Trudi gave in to gloomy thoughts. "We'll never find the place and even if we do, it will be too late. The phone can't work now. You can see, everywhere's wet. You'll *have* to tell Mummy and she'll have me locked up!"

Sven laughed. "You are not a criminal!"

"Not a criminal – an idiot. She'll *really* think I'm mad."

"She's going to be too upset with *me* to worry about you!" The words were out before he could bite them back.

"With *you?*"

Sven straightened up and gazed far away.

"Trudi, can you keep a secret?"

Another secret? Trudi had resolved to give up all her secrets, but perhaps there was room to squeeze just one more in. She instantly forgot the phone.

"I'm going to lose my job," Sven went on. "They are cutting down the University departments, making them smaller. They notified me at the end of term, but I didn't have the heart to tell your mother just then. I hoped something else would turn up. I so wanted this to be a good Christmas - no problems."

"But you'll get another job!" said Trudi without hesitation.

"Perhaps, but it won't be easy. And it may not be near home. We may have to move. They are cutting posts at lots of Universities. There won't be too much money..."

Trudi looked at his face, all rumpled with worry. "Professor Saxmund will find you something," she declared. "He'll take care of us. He always does."

"He may not be so sure of a job either. All the funding is coming from an outside business source. *They* will choose the staff from now on."

"But we don't *need* lots of money! We'll be fine! Besides, you're the best! Everybody will want you."

Sven closed his eyes and opened them with a smile. "You're just about as silly as me, aren't you, girl! Never give in, eh? Larssons never say die!" Such pirate talk was music to Trudi's ears.

"Never!" She tried to picture how her mother would take the news. No more extravagant shopping. No more foreign holidays. But then her mother knew how to deal with every crisis. She was marvellous. "Never say die!" She slipped her arm through his. "Something will come up."

"Then you think I can tell her?"

"Of course! She'll be marvellous!"

At that moment, Jurgen appeared waving something pink.

"It's dead!" he announced with relish. "Full of water."

Sven didn't give up so easily. He winked a smile: "We'll dry it out by the stove and see."

And though drying out didn't actually help, Trudi kept the phone and found to her relief that the issue passed without fuss, for Kirsten, having heard Sven's news, had weightier matters on her mind and Per took no interest.

The family would leave at first light tomorrow, so the car must be packed that night. At dusk the sky cleared and temperatures started to fall again. It was a chilly job carting out the cases.

Trudi looked back at Per's house and the light from the doorway, just as she had seen them a few days before. Her expectations then seemed childish now. Of course adventures didn't happen as she had imagined. What actually happened in life was nothing like a storybook with a plot, but merely a bundle of random events. And people themselves, why, they too were little more than bundles, full of loose ends, incapable of understanding or even remembering their own reasons. In a way she had had an adventure but it led nowhere - meant nothing. And secrets! They hemmed her in on every side, but to no purpose. They were simply pointless and sad.

Per took her by the shoulder and led her away from the house to a clearing under the sky.

"See those stars?" he said. "I will tell you what they are." The heavens glittered with a preternatural brilliance, never to be seen in England. It was dizzying to look up. Trudi felt her grandfather's grip tighten and her heart gave a leap. Of course she knew that the road and the house and her own parents were still nearby, but here, outside the circle of light that encompassed them, the forest yawned silent and dark. The sky felt close enough to touch.

Per traced a figure with his finger. "Those are the seven oxen, Trudi." He paused. "Three bright ones, like a tail. Then a team of four. You will know them by another name, maybe. They are also called the Great Bear and the Elk and in Finland, Otava. The stars have different names in different lands, for as their stories have been carried from tribe to tribe and traveller to traveller over the centuries, they have changed in the telling. But the same thread runs through them, for they all share one beginning and they teach the same truths: what is time - and life and death - and how will life go on? In the far north you spend many weeks without seeing the sun in winter. When this dark time comes, the stars seem brighter. Years ago, before we had electric light, they were everything to us: our clocks, our lanterns, our books. We all knew their stories."

Trudi recognized the constellation. On warm summer camps, supper over, with the fire burning low, she remembered how she and Jurgen had sprawled, relaxing on the ground, hands under heads, as Sven pointed out the 'W' of Cassiopeia, the three stars of Orion's Belt and this crooked figure, the Plough.

But Per was talking again: "Now, follow those two stars. See how they point to another?"

"It's the Pole Star," said Trudi, re-living Sven's lessons. "The star that doesn't move."

"In Sami culture it is called the Nail Star because in the Arctic people believed that this marker held up the tent of the world. A Sami tent has an opening through which you can see the stars." He made a tepee with his hands. "When the wind is still, the hearth-smoke rises from here like a pillar, or the post of a giant mill."

Trudi struggled to hold onto what he was saying for his voice resonated with a sudden urgency. He had come back to life. Here, at last, maybe, was the moment she had been waiting for. He was taking her into his trust. *Remember this,* she told herself trying to grasp the moment. The stars were spinning, dazzling like needles of ice. *No matter if you cannot understand. Remember you were here!* Per pointed through the shadows again.

"But a post is not quite enough. To fix the tent you also need a nail. So this star holds heaven and earth together. Could be a guide for travellers and sailors at sea. And a guide to other worlds too. Old legend says that that the pole that holds up the sky is also a great tree, called the Tree of Life. The roots stretch down to the land of the dead and the branches reach to heaven. Our world, the middle world, lies in between, so a man can travel from one place to another if he can climb this tree."

Remember the words.

Did shamans use the stars to navigate by? Was this how they journeyed to the realms of the spirits and ancestors? And had Per done so? There was no time to ask.

"Now from there, across this darker space to the three bright stars there." He was drawing an arc in the air. "These are hunters in the northern sky. They appear in winter to tell us that evening has come. They are chasing an elk. All across the polar lands the stars play out this story of the cosmic hunt as they have done since the beginning of time. Sometimes they are dogs, sometimes archers, sometimes the elk itself with its mighty horns. Every night they resume their flight. Neither the hunters nor the elk can pause, for though the stars race round the pole, one cannot touch another.

"Look here. Here is the Swan Prince, four stars and another astride the Milky Way. He brings the birds in summer and takes them away along that path to Birdland in winter. The sky is full of such mysteries. Back home they used to say the Milky Way was the ski-track of the sky-hunters. People have forgotten these things now. They do not live so close to nature. But the message of the stars is clear for anyone who hears it. If the elk rests he will be slain. And then - catastrophe. Night after night the hunt must go on. You cannot claim power over life without losing it. This is the course of Nature. Do you understand? If you stop the chase, time will cease. It will be the end of the world we know. Could you find these stars again?"

Trudi retraced her way along the imaginary web they had made. First the Oxen, then the Nail, the Hunter, and the Elk.

She nodded. Yes. She had got it.

Per turned and looked at her directly, his eyes glittering with excitement.

"Trudi, listen. Something is happening here. Something very bad."

Now he was going to confide in her! She was going to hear what she had come for. She gazed back at the shaggy space his figure cut against the sky.

"Is it about Mincke?" she asked.

"About Mincke, yes, but not just him. When I spoke to you in England, I thought that something might be done."

"I brought the shaman's belt. I wanted to tell you. I thought you had forgotten about it."

"Ja, but it's too late for that now. Too late." His voice tailed off and he seemed to undergo some inward struggle. "Things have gone too far."

"You can't put it right with magic?" Trudi prompted.

"Magic." Per dismissed the word with his hand. "Trudi, I do not have much time. Not enough time to teach you what I know. And it may be that I will not be here long enough to put a stop to the evil that I see. Someone is hunting here. They hunted down Mincke. They took from him everything that mattered. Ripped the very soul out of him. And whoever did that to him is now interested in me. They have already found my house, but I know things that must not fall into their hands. Do you understand?

"I am too old now to fight them man to man and they will be hoping that I turn to other ways to help my friend, for then they can catch me easily. But magic is not the right word for the power that was entrusted to me. Oh, yes, Trudi," he shook her arm, "you *were* right about me. I didn't just talk to wise people on my travels, I learned to practise some of their skills. In Samiland, they say, all the cunning arts were destroyed. But people do not always admit all they know. Especially to foreigners. In the old days, the noaïdis died rather than give up their secrets. Their drums were burnt, their songs forbidden. But in Samiland I was not a stranger. I was Sami too. I found teachers who helped me.

"I have been to places and seen things you could hardly dream of. This knowledge is not for everyone. It certainly does not belong to a television company! And it comes at great cost. In my own life, as you know, I had decided to give it all up. I thought there was no more use for it. It seems that I was wrong. But what can I do now? Even to talk of these things is very dangerous. Anybody might be listening."

"What is a noaïdi?" asked Trudi.

Per smiled. "They were the Sami medicine men - spirit doctors and priests of long ago. They dealt with all matters of life and death before Christianity came to the north. In other cultures they are known as shamans, shape-shifters, and they do their work by travelling in a trance to other worlds. Their journeys are secret so they travel in disguise, borrowing a new body to search for cures and lost souls. A shaman might hide himself in the body of an animal, but it is a perilous business. If he or she is named when they are 'flying' this way, they will be trapped in the spirit world, unable to come back. Trudi, they will die."

"What about their magic?"

"Magic, too, can be lost. Many people tried to destroy the knowledge of the noaïdis – and some tried to steal it. But until now no one really succeeded. Those old medicine men simply slipped out of prison and buried their magic where no one could find it. And if the foreigners dug it up they found they had nothing but dust in their hands! But now – things are different. There is a new witchcraft that is able to empty a man's mind... Mincke lost his memory. Remember? So did his bees... You realized it yesterday! They gave up the will to live, but where did their knowledge go? Now it could be my turn. So I must not be here when their spies come back. Hup!" He reasoned now with himself. "The old secrets. That is what they are after. Their power is very strong. I do not yet have the measure of it, but until I do, we are all in danger. Do you understand me? I do not fear death, but I fear that this new magic will steal everything, even death and time itself."

Trudi felt suddenly frightened. "Why can't we tell the police - about the bees - about the television. Why can't we tell Mummy and Daddy and get them to help?"

"Why? Because such things cannot be told to the world. I am only telling you because I think you have the 'eye'. You see on the inside. If we try to explain to others, they will say we are mad. And suppose, by a miracle, they believe us - what will they do? Arrest a television man? And what proof is there against him? Just our word - a child and an old greybeard! No, no. They would think we were mad. In any case it is not the television man who really matters. He is just a servant, obeying orders. Who are his masters, giving the orders? And who is above them? It would take a very great noaïdi to find that out."

"*I'll* do it! Tell me what to do!"

"No, no Trudi. You must go home and forget all this as if you never heard it. Forget that you ever saw Mincke. I thought we could save his stories, but now, as you see, it is too late. If you love me you will do as I say. Go back to England and be a good girl at school. If you try to tell others, even your own dear father and mother, they will not understand you. They are too slow and they talk too much. They would be like snails. Remember the snails in Mincke's drawing?" For a moment he seemed to forget that he had not been there when Trudi saw them.

"Each one leaves a little trail. So easy to follow. That is why I would not go to Litven today – dance to their tune. They used Mincke to find me and they would use me to find others who are greater than me. That must never happen. Now, our best hope is to lie quiet. Let everyone believe that you are merely a child and I have become a fool. For all his carefulness Mincke talked too much and they have finished him."

"But what will become of him? What will become of any of us? What kind of people could possibly want to hurt us?"

Per considered a moment: "Trudi, I cannot tell you just now. Certainly I have made some enemies in my life, for not everyone who deals with magic is good. There are those who are vain, jealous, greedy, just like other people. I met one once. Called himself a sorcerer, but really he was a thief. Such men are dangerous. They have long memories and if they cannot get what they want they will comfort themselves with revenge. Hep!" He shook his head and plucked at his eyebrows as if the memory upset him. Then he returned to his theme:

"Stay away from that satellite company. Mincke recognized the name when Jurgen said it. Laser Wag. I'm sure he blamed them for his troubles. And his bees are not the only casualties. Since that new mast arrived here some of our best trees have died in the forest and the wolves have gone. I used to hear them calling at night. Now silence. No tracks. There is also the old clock-maker in Litven, who went quite off his head after talking to a stranger... Yes, something bad is happening! Mincke hoped that you could solve the riddle of the Sneevelings. Of course, that is impossible. But perhaps in England, you *can* do something. Hold fast, like the Nail Star, to what I am telling you now. Keep your eyes and ears open. Do not accept the lies people tell you. That is the best you can do for Mincke. Be his torch-bearer and hold on to the truth. Knowledge might come to you that way."

Trudi stamped her foot with impatience.

"I don't understand. I can't stop the television company setting fire to things! I don't even know who they are!"

"That is good. And you do not need to do any more than watch and wait. Be patient, and secret, like a hunter yourself. Listen for clues. A twig snapping may mean danger nearby. And then there are false tracks, false notes. You will know them when you find them. Don't be misled. Your heart will tell you. You can trust your heart for it is good. Remember the things that really matter - the places where you feel at home. Mincke's bees got lost but your home is bigger than theirs. You belong to the whole earth and the sky and no one can take those things from you as long as you hold them dear."

"Is that why you showed me the stars?"

"The stars are always true. If ever you are in trouble, think of them. They will guide you."

"Grandfather!" Trudi threw herself impetuously into his arms. "Don't leave us! How will I know what to do? I can't manage on my own!"

Per tenderly disengaged himself. He reached in his pocket and brought out a purse of reindeer hide. "You will not need to. I hope and trust that in England you will be safe. After all, it is far from here. And, you know, trouble never comes without help. I shall watch over you for as long as I can... and then, remember, you have Jurgen - he is a resourceful boy in an emergency. Could help if you are in trouble. Also, take this. It looks nothing but it is a powerful token and has tale to tell. This has sat in my pocket for longer than I can remember. Comes from a special place. But you may need it one day. Look after it for me till this is all over. Perhaps then there will be time for 'magic' again. Can you do that, eh?"

He sniffed, as if he had a cold and folded the purse in her hands. "Hep! And now we must get back. The others will wonder where we are."

Was it all true? It sounded too fantastic. Like one of her own childish inventions! Had she not seen Mincke's undoing for herself, she would have thought her grandfather was rambling, imagining things, as old people do when they slip into a world of dreams. Somehow it hardly seemed to matter. All she knew was that he was in trouble and he needed her. For a moment she thought he was crying, as if he could not bear to say goodbye. She took his cold hand and laid it against her cheek. She would stand by him, come what may.

Later, alone, she untied the purse he had given her. There lay his deer-bone charm: the original carving, of which her hunter's bow was a copy. It was his birth-gift from his mother, and Trudi stared at it blankly, for she knew no Sami who cared about life would give up his amulet so. Beside it, she found a nugget of iron ore, heavy, shiny and misshapen, as if it had been in a fire.

Was Per preparing to die? And yet he did not intend to. He hoped for better times when he could share his magic... This was a truly appalling, powerful secret! She heard her parents moving about in their room next door. They were making final arrangements for the morning. How innocent they seemed. How trusting. They could not imagine the incredible thing she now knew. *The end of death and time...* And of course, Per was right. She could not explain it to them, because they would simply tell her she was making things up. They might even inform the school psychiatrist and then she could be no help to anyone.

No, her course lay clear. She was going back to England but she would *not* give up and do as her grandfather told her. She could not possibly forget something so mysterious and dreadful. That would be tantamount to running away and she was a Sami child – a shaman's child. She was a Larsson and Larsson's never said die! She would be bold and cunning, play good but strike a course on her own. Last summer Per had rescued her. Now she would repay him. The little boy in Mincke's saga outwitted the Sneevelings,

61

didn't he? Well, she would do the same. She would *not* abandon Mincke. She would defy the odds and finish his story for him.

See, the world was turning upside-down already! Here she was, feeling old and wise, while the grown-ups round her looked like children. The change had started that afternoon when Sven confided in her. Now Per had done the same. She would have to watch over them, comfort them, encourage them if things got difficult. And she would save the noaïdis' secrets, so that their magic could come back one day.

Moments later, Jurgen stuck his head round the door.

"You got off lightly over your phone," he chirped. "Are you going to give me a reward for finding it?"

Trudi looked at his cherubic face with sudden sisterly concern. "Yes" she said. "You can have my amulet after all. I think you are going to need it."

Part 2

Processional. Easter

Chapter Nine

Trouble in the Cellar

"Damn! Damn! Hell, Blood and Damnation!"

On a wet afternoon towards the end of March, Barbara was squeezed into a corner of her cellar doing stock-taking, a laptop perched on her knee. A maze of books stretched round her as far as the eye could see: books on shelves, books in boxes, books in piles, teetering skywards - a mini-Manhattan of books. She had plumped herself down on a tea chest and its unyielding form impressed itself painfully upon her flesh. Not only that, the dingy, spore-laden air got up her nose, reminding her that there was a problem down here somewhere - dry rot? - a problem that could cost thousands in such an ancient property - and only added to her general irritation.

"What has happened?" Corky, who had been concealed in a trench behind titles on 'Yoga', jumped up and cracked his head on the ceiling.

Barbara gave him a sardonic look. "See what I mean?" she said.

The mild-mannered Corky rubbed his skull vigorously, as if he intended the drubbing for someone else. He was dusty and thirsty and sick of this uncomfortable job. The cellar could not accommodate someone of his height, and it had no end of knobs and hooks and beams which stuck out of the walls in inappropriate places; booby traps for the unwary. As Barbara explained, you couldn't tidy it up because it had a preservation order on it. It had been a hemp pit in the days when ships sailed up the River Teal to trade with the merchants of Newbridge. All Corky could conclude was that the old rope makers must have been very short, and very thick-skinned. And *they* didn't have to stand almost on their heads to read the titles of books stacked the wrong way up!

"I mean we are not meant to be here, doing this!" Barbara slammed her laptop shut and sat breathing hard.

"Well, we might as well finish," Corky objected. "We're nearly there!" After 'Yoga' came 'Zoology' and then they were done. They would have logged the entire stock of Barbara's bookshop and they could reward themselves with a cup of tea.

Barbara turned to him with a face suddenly full of contrition. "Man, that's the point. It's gone!" Her Boston brogue took on a tragic tone. "It's all gone - all our work for the past dunnohowmany hours. The computer just swallowed the whole goddamn file. Corky, it's *gone!*"

Corky's jaw dropped. He had been reading out titles now since breakfast. He was sore and jaded. He had ripped a hole in his best dungarees on a nail somewhere near the novels section. Brontë - that's where: "Jane Eyre, Shirley, Villette," *rip!* "Wuthering Heights".

Barbara gave up on contrition and returned to rage.

"What stupid idiot devises a programme that poops out on itself just when you're coming to the end?"

"Perhaps you haven't deleted it. Perhaps you just pressed the wrong button."

"Too damn right! Corky, they're *all* wrong buttons! Give me a pen and a piece of paper that's not gonna disappear into thin air and I can do a job. Hell, I can't stay down here any more. I've got to have some coffee!" Wincing, she peeled her ample form off the trunk. "If I'd wanted to mortify the flesh I'd have been a nun, right?" She was now talking to no one in particular, since no one, it seemed, could really understand. "And," she raised the volume, "can you tell me what the hell is going on up there? It sounds like a bear garden! This may be Wednesday-closing, but do we have to scream the place down?" She struck a pose at the foot of the stairs, and the thought of her in a wimple now reduced Corky to tears of laughter. She might as well have suggested squeezing herself into a tutu.

"You - a nun!"

"Yea. What's so funny?"

She thought about it for a moment and then her brown eyes began to twinkle. Perhaps it was a little bit funny. All the same there would be some definite advantages. "If I was in a cell all day, praying, I wouldn't have to produce end-of-year accounts for the tax man, would I? And I wouldn't have a house full of screaming kids!"

She set her foot on the bottom step and yelled indecorously: "Come on, you guys. Get your butts down here. Chocolate Brownie coming up!" Whether this was a reference to her dusty

66

state, or to the lip-smacking cakes she was famed for, the noise on the first floor ceased as if by magic. And by the time Barbara had climbed the stairs, the children from the bear garden had lined themselves up neatly and expectantly beside the kitchen cookie-jar: Trudi, Jurgen and Pedro, looking a bit rumpled and out of breath.

They had been playing hide and seek.

Pedro's only English so far came from his old-fashioned schoolbooks and the Larsson's recent smattering of Spanish consisted of exclamations and convent prayers, so games with words were still a bit tricky. Pedro being blind, they could not use pictures. But then they had hit on this game which needed no language beyond the grammar of rough-and-tumble and despite his pious orphanage upbringing, Pedro threw himself into it with devilish high spirits. They followed the traditional rules: Trudi and Jurgen concealed themselves in the room, or tried to tiptoe from one room to another, and Pedro had to track them, using his ears as eyes and negotiating the unfamiliar furniture with his hands. Sometimes, to make it harder, they turned him round and round. But Pedro always won. He knew exactly where they were without seeing. And he remembered his tracks with such precision, his new friends could only marvel in astonishment.

Corky's boy had been in England two weeks and already he had captured the hearts of all who met him. He seemed young for his age, with an easy, sunny manner, a cheeky irreverence and a spirit of enquiry that made his company a delight. But there was another dimension to Pedro of which he himself seemed hardly aware, which was written in the pure Inca configuration of his face and came out sometimes when he thought no one was listening and sang himself snatches of song. Then one glimpsed in him the lost dimension of an 'other-world', the high, impossible Andes and their secrets, too distant to comprehend. It sent a shiver down the spine. And Trudi loved it.

"Right. One each to start with and you take it back up to the sitting room." Out came the cake. "No crumbs in the shop, mind!" Barbara called after them.

At that moment the doorbell rang and she pushed her fingers into her hair. Her locks were tousled from much tugging and what was left of the topknot sat askew. Her face still glowed with exasperation.

"I'll get it." Corky dived for the door and returned, bringing Kirsten Larsson with two bulging shopping bags, in tow.

"Oh, honey, you're early!" Barbara gave her an encompassing hug. "Kids haven't finished playing, yet!"

"Well, B, I haven't finished either, but something has come up." She lowered her voice. "Something rather awful."

"Okay. Sit! Coffee first."

"Green tea?"

Barbara glanced briefly at God, who was located somewhere on the ceiling. She had been doing a lot of this today.

"Yup. Green tea!"

"I brought some with me," Kirsten began to rummage through her shopping. "I went to that new supermarket by the river. You know? BioDawn. It's an amazing place. Everything is organic. Locally produced or Fair Trade. And the stock is as good and fresh as in any other supermarket – no, better. Beautifully laid out. B, I know you are set against the idea, but you ought to go in and see. Really." She unearthed a packet - fibrous cardboard, hand-printed by a women's cooperative in Rajpur.

Barbara accepted the gift as if it contained a snake. "You know what I think."

"You think a big supermarket will spoil Newbridge and drive out the little shops. And you're upset that they sold the old car park and farmer's market site to the BioDawn company. B, I'm as sorry as you that Corky lost his busking spot. Everyone knows," she smiled specifically in his direction, "that his one-man-band drew more visitors to Newbridge than the quaint old streets and the abbey ruins combined! But they've got a new entertainment area by the supermarket entrance. Someone was painting children's faces there today. Corky, you should reapply. I'm sure you could get in."

Corky nodded and backed away. His busking kit had lain gathering dust now since October, when the market site was closed. Somehow he had lost heart. He had played his saxophone for Pedro - but the top hat and braces, the tramp's trousers, big shoes, knee cymbals, wrist bells that had defined him as a street musician, they belonged to easier times, when he had lived free on his nursery by the chalk-pit. Those were bonny, happy days, but late last summer some snooper had reported his makeshift quarters to the council and they had promptly turned him out. They were quite clear about it: *'No planning permission - no living on site'*. He could garden, they said, but not camp. So he found himself suddenly on the streets, and it was lucky for him that Barbara offered to take him in.

At Prospero's, he had a roof over his head and unlimited cake to eat. Barbara cared for him and he repaid her by helping out with her innumerable odd jobs, but he was not really cut out for indoor life. As bookshop assistant-cum-lodger, he felt like a caged monkey. In secret moments he dreamt of breaking away and roughing it once more. To go crawling back for a contract with BioDawn would be a sorry admission of defeat. Ever apologetic, he ran a hand over his shoulder.

"It's not the kind of place I'd like to work now." Shrugging a smile. "The old market had friendly faces and an easy-going spirit that appealed. I don't want to do publicity for the big boys."

Kirsten shook her head. "You've been listening too much to *her!* Not everyone who's big is bad. This BioDawn business is a new idea. They are doing just what you do on your nursery, Corky. Organic! They would probably even buy your vegetables."

"But I don't want to sell them," he objected, still unmoved. "I'd rather give them away. I've only ever grown things for love. Couldn't do it for profit."

The children reappeared at the sound of voices, hopeful of more cake, but Barbara had other plans.

"Look, here's five quid. You guys run to the pet shop just down the lane and get a bag of swan and duck food. Then you can feed the ducks off the bridge before Trudi and Jurgen go home. Corky will go with you, won't he?" She flashed a smile at his long-suffering person. That neatly got rid of everyone.

Now Kirsten.

"Trouble?"

Kirsten leaned forward in her chair, carefully cradling the tea-glass in her hands.

"I've just had a text from Sven. His father has gone missing."

"You mean Grandpa? In Sweden?"

"Sven received a telephone call from someone who works nearby. The place had been quiet for days and the postman realized that junk mail was piling up. No reply when he knocked. He roused a neighbour and they called the police and the police broke down the door. No one inside. No food left. No note. Nothing. It's still snowing there. He could have wondered off into the woods and... Oh B! What if he's dead?" Her beautiful face suddenly collapsed.

"Hey, Hey! Wait a minute!" Barbara threw her own cares to one side. "What are you talking about? The Grandpa I knew was just about the canniest old geezer I ever met. He's not going to go roaming the forest with no coat on!"

"You don't understand," Kirsten continued. "He'd changed. When we visited at Christmas he was *different*. He was quiet and docile and he kept forgetting things. I thought then... suppose... Oh B, what's going to happen to Sven... and TRUDI! She'll lose it completely. And she's been so much better lately. More her old cheerful self."

"Trudi's not going to lose anything. Now, Kirsten Larsson, you look me in the eye!" Barbara made an effective liar in a crisis. "I don't for one minute believe that anything bad has happened. If Per has gone somewhere he will have his reasons. Might have been nice if he'd told us. But it's no use us panicking all over the place. The police are looking, right?"

Kirsten found a tissue and blew her nose: "Sven is booking a flight now. He's going over straightaway. Thank goodness it's the end of term... Oh but B - I feel so awful. You know I never really made him properly welcome and now - now..."

"Now, when he comes back, you can!" Barbara gave her another of her celebrated bone-crushers. "Do you want me to break the news to Trudi? I can if you don't feel up to it. The kids can all stay here till this evening."

"No, no. I can do it." She folded her tissue and dabbed her face again. "Thank you. I don't believe you. I think he's lost his memory, like the old man we met at Christmas, and wandered off. But you're right, we have to keep going."

"Trudi and Jurgen can come over any time. They're no trouble, really, and Pedro doesn't leave for Kingsbury for another week. They hit it off so well, it's a joy to see them together. And you need time to look after yourself."

Kirsten nodded, not trusting herself to more words and followed Barbara through the shop. By the time they reached the door, she had all but recovered. "I'll go and find the children by the bridge... But I meant what I said about Corky. I recognized some of the old market stall-holders, working in that BioDawn shop. They've got a new ethic of embracing everyone. It could be just what we all need. Work. Security. Cheap, good, reliable food..."

"Out!" Barbara opened the door and pointed a peremptory finger down the street. Her face was wreathed in smiles. "Let me know what happens!" she yelled after Kirsten's retreating figure.

What happened was that Trudi took the matter entirely in her stride. She accepted Barbara's view that events would have a reasonable explanation and she continued to show the same sunny disposition she had brought back from Sweden in the winter. Sven sent regular reports from Litven. Per Larsson had been registered as a missing person and the police had widened their search, even contacting authorities in Finland, in case he had gone back to his place of birth.

All went well until the doorbell rang late on the Friday night.

"I'll get it!" called Trudi, dawdling down the stairs in her flip-flops. Perhaps it would be Professor Saxmund. He had promised to drop by. In the fuzzy glass of the front door she made out a thinner, blonder figure. Dark overcoat. A salesman?

"Trudi Larsson!" the figure gave a little bow as the door swung wide. "Remember me? Your father sent me to see how you are - you and your beautiful mother. Olaf Stromberg, your Grandfather's friend from Sweden."

Chapter Ten

Visiting the Bees

That April turned out unusually mild and dry. The blackthorn blossom at the chalk pit had already turned a dusty brown when Corky next visited his nursery, and the hedgerows of elder and may were breaking into leaf. In their shade, nestled a scattering of spring flowers: violets, primroses, celandines...

The Larsson children had not visited the place for months, for when Scarp, the gypsy, got into trouble and disappeared, leaving his pick-up in a ditch, they had lost their chauffeur. Life was not the same without Scarp. His acid humour and irreverent ways had been a fine tonic to the constraints of 'the system'. But two months ago he had done a runner, abandoning his caravan, his outstanding bills *and* his friends, without note or notice. Only Bella, the little terrier puppy, had gone with him.

Barbara felt it keenest of all. She nursed a more-than-friendly soft-spot for Scarp and she missed his swaggering into the bookshop unannounced and depositing the occasional rabbit or brace of pigeons on her counter, beneath the horrified noses of the customers. A flash of his crooked teeth or skinny carcase, with its green tattoos, would have been a welcome sight these days - and they would have gone through into the kitchen together and brewed up strong coffee and gossiped. Pedro would have loved him. But things had got too hot for Scarp long before anyone knew that Pedro was coming. He had innocently bought a truck that featured on the police computer. (History of theft and GBH, said the constable who came enquiring. Someone, it seemed, had been hit on the head with a spanner.) And then the authorities noticed that the tax disc had run out too, and Scarp was off - poof! - which left a problem when it came to outings.

Since Corky's only means of transport was a vintage motor bike and side-car, and Barbara didn't drive at all, Trudi and Jurgen had relied on Scarp for lifts to the chalk pit where Corky grew his vegetables. And here, last year, they had got used to regular

72

afternoons with him, constructing camps, hunting for fossils and flints and playing rolling down the hill.

"Want to be a proper Stone Age hunter?" he asked one day, as they lounged, belly-down on the grass. They had been firing plantain heads at one another, the way people do on summer picnics, and suddenly he was sitting up plaiting grasses, his skinny, brown fingers working like gear-levers.

"I'll make you a sling. And show you how to use it too, providing you don't go mad and brain one another! This is not a toy, see. It's the genuine article. Weave a loop here... then split the plait... then tie a knot. Now, find me a stone. *Just a small one* – I don't need a boulder. Stick it in there. Give the whole thing a swing to get the momentum going and when you feel the rhythm's right... let go. There!" The stone bounced off an anthill. "Bull's eye! *You* have a go. See if you can hit that tree stump over there. Better mind the greenhouses, though. You could stop an elephant with one of these."

That was Scarp all over. Making something out of nothing. They had spent all afternoon perfecting the art. Another day, it would be another idea.

Today they had to make do without him. No lift and no Barbara either. Barbara stayed at home to finish her accounts and Corky and the three children crammed themselves into a taxi with four bags of seed potatoes, some sandwiches and a digging fork.

"Es muy - es muy bonita!" said Trudi, excitedly practising her Spanish as the taxi rounded a bend in the river. "You'll see Pedro. Good! Pretty!"

Pedro giggled. "You crazy!"

"It's a..." Though gesticulating was no use, she did it anyway to emphasize her point, describing a pudding shape in the air. "Oh, how do you say *chalk pit?* It's a hill - mountain - *com los Andes...*"

"Que?" Incredulous, the blind boy threw up his hands and clapped them on his head as the back of the cab broke into an uproar.

"Foreigners!" muttered the cabbie. "The racket they make!"

They all piled out at the sign that read Lime Pit Hole and heaved the potatoes up the sunken track. Trudi felt a surge of high spirits, noting each familiar bush, fox scrape, bit of burnt-out tractor on the way. She chattered incessantly, no longer attempting to translate,

73

but just revelling in the sense of freedom that the place inspired. And it wasn't long before her tongue ran away with her.

The boys had edged ahead. Pedro put his arm on Jurgen's shoulder and used him as a guide. Corky, unable to carry his bags without stopping to rest, halted every twenty metres or so. And Trudi kept pace with him. She knew she was being kind and grown up, taking special care, because Corky was not as strong as he looked and even Barbara sometimes worried that his face was too thin, and his hair too grey. He had begun to walk with a stoop, as if his crooked shoulder weighed him down and his pony-tail stuck out to one side. Giving up the one-man-band had made him sad. But Trudi did not talk about these things. She unburdened herself on quite another matter. And Corky had no choice but to listen.

"So he's *staying!*" She put one outraged foot carefully in front of the other. "Olaf's staying in our house and he's put all his cases in the hall and taken over the front room as his bedroom. Mummy doesn't seem to mind! She's so busy with her design customers and so worried about Daddy, I don't think she even *notices*. He says Daddy told him to come. I *don't* believe it! He's given us chocolates and he brought Mummy flowers and he buys horrible tins of soup and boils them up in the kitchen."

Corky smiled. "Perhaps he is just grateful for your hospitality. You know, I am a lodger too. It can be awkward to stay in someone else's house."

Trudi dismissed this with the contempt it deserved.

"Corky, what is he doing? He's got cases and cases of stuff - like a salesman. But he never says where he is going, except sometimes it's London. Sometimes it's Tilchester. Next week he's going to France and leaving all his equipment behind. It doesn't feel like our house any more. He's commandeered the computer and put new programmes on it without asking. And he's got pink, soapy hands. And what will the neighbours say?"

Corky set down his bags and laughed outright. "Trudi you sound like the verger's wife!"

"Who is she?"

"She's no one in particular, just any middle aged, suspicious gossip!"

"Well I don't like it." Trudi ploughed on regardless. "I'm glad he can't come here."

Corky abandoned flippancy. "Suppose he is just lonely. He's a stranger in a foreign country. He needs friends." *(The ghost of Mincke slipped into Trudi's mind and sat down on some old furniture.)* "He tries to be kind and helpful. He knows that your father has many worries at the moment. And out of loyalty to your grandfather he attempts to keep an eye on matters here. You know, people are not always how they seem. Perhaps we should give him a chance…"

Trudi looked at him with a critical eye. She couldn't deny the logic of his argument. Put this way, of course, it was the most natural thing in the world for Olaf to visit the Larssons. They were always picking up acquaintances so. How else had they come to know Corky and Scarp, if not by being kind and welcoming? *(The ghost of Mincke beckoned to her from the shadows but for the moment she held him off.)* None of that friendliness, however, seemed appropriate for the interloper from Sweden. Olaf was a special case and Trudi was not going to relax her animosity towards him. If Corky wouldn't listen, she would simply keep her thoughts to herself.

The path now opened out onto a grassy level and the garden came into view: plots of winter cabbage and broccoli and some freshly dug trenches with long, ramshackle sheds and poly tunnels, all valiantly kept in order. The chickens had gone from their chicken run, though. It was impossible to look after them from a distance.

"You carry on, Trudi," said Corky. "I'm going to check the bees and then I'll be with you. Keep the boys away until I come, can you?"

"Oh, please!" *Trudi nodded briefly in Mincke's direction.* "Let me help you. I'd rather stay with you." Ever since the incident at Mincke's she had taken an exceptional interest in bees. But then, she took an interest in everything. *Keep your ears and eyes open… Watch and wait.* That was what Per had told her. *Be patient and secret,* he said. So she applied herself diligently, like a model child, ever eager to please. She had kept her head down at school now for a whole term and she would lie low over Olaf Stromberg too. They would never know what was really in her mind. Her bright eyes shining, round and clear, she hung on Corky's sleeve. "Are you going to feed them? I'll be very still. Just look. I won't upset them."

Poor Corky found it, as always, impossible to say no, though he knew he was taking a risk. Children and bees ought not to mix together. But Trudi always managed to persuade him. And so far they had been lucky. No accidents. The boys had wandered off, out of earshot. "Run and tell them, then," he cautioned. "Say no more than one person at a time can look. I've only got one spare veil. Tell them to stay up at the far end till we come. That's an order. They can lay out the potatoes if they like, ready for planting."

Trudi returned smug as a cat. "They're playing five stones." she announced. "They won't bother us."

Corky had opened one of the sheds and was shaking the dust out of a bee suit. Stiff and white, it was much too large for Trudi. The trousers swallowed her feet and the jacket, made of rough cotton, smelt of sawdust and garden string and rubbed her neck. But she had donned this get-up before and she liked the feeling of danger that came with it. She was a knight dressing for battle, or an astronaut… Gloves. Wrists tucked in. There must be no gaps for an angry bee to crawl through! Corky tied some twine round her ankles in case the elastic was too loose. Then the bee hat. As soon as the veil slipped over her head she entered another world. The mesh blurred her vision and hindered her when she turned her head. Perhaps this was how it felt to be a bee with those large compound eyes and no neck. She could see Corky dimly moving about, a pale, misshapen monster with a smoker in his hand.

All beekeepers had smokers. They were ingenious devices to distract the bees, making them think that their home was on fire. They came in different designs but each one had a little chamber to hold burning tinder and a bellows which drew in air at one end and puffed out smoke at the other through a tin funnel. The whole thing would sit comfortably in your hand. Corky had let her use one before and he now set it going and handed it to her.

"You know what to do? When I open the lid of the hive, you blow the smoke very gently over the bees. Not too much, mind. And no sudden movements. Are you ready?" *And please God, no disasters!* "I'm going for that second hive."

Corky's bees lived in rather scruffy, recycled crates with the original manufacturer's advertisements still painted on the side.

The bees didn't seem to mind. They liked the bright colours. They always produced gallons of amber honey, delicious on new bread. Today though, the second hive looked quiet.

"Something wrong?" asked Trudi.

Corky was rubbing his head, the way he did when he felt out of sorts.

"I think we're too late," he replied. "Should have come last week. The warm weather has caught us out. They've swarmed, Trudi. I think I've lost them."

"What do you mean, swarmed?"

"Gone. They've flown off with the queen to make a new colony somewhere else. All I'll have here is a new queen and a handful of workers. They will have eaten most of the honey. Not good news for us."

"Perhaps they'll come back?" Her optimism fell on deaf ears.

"Stupid." he was saying softly. "Stupid. I knew I should have come last week. Stocktaking! The devil take stocktaking!"

But when they lifted the cover, the hive was empty. Neither queen bees nor even baby bees remained. There was just nothing at all.

Trudi had never seen Corky so upset. She wanted to cheer him up. Tell him not to worry. His bees hadn't died. They had gone off to a new life. And perhaps another swarm would come from somewhere else. It wasn't like Mincke's bees, dying in the snow.

"Oh Trudi, this is disastrous," said Corky. "I've lost the main colony and something must have got in and eaten the rest. Look, there's a hole there. Could have been a woodpecker, or a rat."

Trudi was thinking fast. Perhaps she should tell him about Mincke. For a moment she wavered, but she could not actually bring herself to do it. Corky had decided to defend Olaf Stromberg. If what she knew about Mincke came to the ears of that odious man, he might report it to the television company. And the television company, like Sven and the Swedish Police, was no doubt looking for Per. For a moment she stood once more with her grandfather under the stars. *Stay away from Laser Wag,* he had said. Olaf's business card – she had checked it out with Jurgen - bore the Laser Wag logo in the corner. Televisions... telephones. *Even to talk of these things can be very dangerous. Anyone might be listening.* Although she loved Corky, she decided she could not trust him. Snigels, she thought. *If I tell Corky now, we will be snails, leaving trails behind and then someone will discover us. We'll never catch the Sneevelings and they will do just as they please.* She nodded at the ghost in her head. *It's all right. I shan't tell - not yet.*

The sound of another voice close by made her jump and she spun round as if she had been caught talking to herself.

"Es muy bonita..." Pedro was saying, mimicking her attempts to speak his language. He had crept up on them, following the sound of their voices. "See!" He held out his hand to show a bee calmly sunning itself on his palm.

Corky froze. A blind boy, stumbling about quite defenceless, amongst the hives! Whatever would Barbara say? What would anyone say? If Pedro got himself stung badly now it could jeopardise his operation next week. *Keep still,* he thought, his mind reeling. *Keep calm.*

"Pedro, you should not be here. You must go back. Go away!"

"Look. Look, is no problem." The boy lifted his hand to his face and stroked the bee's back with his cheek. "He talking to me. He good, nice bee."

Trudi gawped in admiration and Corky tried a different tack, offering to give Pedro the smoker if he would just back off.

Pedro, smiling, ignored him, and held out both hands, allowing more bees to settle and group themselves as though holding a conference.

"Is okay. Really," he insisted. "I can do this in Peru."

"What are they saying?" gasped Trudi.

"Is nice day!" He was laughing openly now. "In some countries, in the old days, bee is like god. Ju can pray to him. And he can help!"

"Do you pray to them?"

"No no! Only pray in church now!" Of course. That was why he wore a gold medallion of the Madonna. She was his good luck.

"Pedro, listen, let the bees go, *now*." Corky pleaded.

"Sure, si! They go." He gave a casual shrug, flipped his wrists and the insects took off. "This bee house," he put his hand on the third hive. "This one okay. Bees happy here."

"Let's leave and find the picnic." Corky's nerves could take no more and he herded the children hurriedly away.

But that was Pedro all over: easy, relaxed, and incorrigibly disobedient. He lived by instincts that took no regard of rules of safety. Perhaps he had had to look out for himself for too long. Barbara would find him sunning himself at every opportunity, like a basking lizard, on the parapet of the bookshop roof. And no matter how many times he was told about the drop and the traffic below and the danger of getting splinters from the rotten sash window that gave onto the tiles, and no matter how many times he was led down the narrow stairs with a scolding, he would return as soon as there was another glimpse of the sun. He felt at home on the roof. He liked the air above the town.

Barbara worried sometimes that when he could see he would lose that happy assurance and learn to be afraid like other people. But Pedro anticipated the impending change in his life with the same trusting equanimity. It was all one to him. Life. And there was no way of telling if deeper thoughts troubled his mind. Only once did he betray a hint of unease, and that was when Trudi asked him why he was blind. He had been born too soon, he said, before a soul could come down for him from the sky. That was why his village rejected him. He swiftly changed the subject and Trudi never dared ask again.

Despite the bee trouble, Corky's picnic and potato-planting passed off without further incident and he and the children arrived home in high spirits hoping for tea and cake.

In this they were sadly disappointed. Barbara had been glued to her ledgers all afternoon. She seemed tired and irritable.

"Still can't make the blasted things balance!" she muttered. "I lost another whole section of stuff on that filthy, rotten computer. Two hours' worth of work. And I can't find my security password. Have you seen it? I wrote it on something and put it on the kitchen shelf. Hell, I don't know. I've got the deadline on Monday... Cake? No. *How* would I have time to make cake? C'mon guys! Be fair!" They exchanged rueful glances as she shuffled back to her sums.

"She didn't even ask about our picnic," said Trudi in bewilderment. How *could* Barbara forget to make cake?

"We'll improvise." Corky rallied. "Cornflakes anyone?" In his mind he had already decided enough was enough. If Barbara felt too distracted to make cake, she must be in a pretty pickle and she was no fun to be with while she was fretting so.

He would ask that newcomer, Olaf Stromberg if he could help them out. He sounded a pleasant enough man and by all accounts he understood everything there was to know about computers. He had been helping Jurgen with his homework. And, according to that young chatterbox, he had expressed a curiosity several times about the bookshop. He was a book collector himself, he said. Passionate, in fact. And he was *most* keen to meet Pedro.

Perhaps the bees would settle down if things at home were happier. Corky had read about colonies collapsing before and scientists believed that it happened when they succumbed to stress. Did bees feel stressed when they were lonely? (Corky had neglected them recently). Or did they suspect that all was not well at the bookshop? According to country wisdom, bees are very sensitive... that is why you must always tell them important news. Yes, that was most likely the trouble. Corky had been letting things go. Well, now he would have to make a stand. As he poured out the milk, he nodded to himself. He would put things right there and then. He would send a message to Olaf.

Chapter Eleven

Pilliwig's Circus

Two days later he had his chance.

Tired of sitting in provincial police stations, Sven reluctantly admitted that there was little more he could do in Sweden. His father, it seemed, had simply joined a long list of missing persons. Vanished without trace. The police were sympathetic but not especially helpful. They promised to make contact if any new information came along. In the mean time, he might as well go home. Jurgen would be performing in his music festival class in two days' time, and Sven didn't want to miss that. He fitted new locks to the doors of Per's house and booked himself onto a flight to England, but when he telephoned he sounded glum.

"We'll cheer him up!" said Kirsten brightly. "We'll have a special supper ready when he arrives. We'll go to Newbridge and pick up something from the BioDawn shop. They do pop-in-the-oven chef's dinners. We'll have one of those and strawberry surprise for pudding."

Olaf Stromberg looked up. He had poured himself a tumbler of ginger and elderflower cordial and was stirring the contents methodically, twenty times one way, twenty times the other, to energise the water.

"BioDawn? There are some things I need from there. My muesli, for instance."

For some reason, Kirsten's muesli was not good enough for him. Trudi, sitting in her corner, adopted a scowl. Of course she wanted to make a lovely supper for her father, but Olaf always muscled in on everything! She found it impossible not to show her disapproval.

"Well, give me a list," smiled Kirsten accommodatingly. "I can pick your things up at the same time."

"No, better still," Olaf raised a finger like a Biblical prophet. "I can come with you. You drop me at the Prospero Bookshop and I will have a look at your friend Barbara's accounts while you are busy. You take the children with you. That way I have more time to concentrate."

"You really are extremely kind." Trudi's mother seemed blinded by goodwill. "Are you sure you have the time?"

"Time? Yes. Why not? Life is for friends! I will get my things. I want very much to see this shop."

Trudi's baleful eyes followed him from the room and Kirsten turned on her without delay.

"Now stop this, do you hear? Go and fetch Jurgen. And fix your face! You want to help Barbara, don't you? You want to welcome Daddy home? Well, then, be pleasant. That poor man has tried everything to be nice to you. He's even given you a new phone to replace the one you lost at Christmas."

"It was a sample," shrugged Trudi. Worse still, it was a Laser Wag.

"It's the latest, smartest model, and he didn't have to give it to you. He was being generous and I want to see some gratitude and politeness in return. What would Daddy say if he knew you were so rude and unfriendly?"

"I don't need it," Trudi objected still.

"You go and fetch it now and take it with you to show some respect! Come on, darling," she relented, opening her arms for a hug. "I need your help. How can I do everything without my special girl?" She looked so beautiful, standing erect by the window, her fair hair catching the sun, her slender figure the envy of every mother at school. Trudi could hold out no longer and gave herself up to a truce. It would be good to see Pedro again. Perhaps they would be able to get out of shopping and play on the parapet if Barbara was busy...

Such hopes were soon dispelled. The grown-ups' plans did not allow for free play today. While Olaf paced the bookshop, scanning the shelves in rapture, Barbara made up her own list and commissioned Corky to shop for her too. Principles were a luxury she could ill afford at present and 'pop-in-the-ovens' from BioDawn would have to feed the household till she had finished her paperwork.

"It's perfect!" eulogized Olaf, after his tour of inspection. "Little cosy corners, nice comfy chairs, the olde worlde charm, beautiful books, even the quotations you have written on the

82

walls... such a homely, welcoming feel. And a marvellous selection of titles! This is the perfect English bookshop! Character, passion, inspiration!"

Barbara melted under the praise. "You can come again!" she smiled. "And bring your friends!" Was he short or long-sighted, she wondered. His eyes seemed hardly to focus behind their glasses, yet he missed nothing. "Well?" she went on. "Do you want the bad news now? That's where I've got to with the figures!"

The rest of them slipped discreetly from the room, as though leaving a patient with the doctor.

"Ready?" Kirsten herded the children towards the car. "BioDawn, here we come."

Even the sceptics had to admit that there was something different about BioDawn. For one thing, the building itself didn't *look* like a supermarket. It boasted an elegance of design that actually enhanced its riverside location. There was a car park full of cherry trees in bloom, tiled colonnades, bringing whispers of oriental gardens and a six-sided roof lantern that filled the inner space with natural light. On the walls, hung beautiful block-prints of flowers and butterflies and laughing women harvesting tea. The wine section felt dark and cool, and was vaulted like a cellar, while in the mock-'open market', birdsong filled the air; a profusion of vegetables inundated barrows, bright with decorative labels. Flowers, coffee, pastries... every section had its own enticing smell. Here you could order a salad, or send an e-mail. And there were no children crying!

In fact, no children at all. Where *were* they?

Kirsten paused with her trolley at the door.

"Now listen," she dropped her voice like a conspirator. "I have to be quick because I have an appointment with a client soon and Corky can't shop properly with you all under his feet. There is a children's entertainer over there, where Corky used to do his busking. You'll be much better off waiting there. The show starts in two minutes, and I have to sign you in, so no arguing please. Corky will be waiting for you at the end. He will get you a drink. And then I'll drive us back to the bookshop to pick up Olaf." She whisked them across to a striped tent before they had time to reply. Inside, Trudi saw rows of children sitting expectantly and her spirit rose in revolt.

"I'm not a child!" she hissed.

"Just do it, darling," whispered Kirsten. "Be a spy for me. I want to get Corky his job back. You find out what they do here for me. Mmm?" She gave that impossible coaxing smile.

"*What* they do here?" asked Pedro.

Trudi scanned a flyer that was pasted at the entrance. "Rubbish!" she said, loud enough for all to hear; then read the wording in a sarcastic tone: "'Mr. Pilliwig's Insect Circus. See the master magician at work!'" Unable to restrain herself further she burst out: "It's for *babies!* We're not babies!"

"Hey!" Pedro was smiling. "Is okay. We can go. I don't never see circus. What is circus?"

"But you won't *see* it!" Trudi blundered, impulsive as ever, and the words were out before she could stop them. Oh, what a terrible, tactless thing to say! "I mean," she tried to make amends, "there's probably nothing to look at anyway…"

Pedro ignored her confusion.

"We can see!" he smiled, unperturbed. "Just do it - easy!"

Kirsten nodded in triumph and ushered them into the tent. "Three please." She was digging into her purse. "Oh, a discount? The show is free if I spend more than sixty pounds? And it finishes at four? Well that's perfect. I show the receipt at the checkout and then collect my children? Thank you *very* much."

So far, so good. Now for the 'pop-in-the-oven' counter! Never one to dawdle over a task, she parted company with Corky straightaway and he was left to fumble his way round the aisles as best he could. He squinted at Barbara's list. Did that say 'pears' or 'beans'? The pears looked hard, the beans were expensive. He found some rhubarb instead. Perhaps Barbara would not mind.

Meanwhile, to a rousing storm of applause, Mr. Pilliwig entered the stage.

He was an elderly man sporting a large, black gabardine, a beret perched on his head. He had a powerful, theatrical voice which promised well, but it soon became apparent that he was having trouble with his lines.

"Today - today, children - today I am - pleased - yes, proud even - to present to you - the - er - the…"

"Get on with it!" yelled a precocious boy with freckles.

Uproar in the terraces.

"Today, children…" Mr. Pilliwig began to hunt for something in his pockets. "Ah, yes, the Woodlouse Derby!"

Onto the table before him he emptied the contents of a small sweet tin, rolling out little black pastilles the size of peas. One uncurled itself and began to trot away.

"Can't see it!" "What's he doing?" "Hurry up!" resounded from the back rows. While those close enough to see resorted to:

"Oh, yuck! That's disgusting, that is!"

"Shut up!"

"Squash it!"

"The Woodlouse Derby!" The magician set up a finishing post made of straws and drew a red handkerchief out of his sleeve. "At the count of three …"

He blew heartily behind the bugs and they began to hurry along their track.

"It's *painful!*" objected Jurgen.

"Well he just start. Perhaps he get more good, next one." Pedro, listening to the heckling of the audience was enjoying himself no end.

Trudi sat with her hands over her eyes, groaning.

"Now, next, my young friends," said Mr. Pilliwig, brushing the woodlice unceremoniously onto the floor, "the Spider."

General screams from girls at the front.

"The spider, he makes - yes - a thread, from one thing - to another. He can draw a line - here - between impossible things - to make himself a trap." He was playing cat's cradle now with a creature too small to see. "A trap - or a map… It can be all the same."

Trudi uncovered her eyes. She had been taught to draw by imagining just such a spider, spinning lines out from point to point, object to object, creating pockets of geometric shapes. And was not this just how Per had found his way round the northern sky? By drawing a web between the points of light? Suddenly she was interested.

She scrutinised Mr. Pilliwig again. He had a round, flat face and a mop of wavy, grey hair. Dark eyes twinkling. His hands moved like a dancer's. He had popped the spider into his pocket, amid more gasps of horror and now produced a cricket.

"I want to go home!" wailed a blond, curly child in a pink frock.

The stewards at the door glanced anxiously, one to another. Time seemed to crawl. However had someone so incompetent gained permission to perform? But the show picked up. There were giant millipedes that could walk a tightrope and ants that built a bridge. By the grand finale, most children were hanging on to their seats. A loud buzzing filled the tent and Pilliwig pulled a bumblebee from his ear.

"What did he say?" He tutted and put the bee back in.

"Ah! That's better." The bee flew out of the other ear, circled twice overhead and vanished in a puff of smoke.

"Don't know *what* Health and Safety are going to say!" grumbled the doorman. "I've phoned through to head office but there's no reply. Should we stop him now, do you think? I'm sure there'll be complaints."

Pilliwig now cocked his head, straining after some inaudible sound. The children started to fidget on their seats, listening too, and gradually detected a tiny moan, like a mosquito on a summer night, a high whining drone, that deepened and broadened into a full-throttle roar. Where could it be coming from? The children looked around in alarm.

But a seraphic smile played over the conjuror's lips. He knew. Suddenly he threw back his gabardine to reveal what looked like a leopard-skin lining, amber and black.

"Two bees, children, or not two bees! Ha ha! The golden bee from Italy, or the black bee from Northern Europe. Which do you like the best? With an elegant gesture, he released the double swarm into the air and in a breathtaking performance they described eddies and curlicues like a flock of starlings. Pilliwig conducted. The bees obeyed. Now they flew in a long ribbon, now clustered in a throbbing mass. At last, as though tired of their antics, they tucked themselves back inside the magician's coat and their humming died away.

"That is all, children. Four o'clock." Pilliwig doffed his beret and swept from the stage. A stampede followed. Children in tears, children fighting. You never saw such a commotion.

"Come on!" Jurgen pulled Pedro by the arm. "Let's find Corky and get our drink."

"What happen?" asked Pedro. "What he did?"

"It's a trick," said Jurgen confidently, pushing forward. "They do it with lasers."

"Lasers like what they do for me? In hospital next week? "

"Oh - kind of. I'll explain later!"

Trudi found herself standing alone in the empty tent. She could not share Jurgen's breezy dismissal. She had seen something like genuine magic. A swarm, like the swarm Corky lost, mesmerised, and trained to return again. Perhaps this circus master could help Corky, help Mincke even. Perhaps he would know of the evil sorcerer who had once crossed swords with Per. He said he had black bees. Could he bring them back from the dead?

"You can't go in there, darling!" called the lady steward, but Trudi had already slipped behind the curtain that divided the stage from the artist's dressing-room and now confronted Pilliwig face to face.

He did not look surprised to see her.

"Always one stays behind," he observed, calmly taking off his gloves and laying them on the table.

"Please," stammered Trudi, suddenly unsure of herself. "I need some bees."

"Oh?" Pilliwig scrutinised her with his beady eyes. "She wants bees." He winked at himself in the mirror.

"I need some for a friend."

"For a friend..." he echoed. Then after a pause, he pounced.

"And how would you be going to pay for these bees? You know they're not cheap."

"Pay? Well," she suddenly had a flash of inspiration. "I've got a mobile, a brand new phone - a Laser Wag. Hasn't been released onto the market yet. It can do all sorts of clever things. You can have that, if you like."

"She's got a phone," said Pilliwig, still to his reflection. "Let's see it then."

Trudi pulled it out of her bag. "It's terribly important, you see - for my friend - not to lose his bees."

"Ah well, it would be. Yes, this is quite a phone." He was turning it over in his hand. "This would be a good price. A fair price. For a swap."

"You mean you'll do it?"

"What shall we give her?"

"Oh, black bees, please. They are gentle. They don't sting."

"Knows her stuff, doesn't she? Very well. One black queen and half a dozen workers. Enough to start a new hive." He placed a small white box on the table beside his gloves. "Don't leave her in the sun, or in the cold. And look after her, or she'll lead you a merry dance."

"Thank you! Thank you!" said Trudi. She wanted to take his hand, but didn't quite dare.

For a moment his eyes burned with a different light - almost familiar, almost kindly. He held out the box. "Go well, interesting child."

At the door Trudi paused to say goodbye, but only the figure in the mirror remained.

"Don't know what she's going to say to her mother," it caustically observed.

Of course, she hadn't thought of that.

Chapter Twelve

Cakes to Make You Hungry

She stowed the box in her bag and stumbled out into light of the car park where Corky was waiting anxiously with the boys.

"I thought I'd lost you," he murmured.

Jurgen piped up straightaway: "Oh, Trudi always has to get an autograph." With Pedro for an ally he had become much bolder in his teasing, but Trudi did not react. She seemed quite pleased with his explanation.

"I'm starving!" she said.

"There's a café over here by the news stand," Corky steered them through the traffic and into an open-fronted parlour with art deco lamps and mirrors. "I've left my trolley in the 'shopping crèche'. We can collect it later."

They joined a queue and began to shuffle past glass counters filled with gleaming confections. Cakes of every imaginable shape and size filled the racks: buns and cheesecakes and tarts and gateaux. The prettiest were the children's cakes with coloured icing and sugar writing. There were black cakes like spiders for the boys, and little pink cakes with ponies on top for the girls. Trudi could imagine her mother's disapproval…

But Corky had anticipated her thoughts. "It's all right." He pointed to a certificate on the wall. "They're all organic, healthy and calorie free! No sugar. Only Guar gum and pomegranate juice. Full of alpha-tocopherol and anthocyanides! They actually call it 'Slimming Cake'! You'll have to help Pedro choose."

"I wan' big one!" said Pedro, amiably.

"With chocolate? *Con chocolade?*"

"Si, *si!* Okay. Good."

But the choice didn't end here. There were many varieties of chocolate.

"Do you want pink? Or white, or green?"

"Don't worry about colour," advised Corky, tactfully.

"Oh, no. Of course. Well, do you want strawberry? Er - little fruit - red - no. Help me, Corky!"

The details being lost on him, Pedro could not share such agonies of indecision and he burst out laughing.

"Jus' *beeeg* chocolate. Is good. Okay?" His hand traced the pattern on the counter rail. It was different here from the rail at the entrance - curly spirals - nice to touch.

"Tea for one and three milkshakes. Freedom Banana, please." Corky paid and led the way to a cast iron table under an awning. "Warm enough to sit out, I think. Now eat up or Kirsten will catch us!"

Trudi gazed in awe at her milkshake. The tall glass opened like a lily, fluted at the top and filled with a positive explosion of ingredients: frothy cream, chocolate curls, slivers of strawberry and kiwi fruit and coloured straws with glitter-stripes. Outrageous extravagance! This was real, proper sin, organic or not. And the so-seductive, green chocolate cake on her plate breathed opulence too: something daring, bohemian and very grown up.

Of course, Corky was a terrible sucker. He didn't have the money at all for this kind of thing. He had bought himself a measly shortbread. But he always wanted to live through others. He took his greatest pleasure in giving. Well now, she reflected, with inward satisfaction, he was going to receive something too! She just needed a few moments alone to hand him the bees without the boys mocking and making fun of her. As she leant over and steadied the straws with her lips, a quiver of anticipation shot through her. Which would she enjoy the most? Tucking into this BioDawn feast, or giving Corky his surprise? She couldn't decide. Two treats in one day! It all seemed too good to be true. But as she soon found out, 'too good to be true' summed things up quite literally and neither prospect lived up to its promise.

The milkshake tasted sickly and even Jurgen, who struggled manfully with his, had to admit defeat before he had drunk up half. As for the cake, well it was light and insubstantial and left a curious powdery sensation in the mouth. The emerald icing coagulated into a waxy lump and Trudi hid hers, after some vigorous chewing, under her chair, but it was harder to hide her embarrassment. Poor Corky! She could see that he was disappointed. She actually felt relieved when Kirsten arrived to take them home.

Back at the bookshop, however, the afternoon had gone well and they found Barbara full of smiles. Olaf was a genius, she babbled. He had balanced the books, retrieved the security pass number and filed the whole job online to the accountant. Not only that, he had gone through her stocktaking programme and simplified the system so that even a child could now understand it. And he had scanned the basement with his special laser scanner and located the dreaded dry rot. He knew just the cure for it, a fumigator that he would send her in the post. Barbara beamed like a lottery winner. Her troubles were over!

Olaf sat modestly in one of the bookshop armchairs and blinked behind his spectacles while everyone chattered. Now and then he put out his tongue and moistened his upper lip. Trudi watched him with disfavour. His action reminded her of something unpleasant, but what could it be? As for delivering the bees, that would have to wait. There were far too many people crammed into Barbara's tiny back room for a private tête-a-tête, and in any case, Corky was absorbed in unwrapping the present he had brought and Trudi's resourceful mind went blank. Perhaps later she could catch his eye... Vienna Strudel, it was. A marvel of parchment-thin pastry leaves, wrapped around spiced apple and baked to perfection, the caramel-coloured top lightly dusted with sugar. At the sight of it Trudi instantly felt hungry again. There was one for Olaf too. Barbara eyed hers with caution.

"Well, *thank* you Corky!" As she bit into it she smiled and nodded her head. "It's a LOGDAW," she announced. She seemed quite satisfied.

"A *LOGDAW,* whatever is that?" asked Trudi.

"It's an acronym, honey. You take the first letters of a phrase and make a new word out of them. LOGDAWs are quite common round here these days. Sorry Corky. It tastes of cardboard. I know you tried your best."

"But what is the phrase?" begged Trudi, more intrigued than ever.

"Oh, didn't I say? LOoks Good. Doesn't Actually Work! A bit like that stocktaking programme of mine." She winked at Olaf. "Well, thank goodness, that's fixed now. Corky, it's your turn next. Olaf wants to have a look at the nursery. I've been telling him all about it. You know, he's a keen gardener. He collects seeds of unusual plants. And he's got an anti-swarming device for bees. He's too shy to say, but he'd just love to see how you do things!"

Corky brightened up. He would be only too happy to share what he knew with a fellow enthusiast. He would take Olaf over on the bike. Show him his archive. What, *now?* Well, why not now? He could run him back to the Larssons afterwards.

Trudi felt the last of her expectation ebbing away. She could not possibly tell Corky about Mr. Pilliwig while that ingratiating buzz-fly was hovering near. She could not even warn him to be careful. But she did not want Olaf to go to the chalk pit. She felt suddenly outmatched and inclined to cry. Had she done something foolish at the circus? She hadn't inspected the bee-box. Suppose it was empty? Suppose she had been duped? Suppose she had simply allowed her imagination to run away with her again? Pilliwig's parting words came back to her and she now pictured only too clearly the scene that was bound to follow at home. She had insulted Olaf once more. She had lost another valuable gift... She clung to the slender hope that Sven might return and save her before Kirsten got wind of it. Her father would understand, wouldn't he? She said a subdued goodbye to Pedro and spent the journey home in silence.

But Sven's plane encountered fog at Heathrow and was diverted north. He would be home late for supper and when Kirsten urged Trudi to phone him, the business of the magician's deal inevitably came out.

This time Kirsten really blew her top. All the worry and anxiety of the past few weeks rose in a wall of fury.

"You did *what?*"

"I swapped it."

"Swapped it! With someone you didn't know? Someone we can't even find again?"

"I didn't want it, Mummy."

"And you did want this - this box of bugs, I suppose? What kind of a simpleton have I got for a daughter?"

"They're special bees, not bugs."

"Very well," said Kirsten, in a tone of deadly calm. "If they're so special, we'll give them their freedom. Here and now."

"But they're not for me," cried Trudi. "I was only looking after them. They're for..." Her voice died. She couldn't, she wouldn't say more.

Kirsten fetched the kitchen scissors and cut the tape that secured the box. Then she opened the window and hurled the box into the garden. "There! They've gone. If they are so special, they'll fly home. And you, my girl, you are going to do some very serious thinking." She closed the window and turned around, her hands behind her back. "How is it that you are always so sure everybody must be wrong, but Trudi Larsson is right? How is it that you are the only person to see everything upside-down? People try to help. People try to understand. But oh no! Trudi Larsson knows best. Well, this time you are going to listen. You had better start saving your pocket money, because you are going to buy another phone and apologise to Mr. Stromberg. And there will be no more picnics or concerts or trips to the cinema until you do. You can forget going to Kingsbury to see Pedro next week. Unless I see a dramatic change Trudi, you won't be trusted to do things on your own ever again."

Trudi smarted under the force of the attack. Her mother was magnificent when she was angry and no one dared to interrupt when she let fly. But the destruction of the bees, although a serious blow, only served to stiffen her resolve. In her mind, Trudi saw again Mincke's picture of the little boy who stood on his head. Perhaps it was all right to see things upside-down. She no longer doubted that Mr. Pilliwig was genuine. And she knew that her punishments would be commuted when her father came back. Indeed, Kirsten herself would not hold out forever. She was already looking tearful and before long they would both have a good cry and hug one another and lay the table for dinner. Such storms were not uncommon in loving families. They could even bring people closer together.

Olaf magnanimously brushed the matter aside. Young people were always impulsive. He had another 'Laser Wag', anyway, for Jurgen, who said he was bored with his old phone. And Trudi could always try again when she felt like it. He filed a lengthy report to his company that evening and then casually announced that he was leaving. His work was done.

93

No one considered that he was doing a bunk. In fact, if anyone had then suggested that Trudi's suspicions were right all along, and that the Prospero Bookshop, and all associated with it, were now somehow destined for disaster, they would have met with simple incredulity. Barbara could not possibly have foreseen it. She was far too busy struggling to fill in her Small Business Census to imagine such a thing and, in any case, she had Pedro to think of, for life for all of them would change once Pedro learned to see.

Chapter Thirteen

Beery O'Leary

Yet that is to run too far ahead of the story.

On this wet and blustery day, the very day after the visit to BioDawn, Jurgen was standing at the door of his cello teacher's house. He heard the bell resound inside with a sinking feeling. A whole hour... He had been abandoned here for a whole hour of scales and finger exercises before his music festival class at Tilchester Town Hall in the afternoon.

The door was black, with blistered paint and an oval window featuring a stained glass tulip. Jurgen had an intimate relationship with this door. He seemed to spend some of his darkest moments in front of it, studying the bell whose brass plate read 'Press' and the loose-mouthed letter-box, stained with verdigris. He knew the garden gate that led there, too, the stiff catch, the frame that was curiously fashioned from a wheel. All the other houses in the street had done away with their gardens to make paved parking lots. But Mr. O'Leary hired a garage somewhere round the block and parked his antiquated Beetle there. After the gate, came wet privet that caught visitors smack in the face, (nobody trimmed this plot), and cracked steps down - three in number.

Standing here, Jurgen knew precisely the smell that permeated the hall beyond, the creak of the inner door - the trek down the back yard to the 'music room' that was little more than a shed. The neighbours complained if Mr. O'Leary taught in the house. They had also had enough of scales!

Eternity rented lodgings on this step. Jurgen knew he had not done enough practice. He knew he had not mastered the stretch with the little finger, and that when he got to the run in the third piece, his notes would fall over one another and land in a jumble. It would spell disaster in the festival class and the girl with the glasses, who always won, would scoop the prize again. Jurgen didn't mind much for himself. He made no secret of the fact that he wanted to give up the cello. But everyone said he had such a beautiful tone he could not possibly quit. They didn't have to visit

Acacia Road, or lug the great cumbersome lump around! You couldn't look cool with a cello.

For one brightening moment Jurgen imagined that Mr. O'Leary was out. That he was ill in bed with a cold. Maybe he had forgotten that there was a lesson this morning, or simply didn't hear the bell. Jurgen could find his own way home from this part of Tilchester for it was not far from school. The houses, crammed together in their tight streets, had a neglected feel. Football flags fluttered in the windows. The boys here despised people with music cases. And, anyhow, Jurgen wanted to play his new computer game with Angus. So much more fun than scraping a bow on a string. The sound of a stair creaking, a heavy tread in the hall, dispelled such thoughts at a stroke. He was in for it now. No question.

Mr. O'Leary's polished, purple face appeared fretfully at the door. "Ah, yes. Ah yes, come in, boy. Mind the paint!" There seemed little point in the remark. It was years since the house had been painted and generations of cellists had been knocking off what was left each time they heaved their instruments through the porch. But O'Leary liked to make this concession to appearances. The rest of the house, as everyone knew, lay in chaos: a self-perpetuating clutter - piles of music, piles of washing, recycling cardboard, newspapers and cats. About nine of them.

"Come through. Come through." Jurgen followed, inhaling the yeasty, musty air as he passed the room whose door was always closed.

"That's where he makes it!" Trudi once insisted. "Jennifer Colthrop saw inside when she went for her lesson one day."

"Makes what?" Jurgen could be very slow.

"The beer, silly! He makes his own beer! That's why he's got a fat nose and a funny smell. That's why they call him Beery at school. Beery O'Leary. Get it?"

Some parents wouldn't let their children come here on that account. But Mr. O'Leary was the best. He had played all over the world in his younger days. He had run the mile, too. There were cups on shelves... On they went, down the dingy passage and out past the Russian vine and the chipped flower pots. The 'garden room' had a giant storage heater and a piano and a double-sided music stand in carved mahogany.

"How are we doing this week?" The truth was that Beery felt just as depressed about the lessons as his pupils. A wave of disappointment engulfed him every time the doorbell rang. Ah! They didn't forget. They didn't have the 'flu. Ah well! Scrape away another hour. The cats stayed in the safety of the house.

He found it hard, though, not to lose his patience.

"That note there. What's that?" he would pounce, and, as his quivering pupil hazarded a guess, he'd weigh in with his thin, purple, Irish irritability.

"B? No. It's not B. It's B *flat!* Can you see that? B flat, to be sure. Play that. No. Again. *Flat,* boy! *Down!* That's sharp. *Still* sharp. Can't you hear anything at all, Begod?"

This lad, Jurgen, showed promise, but he was lazy. Didn't apply himself. Once or twice, the master had tried to instil enthusiasm into him, play him a recording of a concert virtuoso, show him a score by Bach.

"Do you know who that is, my boy?"

Jurgen quizzed the cover. "It's Bach?"

"And do you know who Bach was?"

"A composer."

"'A *composer*', he says. No, boy. *The* composer. Will you look at this now? Here's a man, lives in an age when everyone is wearin' wigs with nits in them, and no one has a proper bathroom. All he's got to write with is a feather. Are yer listening?"

"Yes."

"And yet," Beery lifts his hands as though he has seen an angel. "And yet he writes the most perfect, the most sublime music the world has ever heard. You look there. What can you see?"

"Notes?" hazarded Jurgen. The page looked black with print.

"Notes! That's a fugue. Four voices, singing all at once. Four different tunes all in harmony. Do you think you could do that?"

"No."

"'*No*'. He's right. But Bach, even when he was old and blind, he could do it just like that." He snapped his fingers. "No practice at all." Beery came back from the sublime and peered at Jurgen. "You now, sure, you're *not* immortal! You'll need to practise a lifetime, and still you won't manage it."

Jurgen shrugged.

"You've got to have passion, boy, or your life is wasted, see?"

97

The lad was laughing at him. He could see it in his eyes. All the children laughed at him. He knew that. But he wasn't such a fool as they made out. Suddenly he grabbed Jurgen and dragged him back towards the house.

"I'll show you something. I'll show you!" He manhandled him past the creeper and down the stale hallway until Jurgen began to think he was going to murder him, and lock his corpse away. Perhaps the bodies of other children were there already in that forbidden chamber. That would account for the smell... At the threshold Beery paused, breathing hard, then flung the door wide and pushed his captive in.

Jurgen stared about him open-mouthed. The room had been kitted out like a dispensary, or clinical laboratory, spotless and gleaming white. Pigeon-hole shelving covered the walls from floor to ceiling and in each pigeon-hole, neatly labelled, lay a little cask, like a fat-bellied bee. There were dozens and dozens of them. Under the window stood a bench, sporting an array of flasks with stands and complicated glass tubes. Carboys full of amber liquid, air-locks bubbling, gave out the pungent gas that also escaped from frothing plastic buckets on the floor. Jurgen noted a log book under a halogen lamp - an annotated wall calendar. A white lab coat lay draped across a chair.

Beery now stood behind him, a hand still on his shoulder.

"A passion, d'yer understand me, boy?"

"Is this *your* passion?" Jurgen turned to face him.

"You think it's beer, don't yer? That's what they told you? *Beery* O'Leary. Well, I'll tell you something. I'm done with beer. It's okay for beginners, but I'm onto something bigger. Like Bach. You don't need to laugh, now. This that I'm making is the toast of kings. Pure nectar. See the colour of that liquid there? That's honeydew that is. They lost the recipe a thousand years ago. You won't find anything like that in a British drinking cup since the days of Alfred the Great! That's mead, my boy. Honey wine. Have you ever tasted it? Don't worry, I wouldn't waste it on *you!* But what you can buy in the shops is muck. Muck! Sugar water. Not fit for a salesman, let alone a king. I've been perfecting this for nine years now. And at last I've cracked it – how to keep the fragrance of the flowers, and the sweetness of the honey, without it all cloying and turning to slop. Every barrel that you see there contains a different vintage, a different flower, a unique flavour. This is my great work. You know, taste can have a key, just like music. Well, Bach wrote a fugue for every musical key - and I'm making mead for every flower, every flavour bees can harvest. This one I call A flat. Little bit sad, little bit rainy, like a summer morning when the roses are just coming out. That's lavender and sage. Sure, it's a science, and no one else has the key to it. The key, you see?" He laughed at his own joke.

"So what d'yer make of that then? D'yer think yer could do that without passion?"

Jurgen nodded in wonder. "I think it's cool," he said.

"Cool!" Beery echoed in derision, not understanding the term. "He thinks it's 'cool'. God help us!"

He hustled the boy out of the room, and stomped back to his lesson with a defeated air. He had blown his cover in a moment of folly and he knew that when Jurgen told the tale he would probably lose his job. He took refuge once more in waspishness:

"If you want to cross the strings you've got to lift yer arm. Lift it! Look at it - it's stiff like a ramrod. Yer should be fluid - like a dancer. Relax the wrist. Relax it. Let's see it move. Not that much!"

Somehow they got through the hour and Jurgen said an awkward goodbye.

"Three o'clock, the class? Well good luck! You're going ter need it. I won't be there myself. Mrs. Newton'll play the piano for you."

"Thank you, Sir," Jurgen nodded.

"There's your lovely mother come to fetch you. Run along now."

Jurgen ran.

Of course he didn't win the festival class. The girl with the glasses scooped the cup and Jurgen gave his runner-up medal to Trudi. All the way home in the car he did impersonations of Mr. O'Leary, perhaps to cover his shame. If he had tried a bit more, he might have done better.

"Sure the man's weirdo!" He did the accent to perfection. "You've come in a beat early. You can't count, boy. One, two, three. One, two, three. Where are you?"

Trudi laughed till she cried. "Jennifer Colthrop said he once told her she was worse than a puddle. 'A puddle has a note' he said 'like an instrument in the orchestra, but you've got no music at all!'"

"You shouldn't laugh," scolded Kirsten, smiling over her shoulder. "The poor man does his best. I'm sure there's more to him than you think. And you are a hard case to teach, Jurgen. You would try the patience of a saint."

"I'm his best pupil," he retorted hotly and there was some truth in that. "But he doesn't like me. Perhaps he doesn't like anyone."

Inside, he wished his teacher hadn't confessed. The incident had quite spoilt the comfortable caricature he had always been in Jurgen's mind. Now, when he looked, he could see another O'Leary standing behind the first; a sensitive one, sad and rather afraid, and once he had seen him, the figure would not go away. Jurgen did not want his confidence. He liked life to be simple. Knowing his master's secret gave Jurgen an unseemly power over him. After all, he could spill the beans and destroy his career whenever he chose now. He found the whole thing distasteful. It would be easy enough to forget the secret room and he decided that he would only describe it to someone special. That Jennifer Colthrop, the little gossip, would never hear of it. He returned to parody:

"I'll tell you who Bach was, boy," he crowed. "He was a genius with nits in his wig!"

Later he would look up 'mead' discreetly on the internet and find out all about it.

100

Chapter Fourteen

Secret Agent

Ever since Trudi unwrapped her little, pink mobile at Christmas, Jurgen had suffered from feelings of envy and dissatisfaction. He didn't want to possess her particular model, but his own suddenly looked clumsy and old-fashioned by its side. He had scuffed his screen while playing football after school and his paint was chipped. It made hardly any difference that Trudi lost her phone within hours. Jurgen was out of love with his and the craving for a new one gnawed at his soul. When Trudi was given a replacement, he underwent fresh torments and when she so casually lost that too, he felt pangs like a proper tummy ache. But at last his patience was rewarded. On the morning of his departure, Olaf Stromberg came up behind him, put a gleaming Laser Wag into his hands and patted him on the shoulder.

"Your turn, Jurgen," he smiled. "Use it well."

The youngster swung round, jaw agape. "Oh wow! That's wicked! Is this the one that does the satellite mapping?"

"The very same."

"And has it got an 'animus' – the guru thing?"

Olaf slowly blinked in assent. His smile widened to reveal a gold tooth.

"In fact, perhaps you could help us, Jurgen. You could join our research panel and let us know what you think of the product from time to time."

Jurgen's eyes popped.

"Of course this part might have to be a secret between us. You know, other companies have spies everywhere. We have to be very careful. We couldn't pay you in actual money, but we could make sure that you always have a nice new phone, and maybe other things from our toy factory. You would be like an agent for us. 007!" He pressed the pink tips of his fingers together. "What do you say?"

Imagine! Jurgen, secret agent! What a coup! Didn't that just make all Trudi's private schemes and plots look like little girl's dreams? Jurgen would have a secret all of his own to top any of hers.

"When do I start?" he asked eagerly

"Oh, my dear friend," Olaf straightened his cuffs with their shiny cuff-links. "You have started already. Good luck!"

Jurgen decamped to his room and posted a 'Private. Keep Out' sign on the door. A new phone! He sat cross-legged on his bed, gloating over his good fortune. He wouldn't be stupid, like Trudi, and waste his gift! Within minutes he had the device working and the invitation to create an 'animus' appeared on the screen.

This was a unique feature of Laser Wag. The 'animus' would become a friend, a 'pal', a daemon of his own. All he had to do was give his friend a name and profile and instantly the spirit of the phone would come to life, talk to him, listen to his troubles, even give him advice. And if he got bored, he could delete his 'animus' and select a new one at any time.

The 'animus', would remember all the things he had to do, and remind him when to do them. It would send him the football scores as they came in and advise him what to buy with his pocket money. It would even solve his problems in maths. Instead of lists and boring boxes to click, the Laser Wag selected photos for file headings, all downloaded from its own inbuilt camera. His address book would look like a photo album, while his photo album would update itself automatically with pictures the phone took whenever it saw something interesting. Everything was easy, promised the welcome page. The machine thought just the way he did. And when he changed, it would change too.

"Oh well, here goes!" He selected the 'wake up' option and a little bee appeared on-screen, prompting and directing him. What name should he choose? To help him start, the bee offered the choice of a puppy called 'Fig', a girl called 'Wendy', or an alien named 'Zub'. He chose the alien and made him purple with spiky porcupine-quills.

Two seconds later 'Zub' sent him a text, thanking him for being his friend and asking if there was anything he could do for him. He also played a tune and did a funny dance.

Jurgen was missing till lunch-time. When he finally emerged, he looked tired, but he chattered excitedly all through his beans on toast and at the end, magnanimously offered his old camera to Trudi.

"I'll have to keep my mobile for a bit, until I've saved all the information on it. But you can have this, Trood. The lens on my new phone is so much better, I don't need a separate camera any more. That way, at least you'll have *something.* It's all charged up and ready to use."

Trudi smiled and took it thoughtfully.

"Have you made yourself a 'friend', then?"

"Yep! Can't show you. You'll laugh. But Trudi, when these new phones come out, they're going to change the world."

For once, she agreed with him.

Later that day they helped Olaf out to the car with his cases. He gave a characteristic jerk of the head, flicking the hair out of his eyes, and shook hands with them all.

"Tak! Tak! Thanks for all." He gave a kiss to Kirsten. "If my mail arrives, you'll send it on?"

"Yes, yes, for sure."

"And Sven, send me that paper on the Bristle Cone Pine. I have some friends who would be very interested. Something might come of it!"

"Bye, Olaf, thanks for the phone."

"Bye partner. Remember," Olaf touched his nose with his finger and pointed at Jurgen. "We have an agreement. Yes?"

"Good bye."

"Good bye, Trudi. Till we meet again." He put out his hand but Trudi hid hers behind her back and merely nodded in return.

"Trudi, shake hands!" chided Sven.

So she put her hand in Olaf's pink paw and wished him to kingdom come.

Chapter Fifteen

Trudi Takes Stock

That night she sat up in her room, mulling over clues like a detective. The events since Christmas had left her with a collection of random objects - presents and swapses - that she had kept together, hoping a pattern of meaning might emerge. None had come so far, but perhaps the camera her brother had just given her would help, for Jurgen's cast off was not like a satellite phone that could transmit its contents across the world. This relied on a conventional memory card and needed a link to a computer to publish its pictures. Trudi distrusted the computer. In the last few days Olaf had had his fingers all over it! And other people, people you didn't even know, might be able to access the files. But on the camera itself, the information was private and secure. She wondered... she wondered... whether there was any chance at all...

With trembling hands, she retrieved the card from her dead, pink camera and tried it in the one she had just been given. Turn on. There! It worked. By a miracle, the memory had survived. She hugged her knees, incredulous, gazing at the tiny screen before her. Perfectly captured in miniature, were the pages of Mincke's manuscript as they had lain scattered on his desk. She could zoom in closer to see the detail.

There was Mira, the blowfly, tasting his lips with his tongue. There were the ants and the sugar cakes and the little humbug snails, just as Mincke had painted them, and the title page, handwritten in blue. Then a blur, when she was called from the hall and hurriedly broke off. The next picture transported her to the Swedish forest and she stood once more before the cluster of icicles that had caught her eye. Here were the fir needles, crusted with snow. Here the far, blue horizon. Her heart was racing now. And there, way off ahead of her, the bundled outline of Per with his big staff and sheepskin coat, his boots deep in the snow. After that came a strange pattern of strawberry lines, running vertically and then nothing. That must have been the point at which the lens hit the ground but Trudi was no longer thinking of that. Her eyes had filled with unexpected tears and she let her fingers fall.

The actual sight of Per, after all these months, unlocked a great store of emotion which she had buttoned up inside. Since her last glimpse of him, she had denied herself any misgivings about her grandfather, arguing that he was much too clever to come to harm. If he had disappeared, that simply meant he was hiding from the Sneevelings. The grown-ups worried because they didn't understand. But Per had confided in Trudi. She knew.

Now, seeing his outline once more against the snow, she recalled that he wasn't really strong at all. His heart bothered him and made him slow and breathless. And then the Sneevelings were not a wolf that you could dispatch with a hunting knife. They were clever and they were everywhere.

That blowfly, Olaf, for example. With bribes of gifts from Laser Wag, Olaf had persuaded everyone he met to trust him. Even Barbara was now bound to him in slavish gratitude. Only Trudi had refused his overtures and she now felt cut off. If she told the story about Mincke and the Elk Hunt and the television man today, her family would merely think that jealousy had made her spiteful and that she was lying to discredit him. Jurgen would sooner believe an alien!

She laid the camera, with the Sami amulet and the nugget of rock Per had given her, under her pillow and turned out the lamp.

She had gone to Sweden hoping for excitement, believing that she and Per would embark on an adventure together. Now she faced a dreary muddle, all sadness and frustration and her grandfather was nowhere to be seen. She couldn't compete with Olaf. He had all the boxes of tricks - cases and cases of them. And the people in Trudi's world were simply too busy to care about bees and stars. She didn't know if she wanted to care about them either, any more. Being upside-down only confirmed how alone she was and others noticed it too and thought that she was odd. She had already upset her mother. If only she could be more compliant, less hostile to change, life might be easier for them all.

But change happened anyway. The stars moved... winter followed summer... people grew old. When she thought about it, nothing in life really stayed still for a moment. People didn't like that kind of change very much. They preferred to cut out whatever made them feel uncomfortable and keep just the happy bits. That's why they thought Olaf such a godsend, for Olaf brought them Laser Wag and Laser Wag promised to fix everything. The photos that you took with a Waggle Phone were only partly pictures of the actual world - Jurgen had shown her - for the camera itself automatically corrected things, cancelled blotches, erased wrinkles, put smiles on faces and added sunshine. It could make you look thinner, or taller. It could even change the colour of your hair. Such photos were like the fruit from BioDawn that never went off. Olaf's world promised perfection. No dry rot. No bee-swarms. No pain. It was beautiful and radiant with hope and everyone loved it.

Tossing in the dark, Trudi felt she ought to want it too. It would be so much more comfortable to trust that all would be well if only Laser Wag was allowed to make it so. But she had given her word to stay away from their temptations. And even she could see that as life improved it got faster and that living faster brought its own problems. If you could do three things at once, well you felt you ought to. And then that meant that you were always late. There was no escape from the chances you missed every day, the endless things you should have done. Per had told her to hold on to the places that felt like home – but with spies like Olaf watching and directing, nowhere felt like home. Not even the bookshop.

Everywhere might be 'improved', but what was the point if you couldn't enjoy it? She thought of poor Barbara, fretting over her forms and then of Scarp, the tearaway, popping seeds. *He* was the lucky one! Here today, gone tomorrow. An outlaw. You'd never catch him staying still and yet his pleasures were real. Other people had LOGDAWs. Their lives *looked* better, but where was the flavour? She wanted to conform and make her mother happy. But how could she do so when she felt she was an outlaw too?

On one side beckoned the laser world, so smart and inviting. It seemed perverse to resist its charms. But on the other stood that old renegade, Mincke. The man was all blotches and blemishes. Nothing could improve him enough to make him comfortable or easy. Yet he had somehow claimed Trudi's allegiance and she could not forget him.

Mincke was a bigger rebel, even, than Scarp. He had only survived because as a child he resisted everyone. And yet even he must have wanted a home to go to. How many times, during his wanderings, had he not longed to undo the past and race down the Kinkerstraat to his old front door? Longing feeds the imagination and it would have been the sweetest thing in all the world to fool himself. *Maybe his exile was a dream – maybe nothing had really happened and all the while he lay in hiding, his family were at home, still laughing and telling tales! Suppose he could knock and ask for help? Suppose he did not need to be a desperate, barefoot outcast?*

But reality would not allow such thoughts for long and every day brought cruel reminders that the comforts he craved were lost. Trudi saw it all. And she also saw that if Mincke could not change things by wishing, then neither could she.

Mincke, in his nine-year-old's rags, gazed at her with the enormous, brilliant eyes of the starving. His knees knocked together. His hands fidgeted over their open chilblains. No, she could not join her mother and Olaf, for he stood in her path - he and Per, together. Both of them had refused to compromise all their lives. If she surrendered now, she would be unworthy of them.

Her test was only just beginning. She felt a surge of pity for the little Larsson girl, who had such a hard path ahead and her tears fell thick and fast.

In the past, there had always been her toys or grown-ups to turn to whenever she was upset. Her mother would envelop her in her dressing gown and find her a soothing drink; or Sven would crush her in his arms till her hair got tangled in his buttons. And if they were not there, there was always Barbara, soft and ample and smelling of patchouli: *"There, there child! What's your mother going to say? You tell Barbara all about it!"* This time she could tell no one and she was too big to confide in Sticky Bear. She couldn't even lie down to sleep because when she did so the tears ran down inside her nose and then she cried because she couldn't breathe.

Where was Per? Hadn't he said he would watch over her? Somewhere at the bottom of her grief lay the fear that Grandfather Larsson had been defeated and that she would never hear his tread on the stair again. When she tried to recall his face, or his voice, the memories slid about and mixed themselves up and then she felt that he had truly gone forever.

107

Finally she dozed, propped on her pillows and her worries slipped into her dreams.

She found herself in a stately room with long sash windows and gilt furniture, pale walls the colour of lavender leaves. Other people sat there too, perched on the chairs and talking in hushed voices. Trudi spotted Pedro across the room and Barbara, and the girl who won the music prize the other day and then she realized that they were at a hospital. This must be the waiting room, and they were all waiting to see the surgeon. Beyond the windows stretched lawns with beds of flowers, all reflected in great gold mirrors that hung on the walls. In fact there were so many mirrors it was hard to tell which views were real and which simply reflections, or reflections of reflections. Trudi wearied herself with trying to work it out and just as she noticed, with a twinge of unease, that the room had no door, she heard someone call her name. There stood Olaf Stromberg in a white coat, a clip board tucked beneath his arm.

"Trudi Larsson. This way please." She dutifully rose and followed him and they walked through one of the mirrors into a windowless cell.

"Won't you sit down?"

Her hands broke into a sweat as if she was going to play a solo. This must have been how Jurgen felt, she thought, before his Festival class and a wave of sisterly compassion swept over her. She would make him take his medal back. And next year he would thrash that girl in glasses!

"It won't hurt," Olaf held a bee in his hand. "Just a little injection to help you sleep. I thought you might like to see some more of the Sneevelings, since you take such an interest in them."

"No! NO!" screamed Trudi, trying to brush him off. "I won't sleep! I won't. I WON'T!"

"But I've got ice cream for you if you're good," reasoned Olaf.

"I don't want it! I won't be good! WON'T!"

The Swede took a step back. "Well, I shall have to call Matron. In the mean time you can take a look at this. Here is what the Sneevelings look like when they haven't got their clothes on. What do you make of that, Miss Ungrateful?"

He flounced from the room and Trudi found herself in the dark. A gentle murmur filled her ears and before long she began to make out the faint outlines of creatures in the shadows. They were small at first and timid, like pale balloons - naked, white mushroom forms with blank faces - but as they grew larger they gained in confidence and their murmur took on a sneering, malicious tone. Now they were crowding close about her, pressing forward, plucking at her clothes with invisible fingers.

Trudi recognized them as the imaginary phantoms which had haunted her infant mind. Once they had terrified her but now she was a big girl and she would not give in to them. Grandfather Larsson had taught her to stand up for herself. Clear and unmistakable, she heard the rumble of his voice close by: *"...Hold fast, like the Nail Star, to what I am telling you now. Keep your eyes and ears open. Do not accept their lies. That way you can honour the truth that Mincke lived for – be his torch-bearer and keep alive the hope of protecting those you love."*

"I will, I will! I WILL!" She woke to find her fists clenched in a gesture of defiance. Her tears had gone.

Now she sat up straight and put on the light. With renewed determination, she spread her 'clues' once more upon the sheet. This was how Sven laid out his specimens when he was analysing them. He called it his scientific method. She would be a scientist too! She would study the facts with a forensic eye and deduce a theory from them.

First fact: the empty bee box, which she had retrieved from the lawn the morning after Kirsten's outburst, was a dubious item. On proper inspection, it proved to be no more than a plain 'takeaway' packet, probably lifted from the BioDawn cake counter. Even if she ignored the message pencilled inside the lid, she doubted that it was really fit for carrying bees. Was this Mr. Pilliwig's last hoax? His warning read: *"Don't believe everything you see!"* Had she been fooled by him? Into the box she put Per's shiny rock and the Music Festival medal which Jurgen had rejected.

Fact number two: she had laughed at Jurgen for making friends with an alien, but perhaps she had partly driven him to it. Elder sisters were prone to be superior and patronize their siblings, thinking that their feelings were less developed. But Jurgen *did* have feelings, though he tried to hide them from her. If Trudi was to gain her brother's trust at all she would have to be more patient.

Next came the photos she had taken of Mincke's pictures. Though fragments of make-believe, they constituted her only *proper* evidence and represented all that remained of something deep and rather terrible, but true. The memory card went into Pilliwig's box with the medal.

Fact number three: the line between truth and fiction might blur or vanish altogether. Perhaps you simply couldn't trust appearances. Perhaps it was possible for something to be two things at once. It was how you *looked* that really mattered.

She noticed with excitement that a kind of magic *was* at work. Threads of understanding had at last begun to form in her mind. She would carry these keepsakes with her, like touchstones, she decided, so that next time she wavered, they could remind her to be strong.

Chapter Sixteen

Kingsbury

One week later, Sven's capacious Volvo crawled at snail's pace through the outskirts of Kingsbury. It was a Sunday afternoon. Luxury coaches, full of elderly tourists and foreign school parties blocked the road, forming a solid convoy to the out-of-town Park and Ride. Impatient to see past them and glimpse the city's celebrated towers, Trudi leaned forward from the back seat, reading off the names of the side streets, shops and businesses. Surely they must see something famous soon!

"This end of the city is a bit of a muddle" Corky apologized, from the front. "It gets better as we go further in."

Sven turned into a one-way system, past garages, and fishing tackle outlets. They glimpsed a sliver of a canal, a Family Fun Motel, some rather squashed looking Victorian terraces and an industrial business park with a gleaming white and silver sign: *'Honeymeadow Enterprises – Nutritional Research'* it read and beneath that: *'The Toy Forge', 'Laser HoloGraphics'*. Other names were obscured as the traffic moved forward.

Jurgen followed their progress on his phone.

"Turn left here!" he commanded.

Sitting sandwiched between them, Pedro giggled and slumped back, his hands lying loose in his lap. It was all a joke to him. He did not mind where they went. Life carried him on. The others felt nervous on his behalf and tried to reassure him, but Pedro lived only in the moment. He would think about the hospital tomorrow. Today, just arrive and see the house where they would stay.

The nuns at Pedro's orphanage had organised it all, quite at the last minute. And now, instead of putting up in a poky hotel, as originally planned, Pedro and Corky would lodge with some Anglican Sisters who ran a hostel called St. Lucy's, in the north of the city. A letter had arrived to confirm it by first class post.

Normally, Sister Emilia explained, with her usual loftiness, the house was full of undergraduates and they would not consider

111

inviting a child to stay – far too disruptive for the contemplative life.

But Pedro, it seemed, was special. Just now, most of the students were away for the Easter vacation and Mother Carla Maria, in Lima, had put her case for this visit so persuasively that neither the head of the big English convent, nor Sister Emilia, her Kingsbury deputy, could reasonably oppose her. Therefore it was arranged. Pedro and Corky would have their own rooms at St. Lucy's and use of the common room and kitchen. Everything would be quiet and comfortable. And they would stay just long enough for Pedro to recover from his operation and visit the outpatients' clinic. Then home, wherever home was.

Further than that Pedro didn't bother to enquire. People had always taken care of him. No need to worry himself. He was sure Anglican Sisters would be like the Catholic nuns in Peru - sometimes severe, sometimes playful and smelling of incense and beeswax polish. In Peru, the community's sandals squeaked on the wooden floors and Sister Pura, who was very old, had whiskers that pricked your face when she kissed you good night. Trudi and Jurgen would be back for a few days to keep him company in case he got bored. No - there was nothing to worry about.

"There! Look!" They rounded another bend and came slap into the centre of the town - a wide avenue, flanked on either side by buildings in honey-coloured stone.

"These are the colleges," said Sven. "The Cathedral is up there."

"It's even prettier than Newbridge," Trudi cried, spotting a Queen Anne house with a gracious portico.

"Barbara would love it here. She should have a bookshop here!"

The skyline came straight from a fairy book. Turrets, gables, cupolas, spires of every design vied with one another to reach the sky. All gleamed like new in the April sun. And beneath the leaded roofs were latticed casements, oriel windows, lancet windows, Tudor mullions with candle lamps winking inside them and snatches of study walls, all lined with books. The plane trees were not yet in leaf, but as they sped down Longmarket Street they caught sight of gardens behind wrought iron gates, green lawns and snatches of daffodils, sundials... plant pots on window-sills. Trudi thought she had never seen anything so romantic. Jurgen, still engrossed in his map, called out directions:

"Take the right-hand fork here."

From this point on, the college buildings gave way to tall, red-brick villas with bowery gardens and bicycle racks. Brass plates on the gateposts announced the house names and numbers. Trudi noted language schools and outposts of University Departments, a veterinary practice, an hotel... Once they had been homes for University dons, but now hardly any were private houses. They would seem too large for a single family today. Gangs of foreign students, in brightly coloured jackets, thronged the pavements.

"Eighty-one, eighty-three ...eighty-nine," Corky counted the houses off. "Here! This one, with the big lime tree."

Sven swerved into a shrubby, semi-circular drive and drew up at the front door.

"It doesn't look like a nunnery." Trudi felt disappointed. She had hoped for something gothic, but the place appeared quite homely and normal. The ghosts of Kingsbury must live in the pointy archways and ancient passages, tucked away in the labyrinth of the old university.

Pedro laughed out loud. "I will tell when we go inside if is convent or no. I know by this." He tapped his nose.

"Suppose they don't let us out again."

"Well ju can be Sister Trudi." Pedro laughed even more. "Very nice!"

"Don't worry, Trudi. I'll help you dig a tunnel," promised Sven. "There now, someone is coming to meet us."

A young woman in a black habit and long apron opened the door and stretched out arms in greeting. Tall, fair-skinned, athletic-looking, she tucked a lock of loose hair, dazzling blond, beneath her veil and lurched down the steps towards them. Jurgen just had time to finish a memo to Zub: 'We've arrived,' he texted. '3.50 p.m.'

"Welcome! Welcome! I've been looking out for you. You're just in time for tea! I'm Sister Bianca. Let me help you with your things."

She offered a muscular, working-woman's hand to shake. "Are you the guardian?" she enquired of Sven.

"No, no, just the driver," he laughed, extricating his fingers in some embarrassment.

"Ah, then *you,*" she beamed at Corky and turned her attention to the children.

"*This* must be Pedro! Pedro, I'm Bianca. I've got special instructions to look after you." She knelt down and took his face in her hands, then kissed her finger and pasted the kiss on his forehead while he shrugged, laughing over her shoulder. "And who have we here?" she surveyed Trudi and Jurgen.

Better not kiss me! thought Jurgen.

"Just friends." Trudi found her best grown-up voice. She could not help noticing Sister Bianca's rough, sandalled feet. *She's got no socks on, and it's freezing!*

"Well, you must come and find the cake!" Bianca took Pedro's hand and led the way into a hall with a staircase curling out of it. By the door stood a little table displaying postcards and a visitor's book and beside that, a carved wooden trunk surmounted by a long row of pigeon holes for post. The hall continued past an office, sparsely-furnished with a bed and crucifix, and disappeared out of sight. Straight ahead lay two more doors, one opening onto an old-fashioned sitting room, the other to what looked like a classroom, with long, formica tables and plastic chairs. An ancient toaster sat incongruously in one corner. French windows overlooked a terrace and delightful, rambling garden beyond.

Pedro stood grinning, and testing the parquet tiles with his toe. He tugged at Trudi's jacket. "Is proper convent! Ju smell it? What you put on wood!"

Now he mentioned it, she did. Everything gleamed, polished and scrubbed. She pinched him back, but there was no time for more. Bianca wanted to show Pedro to his room in the student wing and they all trooped up the stairs to a maze of landings and banisters and cream-painted doors with numbers on them. There were curious memo boards and little notebooks attached to every door, several had pencils dangling by a string. What were they for? It all seemed as exciting and confusing as a new school. How would Corky and Pedro ever find their way about?

Up they went again. Fire extinguishers and lists of Fire Practice rules. On a little mat outside one door sat a pair of muddy climbing boots. When at last they reached the second floor, they found themselves level with the treetops. Each room had a wardrobe, bed,

114

desk, bookshelf, and mirror. There were clean towels on the bedcovers.

"Will you manage the stairs all right?" Sister Bianca cast a doubtful eye at Pedro.

Everybody laughed, and Corky pulled a comical face.

"Just don't leave any way open onto the roof, or you will find him sunning himself on the ridge tiles!"

At that moment a gong resounded from the hall below.

"That's the signal for tea. We have tea at four thirty every day. Usually it's just toast and jam, but on Sundays we get cake. Breakfast is any time between eight and nine. Supper, if you sign in for it, starts at seven. The Sisters eat their breakfast and lunch in silence, but the students have a big kitchen where they cook for themselves. You can eat with us or with them. You should meet one or two of them today. We have a sort of open house on Sundays. A priest gives a communion service in the afternoon and several regulars come for that and, of *course,* the cake and chatter afterwards. You'll soon get into the swing of it."

If she closed her eyes, Trudi could imagine Sister Bianca, not as a nun, but as Head Girl in an old-fashioned school film, wearing black tights and a gym-slip, her hair tied behind, like Trudi's, in a plait. Good at hockey. Probably clever at maths. And remarkably pretty, in a reflective way. Of course you couldn't ask why someone ended up in a nunnery, but Bianca didn't match the stereotype at all. Her engaging frankness inspired an instant trust, yet there was mischief in her eye too, a rather daring promise of fun.

By now, the congregation from the Sunday service had drifted back and dispersed. Some hovered near the plates of fairy cakes, or queued by the giant teapots on the tables, pink, plastic mugs in hand. One or two had already collected their scoff and made for the comfort of the 'common room' where they immersed themselves in conversation too deep for Trudi to fathom. The Sisters, conspicuous in their convent black, shuffled about, officiating with the kettle, or handing round the plates. All came up to introduce themselves. Trudi reckoned there were about six. Mostly elderly, with plain glasses, and smooth faces, warm smiles. They seemed genuinely delighted to see children.

"Now you must meet Sister Matilda," said one gripping Corky's sleeve and propelling him through the crowd. "Sister Matilda has been here since 1980. And like Sister Julian she trained in medicine, so she will take a special interest in your stay here."

Seated at the round table in the window, engrossed in a cryptic crossword, tiny Sister Matilda sat with a grey-haired gentleman, their heads almost touching. She held a pencil in the paper-fine fingers of her right hand, while her left thumb drummed softly on the table.

"Well," she mused, "Sixteen Down. *'Afterthought surrounds argument for an ancient city'*... That can't be very difficult. How many letters? Eight? Beginning with 'P'..."

"And there may be an 'i', letter seven."

"Afterthought... P.S.?" There was something rather touching about their familiarity.

"May I butt in?" The sister at Corky's elbow took advantage of the pause. "Sister Matilda, this here is Mr. Farthing who's brought the blind boy. I know you want to meet him."

Sister Matilda looked up, beaming.

"Now, *how* do you do?" she made to stand up though Corky protested.

"No, no, please. Don't let us interrupt you."

"It's not interrupting at all! We're stuck, aren't we, St. John? We need a younger brain! Are you a crossword fiend, Mr. Farthing?"

"I'm not much use at puzzles, I'm afraid. But please call me Corky. Nobody but the tax man uses the Farthing thing. I once played a one-man-band and Corky was my street name. It stuck with friends and now when people use my formal name I feel I must have done something wrong."

The old gentleman chortled merrily. "Another musician! Wonderful. Sister Matilda here does a terrific trombone on the comb and paper and I am an indifferent cellist. We must get together and have a jam!"

"Ah, that lad there is the one you want," said Corky, modestly backing out. "He is a cellist, like yourself - and has a real talent, if he ever puts his mind to it.

For a second, narrowing his gaze, Matilda's companion took in the blond, slightly bored boy, standing by his father and made a mental note. "It's a date!" he twinkled. "Have you got tea?"

Later, on the journey home, Trudi reconstructed the room in her mind. She was used to her parents' gatherings at home, but this afternoon she had glimpsed another world entirely; the nuns in their fancy-dress habits and their elderly visitors, speaking through their noses in antiquated, sing-song voices and then the few students who had stayed on: a hugely tall, energetic Scot with a long chin and curly hair; one little mouse of a girl who sat on the floor, earnestly berating an Indian in thick glasses; another, wearing glass jewellery, legs encased in white leggings, and then the minister's wife, ample and loud, who smelt of lily-of-the-valley and innocently sported the price ticket on her new, pink dress.

She worried about Pedro. They were all very kind, but would he fit in? Would he be a fish out of water? Of course, she didn't really know where he truly belonged. Which was his proper home? The Andean village of his birth, or the convent in Lima, or Barbara's bookshop? Just now, he didn't seem to care. It made no difference to him. But tomorrow his world would change. Tomorrow he would go to the Kingsbury Infirmary and they would start to give him back his sight. Then he would see everything for the first time and perhaps he *would* care. According to Corky, it would take a while for him to recover and learn to make sense of everything. There might have to be several operations.

If he was still at Kingsbury by half-term, Trudi and Jurgen would come up and stay to keep him company. She hoped they would. She felt somehow she wasn't finished with Sister Bianca and the crowd at St Lucy's, or with the tramp who rang the doorbell so insistently just before they left.

The tea pots were running low and the little cakes had mostly disappeared from the tea-plates. Guests were beginning to depart when this interruption occurred and Sister Bianca, who was chatting, perched on the low piano stool, glanced briefly at her Maker. "Edmund!" she said, getting to her feet. "Come on Trudi, you can help me make a sandwich."

In the entrance porch stood a character from a Russian novel. A hollow face looked out from a mane of dishevelled, hair, dark with silver in it, and a beard that straggled to his chest - perhaps it had

117

never been combed - there were lumps of what looked like porridge in it - while his white shirt, unbuttoned to the waist, revealed a once athletic but somewhat wasted torso. This shirt, and a pair of ragged trousers, tied with string, seemed his only protection from the weather. He wore big boots with broken laces. Trudi's jaw dropped.

The figure made a menacing bow and brandished a club in his right hand.

"Edmund!" he announced. *"Namas te.* Have you seen His Holiness?" A moment later he added: "Shalom!"

"Bread and marmite, Edmund?" asked Sister Bianca brightly.

"Marmite? No. No time. Beef and horseradish! First class. Edmund!"

Bianca smiled and shut the door.

"He's been coming here a while now," she explained as she led the way to the kitchen. "Turns up regular as clockwork. Won't step inside. We offered him a coat but he won't wear one. Lord knows where he sleeps. We have quite a few tramps who call for food. This is a new thing, refusing marmite. Quite a cheek! He'll have to put up with it anyhow."

Trudi stood on the kitchen step, marvelling at the high ceiling, the giant cooking pots and old-fashioned sinks beyond, while Bianca buttered bread and made a fresh mug of tea.

In their absence, Edmund had turned his back and stood conducting the traffic with his staff. On hearing the door, he swung about face and slipped his stick down at his side, like a soldier doing drill. "Far out, man!" he called to no one in particular. Then he reached greedily for the food. After a moment he peered down at Trudi and tapped his nose. "Don't believe everything you see!" he confided. "I was top of my year, you know: Biochemistry and Computing Science, Artificial Intelligence I knew it all. I was on to something big." His glittering eyes bored into her till she quailed and took refuge behind Bianca's skirt.

Then he waved the matter aside. "All gone now. You think I'm crazy. One day, though – one day." He whipped round again on his heel, as if trying to catch a stalker, stuck his nose in the air and, rudely ignoring his benefactors, tucked into his bread.

"He's harmless!" laughed Sister Bianca, as she closed the door once more. "He *was* a scientist once, we think. If you come back

118

you'll see plenty of him." Then she gave a smile that went to Trudi's heart. "Don't worry about your friend. We'll look after him. No one can come to harm here."

Trudi wished she hadn't said that. The words sounded so confident and carefree. But it seemed that wherever Trudi went just now, trouble was sure to follow. She counted off the disasters. First poor Mincke and Per, and then Barbara, who had always been so jolly, suddenly out of sorts and struggling with her shop. Now Corky had lost his bees and her own father looked so unhappy. He would be out of work in a couple of weeks and every time the phone rang, he leapt to answer it, hoping for news from Sweden. But none came and Trudi longed to put her arms round him and comfort him, as he had comforted her innumerable times before. *Per would be safe, wouldn't he? He could navigate his way from world to world. Surely he could dodge a television man!* But having taken on the habit of secrecy, she did not even tell about the tramp, in case he too had a part in Mincke's plot

Part Three.

Octave - Simples and Doubles

Chapter 17

A Glimpse through the Door

Life flowed on in the Larsson household for about a month without further problem. Letters brought good news from Kingsbury. Pedro's operation had been a success, and he was now able to detect light with both eyes. But he would have to stay on longer in Kingsbury. His surgeon predicted confidently that once the scarring had healed, the next laser treatment would bring proper results and that 'the imp', as he liked to call him, would soon be able to see, really see things! Pedro counter-signed each account with his own inimitable flourish.

When Easter passed and the students returned for another term, Corky and Pedro prepared to leave St. Lucy's, but the Sisters declared they had been such model guests they would not hear of them moving out and found room for them to stay in their own private wing. This, though irregular and against Sister Emilia's better judgement, showed the great affection and trust in which they held them. Luckily, none of them knew about Pedro's midnight ramblings and his fondness for shinning down fire escapes and sitting out in his pyjamas under the stars!

Back in Sussex, things were also looking up. Kirsten had put her skills to good use and temporarily saved the family finances by securing an important job in Tilchester. She was to design the interior of a health clinic offering a marvellous new, stress-busting therapy, known as 'Tranquillity Parasympathism'. Nobody could say for certain what 'Tranquillity Parasympathism' actually was and Kirsten herself became far too busy to care, poring, as she did, from morning to night, over fabric samples and enormous sheets of plans. In fact, she was so pre-occupied with checking her emails and texting suppliers, overseeing the painters and consulting textbooks, she hardly set eyes on her nearest and dearest. But just at the moment that seemed a small price to pay. For the foreseeable future the Larssons had money, lots of it, and no longer needed to think of moving house.

Then, just before half term, Sven received an invitation on very important looking paper, to visit an Institute for Global Science in Kingsbury. The directors were looking for lecturers in ecology, it said, and might be able to offer a Fellowship. They would very much like to meet him. Perhaps Professor Saxmund had been putting in a good word, for the timing seemed perfect. Sven would take the children with him and leave them to play with Pedro, while he attended his appointment. Kirsten would have a much needed week of peace and quiet to crack on with her work.

Only Barbara still seemed down at heart. Before leaving for their trip, the Larssons were summoned to Newbridge to pick up a parcel. Barbara was sending gifts, she explained, because she could not spare the time to go herself. Things had got so much worse at the bookshop since Olaf fixed the computer, that in desperation, she had advertised for an assistant.

"Tell Corky I miss him," she added tearfully. She really meant it. "And I need him home soon. That's lemon cake, and some shortbread for the nuns, and new socks for Pedro, oh, and some books for them to read together. Tell him also that I've been out to the nursery and everything is fine. The potatoes are coming up - oh - and it looks like some new bees have moved into the old beehives. Dark ones. Never seen 'em like that before."

Trudi clapped her hands. "*I'll* tell him," she said.

She could not wait to return to Kingsbury. In the few weeks since they last visited, spring had truly arrived. The chestnut trees along the Pinkney Road, stood resplendent, their emerald leaves pricked over with creamy flower-spikes. Beneath them passed the holiday buses, now contending with a new complication on the roads. For this was term-time and every kerb, every lane, now swarmed with university folk on bicycles. Trudi gawped as ageing dons spun by, their handlebar baskets crammed with books. Wherever you looked there were students pedalling, nonchalantly chatting two abreast, or racing, late for class, swerving in and out of the traffic. Cyclists had quite overrun the place: girls in streamlined helmets, long hair flying, and straight-backed youths, free-wheeling, their arms casually folded in front

"Don't they hold the handle-bars?" she asked primly. That was not how they had been taught to ride for Cycling Proficiency at school.

"'Course not," retorted Jurgen, as though he knew it all. "That wouldn't be cool, would it?"

A genial welcome awaited them at St. Lucy's. The French windows had been thrown open and the sisters, taking advantage of the May weather, had carried tea out into the garden. There were hugs for the adults all round, but the children stood embarrassed, unsure how to say hello.

"Is okay," Pedro laughed at last. "I no can see you. Not yet! Next time, maybe!" But he had developed a new habit of lifting his face and tilting it towards the sun.

"What *can* you see?" asked Trudi.

"All things," he parried, "in my head!"

Sister Bianca moved aside to make room for the Scot with the jaw who had been there in April.

"Hamish!" he announced, sitting down and then rising again to shake hands and spilling his tea. "Hamish Wall. Physics at St. Gregory's. Second year. Ye've picked a grand day to come up."

"Hamish has been our invaluable guide," explained Corky. "He's a great walker and I reckon we've visited just about every corner of the city on the guided tours he's given us."

"Nothing like walking for expanding the lungs," Hamish jerked his head in approval, sending his tea slopping again.

"St. Gregory's?" noted Sven, with interest. "That's the very College which has invited me here."

"Old, poor, rather deplorable at academics, but friendly enough if you can down a pint of beer and shout lustily at a boat race! We're the last 'dirty' college in Kingsbury! You'll have noticed how clean and new all the others look? Well, up till now, we haven't been able to afford the restoration. We've got the only genuine soot-blackened, moss-encrusted walls in the city. Myself I prefer them. Like 'old master' paintings. Too much scrubbing has made Kingsbury resemble a Hollywood set in my view."

"My invitation is from the Institute of Global Science."

"Ah!" Hamish pulled a face and set down his mug. "That would be the new money. Sir Maximus Bligh. Don't tell me you haven't heard of *him*? He's the chairman of the supermarket BioDawn. Got fingers in just about every pie. And his latest idea is to be fairy godmother to poor old St. Gregory's. I said we had no money up till now, but suddenly, everything is going to change. We are to

125

have shower rooms instead of the ancient baths. They have even stopped serving up soggy cabbage for supper! We're to be re-branded. New college crest. New logo. New patron. Why we need them I can't imagine. I was quite happy with the old ones. Now they want a new statue. Poor old Wallis has been pushed off his pedestal for some foreign upstart and no one even knows who it is..."

Such matters did not interest them and the children wandered away down the garden.

"What was it like?" asked Trudi, still feeling nervous. "Was it horrid? The operation."

"No, no!" Pedro shrugged. "'S okay. They give you bananas. Everyone very nice."

"But you have to go again?"

"Next month. Look, I show ju sunthing."

Past the lilac and the late-flowering tulips, a path led down to a separate patch of lawn. Here the convent wall created a secluded corner with a wooden bench tucked beneath some cordon fruit trees. The rosy brickwork glowed between peach and pear blossom and then ran out at a height of nearly three metres. Beyond it, you could see nothing but blue sky, bright clouds. It might have been the end of the world.

"This my place," said Pedro, feeling his way and sitting down. He patted the seat. "Ju sit!" He had a way, all his own, of pronouncing certain words with this soft sonancy, like the '*zh*' in pleasure. "Now, tell me. What ju can see?"

"A wall," said Trudi obtusely.

"No, but here I hear sunthing. I hear peoples talking on other side. There is door, no?"

True enough, behind the branches was an arch with a wooden door, long out of use.

"It's locked," said Trudi. "But it's half rotten. Broken. Splitting apart at the top."

"What ju can see through?" asked Pedro. "Careful. Don' to let the Sisters know."

"Jurgen, give me a leg up. Then I can tell." Jurgen obligingly lent his back and Trudi scrambled up and put her eye to the gap.

126

"It's a garden, like this one," she whispered. "But that one is just grass, with people walking about. Some old, some young. Most are on their own." She paused.

"Well?"

"Well, it's odd. They all look very slow. There's a fat girl trying to do a handstand. And a man sitting at a bench, pretending to play the piano. I can't hear what they are saying."

Pedro nodded.

"Can you get off now?" gasped Jurgen. "You're squashing me!"

Trudi let go and slithered to the ground. "It looks weird. What did you hear?"

"Nuthin' special. Jus' voices." Pedro had become evasive. "There was a girl crying."

They wandered back to the house, wrapped in thought.

Sven was waiting for them, rubbing his hands. "Well, Jurgen, how would you like to play with a real grown-up orchestra? Hamish plays French horn in the Pinkney Symphonia, and he's offering to take you with him."

Jurgen thought he wouldn't like it at all, but he had the perfect excuse.

"Oh – no cello!" he contrived a crestfallen expression.

"No problem, man," cried the ever resourceful Hamish. "My friend Archie can help. He's a violin-maker with a music shop close by. He'll fit you up with something. I'm sure of it. You'll have a fine time."

Jurgen's blue eyes widened. He knew it was pointless to struggle. Whichever way he turned he found the world full of people determined to help improve life for him. He didn't want to be helped. He wanted to just mess about like other boys. But Fate had decided otherwise. Fate sent him to Beery O'Leary and now it would drag him off to Pinkney, whether he liked it or not.

"I coming too!" giggled Pedro. "In the smart car."

"Smart car?"

"Och, wait till you see it!" laughed Hamish. "There never was a car like mine!"

"Has it got sat-nav? *I've* got sat-nav."

"Well then, you can lead the way."

"Why don't you all go?" said Sven. "I can prepare for my interview and Corky can have an evening off." So that was settled.

127

Jurgen put it all succinctly in his night report to Zub: *"It's boring here already. No football in the garden. And there are mad people next door. We're staying at The Phoenix Hotel on the Pinkney Road. Logging off now 9.30. p.m. Pizza for tea."*

Chapter Eighteen

Nutters!

Archie Gunn's violin shop stood on the corner of Humboldt's Walk, a small parade where students could buy all the necessities of life. The shops here sold everything from milk to bicycle repair kits, but anyone in a hurry could be forgiven for missing Archie's altogether. For one thing the window had not been cleaned for years and wore a thick coating of carpenter's dust. For another, the interior was very dark and those who did peer in were greeted only with sight of a workbench littered with tools and wood chips. Overhead, hung templates for fiddle backs, displayed like the pheasants and rabbits in an old game-butcher's stall, but the shop advertised nothing visible for sale at all. The door creaked as it opened and set off a distant bell. Inside, the air reeked of cigars and linseed oil. How was it, thought Jurgen, that houses with cellos always had a funny smell?

Archie himself came lumbering through, rubbing his hands on a cloth.

"Hamish!" he exclaimed pleasantly and then paused in doubt. "Not broke again, are you?"

"No, no Archie. I'm here on serious business. We want to borrow a cello for this here laddie to play at Pinkney orchestra tonight. Have you got anything small enough for him?"

Archie took a longer look at his visitors, and raked one hand through his hair, from brow to nape. Dark hair, Trudi observed, a whole shock of it, with just a little grey threading through. And heavy, dark-rimmed glasses, which he now took off and polished on his duster. He was a biggish man, not tall, like Hamish, but stocky - too big really to fit inside his own shop. But he popped the lenses back on his nose, peered at the children, as older people do, with his head thrown back and gave an enigmatic smile.

Then he turned on his heel. "Follow me!" he boomed. "Sorry about the mess. Mind out for splinters!"

They waded through a muddle of wooden cut-outs, discarded panels, fretsaws, pots of paste, clamps, chisels, slivers of mother-

129

of-pearl and ash-trays, liberally furnished with dead cigars. There were un-drunk cups of coffee dotted about amidst old newspapers, sheets of music manuscript, and crumpled star-charts, and the whole effect was topped off with a set of photos of crop circles and a rather rude cartoon.

Ducking the low doorway, Hamish waved them on to a second chamber, darker than the first - a veritable Aladdin's cave.

And here they stopped in astonishment. Musical instruments covered every inch of wall. They cluttered the floor. They lolled in corners, reclined in the armchairs. Dark, sweet-smelling violins with fine-ribbed backs and fancy pegs; a pale, honey-coloured viola; two fat-bellied lutes, in stripy waistcoats; a double-bass, sporting a lion's-head scroll and cellos of all sizes, posing like chorus girls in a line. A selection of bows swung from a rail above.

"Can you get through?" called Archie. "There is order here somewhere in the chaos. Look at that now!" He held up a naked, half-constructed piece, the inside as fine and intricate as the fluting of a shell. "Sycamore wood from Tuscany that is – grown on a southern slope. See the bars on it? Get some varnish on that and it'll sing like a bird!"

"Have you made *all* these?" asked Trudi, captivated.

"Good gracious, no. I mend 'em. And sell 'em. This one is my pet hobby."

"*One* of his pet hobbies!" corrected Hamish. "Normally he is to be found on a hilltop somewhere, star-gazing and listening for aliens!"

"You may mock, my son," said Archie. "You may... Here, what about this one?" He pulled out a dapper cello with a narrow waist and deep-curves in the back. "Try this," he selected a bow and tensioned it. "You know not to pull the hair too tight, do you? I don't want to get it back all bent like something from Agincourt, you know!"

Jurgen stared at his feet, and scuffed the dusty carpet. Dignity required that he rise above this patronizing with disdain, but he did feel a curious desire to play. He invariably blamed the cello at home for all his faults: it was too big, too new, too squeaky. It had sticky pegs. The spike was prone to collapse. How could he sound right on a thing like that? Just out of interest he'd like to hear this one.

He gave Archie a mirthless smile and muttered: "I know how to do it."

"Well, sit yourself there, then. Let's hear what you can do."

Perched on the prickly sofa, Jurgen teased his bow across the strings and brought out a yawl as he landed too near the bridge. Not enough pressure. He fiddled with the screw, frowned and applied himself again and this time he found the voice - sweet, rich - unlike anything he had ever produced before.

"Ooh - not bad!" said Archie, falsetto.

"He's the best!" Trudi crowed, taking the compliment with proprietary pride.

"Let's hear some Bach then." Archie fished out a sheet of music.

"Don't really like Bach," said Jurgen, thinking of Beery.

"Don't like Bach! What's he talking about? Listen, when the rest of Europe was splashing about in the mud, Bach was composing the most perfect music ever written. Do you know he could write a tune you could play forwards and backwards and you could turn the music upside-down and it would still sound like a tune? He was a magician. He could even write a tune that you could play forwards and backwards *simultaneously,* as a duet. Don't believe me? Go on then, I'll show you. You play that there and I'll play too."

Archie grabbed a violin and read off the second part, transposing as he went. The result sounded strange, but pleasing. "Try this one here!" This was a furious round, the second voice in pursuit, just one note behind, but still the harmony held. By now everyone in the room had burst out laughing.

"Jesus!" cried Pedro. "Is crazy music!"

"They are mazes. You know what a maze is? A place where you get lost and then come out right. What do you think *those* are?" He pointed beyond the door to some prints of whirling galaxies and, without waiting for a reply, went on: "Mazes. What do you think that is? Yes, it's a crop circle, but it's a maze too. See all the lines weaving into the centre and out again? Ever heard of the 'music of the spheres'?"

"He's off!" howled Hamish.

"It's the celestial sound the planets make as they travel through space. Once upon a time scholars really believed in heavenly music. Every planet moved in a crystal sphere, they said, and the spheres rang with their own notes, just like a…"

"…A puddle?" suggested Jurgen.

"What about stars?" Trudi cut in, impatiently dismissing the joke. "The stars in the Great Bear? Can *they* sing?"

"I'm sure they have their own music too. A Bach Fugue is a piece of code, a musical maze that winds round and round, just like them."

"What does the code say?"

"Ah, well!" Archie put down his fiddle and stroked his chin. "Haven't cracked that one, yet. Perhaps young Jurgen can do that for us."

Jurgen reported to Zub that night:

"They're all nutters here in Kingsbury. But Archie's okay. He's got a passion. He and Hamish are going to take us on a picnic to see a chalk maze on a hill near here. His cello is awesome. Pinkney orchestra was rubbish, but very funny. Met a bee man."

Trudi had also begun to keep a journal:

"So many things happened today, I can't remember them all. At half past six Hamish called and we all climbed into his car with the cello. His car is a total wreck, all rusty and the windows are falling out. The boot doesn't shut properly and there are weeds growing out of it! I sat in the front and Jurgen was so boring, he read his map all the way. Anyhow we went to Pinkney, which is a lovely village built of stone. The orchestra practises in a church hall. All the old people from the village play in it and they make a dreadful racket! Pedro and me had hysterics, sitting at the back.

"The old man next to Jurgen turned out to be the jolly gentleman we met at the convent the first time we came. Jurgen said he kept playing all out of tune and twisting his head round, pulling terrible faces. At half-time they had cups of tea and we had squash and the orchestra people talked about their gardens. The old man next to Jurgen is called Mr. Brambling. Very important. He keeps bees. He's a lovely bumbling man and he advises the Sisters on how to look after their bees at their big convent. Archie Gunn is important too. He follows the stars, just like Grandpa said you should. And he makes violins.

"I think I'm on to something. I told Corky about the black bees arriving at the chalk-pit, and he seemed very excited. He has great

plans to improve the nursery when he goes home. Can't write any more. Hamish has got a lecture tomorrow morning and then he's going to take us all to Mr. Brambling's house to see the garden and the hives."

"Well, why don't you come?" Mr. Brambling proposed, stroking his waistcoat and beaming at them each in turn. "Why don't you all come along and bring your friend, Cronky, or whatever his name is, and we can have tea at the cottage – eh? Oh, and you can meet my new friend Mordred. You'll love Mordred!"

Mordred sounded warm and comfortable, and Trudi instantly decided that he must be a cat. She pictured him to herself, sprawling a marmalade tummy across the step and blinking in the sun. Life likes to play these little jokes. Of course, in reality, he was nothing of the kind...

Chapter Nineteen

The Secret of the Seed Pattern

The next day, Sven took himself off early to get a special pass for the library. Hamish cycled back from his lecture with the wind behind him and Trudi, who spotted him from the landing, gave a little gasp as he freewheeled full-speed into the drive, leapt from the saddle and slammed the bike into its rack. He was quite an athlete. Within seconds he had breezed into the kitchen and carved himself an enormous tomato sandwich. Hamish did nothing by halves.

He kept his car at the side of the house and it more than lived up to Trudi's description, being a general dump for climbing gear, tatty maps, boots, old socks and mildewed tarpaulins. Its pungent, mouldy smell would have been enough to deter the stoutest-hearted thief, so it didn't seem to matter that the locks were broken and Hamish routinely left it with the key in the ignition. When he had eaten his fill, the children piled onto the back seat and Corky slipped into the front and they all set off for Pinkney together. The river passed that way and once they were out of the city, they could see the green line of willows that marked the banks quite clearly from the road. The Kingsbury Canal also ran briefly alongside.

"That's Pinkney Lock," said Hamish, pointing way over to his left. "It's a deep one. Quite tricky to navigate, they say. They had a big murder there in Victorian times and the cottage beside it was once a pub, 'The Stranger's Arms'. People took to calling it 'The Stranglers' and then it closed and became a lock-keeper's lodge. Don't know what has happened to it now."

"And what about over there?" Trudi pointed to a high fence further on, which enclosed an expanse of woodland."

"Ah. *That's* Pinkney Forest."

"Looks like a prison!"

"Well, it's private, you see. Ministry of Information, or something. I peeked in there once with Archie, when we were out on one of our walks. You know if something says: *'Private - no*

134

trespassers' he has to try and get in! They are extensive woods, but they weren't my cup of tea. Quite creepy, in fact."

"Why creepy?"

"Well, there were weird things in the trees - experiments going on. Warnings. I'm not too keen on guard dogs!"

Trudi shivered.

"I think the University does research there." He softened his tone, realizing perhaps he was on sensitive ground. "Probably perfectly harmless. Just monitoring the environment. I suppose it's the kind of thing your father does. Conservation studies. Insects are dying out. They count them and try to discover why..."

"But why is that so secret?" asked Trudi, glancing back at the notices in red, the razor wire.

Hamish should have known better. Children can be frightened by the silliest things and it is unwise to scare them with suspicions and rumours, but Pinkney Forest held a private fascination for him and this prompt was all it took to set him off again: "My hunch is that there is something else going on. Something they don't want us to know about! Every so often snippets leak into the press. They've got radars and satellite masts and all sorts of paraphernalia in there. Armed guards even."

"Sounds neat," said Jurgen.

"You're a zombie!" Trudi rounded on him, forgetting her resolution to be kind. She felt suddenly alarmed. To think that there were sinister masts here, of all places, and that Jurgen could actually *approve*... "You're only fit to talk to aliens! You should tell Archie about your 'alien'. I'm sure he'd be impressed."

Jurgen smiled. Trudi could say all she liked, but she wasn't a secret agent, and she didn't have a contact to report to. He could probably see what was in Pinkney Forest, just by consulting his Laser Wag - but frustratingly, as they neared the perimeter, something happened to the signal and his phone blacked out. It didn't revive again until they reached the road works, half a mile further on.

"This is Nether Pinkney, noted for its Annual Flower Show," Hamish resumed his commentary, "and Pinkney proper, famous for its Symphonia, is just down here." He turned off at the roundabout, down a narrow lane and past a village 'welcome' sign.

Daylight confirmed what Trudi had guessed the night before. Pinkney was an idyll - the stuff of picture books. There were stone cottages with steep-pitched roofs, magnolias, clematis, blackbirds practising snatches of song, and little flyers pasted up on notice-boards advertising local events: the Drama Society Dinner-Dance, the Pinkney Artists' Garden Party, a sausage-sizzle for the Girl Guides... Those same elderly people, who had been blowing and scraping in the orchestra the previous evening, were now doing their shopping. Everyone seemed to have a wicker basket and a little dog on a lead and all the little dogs yapped ferociously at one another while their owners popped into the baker's or the Post Office and tied them up outside. Pinkney had kept its Victorian street lamps and its verdant village green. The groundsman was even now, rolling the cricket pitch with a cast-iron roller. And on the far side of the village green, under a bower of blossom, stood Humbug Cottage.

They drew up at the gate, ignoring a sign which read: 'Residents' Parking Only' and Hamish took the lead and Corky brought up the rear and they progressed in single-file along a narrow brick path, stooping to avoid the overhanging shrubs. Late bluebells and starflowers winked in the lawn and delicious pockets of lilac and viburnum scent lingered under the boughs, where early campions flowered in a tangle. The cottage came into sight at last, a dear, low, crooked building with dark timbers and a monstrous thatch, like a tea-cosy. The name 'Humbug' described it exactly: all cream and brown stripes. As they got closer they could see diamond-paned windows and a Tudor door mailed with massive iron bosses and bolts.

The door swung wide in welcome and there stood Mr. Brambling, grinning and tugging at the buttons on his jacket.

"I was so worried that you might not find it!" He led the way in, down a step and then across a flagstone floor. Light from the back garden poured into the kitchen.

"It's perfect! It's *perfect!*" cried Trudi.

"Oh, *do* you like it?" Mr. Brambling really seemed to care. "I am so pleased. I'm afraid it's too late for me to modernize. But this suits me here. I've got the shops nearby and good neighbours - oh and the orchestra of course! Well, what a revelation it was sitting

136

next to young Jurgen, here, yesterday! My dear fellow, you're going to go a long way with that cello."

Jurgen cringed. "It's not my cello. I only borrowed it."

"No, no, it's the *hands* that matter. The hands and -" he tapped his head, "what goes on up here. You've got a talent there, my boy. Oh-ho dear!" He broke into a chuckle. "I must have given you quite an earache. What?"

"Well, I'll leave you all to it." Hamish spotted his escape. "I'll pick you up at twelve thirty and take you back for lunch. I've got an 'infinity' problem to solve before tomorrow. Tutorial first thing. Do a bit of study by the river." He would sneak off now while they were talking. An hour and a half would give him time for a snooze in the sun. But no one actually noticed him go.

"I'm not the best," Mr. Brambling continued as if there had been no interruption. "I joined the orchestra for the fellowship, the fun of the thing, but I do genuinely love music." He was now fiddling with tea things on a tray. "I expect you children would like something sweet. There's lemonade. That's what I used to like. We'll go into the garden and then we can have a *proper* chat."

A pause and he was off again, musing. "Pedro - Pedro that's an interesting name. Yes, we must have a proper chat."

Some gardens are like great works of art. You can see the huge amount of effort that has gone into making them. Long yew hedges, lawns, and formal flower beds require armies of gardeners, weeders, mowers. You would need great compost heaps, glasshouses and potting sheds behind such gardens, where all the planning and preparation could go on. But the garden at Humbug Cottage seemed to have happened spontaneously, all by itself. A little brick terrace, bordered with honesty and old-fashioned pinks, sloped off into an orchard where the ancient apple trees, all crusted with lichen, inclined at crazy angles, and branches, foaming with blossom, dipped down to touch the grass.

Trudi was entranced. The snow in Sweden had been beautiful, but it was cold and its beauty was shot through with danger and fear. This garden, by contrast, seemed never to have known a winter. All spring sap and sunshine, it simply pulsed with hope and life. They emerged from the orchard to find a picnic spot prepared: a stone table and comfortably cushioned chairs.

137

"Will this be all right?" Mr. Brambling set down his tray. "The herb plot, which I'll show you in a moment, is just over there. You can see the lovage and fennel stalks from here, and then the bees live in that wall over there." He turned to Corky with a stiff, sideways movement of the head. "We've got a medieval apiary here. Quite a rarity. It was part of the old Pinkney Abbey estate. After the dissolution, the monastery stone was plundered to build the village here, but someone who knew a thing or two kept the bee boles. And I am so lucky. They happen to be in my garden!"

He stirred the tea and put out jammy dodgers.

Nobody else got in a word, but who minded?

It was delightful just sitting in the sun, absorbing the atmosphere, and the boys were happy picking the cream out of their biscuits. After tea, they set off exploring once more. Mr. Brambling helped himself to a garden fork and pointed things out with it. This long wall here was part of the monastic boundary, which once stretched down to the river. This was where the old bee-masters tended their bees.

"I know it's foolish and sentimental, but I like to keep traditions going. I'm afraid I still favour the old-fashioned hives, the straw skeps that they used all those years ago."

Corky shook his head in a daze of pleasure. "And you still find a maker for them?"

"Well I've been very lucky." Mr. Brambling confided. "I managed to track down a man who had the skill to do it and I got the knowledge from him. I could make any number now! Of course the sad thing is that you have to kill the bees to harvest honey this way."

"Kill the bees?" objected Trudi.

"Seems ungrateful, doesn't it?" Mr Brambling looked genuinely distressed. "But I make sure they have the best of everything while they are alive. The herbs, the trees, flowers, are *all* planted for them."

Trudi felt a surge of compassion for the old man. How terrible for him to have to kill the creatures he loved so much. As they stood beneath the wall they could see the skeps, like fat, golden cobra-baskets, each one tucked into its own alcove to protect it from rain and wind.

138

There must have been eight or ten hives contentedly foraging here. Corky counted them off, but suddenly he seemed sunk in thought. Perhaps he was reminded of his missing bees at home. He began to rub his brow.

"And they stay healthy?" he enquired.

"Ah!" Mr Brambling clasped his hands together like a vicar about to deliver a sermon. "The great question! Our little friends here face such terrible hazards in their lives. The weather is often against them. They get eaten by birds, attacked by hornets, invaded by moths - mice - not to mention the dreaded mites that carry fatal disease. Chalk brood - foul brood. The list is forever getting longer. Now colonies are collapsing for no apparent reason at all! You, Mr. Corky, how do you help your bees to survive?"

"Well, I must admit, I've been lucky until now. My bees are quite isolated so perhaps that has kept them safe. They pretty much do their own thing," Corky gave a wistful smile. "Of course I make sure they have lots of flowers and forage trees nearby and I protect them from predators, talk to them. But this year I've lost two whole colonies. Can't explain why."

"Worrying times!" Mr. Brambling shook his head. "So many things find life a struggle nowadays. I'm afraid we humans are too careless with our planet. But if we lose the bees, we shall starve for it. Who else will pollinate all the orchards and gardens and field crops for us? Imagine life without honey, without fruit or flowers!"

Trudi tried to consider a summer without strawberries and gave it up.

"We must save them," she said passionately.

"Exactly!" Mr. Brambling bestowed an approving smile upon her. "We must do what we can to save *everything!*"

Pedro, all this time, had been very quiet, but suddenly he pricked up his ears. "Oh-oh!" He gave a little warning whistle.

Trudi started, hearing something behind them, and Mr. Brambling swung round with a practised readiness, his garden fork raised like a bayonet, and all but speared a cockerel which came charging out of the shrubbery.

The creature stalled, with the fork tines at its breast, backed up a little and tried a flying attack, feet foremost. Mr. Brambling beat him amicably off once more.

"Meet Mordred," he said. "I thought he would turn up sooner or later."

Mordred had a devilish look about him: black, glossy plumage tinged a metallic green; blood red comb and wattles; dark legs and muscular feet flushed with crimson webbing. His claws and beak gleamed like polished stone and when he wanted to make an impression, as he clearly did now, he dropped one wing and skipped along sideways, brandishing his spurs. For a cockerel he boasted an impressive size. The tip of his comb and the crest of his free-flowing tail reached easily to Mr. Brambling's knee. Oh, but his eye! - and it was his dark eye which transfixed Trudi - that seemed a bead of pure malice.

She shrank behind Corky for safety, pulling the boys with her. But Pedro, who could only hear the beating of Mordred's wings, broke away, curious:

"What is? What is?" he tugged at Trudi's arm.

"It's a huge cockerel - you know? *Cockadoodledoo!* But *big, black!* It's going to kill someone."

"Oh, my God!" laughed Pedro. "Better not stay here!"

"Don't worry, you're quite safe," beamed Mr. Brambling. "It's *me* he doesn't like. But he's very good with the hens. And he warns me of any intruders."

"Is that a good enough reason for keeping him?" Corky looked on, bemused and wary. He knew well enough how to wring a chicken's neck if Mordred turned on the children.

"Well," Mr. Brambling began to drive his adversary back towards the house. "I feel rather like the Sheikh in the story, you know? He kept a ferocious dog that guarded the door of his tent and attacked him every time he ventured in or out. There was no doubt that that beast wanted his blood. But when his friends asked why he kept it, he replied that it was his teacher. It saved him from being complacent and taking too much for granted. One must stay on one's toes you know!"

Trudi wondered why that was necessary here in Pinkney, but she did not like to ask. Perhaps if Mincke had had a Mordred, he would have been warned of his intruder.

"Don't you worry about him!" called Mr. Brambling. "I'll shut him up. Then we can relax once more." He and Mordred receded out of sight like dancers in a mad minuet, the cockerel hurling himself upon the fork, the old man warding him off.

When he returned, Mr. Brambling was sweating.

"That was *wicked!*" said Jurgen appreciatively.

"You think so? I've taken on bigger terrors in my time. Well, at any rate, now it is safe for you children to see the maze. I have planted it with herbs and all are labelled according to their use. I like to dabble a little in home remedies, you know. You might enjoy getting lost there. Here's the entrance, look. Follow the path to the middle and then, good luck! We'll time you till you come out," he fished out a silver fob watch. "I'll wager you can't do it in less than fifteen minutes!"

"Come on, Pedro," said Trudi, grabbing him by the hand. "We'll memorise the way. Jurgen, you try to remember the names of the herbs we pass. I'll take the lead."

"I could guide you on my phone," objected Jurgen, but Pedro interrupted:

"*I* could guide you - *easy!* Look!"

After the first circuit, Trudi lost her sense of direction completely. Her system of counting off the herbs proved useless for Mr. Brambling had planted them at random. There were purple-budded chives dotted all along the path and the creamy tops of sweet cicely mixed up with lavender and sage, round every bend.

Here were mints by the dozen: pineapple mint, silver mint, peppermint, even one called eau-de-cologne - and all the foliage looked similar to an untrained eye. Then the names themselves bore a confusing likeness to one another: tansy and pansy, borage and bergamot, wormwood - southernwood. Sven would have known them! As they pressed forward, the scents floated up to meet them, bitter and pungent and refreshing. If only they were not being timed it would be nice to stop and sniff them properly. The path wound on, switching back on itself whenever it reached an impasse. They could not see an end or a middle, but Pedro pushed confidently ahead.

"I don't like it," said Jurgen, feeling suddenly nervous. "Suppose that cockerel gets out now. No one will ever find us to rescue us here!"

Trudi pounced straightaway. "Trust you to say that!" This was no time to show weakness, though in her heart she had been thinking the same. She took hold of his hand too and let Pedro lead the way.

"Left here..."

"That's rosemary, remember that!" She could not quite relinquish giving directions.

"... And left here."

"Foxgloves."

The circles were getting smaller. "You don' need remember," said Pedro. "You won't pass them again - unless we going wrong." All the same he brushed the leaves of the plants they passed with his free hand, rubbing them between thumb and forefinger, making mental notes.

"Here should be the middle," he announced as the path opened out and they found themselves in a clearing.

"Pedro, how did you *know?*"

"Ah," he laughed, tapping his nose. "I knows many things. Many secrets too! This maze is old pattern ju find in many places. Is on old rocks, on baskets, on paintings too. Is called the 'Seed Pattern'. Ju can find it anywhere in the world - even in Sweden! What you can see here?"

"It's like a little grassy plot, cut in half. The herbs meet in the middle, but there's a metal arch with plants climbing up it, making a kind of doorway. The sign says," she squinted to read, "'Hops' and 'Honeysuckle'. Do we go through?"

"Si – Ju must go through. Then you can go out. It means there are two paths. Will be quicker on the way back."

"Pedro, *how* do you know? Have you done this before?" Trudi struggled now to keep up.

"On paper! Yis. Old friend in Lima taught me. He taught many special things."

"What's his name?"

"He gone now. He was call Father Hieronimo. French. Jesuit. Very old. He work in the mountains with the Indian people, digging up old things! Funny man! I liked him."

Trudi was not yet satisfied. "But what is a 'Seed Pattern'. Why is it everywhere? Why is it special?"

"I don' know. It's a path goes round, round, round like the sun - like the stars. Like water going down the sink! Like a little snail - back to the beginning of time, or middle winter – what is called?

142

"The Winter Solstice?"

"Maybe. Now we can come out."

"Through midwinter?"

"Oh, yis. You pass through midwinter to come back to summer. Is like a new life. When we come out we are in a new world. Now we can't be lost."

The path snaked on in widening coils and then abruptly ended. They tumbled out exactly where they had begun and where Corky and Mr. Brambling still stood waiting. Trudi felt a shock seeing them together. In the short time they had been away Corky seemed to have aged so that the old man, though shorter by a foot, now appeared the stronger of the two. There he was, consulting his watch and referring in an animated way to his companion, as though taking the measure of him. Corky, swayed, grey-faced, at his side. For a moment she found it hard to believe this was the friend she knew. What had happened to the exuberant clown, who had jigged in his top hat and braces to the strains of his one-man-band only a year ago? The joker, the life and soul of the Farmer's Market? Now he looked positively ill - crushed by his crooked back. She hated to see him so.

"Bravo!" cried Brambling, enthusiastically. "Excellent time! Twelve and a half minutes. What clever children you are!"

"Pedro did it," said Jurgen. "Pedro knows how to do everything."

Mr. Brambling nodded at the quiet slip of a boy, his eyes shining.

"Extraordinary!" he pocketed the watch and rubbed his hands together. "Perhaps he can teach me! Next time you come, Pedro, I will show you something too. You know I am quite mad about your country. I'm a secret collector. I've been to Peru. What a marvellous civilization! I've got ancient pottery from Machu Picchu, from Cuzco, all the big Inca cities. Well... perhaps you have a moment to see it now?"

Corky gave a passive nod and Pedro shrugged, as Pedro always did. Why not? So Mr. Brambling hobbled back through the orchard, beckoning them to follow, excited as a schoolboy.

In the cool dark of the parlour, he opened a glass-fronted, cabinet. Out came a little figure of painted clay, which he pressed into Pedro's hand.

"There. Have you ever seen anything like that before? That was made by your ancestors, seven hundred years ago!"

Pedro explored the figure with his fingers.

"Si, si."

Mr. Brambling watched him intently.

"Know what it is?"

"Si," Pedro handed it back. "Is Wiraqocha. God of Inca people."

Mr. Brambling twinkled back.

"What about this?" A bracelet.

"Feels like gold," said the boy, weighing it lightly.

"Marvellous! And this?"

'This' was a heavy, straight-sided bowl, more impressive in style. Pedro did not seem to recognize it and Trudi felt glad, because although she would not say so, for fear of hurting Mr. Brambling's feelings, she did not care for it very much. It had been worked in black on naked, red-hued clay and bore a formal decoration, beautifully executed round the rim, of painted heads. But these heads felt out of place in Humbug cottage. Unlike the quirky animal faces on other pots, or even the sun face of Wiraqocha himself these expressed an alien, unfriendly power. They were ugly, severed heads, with staring holes for eyes.

Pedro shook his head. "Is a bowl," he said simply.

"Exactly!" Mr. Brambling popped it back in the cupboard. "Next time you will see. How wonderful!"

Moments later Hamish knocked at the door. Already they were leaving, shaking hands, exchanging formal smiles.

"Thank you for the lemonade and the bee tour."

"Thank *you*. What a delight it has been. But we shall meet again soon. Perhaps on Sunday afternoon, at tea. And please, take some honey – sage and lemon balm from last summer, when the herbs were at their best. Oh, and some apple blossom for the convent chapel. There is so much this year, it won't hurt to steal a little."

Pausing to wave at the gate, Trudi ducked down and caught a last glimpse of the cottage nestling amidst its leaves. Cream and brown, she thought, just like a bee. How perfect!

Sister Bianca met them at St. Lucy's with a grin. "You're late! You've missed lunch with us." Trudi felt secretly relieved for it was an awful thing to eat lunch in silence. She simply couldn't keep quiet and she knew she would get the giggles if she tried.

144

"We've left you helpings in the student kitchen." Bianca waved them through. "Oh, and Trudi, you were asking about Gallipot Hill. I'm going to the Co-op there this afternoon. Want to come with me?"

After lunch, Corky said he would take a nap in the garden. The boys sloped off to play some game Pedro knew with knotted string.

Sister Bianca assembled her shopping bags and wrote out a list. She and Trudi would do the shopping first, then look for the coaching inn where Long Ned, the highwayman, once kept his horse. The Three Purses, it was, Gibbet Lane. What more could Trudi want? The very name signified romance and adventure. They were all set to go when the doorbell rang.

Edmund again.

"One moment!" Bianca swept off to the kitchen to boil a kettle, leaving the door ajar, and Edmund paced up and down the drive, swishing his stick and muttering crazy things to himself. Trudi spied on him through the gap.

At last, becoming impatient, he returned to the porch and nudged the sill-board gently with his toe. The door swung open, on its well-oiled hinges and tramp and child found themselves suddenly face to face. It would be hard to say which of them had the greater shock.

"Tea's coming," stammered Trudi.

Edmund sprang back. Then crouched towards her again.

"A lot of Russians about today," he confided, jerking his head towards the road. "Have to be careful. Don't let them see what you're doing! Control A. Delete. Got it?" He took in her diminutive figure, clad for summer in cropped jeans and jelly shoes. Her tee shirt, which had been a present from Barbara and Corky, bore the slogan "I love honey!" in curly script, and showed a swarm of bees cavorting above a hive. Bianca's bags lay at her feet. He stared rudely for a while, then straightened up:

"Ah! Going out?"

"We're shopping. We're going to the Co-op at Gallipot Hill." She was gabbling now to fill the time. *Please come back Sister Bianca. Come and save me!*

Edmund sniffed, looked down his nose and consulted the sky like a mariner. "Half a mile, as the bee flies," he observed, pursuing the honey theme. Trudi wished she had put on a plain top

– her swarm must have got into his head - but she could not help correcting him.

"Don't you mean as the *crow* flies?"

He turned back with a frown. "A *bee*, I said. Bees are better navigators."

"But they can't see properly." She knew that. She remembered just what it was like inside the bee-veil - all fuzzy.

"Don't need to." Edmund pressed his face closer, frowning, as if troubled by an inner conflict. His next words startled them both:

"They can detect patterns in the sky to guide them. Ultra-violet. Better than that – they have got magnets in their brains. Tiny grains which tell them, like a compass, which way they are going." *Where did he get that from?* "Have *you* got bees?"

Sister Bianca arrived with her beaker and plate and Edmund retreated.

"I'll put your food on the bench here for you." She shot him a searching look. "That all right?"

And he grimaced back, resuming his idiot role. "Muchas Gracias. Bull's eye!"

But he did not touch the tea.

As Bianca and Trudi set out, he overtook them and marched ahead along the street, brandishing his stick and calling things out till passers-by scuttled anxiously off the pavement. He kept it up all the way, glancing back every now and then to be sure his friends were following. Bianca said afterwards that she had never been so embarrassed. Not only that, he parked himself noisily outside the Co-op while they bought their purchases and then escorted them all the way home.

As they let themselves in at the door, he crept up behind Trudi and shouted: "Buzz! Don't forget!" in her ear.

When Sister Matilda heard of it she slapped her hand on the table. "We can't stand for that kind of behaviour. I shall have words with him next time he comes. He must treat our young visitors with respect."

"I don't think he meant any harm," murmured Trudi. Secretly, she felt sorry for him. She thought he must be lonely, even though he filled her with trepidation.

146

"A man like that doesn't know what harm is, my dear. He's quite in a dream. I think perhaps it would be better for you to keep out of his way for a while."

Trudi thrust her hands into her pockets and fingered the feather she had picked up earlier in the day. It was one of Mordred's, black, with a viridian sheen and a downy quill. She had spotted this trophy, caught in the grass soon after the battle with Mr. Brambling and secretly hidden it away. Though she could not say why, she felt it might be important, a reminder that threats lurked, even here, in Gloucestershire.

Mad cockerels… Mad tramps… Back at the hotel she placed the feather in her box of clues and noted in her journal:

"Important developments. More bees. And another maze. Humbug Cottage is just perfect and Mr. Brambling very kind and eccentric. Gallipot Hill, though, was a dead loss. Just houses and shops. No gibbets at all. But there are dangers to watch out for!"

Neither Edmund, nor Mordred, however, did any harm that day, for trouble, as Trudi would learn, prefers to strike where it is least expected.

Chapter Twenty

Mambo-Hambo

Mrs. Sparks, the cleaner, answered the door next morning when the children returned to St. Lucy's. She was busy polishing the banisters on the stairs, down on her knees, where she seemed to be happiest, her buckets and dusters spread all around her. The nuns had warned her several times that someone would fall over so many buckets, but Mrs. Sparks liked to make a thorough job of her cleaning. She hummed softly to herself as she worked, like a bird, thought Trudi, chirruping to no one in particular. She wore a skirt and an old-fashioned, large-pocketed apron, and her little sparrow legs ended in flat shoes with leather toggles on the front. Yes, like a bird. She had her head on one side now, a little round face like a pippin apple, curly brown hair, though she must be far too ancient for it really and loose rings on her big-knuckled fingers.

"You come for the little Peruvian boy, have you?" She had a curly brown voice, with a Cotswold burr. "He ha'n't come down yet this morning. You better wait here and I'll go an' find Sister Emilia. She knows what's goin' on."

Perplexed, they waited at the foot of the stairs. Sven would be hard pushed to make his appointment at nine-thirty if there was a delay. He shifted uneasily from one foot to the other.

Then they heard footsteps in the big kitchen and a rustle of clothes and Sister Emilia sailed out on her dignity, her pectoral cross a-gleam on her substantial bosom. She clasped her hands, smiled over the heads of the children and ushered Sven into the office.

So something was up then - something important. Trudi stared as the office door closed, then turned back open-mouthed.

Mrs. Sparks wrung out her floor cloth and gave a reassuring nod. "Don't you worry. I don't s'pose it's nothin' serious. Just a summer chill. Anyhow, Hamish tells me that you're all going on a picnic, so it can't be anything serious, can it?"

"We're going to Drayholt tomorrow, with his friend Archie, to see the Worm on the hill."

"'S lovely up there," Mrs. Sparks recalled, with a dreamy, far-away look. "We used to go as children, for our Sunday School treat, once a year. Midsummer, you're s'posed to go."

"That's what Hamish said, but we won't be here at Midsummer. He said the Worm is very ancient. It's meant to be a dragon."

"Oh, that's right enough. But it don't look like a dragon. It looks more like a funny, squashed kind of doughnut. Don't be disappointed will you? I 'spect most of the design got lost in the grass, you know, grew in like, over the centuries. It's a lot of work to keep that figure cut clean, and now they're talking about not letting people walk on it no more - to preserve it, like. I call that a shame. You can't do your wishing if you can't walk on it, can you?"

"What wishing?" asked Jurgen. He was looking up Drayholt on his mobile.

"Well," the old lady got to her feet. "Tradition was, in my day, that you had to stand on the eye of the Worm, turn round three times, look out towards Drayholt and make a wish."

"It says here it's a lem-nis-cate," Jurgen pulled a doubtful face and tried the word again. "Lem-nis-cate." He went on reading: "It's a figure-of-eight – an ancient symbol - like the snake of legend with its tail in its mouth…"

Trudi shot him an irritated glance.

"…It's also a prehistoric solar calendar, depicting the sun's path from summer to winter."

"Archie already told us that." She did not want to be informed by Laser Wag.

"I don't know 'bout any of that," said Mrs. Sparks. "I just know it's supposed to mark the place where Merlin, the magician, had a fight. The church at Drayholt has got a picture on the wall."

At that moment, the office door opened and Sven and Sister Emilia emerged. Mrs. Sparks applied herself once more to her paintwork and Sven beckoned the children close.

"Listen scamps," he confided. "Today we've got a problem. I *have* to go into Kingsbury for this interview, but Corky is not very well. He must have caught some kind of bug. He's going to stay in bed today, but Sister Bianca will look after you. I'll be back at about four. You will be good for me, won't you? And try and keep Pedro cheerful? He's a bit upset."

"What kind of bug?" asked Trudi, remembering how terrible Corky had looked outside the maze.

"He just… doesn't feel good. Needs to sleep a bit. He'll be fine tomorrow."

He could not repeat what Sister Emilia actually told him, which was that Corky had been raving, incoherent; thought he was in a shack, on a mountain in Peru and kept clutching his shoulder and asking what they had done with the baby. Nor did he mention that Pedro had dug in his heels, and positively refused to leave Corky's side. He had actually bitten Sister Caroline when she tried to pull him away! The nuns had telephoned for a doctor that morning, but since the lines were all busy, and Corky's pulse and temperature seemed normal, Matilda had recommended rest and lots to drink till help could be summoned.

"Now, my dear," she said taking Pedro's hands in her own, and applying her eighty years of human understanding, "the best *you* can do for Corky is to fetch him some medicine. I am trusting you because I know you are the best person to ask. I will write what you need on a piece of paper and you can hand it to the pharmacist in Kingsbury. Meanwhile, *I* will speak to the doctor. Sister Bianca is going into town this morning. She will take you with her and bring you back before lunch. The doctor will no doubt prescribe something else but my medicine is a tonic and will do Corky no harm. Much better than waiting, doing nothing. You must *not* worry, you know. Nothing upsets a patient like worry. I've known people look a lot worse than this and they always got better!"

Under her influence, Pedro grew calmer and agreed to cooperate, but the boy who appeared downstairs, moments later, was grim-faced, listless and silent, and the shrugs he gave as answers showed that, for once in his life, he cared about things all too much. His light had simply gone out and the whole house felt the darker for it. When Jurgen suggested playing the string game again he turned away and Trudi once more forgot her resolution to be nice and said string games were for babies.

Sister Emilia shut herself in her office and fumed.

Was this not exactly why she had doubted the wisdom of having the blind lad, in the beginning? Disruption and distraction. She had seen it all coming. Disastrous for discipline and heaven knew where it would end! The University students were bad enough,

150

with their irregular comings and goings, but to have parties of children hanging about on the stairs, sulking in corners...

If only the orphanage in Lima had not insisted so passionately that Pedro must come *here*. If only Mother Constance had stuck to her original plan and persuaded the Sisters of Mercy to have him instead... They were Catholics, after all, and only streets away... Much better and more homely for a Peruvian. But they had all acted under the impression that a stronger and higher power was mysteriously at work and that Pinkney Road had, in some obscure way, been specially 'chosen'. St. Lucy, after all, was patron saint of the blind. Emilia had submitted, as she thought, to the will of the Lord. Suddenly she wasn't sure that the Lord had anything to do with it and her misgivings came flooding back. True, Corky had always seemed a perfect gentleman and nothing untoward had happened until today, but his present collapse suggested dark and disturbing possibilities. Had he been drinking? One could not entirely rule it out. And then there was the boy... He had changed from an angel into a devil in a matter of minutes. A most shocking affair. Did his own Peruvian family reject him because he was given to biting?

Emilia put her head in her hands. These things were bad enough, but they came on top of still graver matters.

The question of the fire doors, for instance.

Every day, it seemed, some new problem landed on her desk, preventing her from praying or sleeping quietly. There had been the accountant, the leaking roof in the chapel... now the Fire Department, insisting that new fire doors must be fitted. And where was the money to come from? The world hardly gave her time to think. Old ways, like the old monastic vestments, were dying out. The Sisters of Mercy wore short skirts, and little headscarves. No one would suspect that they were nuns at all!

Her thoughts ran on unchecked.

She knew she should not criticize. She knew it showed weakness and lack of faith to give in to hopeless thoughts. But these new fire doors would bankrupt St. Lucy's. The quiet life, to which all the Sisters had devoted themselves, was little by little changing into a very busy life, full of pressure to change. Now they were being advised to put everything on computer - have a website - prayers online - a daily blog. And who would do all that? She envied Mrs. Sparks her dusters and polishing cloths. Even if the woman was always under her feet, at least she knew her job and she would not change her ways - not for anyone! She spent more time on her knees than the Sister-in-charge!

Emilia wiped tears of frustration on her scapula. She must try harder to move with the times. Would St. Lucy have had a website if she had been alive today? She had a nasty suspicion that she probably would: a special website for blind people with a cyber wall for prayer requests and virtual candles to light. If they charged fifty pence per candle, she thought sarcastically, it would pay for the chapel roof!

She ought to repent for such impiety, but instead she started as if she had received an electric shock, leapt to her feet, shook herself and tripped back to the kitchen. Perhaps the Lord knew best, after all! A blind boy at St. Lucy's might be *just* what they needed... Sister Caroline, rubbing arnica into her bite-wound, later heard her singing over the soup.

Meanwhile Bianca had marshalled the children in the hall.

"The doctor is coming at eleven o'clock. There's an excellent chemist in the old city centre. They'll make this up for Corky. And maybe we can get an ice cream at Gulliver's!"

She set off before they could object, leaving them to keep up as best they could. At first Pedro struggled along refusing any help, but after a couple of stumbles he reached out and shyly gripped a fold of Bianca's habit. When they came to a kerb, the young Sister laid a hand on his shoulder and he did not shake her off. Then, as they stepped out into the traffic, he took her palm and kept it, so they reached an unspoken truce and by the time the old colleges came into view, he had dashed away his angry tears, and Trudi and Jurgen, trotting along behind, had exchanged grown up glances and they were ready to confront the day.

"Medicine first," said Bianca, steering Pedro round some sightseers.

The city had a buzz that morning. College walls and weather-cocks gleamed in the sunshine. Clocks in every tower and steeple tolled out the quarters. There were groups of students hurrying here and there or debating where to go for coffee. A cluster of protestors chanted outside the Town Hall waving 'global warming' placards.

Bianca and the children passed two jugglers arguing over a patch of pavement.

"This is my spot and everybody knows it!"

"Well, I got here first. And I'm not budging."

The owner of a nearby café came out and threw water over them. "Clear off! Both of you! You haven't got a permit anyway!"

How exciting! From somewhere else came strains of music. Just around the corner... A busker.

This character had staked his pitch with more aplomb. A huge paper kite in the shape of a condor fluttered overhead. Amidst a clutter of aluminium cases and amplifiers, he strutted, resplendent in a coloured tunic, selling lucky bracelets, wampum and wooden snakes. What he lacked in height, he made up for with swagger, puffing out his chest, and proudly cocking his nose to reveal a profile like a hawk. He wore a felt hat with feathers in it. His hair, in two thin plaits, reached down to his waist. He breathed Mystery. A sign beneath the condor read: *Mambo-Hambo - the Man of the Mountains"*.

He looked, to Trudi, like a shaman.

"Listen Pedro - it's your music, from South America!" She had succumbed instantly to the showman's spell.

But Pedro seemed unimpressed. The tune, a plaintive melody on the pan-pipes, wheezed from the loudspeakers, to the accompaniment of sounds of Nature: a waterfall, a macaw, a wolf, a boatman calling... "Is no real!" he dismissed it with a shake of the head. "Not from Peru. That wolf can't live in my country!"

Trudi looked at Mambo-Hambo's face, and the beaded bracelets, drums, llama-patterned purses which he handled as reverently as if they were sacred relics. And Mambo-Hambo, from his pygmy mountain, stared back, inscrutable, searching her soul.

She *wanted* him to be real. She knew that Pedro was dismissive because he was upset about Corky. He would have rejected the god Wiraqocha as an impostor today. But he had a point. Several other things about Mambo-Hambo suggested he might be a fake. That dark complexion, for instance - it finished in a line at his neck. Was it painted on? He was certainly wearing jeans beneath his tunic and some of his stock looked suspect too. She knew for a fact that wampum came from *North*, not South America - Professor Saxmund had told her that. And doubtless Pedro was right about the wolves. Grey, howling wolves, like the ones Per knew, belonged above the equator. None came south of Mexico. But she liked Mambo-Hambo's charade. Didn't one of Barbara's quotations on the bookshop wall at home read: "Deceit is enchantment"? *("That's Plato,"* said Barbara. *"If anyone knows, he does!")*

She gazed lingeringly at the trinkets for sale. The wampum came in beaded belts, adorned with shell-patterns of birds and frogs, but there were also coloured braids hooked up in figures of eight. Seen thus, they brought to mind the pieces of string that Pedro played with when he was bored. Was that what Jurgen meant by a lemniscate?

"Come along, Trudi. There's nothing for us here!" That was Sister Bianca, propelling Pedro forward, in her breezy, practical way.

At that, Trudi rebelled. She didn't care if the Indian *was* a fake. She didn't have to believe him. After all, Corky was not really a clown in a top hat. He merely dressed up when he played his one-man-band. Perhaps Sister Emilia stopped being so frightening and saintly when she took off her wimple at night... Impulsively, she fumbled for her purse. She would buy a string for Corky, to cheer him up. No one need know, if she was quick.

Mambo-Hambo saw her and in a flash pressed the braid into her hand. "You are the lucky one! No need to pay, today!" He made an expansive flourish with his hand. "Not everyone can see. But you – you have the eye. You see further than most. Here is something special for you. The pattern is a code. It says the path ahead is long but the spirit of Mambo-Hambo will go with you." He peddled the usual fortune-teller's patter. "Fix like this and you can make a loop. Then you can wear it as a bracelet. Can have many uses. Good in times of trouble…"

As he slipped the knot into its fastening, his beady eyes rested on her and softened for a moment. Then he turned away and she pushed the braid into her bag and hurried on.

At St. Lucy's, Sister Roberta greeted them with news that the invalid had rested well. He was still sleeping, so Trudi kept quiet about her string and stowed it, for safety, with her keepsakes. If Mambo-Hambo was right, things would soon be looking up. There would be no more need for lucky-charms. Already there were

154

encouraging signs. Sven returned from St. Gregory's smiling, having secured a second interview.

The next day Hamish would drive them to Drayholt.

Chapter Twenty-One

Lemniscates and Spindle Whorls

Archie Gunn presented himself at St. Lucy's at ten o'clock, resplendent in a pair of old leather hiking boots and combat fatigues with multiple pockets. He had stuffed his trouser bottoms into coarse-knitted, red, woollen socks and jammed a tweed cap on his head. Something which looked like a metal coat-hanger protruded from his rucksack. To Trudi and Jurgen he appeared perfectly ridiculous, but Hamish paid no attention to appearances. Hamish was too busy poring over his maps.

"Too bad about Corky," he said without looking up. "Poor fellow has, gone down with something. And Sven Larsson has been recalled to St. Gregory's. Looks as though we've got charge of the children."

Archie pulled a face. "How's my cello, more to the point?"

"Your cello is fine. Young Jurgen shone as the brightest star in the orchestra. Mr. Brambling was most taken with him and invited us all for tea next day. So you see, we are moving up in the world! Old Brambling's never noticed me before!"

"Well you're a brass player. Not refined enough!"

"True. Anyhow, we may have to cut down our plans a bit today, for the kiddies. I don't suppose they're used to twenty mile rambles."

They talked as if the children, seated nearby on kitchen stools, were quite invisible.

"Going to do the Worm, though, aren't we?" Archie insisted. "I've brought my gear." He tapped his coat hanger.

"Yes, Archie." Hamish swung round to address the youngsters and his voice assumed a sardonic tone. "Archie has a theory about the Worm. It's not a wizard's magic sign and it's not a dragon, or rather, what is left of Medraut's horse, as the guide books would have you believe. No. It's a launch pad for alien astronauts. He's a UFO freak. Don't you find that curious in an otherwise intelligent man? *You* don't believe in aliens, do you?"

156

"Jurgen's *got* one!" Trudi blurted unkindly. "He's called Zub. He lives in his mobile."

Jurgen squirmed: "It's only a game. You can see it if you like."

"Oho! Laser Wag, is it?" Hamish took a squint. "But not the latest model. I'm told that the new design now has 'personal recognition' - it knows exactly who is using it. Supposed to be for security - you know - stop theft and all that. But it means the phone is watching you. I call that sinister! In any case," he continued, talking once more above the children's heads, "they shouldn't give them to bairns. Fries their brains. Not only that, it's bad for the environment. Think of the poor bees. They can't fly straight with all that radiation buzzing about."

Trudi looked up to Hamish. Though he did not really know how to behave with children - he did not understand that grown-ups were supposed to be especially nice to them and make them feel important - he was funny and outrageous and said things with such confidence he often fooled others, even his tutors, into thinking he knew more than he really did. However, this time Trudi felt certain he was wrong. Mobile phones had nothing to do with the disappearance of the bees. She had heard Corky say so. What was more, scientists had proved it. Bees were vanishing for other reasons, though nobody yet understood them.

Archie stuck to his own view: "You're behind the times, young Hamish. The bees are being stolen for the great knowledge that they have. Think of a beehive - how it functions in perfect harmony, each bee performing its separate task, like the cells in a super-brain. They've got the keys to navigation, time, gravity, architecture, social organization, information codes... They are masters of memory, nutrition, medicine, defence. Bees know it all. Humans are nowhere near building a society as peaceful and efficient! Now if you were an alien and you wanted to start a new civilization, which would you choose for your model? Not homo sapiens. Why, bees, of course! They've simply been stolen, man. They're up there, in the stars!" Trudi jumped at the words.

"Bees in space?" scoffed Hamish.

"I'm perfectly serious. Look at old legends. You'll find plenty of examples!"

Would Mincke's bees be there? Had Trudi and Per somehow overlooked them when they scanned the winter sky?

"Yes, yes, and those aliens have stolen your brain cells too. *They're* a model of perfection you'll find nowhere else!"

"Come with me to the Worm at midnight, if you doubt me then, and I'll show you!" Archie had taken enough ribbing.

"Well, I just might do that! I like a midnight walk now and then!" The sceptic folded his map and, sticking his foot up on the table, began to retie his laces. "Pedro here would be our best guide, wouldn't you? You going to come along quietly? You know the doctor is due to see Corky today, so everything will be fine here. Don't you worry!"

Pedro nodded gravely. "Si." He had been talking again to Mrs. Sparks. "I want make my wish."

"Well, all set then!" Hamish shouldered his pocket-sized knapsack and flashed a decisive smile.

"Please," hazarded Trudi. "What about the picnic?" She was remembering the companionable feasts that Auntie Barbara always prepared for a country outing at home: the pies, pasties, buns, fruit salads... Normally they could hardly stagger along under the load.

Hamish seemed to have given this no thought at all. He liked to travel light. "Ah," he put his hand on his chin, then shrugged. "We'll call in at the Merlin Arms, if we need to. Don't worry. I've packed essentials."

With this breezy comfort, they trooped to the car. Sister Bianca waved them off from the doorstep. "Have you got everything you need?" she called. "Food?"

Hamish nodded and tapped the roof.

"Don't be late back!" Bianca watched them drive away. *"And don't lose my little ones!"* She was not sure about the wisdom of this trip.

West of the city lay the Rump, a ridge of chalk grassland, much like the downs at Newbridge, though steeper in places and riven by wedges of beechwood. The summit gleamed invitingly beneath a blue sky. They parked at the foot of the hill and set off along a path – Hamish had walked this way before.

"This your first mountain?" he asked Pedro.

"Si." The boy had dressed himself in plimsolls and a flimsy jacket. As the trees thinned out and the wind picked up, Trudi thought she could hear the ghost of Auntie Barbara tutting. *"Saints alive! How did you let him go out like that? He's going to catch his death, or fall down a rabbit hole, or something."* But Pedro seemed content and kept up as best he could. Half way up, they rested and he bared his arms and stretched himself out on the grass like a lizard, to catch the sun.

"If ju lie down," he said "is not so windy. Look!"

Trudi tried it. It was true, but now she could hear her mother: *"Sven, you let the children go all day in the sun with no sun cream! Do you know how dangerous that is?"*

Hamish and Archie didn't 'do' precautions. They were now arguing amiably over the map.

"I say come down this combe here, then follow the stream to the road. Two miles to Drayholt. Lunch. Back to Kingsbury."

"But the Devil's Dewpond is in the next valley. It's so close Hamish. We could just *look!*"

"There's no path."

"We don't need a path. You can't get lost, you can see everything. It's open downland. You can probably even see the car."

Along the ridge, the wind blew the grasses flat. Thorn trees here had been weather-carved over the years till they looked like staggering men, all blown one way. The ground undulated with the pits and pockets of ancient earthworks. From the horizon, a band of low cloud started to roll in across the vale.

"It's spooky up here," said Jurgen. "Do you think they have witches' covens and things?"

"Oh it's a magnet for witches!" laughed Hamish. "Witches, warlocks, herbalists, UFO hunters, circle dancers. All the crackpots on the planet come here!" As they reached the summit, the flank of the hill unfolded eastwards, disclosing a section of the Worm. Bare chalk glowed in the thickening light.

"Come on." Hamish broke into a run, long legs flying. "Who's going to make the first wish?" They tumbled after him. All except Archie, who liked to prepare himself before approaching holy ground. First he put on his binoculars; then reached out his notebook in its protective plastic sleeve. Last of all, came the coat-hangers, which he began to wave about, solemn as a priest.

"What's he doing?" asked Trudi, feeling the first rumblings of hunger.

Hamish was dismissive. "Oh, ignore him! He's divining for cosmic energy. It's called dowsing. Sheer nonsense, believe me! He honestly thinks he can pick up astral influences. Give the man a violin and he's a genius. Give him a coat-hanger, he goes to pot!"

They all laughed. Of course twirling round on a lump of chalk and making a wish was much more sensible!

"Right. Youngest first. Off you go, Jurgen. Really you should walk the whole Worm first. But the weather's changing. I don't think there's time. Let's just do the eye. I'd say it's that bulge over there."

The turf here was springy, close-cropped and the chalk scar cut deeply into it, and wound, in a wide path, out of sight. Seen this close, the scale of the figure came as a surprise. Jurgen duly stepped forward, feeling the first rain-spots on his face. "Which way is Drayholt?"

"That way - oh do get on!" Trudi suddenly sensed that they had been here long enough. Hamish was right. Swathes of farmland below were disappearing as the mist moved in. She wondered what Jurgen would ask for, but she never found out, for the wind took his words and blew them away over his shoulder. He, however, knew exactly what he wanted. The very moment Hamish disparaged his phone at St. Lucy's, he had lost interest in it: "I wish I could have the *new* Laser Wag – the one with 'personal recognition'!" That was Jurgen all over. Short and sweet. No fancy frills. He nodded and moved aside.

"Trudi!"

Trudi stepped onto the eye and summoned all her concentration. "I wish," she breathed, holding the hair out of her eyes as the wind whipped round her. "I wish Grandfather Larsson could escape from the Sneevelings and be with us here in Kingsbury. I wish I could go home and find everything like it used to be, happy and safe. I wish I could understand what was going on. I wish a hundred thousand things. And I know I'm not allowed to ask for so much. But everything has become so complicated. I want Corky to get better. And I want Pedro to see. And ..."

"Come on!"

"And *please* can we have lunch soon!"

"Finished? It's Pedro's turn!" Jurgen guided him forward.

"I'll help turn you, so you don't fall," Trudi took his arm. "There - "

She dropped her hand and Pedro said something solemn in Spanish. Then, as though he had forgotten she was still at his side, he called aloud:

"I wish there will not be a *pachakuti*. Wiraqocha, sun father, don't to let the world end now."

After that, Hamish's request to postpone his next tutorial sounded rather tame. A steady drizzle set in. Archie folded up his aerial, declaring the 'energies' were not propitious - and they moved off in search of a shortcut.

"This will be the path," said Archie, wiping his glasses.

"Rubbish man!" Hamish was having none of it. "It's the next one. Remember, *I've* got the map." He ran his hand over his scalp. Little runnels of water were seeping out of his hair, and trickling down behind his ears.

Trudi, starving, put her plait in her mouth and chewed on that. Beside her walked Pedro, hunched in his nylon jacket. Last of all came Jurgen, filing a text to Zub.

"I say it is here," Archie persisted. "Who's the mountain guide? Who checked the weather before we came?"

Hamish shot him a scowl. "I checked everything. It's all under control. This is just a spot of rain. In any case, I'm prepared for an emergency. Flashlight, survival blanket, blister-plasters, chocolate."

"Chocolate?" Trudi's ears pricked up.

"No, no lass. Not what you think. This is for disasters only. It's climber's chocolate - completely horrible to eat."

Trudi thought she would be willing to try it, but Hamish strode ahead. He must keep them all together, all involved, as if they were out in the wilderness: "Well, Pedro is mountain guide. Which way does he say?"

Pedro faced into the rain. The hillside, now obscured, sloped blindly at their feet. "This way," he said.

Hamish backed down. "Okay, we'll bush-whack. The car has to be at the bottom, anyway!"

Scrambling and stumbling on the slippery grass, the party made a ragged descent. Ghosts of bushes loomed up and vanished again. The elder trees dripped, draggling last year's brambles. Startled rabbits shot out of the way. And beneath their feet the ground plunged down, first it seemed to the west, then to the east, until all sense of direction was quite confounded.

Pedro alone pushed on. He had caught a hint of wood-smoke on the wind and knew there was a house nearby.

A few steps further brought them within sight of its gabled roof. Soon they stood level with the chimneys and the tops of some beeches which had grown in a hollow behind. Walls, whose window-lights peeped cosily at their feet, snuggled half-buried in the hillside. Every part of the building was hewn from solid stone and the tiles, mullions and gateposts gleamed as if lacquered in the rain. But for all its pretensions to grandeur, this dwelling was tiny – hardly larger than a labourer's cottage. The wind drove the chimney smoke down and chased it round the gutters, giving a spectral look.

"Ask here," demanded Archie. The wet had saturated his notes, and dripped forlornly from his binocular-case. He had been dreaming of sausage and chips at the pub, but any kind of shelter would be welcome now.

A shamefaced Hamish hammered the door.

No reply.

They all listened, straining after a creak or footfall that might denote someone inside had heard.

Hamish knocked again and called, for good measure, through the letter-box.

Instantly, the door flew open and there stood a striking woman dressed in black, a woodman's axe in her hand.

She was fifty, perhaps, dark-haired, statuesque, and her broad, intelligent face looked in surprise at the party on the step.

She's a witch, thought Trudi. *We've made a terrible mistake.*

"Sorry to be a bother. We're looking for the Drayholt Road. We've parked below the Worm. Got a bit lost. Wonder if you could point us in the right direction?"

"Oh, my dears," said the witch in a voice like a turtle dove. "You're miles out of your way. And look at you! You're drowned! Look at the children!" Hamish did so and admitted, ruefully, that they cut a pitiful sight. He would be in disgrace when they finally reached home and developed pneumonia.

162

"Won't you step in a while and dry off? You must have been walking for hours."

If we go in, she will feed us on toadstool soup and lock us up and no one will ever hear of us again.

"Och, no, no." Hamish demurred. "That won't be necessary. Very kind of you though."

At which point Archie pushed himself forward, herding Trudi and the boys ahead of him.

"Thank you, *I* will be delighted," he bugled. "We were caught out by the weather."

Hamish had no choice now but to submit and, abandoning any further claim to leadership, tramped in last, closing the door behind him.

"That's the thing about this place. Everything is so unpredictable. I suppose it is the altitude that does it. We're the highest point for miles. On a clear day, you know, you can see all the way from the Black Mountains to the Kingsbury Vale. Come through this way. At least the stove is alight. You caught me chopping wood. I do hope I didn't alarm you, appearing with my axe! I'm afraid I'm not very used to visitors. This house is really a workshop, so it is a dreadful mess. But you won't mind that, will you? Put your coats here, look, by the burner and I'll boil a kettle. Have you had lunch? Can I get you something? Toast? With cheese? I'm Eleanor Partridge. A weaver, as you see. Just push the wool off those chairs and sit yourselves down. I'll be back in a jiffy."

Not toadstool soup, then. Cheese on toast! Heaven! And what a place!

On the inside, the house seemed surprisingly spacious. The visitors tiptoed into in a barn of a room, open to the beams like a Saxon hall, with a wooden gallery at one end. The grasses of the hill could be seen, nodding damply at the windows. In the centre of the floor stood a vast, upright loom and hanks of wool, dyed green and yellow and blue (in shades reminiscent of the sea, or of summer leaves) hung from the joists. There were bales of raw wool, too, stacked against the walls and what looked like finished weaving - rugs and shawls – slung across the gallery rail. Stone weights, with holes bored through them, decorated the chimney-breast and the hearth recess was filled by a stove, whose black flue took an eccentric route along the wall, seeking a way out somewhere amongst the rafters.

Stacks of books littered the floor.

Hamish took the children's jackets and hung them up, using the chair backs as airers, and in a few moments their hostess returned.

"Hot chocolate," she said, setting the tray on the floor. "Thought it would be more warming. Here, you children can sit on fleeces, can't you? Drag some over. And those wet trousers had better come off, too." She pointed and then put her finger on her lip. "Don't worry. I can fix you up."

Vanishing this time to the gallery, she reappeared with what looked like armfuls of felt. They were kaftans, patterned in the Mongolian style. "These will keep you warm while you drink up. Sit this young lad close to the fire." Without alluding at all to his blindness, she helped Pedro to the warmest place. "Toast's coming."

How delicious!

Cocooned in her nest of wool, cosy as a clothes moth, Trudi listened to the rain spitting on the window panes and wondered how they would ever get home again. Glistening, cheesy toast arrived, with chocolate biscuits for afters. And Mrs. Partridge perched herself on the end of the loom and gave them all an expectant look.

"Our expedition went awry," Hamish began. "These are not *our* children - only borrowed for the day. Pedro is up in Kingsbury for an operation to remove his cataracts; Trudi and Jurgen just visiting, while their father applies for a Fellowship at St. Gregory's. I'm a physics undergraduate. Archie here is a violin maker and climbing companion. Should have been a jolly, communal outing, but Pedro's guardian felt poorly today. And then the weather…"

"The weather is always strange here," cooed Mrs. Partridge. "Did you see the Worm?"

"We made our wishes," Trudi assured her, wiping the crumbs from her mouth.

"Good."

Now that she could observe her hostess more closely, Trudi noticed little snippets and wisps of wool stuck all over her. They were on her skirt and in her sleeves, even in her hair.

164

"Have you been weaving today?" she ventured. It was probably rude to ask, but she couldn't resist it. Hunger could be satisfied so much more easily than curiosity. Mrs. Partridge did not take offence in the least.

"I weave obsessively all the time! It started as part of my research but has become a consuming passion. Once I start I can't stop. I forget to eat, to sleep even. You've done me a good turn, arriving like this!"

"How do you know what to make?"

"Oh the designs are all from ancient sources. I'm really a historian. I study the myths and meanings in patterns. Did you know that many depict very interesting things, legends and starlore and so on? All sorts of fascinating secrets! And then cloth-making - spinning and weaving - is such an essential part of our human journey, understanding who we are...

"Those stones by the fireplace, for instance, are spindle-whorls. They belonged to our great-great-great-great-grandmothers. Treasured possessions! With one of these and a spindle-shaft you could make all the yarn you needed to clothe a family. The women carried them with them wherever they went. Archaeologists find them in the most unlikely places. And they, too, have secrets to tell. There's a Viking spindle-whorl that turned up in Newfoundland! Imagine that. That tells us that some brave woman crossed the Labrador Sea a thousand years ago with her spindle in her pocket! The wool she spun and the tales she told will never be found but we know she came from Greenland and the Greenland Vikings came from Norway...

"Navigation! I am a navigator too in my way. I follow the thread of an idea and it leads to something else, so I never get bored. And if I make a mistake, I unweave it and start again. I've got big cauldrons for boiling up the dyes, but I do that in the garden on fine days. I can collect most of the herbs I need for my colours here. The wool is from Iceland. Very soft... Forgive me, I'm rambling on!"

"And what do you do with it all?" asked Hamish.

"Oh, I sell it. I'm forever staggering off with giant parcels to the post. But just recently I've gone 'online' – started a website - to try and stay abreast of things. Many of my old contacts have gone out of business and there are a thousand foreign weavers producing

165

what I make for a fraction of the cost. Modernize or die! That's what my bank manager tells me! Get a digital power loom!"

"You won't, will you?"

Mrs. Partridge smiled. "And spend all my life filling in forms? No thanks. I'm a scholar, not a businesswoman. This is my place for thinking. And for much of the time, in any case, I am away in distant places, attending conferences and digs and talking to anyone who can remember what the old patterns mean. But this is my favourite place. At night, in the dark, the hills are quite magical."

"We were thinking of a midnight ramble on the top. Archie here is very interested in the stars!" Hamish gave a knowing wink.

"Then you absolutely must come here! You see, legend says that the Drayholt Worm lies directly under the Pole Star. Stand there on midsummer's eve with your broomstick and you can fly straight to it! The Worm is..."

"A lemniscate!" Jurgen interrupted. "I looked it up."

Mrs. Partridge smiled. "Ah, well. You probably know more than I do, then. But your friend here is a physicist, so he will know too." She nodded at Hamish. "Physicists love to talk about infinity, just as weavers love to talk about wool! And we can both go on forever! Physicists, like stitchers, write their ideas in code. We are both pattern-makers. But some are greater than others. Ask him, one day, to tell you about Wallis, the mathematician. He was interested in lemniscates and there's a story that he once visited St. Gregory's. Had one of his finest ideas there, so they say. He was a code-breaker and I suppose that's what I am too.

"Ah! Poor Wallis..." sighed Hamish.

Trudi listened as she listened when her father spoke in Swedish, letting the words wash over her without bothering too much about the sense. At times, the talk receded like the murmur of the sea, but individual phrases resonated here and there and mingled with her thoughts. Her mind wandered away to the loom and the web of patterns on it, the shuttles hanging down, skeins of yarn suspended nearby. Twisted wool, just like Merlin's worm, wound in an infinite loop...

Perhaps all people were pattern-makers and code-breakers, for the world, it seemed, was full of secret messages. They might lie right beneath your nose, and you would never guess they were there till you found a key to read them by. Finding the key was everything. Without it the world was boring and blank; but if you had a key even the most ordinary things came alive and were beautiful. She thought of the invisible threads that Per had used to steer a path across the sky. They wove whole worlds together, and they were everywhere, weren't they, if only you had eyes to look? Hamish and Archie had been drawing them with their fingers on the walking map that day. Pedro followed them to find his way in the dark. They had all laughed at Archie with his binoculars and his dowsing rods on the hill, but maybe he was only doing the same. Feeling for lifelines you could not see…

"Could you watch the Celestial Elk Hunt from here?" she asked, to everyone's surprise.

"You could do better than that!" Mrs. Partridge stood up and shook Pedro's jacket. "Come back in June and you could see a lunar eclipse. It coincides this year with Midsummer. It will be a great and memorable event."

"Well thank you," said Hamish, stretching his legs. "I think we shall! So kind of you, taking us in. You've saved the day!"

"These things are dry enough to put on," she patted the clothes approvingly. "And I think the weather is cheering up. I'll walk with you, if you like."

As they left, she scooped up a large black hat and placed it on her head. "Here. Mementos. You must take a memento from the Worm." Helping herself to what looked like buttons on the window-sill, she pressed them into the children's hands. "Priceless these are! Look after them! All the secrets of the universe are locked up here!"

A short journey brought them to the car.

"Goodbye and thank you," said Trudi, remembering her manners.

"Goodbye children!"

"Adios!"

"Cheerio!"

They piled from one vehicle into another and as Hamish started his engine, one windscreen-wiper began to clear the view.

"What happened to the other?" Mrs. Partridge's face appeared at the window.

"Och," said Hamish. "It got jammed somehow. Don't worry. I can see."

And off they went beneath the dripping hedgerows, while she waved, laughing in the lane.

"What did she give you?" Trudi wrestled with her seat-belt.

"Esmall creature shell. Esnell?" Pedro looked bemused.

"Snails!" agreed Jurgen. "She's bonkers!"

"*I'll* have them, if you don't want them."

"Don't tell me - *they're magic!*" he mocked.

"They're 'snigels' - pooties. They might be important."

Jurgen screwed his finger into his temple. "Here you are then. Have mine. I don't need snails." And he dropped them unceremoniously into her lap.

All different they were. Some had yellow bands on a dark ground - some the reverse. Some were white, coated with chalk where they had lain on the hill. Some tiny. Others polished like seeds. As the car bumped and rattled along, Trudi began to feel sleepy. In her mind she saw again the page of Mincke's manuscript with the snails trailing round the margin. On Drayholt hill they must leave innumerable trails, a web of paths as fine as the paths between the stars above... But where did they lead? The shells would go in her collection for now, but they couldn't yet point her in the right direction. It would take something more to unlock the secrets of the Sneevelings. And what, in heaven's name, was a *pachakuti?* How lovely the smoke had looked, hanging in the beech trees. She would ask Pedro about *pachakuti* when they had a moment alone, for if Jurgen heard, he would be bound to blab it all to Zub... and then Laser Wag would come up with an answer and put an end to wonder. And wondering, wandering, led to all life's surprises. They would never have found Mrs. Partridge, today, if they had not first lost their way...

Chapter Twenty-Two

Supper at St. Gregory's

As they pulled in at St. Lucy's something odd caught Trudi's eye.

The convent's neighbouring property had a forbidding air. It was white and stark and silent; a slab of a house, surrounded by dark laurels. This was where the mad people lived who did handstands in their garden. The grown-ups wouldn't talk about it but Pedro called it a 'carcel'. He insisted the place was a prison. Certainly it held secrets. Neither name nor number identified the building from the street and the windows here stared blankly down with pale blinds drawn. But today, just as the Drayholt expedition drove past, the front door opened and a lumpy looking girl in a white bathrobe - bare feet, pale, moon face and hair wrapped in a towel - dashed out and raced towards them, wildly waving her hands. Almost immediately, she was pursued by a man who ran her down, pinning her arms to her sides. Two women, dressed like dinner ladies, flew to his assistance. Between them, they bundled the girl inside and closed the door. The house resumed its inscrutable calm as though nothing at all had happened.

Trudi gasped. What a scoop! It seemed Pedro must be right, after all. She turned with an exclamation on her lips: *"Did you see that?"* but never found the words, for at that moment Hamish slammed on his brakes, and everyone lurched from their seats. When they recovered, they found themselves nose to nose with an ambulance that was calmly usurping the drive. In fact they had almost hit it. Instantly, Trudi forgot about the drama next door. This was stranger and more sinister by far. On the convent step stood Sister Bianca, watching, as green-suited paramedics gently posted a stretcher on board... Who was it? *What* was it? Hamish and his passengers sat dumbstruck. Had a bomb exploded? Someone, it seemed, had turned off the sound. Limbs froze.

Time stalled. Beyond the windscreen, the blue emergency lights flashed silently - the ambulance men, in their crêpe-soled shoes, went about their business with noiseless efficiency. The only sound they could later recall was the flip-flap of Hamish's windscreen

wiper as it laboured ineffectually back and forth. At length, Sven
appeared, put up his hand in greeting, and, like an underwater
diver, waded down the steps and pressed towards them through the
rain.

"Nothing to worry about," he assured them, sticking his head in
at Archie's window. "They're just taking him in overnight, for
observation."

That broke the spell and suddenly they were all yelling:

"What happened?"

"Who?"

"Why?"

"What 'observation'?"

"What *happen?*" Pedro, like a wild animal, began to fight with
the door. "*Where* the handle gone?"

"Pedro, calm down, it came off a long time ago."

But Sven was still explaining: "Corky's fine, I promise. I'm just
going with him because he's sleepy. The doctors say there's no
problem but they don't know why he can't wake up, so they want
to do some tests. That's all. He'll be home tomorrow. Sister Bianca
has made tea for you. Be good, children. I'll be back in an hour.
We're only going to the Infirmary down the road."

His curly head disappeared and he sprinted to the ambulance,
hopping on board as the driver swung the big door shut and took
his seat at the wheel. Hamish backed up to let them through and,
the vehicle, with the stricken remains of Corky on board, crept soft
as a hearse to the roadside and pulled out. Moments later, absorbed
by the traffic, it was gone.

Those next few hours passed in a blur. The children picked at
their tea and Archie collected his cello and bade them a rather
emotional farewell. He no longer seemed ridiculous to them in his
wide trousers. He belonged to a different, carefree world and his
departure affected them all as though it was final. More upsetting
still, was the sudden respect the rest of the household showed
them, which effectively severed their last links with normality. All
at once they were no longer 'children'. They had become objects
of compassion. The nuns spoke in hushed tones in the hall outside,
or peeked in at the door, smiling anxiously, as though they were
looking through a grill. Sister Emilia exuded such solicitude, they
began to believe that Corky had already died.

170

When Sven returned with his usual chirpiness, it struck an unconvincing note.

"He is very comfortable and he'll be back before you know it!" He rubbed his hands, to dust off any doubts. "Now, tonight, I have to go to St. Gregory's for supper. I've been invited by Sir Maximus Bligh to dine on High Table and I can't really wriggle out of it. It seems that I've passed the first stage of my application. After this, there's a lecture to give and if that goes well, the Fellowship is mine, so the Institute and Bligh Corporation will be my bosses. It's good news children! Mummy will be so pleased."

Trudi knew that she ought to congratulate him. His appointment would put an end to all his practical worries. But her jealous heart resented this magnate, Sir Maximus, with his ability to order people's lives as he chose. She had wanted to spend the evening with Sven herself that night. She felt sick of new faces, new places. She looked for a moment as though she was going to cry.

Hamish took a deep breath and swallowed his own frustration. He had been looking forward to getting rid of the children and indulging in a nice evening off, but seeing Trudi's melancholy face, he magnanimously rose to the occasion.

"They're having a Guest Night in Hall tonight. I'm sure I can scrounge tickets from somewhere. It's part of Sir Maximus's new 'open college' policy that anyone can come to dinner if they've got a ticket – even children. Why don't you eat at St. Greg's with me and then you can see your father dining with the nobs. No waving mind," he cautioned. "We have to be very mature."

Trudi, who thought she was always very mature, overlooked the insult and, curious, agreed to go.

"I wan' stay here," said Pedro. "I don' to need a supper."

"*We'll* look after you," promised Sister Emilia unctuously. Her plans for the website were coming along nicely and she now needed Pedro to feel part of the fabric of the place. "St Lucy's is your home for the time being, so you must do just as you please."

Jurgen demurred. He also wanted time alone to write to Zub and download all the messages on his phone. He did not like Trudi always peering over his shoulder. His work was private and sensitive. At least Pedro could not spy…

"I'll stay with Pedro," he voted.

171

Sven smiled with relief. "Hamish you are a brick!" He clapped him on the back. "I would have turned the invitation down, but I need to make a good impression at the beginning. I'll get away as soon as I can. Is that all right with you, Trudi? You'll love seeing the college. Such a beautiful place."

"It will be a night to remember!" Hamish winked.

Supper started at seven. They left the car in a private yard belonging to the Abseiling Club, and skirting the traffic, turned in at a narrow archway. "Look your last on this!" Hamish tapped the crumbling wall. "This is now the only true dirt in the city! And we're having the cleaners in next term! I tell you Trudi, things have come to a sorry pass. St. Gregory's used to pride itself on being bottom at everything. It took them years to install computers! Now we're going to be top. With Sir Maximus as Rector, the money is simply pouring in. They are building all over the old quad. They've re-vamped everything from the library to the kitchens. The Tiffin Club Bar is now a children's crèche and that's just the beginning."

Trudi, scurrying along beside him, heard only part of what he said, and comprehended still less. But she felt flattered that he told her all the same. She, too, liked the medieval grime, the doorways with spiral staircases leading to hidden rooms, the wisteria, the sound of laughter from open windows. And the cloisters, though smaller than those of the grander colleges, had a magic all of their own. She had washed and changed for the evening with special care, letting her hair flow loose, like a grown-up. For a moment she imagined she could pass for a student - one of the young women, say, who brushed past them in the corridor and loitered, laughing on the steps. Hamish seemed to know them all. But they weren't taken in for a moment. They teased him and gave his young guest distant, patronising smiles, which hurt her pride. Nevertheless, Hamish did not want to talk to them tonight. He was enjoying showing off to Trudi and pressed casually on.

He had donned a black scholar's gown that looked too small for him. Almost everyone wore a gown of some description. "That's going too," he said wistfully. "Gowns are out in the new administration. And wait till you see the food!"

But it was the Refectory that Trudi liked best of all. The Refectory *breathed* history and its dark portraits, stained glass windows, and fancy Jacobean plasterwork whistled up romantic dreams of long ago. If ghosts lingered anywhere, why, surely it was here. Who could ignore them in their ruffs and periwigs? Long, polished tables, ran the length of the room, culminating in a dais where, swathed in white damask, High Table gleamed like an altar. Up there were carved chairs, silver place settings, decanters of water and wine, and elaborate baskets of fruit. Down here they sat at splintery wooden benches and though Trudi hopped over with ease, larger folk had a job to climb in. She could not help smiling at the attempts of girls in tight skirts. And no sooner were they settled than they all had to rise again and stand half crippled, with knees bent, as the dons filed by.

Hamish gave her a nudge and Trudi saw Sven go past, led by a florid-faced man who towered head and shoulders above him. The man was holding forth in a self-important way but Sven did not seem to be listening. He was looking about him as if he was lost - like a child at the zoo, Trudi thought. Of course, she knew he was not lost; he was looking for *her*, but in the sea of faces he could not find her and his head bobbed along with the others, till it was finally hidden from sight. There followed 'Grace' and an undignified scuffle as the catering staff brought in the food.

"In the bad old days," said Hamish, helping himself to a hunk of bread, "dinners were for men only and rather rowdy affairs, with food flying about, and forfeits and the waiters were little old retainers who had worked for the college all their lives. Now we've got a new system. We employ catering staff from local institutions. All part of our new 'social conscience'. I can't think it's much fun for them. They never look happy."

He had a point. Dressed in ugly blue overalls, the waitresses shuffled to and fro like robots with blank faces. The big serving dishes were heavy to hold yet no one seemed to notice if they kept them waiting. No one really spoke to them. They were young girls, mostly, with older women supervising. They wore netting caps and flat shoes. No make-up. No earrings. They scarcely glanced at one another as they passed, and they seemed divided from the animated chatter of the diners by an invisible partition. Trudi, with her Swedish upbringing, decided to strike a blow for equality, and when the vegetables arrived, sought out the waitress's eyes and smiled into them. "Thank you." She meant it. But the girl stepped

173

back, staring hard as if she had uttered an insult, and hurried away with her tray.

"No use," Hamish confided. "I've tried it before. I don't like to say it, but they are zombies. You can't talk to them. And I think we're going to become the same if we eat this food much longer."

Trudi winced. She would never hear Sven or Corky speak so rudely.

Hamish, oblivious to public opinion, gave his dinner a liberal scattering of salt, smiled all round and settled himself comfortably for a rant. His friends exchanged exasperated glances and grinned at Trudi.

"Here we go!" they warned.

"Last year we had rissoles and watery greens. It was grim, but it filled you up. We had tinned sponge pudding with pink sauce, which stuck to your insides. I quite liked it. But now – now we have," he squinted at the menu: "Salmon remoulade, with timbale of spinach and celeriac. Did you ever see such a thing in your lives? It tastes faintly of," he pushed a little round his mouth and pursed his lips, "anchovy essence, I should say and bath cleaner. And why?" he was flirting with his audience now. "Because it's not food! That's why. It comes from that BioDawn factory out at Rushlea. It comes from Sir Maximus up there and his giant food emporium. It's *organic!* But it was cooked up by scientists in the String Kitchen and it has never seen an animal or a plant before!"

"Hamish, shut up and eat, there's a good chap," said a burly geographer across the table. "You talk such rot."

But having got into the saddle Hamish meant to ride a bit further.

"It's not rot. It's true! He has a laboratory on the outskirts of the city where they are re-inventing food. Not to mention his sinister BeeDome at Pinkney - and nobody knows what *that's* for. They are already concocting monster lettuces, with their proteins scrambled back to front. Can you imagine it? You might as well unravel DNA and make it spiral round the other way. In fact they would probably do that, if they could! Everything will look normal, but it will taste... like this!" He gave his timbale a derisory prod.

At that, a stony-faced woman sitting opposite rose to the bait.

"If you were not so ignorant," she snapped, "you would know that the 'String Kitchen' as you so wittily call it, is our best, if not our only hope of saving the world. The BioDawn lettuce will be able to grow organically without fear of slugs and snails. No viruses, no fungi can attack it. When the conventional lettuce with its reliance on pesticides, dies out, the new lettuce will be all that's left to feed the starving."

"Ah! The lovely Marina! Marvellous!" Hamish dropped his knife and fork and sat, smiling provocatively. "Only you have forgotten one thing, my sweet."

"I am *not*…"

"*Not* going to score over me with your fancy arguments," he interrupted, "because you have forgotten that I am a scientist too and I know that if slugs and snails cannot eat a back-to-front lettuce, then neither can a student at St. Gregory's, whether he is starving or no! Mirror image proteins cannot be digested by us. I remember enough of my chemistry to be sure of that. You would have to turn us round the other way too, before you could feed us on your 'Honeymeadow' lettuces!"

Marina fell silent and began a savage dissection of her salmon.

"Point?" Hamish wanted a proper victory.

"The point is that you see only a tiny part of the picture," she muttered. "Nutrition can always be *added*. Perhaps you should visit the 'String Kitchen' one day."

"To be reconstituted?"

"You judge things you do not understand. You may sound clever, but you are out of your depth, Hamish Wall. You're quite pathetic. Sir Maximus has *vision*. Yes, he is helping to rehabilitate social outcasts, and planning for the future that is only just around the corner. Earth's natural resources won't be able to sustain the human race much longer! You should know that. In a year or two, you'll be crying out for the likes of Sir Maximus to save you. I'm almost sorry that I am coming to live at St. Lucy's this summer if I shall have to listen to ravings from the likes of you!"

This news came as a surprise. "*Are* you now?" he lifted his eyebrows. "Well that *will* be a delight!"

She returned a venomous scowl.

Though Trudi may have missed the finer points, she picked up enough of the exchange to get the general gist. She had a vague memory of passing a 'Honeymeadow' sign on her first visit to Kingsbury. Was that the place Hamish meant? And what would Mincke say about a kitchen where the food was made the wrong way round? Those cakes they ate from BioDawn in Newbridge, for instance – the LOGDAWS - were *they* baked in a String Kitchen? And was back-to-front the same as topsy-turvy? The Sneevelings made cakes that were upside-down...

Now Hamish talked again about something odd at Pinkney. Whatever could *that* be? You would think that Pinkney, where even the bees lived simply under their own straw thatch, would be the last place to harbour unnatural practices. But Sir Maximus, according to Marina, had designs to re-fashion the whole world. And now he was to employ her father. Would Sven become sucked into his conspiracy? It did not feel right that this woman should stay at St. Lucy's. Perhaps she would want to turn that place on its head. Trudi took a defensive dislike to her and wished a curse on her mousy hair and freckles.

If only Corky was here, he would have explained things to her in language she could understand, but Hamish turned affably to other subjects and besides, the second course was now on its way. While half the caterers collected the dirty dishes, the others trudged forth with trays of summer pudding and quivering crimson jellies. Returning to the table, the lumpy girl in blue began to dispense her dishes. This time Trudi avoided her eye, but as she passed by, the girl leant forward and thrust a fold of paper into her hand. "Hide it!" she hissed in her ear. "Read it later!" and passed on, her face impassive as clay.

Startled, Trudi tucked the scrap into her sleeve, and stared after her. Had she written to complain about the smile? Or had she overheard Hamish running on in his tactless way? Something about her seemed familiar but she could not think why that should be and before long coffee came and another 'grace' and people began to drift away to their rooms.

"Come on," Hamish eased his long legs over the bench. "I'll show you the garden. We're to meet your father at the Main Gate at nine. That gives us half an hour."

Trudi hurried along behind.

"Is that girl really coming to St. Lucy's?"

176

"So she says. *Aren't* we lucky? She's one of the BioDawn Scholars – so I was a bit naughty teasing her like that. But there's some truth in what I say. Sir Maximus and his minions are up to something. Public philanthropy and private skulduggery. Don't know what it is, yet, but I'm on the trail! I shall probably be reported and sent down before I catch them!" He didn't seem concerned.

The spring evening wrapped the college buildings in a cosy darkness. Lights burnt here and there in wall-mounted lamps and in student room windows. Footsteps came and went on the flagstones. The garden gleamed under a rising moon.

"When I grow up I want to be a don," said Trudi, as ever captivated by the moment.

"No you don't." Hamish replied. "You're going to do something much more exciting than that. You need adventure. Come and join my Everest expedition. I've invented a grappling-iron harpoon for rock climbers that I want to try out. It will make abseiling down mountain precipices much safer. If I get it patented I'm hoping to scoop a fortune."

"What do you mean?"

"Well, authors have copyright, to make sure other people don't steal their stories. Inventors have patents. This will be the 'Hamish Wall Grappling-Iron Harpoon' and the devil take anyone who tries to steal it!"

Trudi thought a moment. "I couldn't come to Everest for a while. I'm busy solving a mystery."

Hamish took his time. "Is that so?" He didn't mock, but she knew he was indulging her. Then, without warning, he grabbed her hand and tugged her into the shadows. "Quick! This way – through here!"

She just had time to glimpse the outline of someone approaching before she found herself in a poorly lit passage. Hamish was striding ahead now, dragging her after him. His head almost brushed the vaulted roof. As she stumbled along, she felt the clammy cold that emanated from the walls and the pavement beneath her feet. The passage took a sharp turn to the right - they must be passing under the main body of the college - then left, and suddenly they were out in Nostrum Street, just by the entrance. She recognized the heaps of bicycles, the new-looking, sharp-faced statue in an alcove in the wall. And there was Sven, pacing up and down with a preoccupied air.

"Perfect timing!" Hamish pulled up beside him.

"Oh, you have been running. There was no need. I'm early."

"We had a narrow escape," Hamish admitted. "Almost bumped into the tutor whose lecture I skipped this morning. Sometimes I'm glad the college is a labyrinth!"

"And dinner? How was it Trudi?"

He looked so handsome in his borrowed dinner jacket.

"Perfect," she smiled.

Hamish snorted.

"I see Sir Maximus was on form."

"A strange, tense man," Sven nodded. "But kindly enough. He's trying to do good with his money. I mean, I think he genuinely cares. My lecture is to be about oak trees – the new disease that is wiping them out. Oh - and he has offered us a tour of the research facilities tomorrow - especially for you children."

"There you are," Hamish made a flourish in the air. "You will see the String Kitchen for yourself! You're honoured indeed!"

Trudi's head was spinning from it all when they returned to St. Lucy's. Sister Bianca had waited up with the boys, and then there were stories to tell, 'goodnights' to give and it was not until she reached the privacy of her hotel room that she could open the note she had been given.

Scribbled in pencil, in an almost illegible hand, it filled the corner of a college menu sheet:

"Don't believe what they tell you. Im not stupid nor mad. Nun of us are. Wait for me by the garden door at the convent and I'll explain. You must be alone and don't tell ANYONE. They are watching all the tim…"

The writer must have been interrupted, for the message broke off there. In a flash, Trudi remembered the incident she had witnessed earlier that day: the runaway girl in the bathrobe who had signalled from the drive next door. Same build, same moon face. And the girl she had seen trying to stand on her hands in the garden. Was that her too? And who were *'they'*? The orderlies who had forced her back indoors that afternoon? The catering overseers at St. Gregory's? But what were they really up to? Did they work for Sir Maximus too? And how could she ever find a moment to be alone in the garden? Sven would be taking them home the day after tomorrow. And then what was going to happen about Corky?

She drifted into an uneasy sleep with none of these questions resolved. Corky knew better than anyone how to grow lettuces – she had seen them at his nursery. He grew them with love and though the snails ate a little bit, nobody minded much. In Corky's world there was room for snails and humans. And perhaps, in some way that was not immediately obvious, that was how things were meant to be. Perhaps mankind needed snails. What was it Mrs. Partridge said? *"All the secrets of the universe"*...

True to promise, Corky woke up and came home the following morning. He seemed slow and dizzy and sat in the wicker chair in his room under a pile of blankets, smiling inanely at his friends.

"You go. Go and don't worry about me. I'll write a letter to Belinda and tell her what is going on."

"Belinda?"

"Yes, back at home, back in, in ..." he fumbled for a moment.

"You mean Barbara, in Newbridge?" prompted Trudi.

"Barbara!" he giggled, clutching his head. "I'll forget who I am next!"

They all laughed with him. All but Trudi, whose memory pricked her. For a moment she was back in Sweden, trudging with Per through the snow. His voice came back, clear as the wind in the trees:

"Almost as soon as he has gone," he was saying, *"Mincke falls into a deep sleep and it is several days before he wakes up. The house is cold. The milk has gone off. But what really worries him is that he cannot remember the television man's name. This is most unusual. His mind is always sharp as a razor. By the end of the day Mincke has discovered other things he can't remember..."*

The echo brought tears to her eyes.

Other voices were dear. She could not wait to hear Auntie Barbara scolding and gossiping again. During these last few days, she had missed the calm reassurances of her mother, but Per spoke from a different place in her heart, a world that seemed infinitely far away. Did he still remember *her* name, from his solitary hiding place? Or the names of the stars that shone above his roof?

Chapter Twenty-Three

The Toy Forge

Sir Maximus sent a car the following morning: a large limousine with black windows and leather seats, so generous, they swallowed you up. The chauffeur, in his peaked cap, started the engine and cruised through the Kingsbury traffic like a fish slipping currents in a stream. Indeed, after the bumps and jolts of Hamish's old banger, this journey felt strangely unreal. Traffic lights, cyclists, buses, all dropped noiselessly behind them and they purred to a halt at the gates of the Rushlea Business Park before the children had half drunk in the novelty of it all. Just as she thought, Trudi had seen the signs before: *Honeymeadow Enterprises – Nutritional Research...*

Ahead, lay an expanse of neatly clipped lawn and then an eruption of buildings. White and windowless, they appeared to Trudi's eye like newly sprung mushrooms, pristine domes gleaming. A sentry popped out of his pill-box to question the driver, and then popped back in and raised the barrier and they advanced along a gravel drive. As they drew nearer, Trudi made out two commissionaires in green and gold braid uniforms standing at the entrance and beside them, gesticulating in an expansive way, the crimson-faced man who had accompanied Sven at dinner.

Otherwise, the place looked deserted. No sign of a car park – or of cars, or of people either, come to that. It seemed odd. Where was everyone? A doorway gaped behind Sir Maximus like an open mouth and Trudi suddenly felt uneasy. Was this the String Kitchen Hamish had joked about last night? She had seen Honeymeadow products on the shelves of BioDawn, at home. The jars sported pretty labels, with pictures of butterflies and wild flowers. There were jams, chutneys, old-fashioned cordials, and of course the honey itself, pure English honey. Did they come from here? If so, the angry girl, Marina, must be here somewhere and Trudi fervently hoped that they would not meet her.

Sir Maximus finished his conference and came across to greet them, shaking Sven by the hand and smiling down at the children.

On this warm day he wore a close-fitting cashmere suit. He looked constrained, like a parcel too tightly wrapped, but since the wrapping was expensive, and told the world he was a man of substance, he could not very well undo himself without spoiling the effect. His scanty hair, slicked and plastered down by a habitual movement of the hand, stuck to his head with only a few curls escaping. Eyes green, Trudi noted, unusual in a man.

"Well, come in. Come in! Come and see what we are doing!" He ushered them into a foyer, plush, like an old-fashioned cinema, with large fish tanks set into the walls. A manicured receptionist graced the desk.

"Going through to the laboratories, if anyone needs me." He led the way towards the lift, swiping a security pass to open the doors. "We have to be careful," he explained. "Industrial espionage, you know. Business spies will stop at nothing to steal the finest ideas. It looks like an observatory from outside, doesn't it? But, you'll see… inside is a surprise!"

They entered a hall the size of an aircraft hanger, where scores of people in white overalls pored over microscopes or typed at computers, some performing delicate autopsies, others working tabletop centrifuges. There were rows of open-plan desks and laboratory benches, banks of cages with small animals in them and monitor screens everywhere. Vast windows, the length of the walls, let in sunny light from a world beyond – rolling hills, covered in heather. You could even hear birds calling. As Trudi watched in disbelief, the scene changed to a redwood forest.

"The joys of plasma!" extolled Sir Maximus. "Everyone loves it. They can tune in to their own sounds of nature, music, radio, and they can sample the fruits of their labours in their own canteen. Welcome to the workplace of the future!" It must have been his sense of pride that filled out that capacious suit. "Through here is the garden." Rows of immaculate greens under an ultraviolet canopy. Were they Marina's lettuces? "Fertilisation. Pests and diseases." He whisked them on now. "But what you will really want to see is the fun stuff. The Toys!"

Trudi understood that they had entered a different building.

"Here we are developing holograms for the entertainment industry. In time holograms will replace television altogether.

People will have laser shows in their own sitting rooms. Ever seen one?"

Jurgen nodded in an ambiguous way. He didn't want to be thought behind the times. But Trudi shook her head. Sir Maximus had no idea how to talk to Pedro, so he ignored him, hoping that, since he was blind, he would not notice.

"Well, let's see." He brought them up before a plate glass window. Darkness filled the space beyond, but peering through, they gradually made out the contours of an unlit studio - walls, floor, ceiling, all painted black. "Pirates. Do you like pirates? Let's call up Blackbeard." On a handset no bigger than a business card he began to thumb instructions. "Oagh! What have I done? I can never remember the codes. Not sure if this is Blackbeard or not. Never mind. We'll soon see!"

Deep in the shadows, something was happening.

A beam of light appeared centre stage, revealing a concert grand piano. And there, dressed in formal tie and tails, so close you felt you could reach out and touch him, sat a young man with staring eyes. His hands briefly caressed the lacquered frame. Then he took a breath, laid his fingers on the keys and muttered something like a prayer. The next instant he threw himself into action. His arms flailed as though in the grip of some demonic force. Up and down went his hands, executing trills and arpeggios at breakneck speed, now pounding notes out with high hammer strokes, now huddling low, his fingers working like spider's legs. He frowned in concentration and sweat began to drip from his forehead. The faster the he played, the more he seemed to suffer, but the music would not let him rest.

Trudi tried, but could not identify the piece, for the sound was missing and this was a punishing virtuoso work, way beyond her competence. Finally, the pianist turned his head and stared directly through the window in a desperate appeal. It was impossible not to feel disturbed by that demented gaze, the music plunging wildly on, the face in anguish, pleading. You could see he needed to stop...

"Help him!" cried Trudi, unable to bear it any longer. But Sir Maximus laughed and lightly pressed a button and the vision faded, no more than an optical trick.

"Who is he?" asked Trudi, suddenly thinking of Mr. Pilliwig and his insects. Jurgen had dismissed that spectacle as no more than a laser stunt and the old scoundrel had vanished into his mirror just as abruptly.

"Who knows?" The big man shrugged. "As I said, I forget the codes. Don't do it often enough. But they use these effects already in the theatre. And you'll be seeing a lot more of them before long. Exciting stuff. Soon you will be able to have a concert pianist of your choice at your own beck and call. And not just pianists... dancers, horse jockeys, tennis players... The whole world at your finger tips! No need to go out for pleasure ever again!" Now, as he marched them along, his voice took on a new urgency: "But this is just the beginning. Through here is what we affectionately call the Toy Forge. Here we manufacture inventions – the best designs, the latest technology, the fastest software – we aim to put the spirit of fun back into everybody's life. That is our goal. Save the world with a smile!"

At the end of a corridor they passed through double doors and came out onto a viewing gallery high above the factory floor. Vast, automated assembly lines stretched below as far as the eye could see - not a human worker in sight - and Trudi began to understand why the entrance had seemed so deserted. Of course, robots did not need car parks. "What you see here is the cleanest, greenest engineering," boasted Sir Maximus. "We can take hold of anything in the world, and, once we have worked out the blueprint, we can manufacture and sell it! All we need are the codes. Wrinkle cream, Waggle Phones, safety ropes, chocolate cake... You name it, we can make it! I daresay, Sven," he allowed himself a chuckle, "that if all your oak trees died, we could even replace *them*. Super Oaks, eh? I can't actually take you down there. Health and safety, what? But the scale of our production, as you see, is huge and *growing*. There are three new buildings planned for this site alone. And very shortly we shall be going global. There will be no stopping us then. Excellence and innovation!"

The whiteness and the eerie silence of the processes below struck them all dumb, till at last Pedro spoke up.

"You making these thing here?"

"Yes, yes. Toys, too. Well, they are all toys, aren't they? We'll go down to the shop and I can show you. You can all choose something to take home."

Since no one responded, he went on: "I expect you are amazed. It's understandable. We live in very exciting times and Kingsbury is the dynamo, the beating heart, driving the action forward. Now, you can ask me another question, if you like. You will be young ambassadors for us when you go home!"

After a further pause Trudi took the plunge.

"What is the Beedome?" she asked sweetly.

Her words had an immediate effect. Sir Maximus grew rigid as a corpse and all the ruddy colour drained out of his face.

"Who talked to you about the Beedome?" He shot a searching look at Sven.

"Somebody mentioned it last night at dinner," replied Trudi, all innocence, lacing her answer with a lie, "I can't remember who."

"Well the Beedome is a very sensitive project." Sir Maximus was huffing now, trying to hide his discomfort. "Just at the planning stages you know. It will all be in the press when the time comes. At the moment it's hush-hush. I have already told you, the spies are out there and one can't be too careful. If anyone talks to you again – well – I wouldn't pay too much attention to anything you might hear, but you could let us know perhaps. Yes! That would be the thing to do. It's *very* important that nothing gets out to the media. So much jealousy and spite surrounds any brave new endeavour."

As though he was late for an appointment he began to hurry them along, his mind already fixed ahead. At the door of the showroom he nodded curtly to Sven and consulted his watch.

Then he turned to the salesman.

"Give them whatever they want and get them out," he blurted and off he strode, swaying on his patent leather shoes.

Such rudeness left behind an unpleasantness, difficult to dispel. But the assistant did his best:

"Samples are here!" He gestured towards a counter, suitably laden. "Take your pick! You can have anything you like. Everything is brand new. These designs have hardly touched the shelves. *You,* I know," he pointed at Jurgen, "would like one of these!"

He held out a mobile phone, *the* phone, the new Laser Wag with 'personal recognition' which Hamish had recently described.

"Wow, *thanks!*" Jurgen gasped, eyes round as saucers.

"And you," the man considered Pedro next. "You like music. This little micro-digit tune-scanner can mix and mash any melodies you care to download and play them straight into your ear. No wires. No batteries. It's solar powered so you simply sit it in the sun for a few minutes a day to charge up."

Pedro, impassive, accepted the gift that was pressed into his palm.

"Now the little girl…"

Trudi avoided his eye.

"An electronic beauty pack? Does nails, eyebrows, skin-massage. No? What about a pop-icon mini-cinema? Or this virtual play-pony with laser graphics?"

Her lip curled. In the end she chose an ice-cream-waffle machine for Barbara and they beat a shabby retreat. A taxi was waiting for them by the gate.

"You for St. Lucy's?" asked the cabbie. The big limousine had been requisitioned for someone else.

Back at the convent Corky had a visitor. Archie Gunn had called by, and, having squeezed himself into a chair beside the bed, was entertaining the invalid with a booming rendition of *The Pickwick Papers.* Corky looked up as the door opened. "Had a nice time? I'm being thoroughly spoilt here. Dickens. That nice man with the bees brought me books and honey this morning. So kind. You know he's a marvellous writer, this chap Dobbins – did I say Dickens? Yes, I must tell Brenda – see if she can get some of his stories for the bookshop."

"Perhaps you should rest now," said Archie, rising.

Corky placed his hand on his forehead, suffering a moment of doubt. "It *is* a bookshop she's got, isn't it? You know my brain's not what it was! I've been so lazy. Not looking after you at all. We must get back to work as soon as all this is over. I wanted to plant potatoes this year and I've had a wonderful idea. You know we could try and keep bees down at … at … oh, what's the place called? We'll miss the season if we don't get started soon!"

Sven took charge.

"Sleep!" he ordered, tucking Corky under his quilt and plumping up the pillows. "We've had a very interesting morning and I'll tell you all about it later, but Sister Matilda says we're not to tire you. Besides, the children have not yet had their lunch. I've spoken to Barbara. Everything is fine at Newbridge. Oh, and I've practically got the Fellowship." He halted, then went on: "At least, I *think* I have. The inaugural lecture is booked for next month – on *'Sudden Oak Death'*. Pedro is doing marvellously. No worries!"

Corky nodded and closed his eyes. "Pedro... Pedro... I swear that name rings a bell... Stupid to feel so tired." His face looked like old pastry.

Pedro crept up and shyly took his hand. "Come back, Corky! We need you!"

When they left the room, they found Archie waiting on the landing.

"The real reason for my visit" he explained, as they tiptoed down the stairs, "is this young lad here. Hamish tells me he's something special on the cello."

Jurgen groaned. Not the cello again!

"Now, I hope you won't take offence, because I'm sure you've got him a very good instrument at home, but sometimes the *right* one can make all the difference. It's like rather like an aerial or a transmission mast. The balance is everything."

At the word 'mast' Trudi sprang to attention. Masts to her meant Laser Wag and trouble. Was it possible to have a good one too? Fresh in her memory, she still had a vision of Archie on Drayholt hill, with his rain-spottled glasses and his wind-blown hair, dowsers aloft, waiting for a sign. Was he too raising a mast?

"I have a cello I made some years ago – my first 'good'un', actually," he was saying. "Well, a new instrument has to settle and wear in, you know. Raw, new wood and varnish normally have a sour tone and have to be played before they will mellow. I can't tell you why, but this one just worked right away. Only it had a wolf note in it, so I couldn't sell."

"A wolf note?"

"It's a technical term. Sometimes vibrations build up in the sound box when you play and produce a discord, like a howl, that appears without warning, and spoils the music. Of course a wolf note is a construction fault and I've been working on the

186

proportions, over the years, to see if I can drive it out. It's not perfect yet, but - better! You'd hardly notice now. If Jurgen likes, he can borrow the old girl and put her through her paces for me. See how he gets on. The practice might be good for them both!"

The cello was waiting, leaning against a chair, when they reached the common room. Unlike Jurgen's instrument at home, this one had been treated only with love and respect. It had never banged the paint off a music-master's door, or fallen off a bus, or improvised as a goal post in the park. The honey-toned wood shone sleek and glossy, plain at the front, but ribbed with caramel stripes on the back. It looked more like a friendly tiger than a wolf and everyone wanted to touch it, but Jurgen held it out to Pedro first. He plucked two strings, grinned and handed it back.

"*Ju* go! Make it play."

"Bach – there you are – the one with the nits in his wig!" laughed Archie, putting some music on the stand. But Jurgen was not prepared to give a concert. He had spotted two nuns already, hovering at the common room door.

"Just you and you!" he insisted, pointing at Sven and Archie. "All the others, out!"

Trudi and Pedro wandered off into the garden and, by common consent, made for the bench by the wall. Here was a corner for reflection: blue sky soaring above and the air drugged with the scents of spring. A blackbird, buried in some chestnut leaves, began to clear his throat. Trudi squinted through the gaps in the garden door, but the grounds of the neighbouring house stood empty. No cartwheelers, no piano-players, no people in pyjamas today.

They sat for a while in silence.

Then Trudi said: "Pedro, what is a *pachakuti?*"

She was thinking about Drayholt again. Perhaps he had been doing the same. He did not seem surprised by the question, though he took his time to answer:

"*Pachakuti?* It's like end of the world. It's when, the Inca say, everything turn upside down."

She gazed freely at his unsuspecting face; the cloudy eyes that seemed to see things others could not see.

"Do you really think it will happen?" The grown-ups talked habitually about the end of the world - global warming, mass extinctions, water wars - but Pedro seemed to mean something else. The end of the world for the oak trees, or the polar bears, or the honey bees - that was really sad, but everyone had become more or less used to the idea of it. *Pachakuti,* on the other hand…

"Tell me," she said.

"Is jus' a feeling." Pedro paused, then shrugged. "In old stories from the mountains in my country, they say it is end of the world when the stars fall out of the sky. Because stars are how you tell the time. If ju lose them, ju lose the path to the ancestors, who know everything."

Trudi leant forward now, devouring his words.

"Go on!"

"Well, ju know what is Milky Way?"

"Yes, of course. You can't see it here because the city lights are too bright. But everyone has heard of it, just like they have heard about the Northern Lights." She felt sparks flying in her mind. So Pedro already knew what Grandfather Larsson told her about spirit paths. It seemed that sky wisdom, like the ancient-spindle whorls Mrs. Partridge collected, had travelled all round the world. The Indians in North America believed that the Aurora was a bridge to the land of the dead. Professor Saxmund once told her that. A medicine man could cross the bridge and go there. For the Sami, the Milky Way was something similar - a passage to a hidden world. Per had shown her the ski-tracks, sky-tracks the Swan Prince made as he led the birds away in winter. Now, far south, in Peru, here were more star legends, and more magic roads... Pedro was speaking again:

"Well, when ju die, Inca say, ju follow this path to what is spirit home of the ancestors. If this path is broken, if the stars fall down, ju cannot go. So there is no future time after life. And then wisdom of the ancestors cannot return to earth, so we have to start learn everything all again. Can take a long time. The old spirits will be lost. And how can new people find a soul?"

"You mean we would forget everything?"

"Everything, like Corky forget…"

"…And Mincke."

"Like the oak trees can forget how to be well."

"And Barbara has forgotten how to be happy."

"So I wish that Time will not turn everything upside down."

"And?"

"And I want that Corky come back home and not be lost any more. He know *everything*. Everything we need, like Father Hieronimo, in Peru. But *he* gone. Now I lose Corky too. I rather give up and no try to see, if I can jus' have Corky back." His voice trembled on the verge of tears. He seemed to think it no disgrace.

"What happened to Father Hieronimo?"

"He jus' disappear. One day he go up in the mountains. Perhaps someone kill him. Perhaps he go mad, like Corky, and forget the way home. "

Another one!

Trudi leaned forward. "Pedro, listen, listen! Of course, you *must* carry on with the doctors till you can see. That's what Corky wants for you more than anything. He hasn't gone away forever. I'm sure we can find him and bring him back. Just as I'm sure I will one day find my Grandfather. And we've got friends here who can help – Sister Bianca and that lovely Mr. Brambling. He understands lots of the things that Corky knows. *He* won't let us down. The things that have happened are not because of the stars – I'm sure of it - they are because of *people*. Bad people *made* them happen. My grandfather knew all about it. And I think Hamish suspects something. But it's so secret, Pedro. And the ones who mastermind it all are very dangerous... At dinner last night, the waitress gave me a note. A kind of S.O.S. Pedro, do you understand me? Are you listening?"

"Si, si, I listening but ju speak very fast. Is no easy – and that bird he talking up there too."

"She was the girl we saw doing funny handstands in the garden next door. Yesterday afternoon she tried to wave to me from the drive, but she was dragged indoors. She wants to speak to us, but I am going home tomorrow and today the house is all closed up. They haven't let anybody out. *Is* it a loony bin? What goes on next door? Why did she write a note to say: 'I'm not mad'?"

She paused for breath, but her mind was racing on. All the while, Pedro sat with his hands idle in his lap, the blackbird on one side and Trudi on the other. You could not tell, just from looking, whether he was listening to either or whether he gave himself up to his own thoughts. Trudi gabbled on regardless:

189

"We can't tell anyone, because for one thing they won't believe us and for another we might get that poor girl into more trouble. When the world goes mad, it's the sane people who get locked up. I was told that by a man who really knew. Perhaps that is what is happening. The world is already turning upside-down, Pedro, and nobody has noticed. Perhaps it looks all wrong to us because someone is *making* a *pachakuti* happen here and now. And that is what is making Corky ill – just as if he was sick at sea.

"My grandfather, like your old priest, maybe, has gone to take his knowledge where 'they' can't find it, just as the Sami and the Inca shamans did long ago. They didn't tell the missionaries everything, did they? They don't tell modern people either. Professor Saxmund says so. I don't suppose even your Father Hieronimo found out the really secret things. They don't want foreigners to know. But companies like Laser Wag have spies who can root out the deepest secrets. They want to steal people's ideas, even their memories... They are like New Conquistadors, but more terrible because they are invisible. And they are here, in Kingsbury, Pedro. How else did the people at the Toy Forge know that Jurgen wanted a new phone? They are in Sweden, and in Newbridge, too. Who knows, perhaps they may even have visited your convent in Peru! They are like that horrid man this morning. They want to own everything so that they can turn it into money. If your Milky Way ever fell into their hands, they would cut it up and sell it back in little bits, but it doesn't belong to them, nor does the ancient magic that goes with it. I don't properly understand what is going on yet, but I mean to find out. Will you help me fight them?"

Pedro whistled. How could anyone talk so long? "What ju can do? Ju are just one girl!" he objected.

Trudi flashed back, undeterred. "Help me and you'll see what I can do!"

"Santa Madre! Okay, okay I help, warrior girl. At least ju make me laugh when I feel too sad!"

"We'll show them!"

"Sure!" Were all English girls this crazy? At any rate he was glad to laugh. Since Corky's seizure he had suffered from a horrible vertigo – a feeling inside that he was falling - and laughter stopped it for a while. Now he roused himself: "There – he stop singing too – that bird. That mean it's time to go back. We find Jurgen now? Perhaps he finished playing his music."

Trudi put his hand on her shoulder and led the way back to the house. It gave her a curious, tingling feeling to touch him and a warm, dark happiness spread over her. She did not know if she had said too much or too little, or if he had paid attention at all. But she no longer felt so alone. At the dining room steps he paused:

"Maybe we can make a string figure – so bad guys go away."

"A string figure?"

"Si. Like I show Jurgen the other day. He call it *cat's sunthing*."

"Cat's cradle?"

"Si – cradle – si. Is like magic in the old days. To give power or take power away. Very old game. I could show you. In Peru ju should do it only in winter, but here could be different, and is special occasion …"

Later that night, long after they had all gone to bed, Trudi could hear the muted strains of Jurgen's cello through the cheap wall of her hotel bedroom. He was not sending messages to Zub. Nor was he looking up things on his Laser Wag, or texting friends at home. He was working his way round the instrument, like a secret lover exploring a mistress, trying every note on the fingerboard, hushed, but intent. Trudi wanted to knock and ask what he was up to. Why didn't he play a tune? She knew he hated scales. And suddenly she heard a jarring sound and she knew exactly, without telling. Her brother was wolf-hunting, looking for the combination of sounds that would bring out that secret howling note! She almost laughed aloud. Now Jurgen had a secret too! He had discovered a passion that was momentarily more pressing than his love for Zub, and it was something as simple as the note she had listened for at her Grandfather's window in Sweden.

Wolf-notes. They were everywhere, if only you could hear them. In the sound of the wind across Arctic snow, in the groan of forest trees, the wing beat of a goose. But these were the obvious places. Anywhere, where the walls grew thin between this ordinary, everyday world and Per's Big World, would do.

If you put your ear close, you would hear the unmistakable peal, roar, yawl, like the gear-changes of a giant heart or mill, the engine of the universe at work. *That* note rang true. But there were other, local discords that did not. Sir Maximus made them when he tried to be pleasant. The odious Stromberg positively resounded with them. These were not wolf notes, just wrong notes, but they also hinted at immensities. Sir Maximus, with his toys and his lettuces and his mysterious Beedome, was a vast enigma. And Olaf, who the devil knew what made him sing?

Chapter Twenty-Four

A Cure for Dry Rot

At five o'clock the following morning, the first curl of smoke lifted above the rooftop of the Prospero Bookshop, in Newbridge. The town lay quiet. Early lorries purred in their loading bays behind the BioDawn Superstore, but most people were innocently asleep. Downstream of the bridge, a pair of mute swans dabbled beaks with their reflections, enjoying the peace of the river. No common ducks about to break up the milky gleam of the water. Traffic lights signalled to empty roads. It was going to be a beautiful day.

By six, a passer-by might have noticed that something was not quite right. Prospero's crouched between later buildings, its beams a little crooked, as if the neighbours had pressed in too hard on either side and elbowed it out of shape. As proof of its antiquity, a date, imprinted over the door, made a decorative flourish: *'1573'*. So Queen Bess herself could have glimpsed the house, standing new and straight, when she made her Progress through Sussex, six years later.

A perky display now filled the bow-fronted window, promoting the 'Adventures of Sherlock Holmes'. With theatrical gusto, Barbara had recreated the hero's study. A green, buttoned, leather chair took pride of place, with Turkish slippers set before it and the detective's celebrated Inverness cape and deerstalker thrown casually over the back. There were hints of his other interests, too. A violin sprawled in an open case. There was pipe-smoking tackle on a table nearby and, amongst scattered papers and *books* - after all, this *was* a bookshop - some antiquated scientific equipment, comprising flasks full of brightly coloured liquid. The whole effect had been liberally sprinkled with crumbs from a plate of Mrs. Hudson's rock cakes. Realism was further enhanced by quantities of smoke, now seeping in from the shop behind and looking, at first sight, like London fog, or a fiendish Holmesian experiment gone wrong, or a sign that someone had left their crumpets too long on the hearth. But a second look, had there been a neighbour or a passer-by to take a second look, would have dispelled such fancies instantly, for there could be no doubt about it, Prospero's was on fire.

Barbara had been tossing and turning in her bed all night. First she worried about Corky and Pedro *and how was she to get away to see them both, when she had no one to man the till in her absence and the trains were all disrupted on a Sunday?*

Then she worried about the shop and her mind started to make an inventory of all the other anxieties she could think of: *the summer tourist season about to start and she so behind with her paperwork and would anybody be buying books anyway, when they could download everything electronically from the internet? She needed an assistant, but her advertisement in the local paper had brought a hopeless response: a housewife who couldn't stop talking and admitted she wasn't very good with her alphabet; an elderly bank manager, retired, who had a bad back and couldn't bend down; a rather militant ex-financier who spent the interview telling her what was wrong with the business... To cap it all, the Council had come to make a Health and Safety inspection, condemned the cellar stairs and given her a weighty dossier on Employment Law. Give up? But then what? Her books were her passion. What would be left of Barbara without her books? She really ought to lose some weight. And that tap in the kitchen was dripping again...*

Her mind made a short-cut, via the computer and Olaf Stromberg to the dry-rot and the special laser device she had received in the post the day before. *Simply plug in overnight. Kills all dry-rot spores in twelve hours. Thank heaven for people like Olaf! She was sure he could help Corky with the bees. Oh Lord, she ought to go and look at the bees and she was so nervous about them, and how was she going to get there with no transport? Poor Corky! What rotten luck to fall sick, just now.*

The tour of these problems took about twenty minutes, with drifts of sleep in between, and she was just about to begin another circuit, when she caught a whiff of smoke from under the door. *Funny,* she thought. *Was Corky making toast?* Then she remembered that she was alone in the house, and for several moments struggled to get her bearings.

At length, her mind cleared. *Of course, the fumigator! Must have been on too long. She would go down and turn it off. Make some coffee maybe, and get a grip on things.* She rolled out of bed in her long white nightie, shuffled about for her slippers and paddled to the door. *Light switch. Handle... Disaster!*

No sooner did she open the door, than she found herself engulfed in a pall of smoke - a choking cloud, which poured into the room, stung her eyes, making them water and seared the back of her throat. Down below, she made out a lurid flicker of flames, while an ominous hissing and crackling issued from the stairwell. Heavens above! It was the swansong of the oak partition that divided shop from house.

"Oh my Lord! Oh my!" Now fully awake, Barbara made some rapid calculations. There was clearly no escape that way. The only possible exit would be via Pedro's route, up the narrow stairs to the top floor and out on to the roof. For once she was glad of his madcap antics for they had given her practice, hauling herself up there after him, time and again. Grabbing the dressing gown that hung behind the door and holding it in front of her face, she launched bravely forth and had already climbed some way, when the voice of reason butted in. *"What about the Fire Brigade?"* it said. *"Telephone is in the sitting room. What's the use of frying up on the roof if no one knows there's a fire?"*

"Oh Lord, yes." Barbara stumbled down once more. No time to find a mobile. *"And what about the books?"* The sitting room shared the first floor with the bedroom she had just vacated, but whereas the bedroom, being backward-facing, had a rather poky aspect, this, her best loved room, was expansive and overlooked the street. As she stood on the threshold, she knew that she would no longer make a practical escape.

From floor to ceiling, this room, like the floor below, was lined with shelves of books - perfect fodder for a fire. But no insurance could cover these, for they were the treasured volumes of Barbara's private library. They had been collected, item by item, since she was a girl, foraging in the second-hand bookstores of her native Boston. Each one had its own story, its own particular smell. She knew every dog-ear and thumb-smear of the cheaper volumes. And the fine bindings, which she had purchased later, well, they were irreplaceable. There were first editions amongst them, with author's inscriptions and precious colour plates, and unique items, like the bird-pecked copy of Doctor Johnson, once given by a friend.

What would become of Virgil now? And Smollett? Why, there was even an original, sixpenny pamphlet of *The Rights of Man*... Were they all to be lost? Unthinkable! Then her eye caught sight of Corky's saxophone in the corner. She must certainly save that. That instrument had been everywhere with him. And one day, when things were better, he would play it again, just like he used to.

"Hello, Fire? Yes Hello – It's the Prospero Bookshop. Lion Street. We're going up. Hurry, can you? People trapped? No, no, no. Just me. But there are some priceless... *What?* Oh, NB7 4PS – no, S like in Shakespeare! Sorry? The fire's just on the stairs here. I'm fine. I can get to the roof. It's the books... if they spray water in here, they'll ruin them! What? Oh sure, yes. Thank you." She hung up in frustration. Have to do something herself.

The street below lay deserted. Perhaps she could call for help and throw her volumes down. Though the spines would be damaged the books themselves might survive. But as she loosened the window and fresh air rushed in, she remembered that oxygen would only feed the blaze. No, no. Not that way. She closed the catch again. She would have to abandon most of her collection. If she picked out selected items, she could cart them up to the roof with her - that was the best she could hope for, beginning, for Corky's sake, with the one-man-band.

It is not easy, when you are large and encumbered by an accordion, to climb narrow stairs in a nightie, especially when there is an inferno raging at your heels. The heat of it and the unusual exertion brought the colour to Barbara's cheeks and she began to rail against fate and everyone who lay within reach of blame: that Goddamn Swede for one, with his 'I-can-fix-your-dry-rot' device. And the girl at Fire Control, who couldn't spell Shakespeare...

Hell-fire and Buckets of Blood! How was she supposed to manage on her own? Two more journeys brought her best-loved titles and a photo of Tod to the roof-light. Being angry somehow helped. Not that she blamed Corky and Pedro. The dear innocents had nothing to do with this and she felt glad that they were out of the way. Tod, her old partner, who had set up Prospero's with her

196

so many years ago, was also in the clear. Poor man, he couldn't help dying, could he? But Scarp the gypsy, was a different matter. Scarp, who had cleared out of Sussex last year without so much as a *'cheerio'*, who was always in trouble anyway and had somehow tweaked at Barbara's heart-strings, *he*, hapless soul, bore the full brunt of her rage.

"God damn you Scarp, where *are* you?" she cursed, balancing too many things on her pile. "Cluttering off, just when you're needed and not giving a goddamn care about your friends. You could have been some use around here. You could have saved something. You could have *helped* me! No good fly-by-night!" She missed her step and *Oliver Twist* toppled off the stack and plunged over the banisters into the flames below.

That was it! She reached the window and began posting things onto the parapet beyond. By now she had an audience: Wally, from next door, in his pyjamas and a postman and the people who lived across the street. Barbara kept her mind fixed on Scarp and his misdemeanours. That way she needn't remember that she was frightened and that she had bumped her head when she slipped.

To the onlookers below, the tableau on the roof-ledge took on surreal proportions. With smoke now billowing freely from the ground floor, and the sound of sirens threading the morning air, Barbara's white-gowned figure could be seen, calmly busying about, like a roly-poly Lady Macbeth with a top hat and a pair of cymbals, as though she had no concern in the world beyond arranging a stall for a jumble sale. A police car arrived and two officers leapt out and began to marshal the public away.

"Move along now, thank you. Down to the end. Health and Safety. The Emergency Services will be here directly and need free access. "

"Hold on, Barbara!" shouted Wally. "They're coming for you!"

Barbara waved nonchalantly back and sat herself down to wait. Then suddenly jumped up again and gave an audible gasp: "Oh my God, Keats and Milton!" To general cries of horror and dismay she staggered to the skylight and vanished once more inside.

The police sergeant, a youngster, newly promoted, was hopping up and down as the first fire engine drew up. "There are 3 people in there!" He confided excitedly. "There was a woman on the roof, and now she's rushed in to rescue two more – hasn't been seen for three minutes."

Oh marvellous! thought Bert, the Leading Fireman. (His retained crew had scrambled first, since the Newbridge full-timers were on another call.) That wasn't what he'd been told on the radio. He had just started his breakfast when the bleeper went. Now he had a real emergency on his hands, but he maintained his outward calm. "Don't worry," he said, with what he hoped was a rugged professionalism. "We'll start the search. There's a platform tender on its way. They can bring the survivors down with that."

Or the bodies... The young sergeant nodded and stepped back, suitably awed and the crew, in their thick mustard-coloured trousers and yellow hats, jumped off the machine and set to work, some rolling out hoses and locating the nearest hydrants, while others fitted on their breathing apparatus. By the time they were ready, two more pumps had arrived, the street had been evacuated and flames were licking the *'1573'* plaster panel off the wall. Barbara re-emerged triumphantly waving a book in either hand, just as a Fire Officer reached the scene.

"Got them!" she shouted. "Got them safe!"

"What's she talking about?" The officer swiftly took charge, calling back: "Where are the other people?"

"What people?"

"What are their names?" he turned to Bert.

"Keats and Milton, sir."

"Oh, for goodness sake, man, they're poets, not people. Can't you see? She went to rescue her books!"

She's a nut-case, thought Bert with some feeling. He didn't like being treated like a fool. "Couldn't take the chance, sir," he replied stiffly.

And his superior had to agree. "Quite right. Quite right. People have the oddest names, these days. Well, let's get the platform up there and fetch her down. She's insisting she's alone."

Bert was the man to go.

By now, bloodied, dirty and coughing, Barbara had begun to tremble uncontrollably. Despite the nearby heat, an icy chill gripped her bones. Her dread of heights swept back in a nauseous wave and she wondered if she was going to fall. Clutching the saxophone, she staggered into the arms of her rescuer, almost knocking him off his feet. But she was not going to abandon her gear.

"This lot has to come down with me. I'm sorry. It's life and death. I'm sure it's against all the rules, but these things are priceless - I'm not budging without them. That Milton there belonged to Charles Lamb. It's got his marmalade on the fly-leaf. I don't expect you to understand, but please... humour me... or I'm not coming. I need those leather boots there, too..."

It was easier to agree than argue. There was not that much to move after all, no other lives were at risk and the crew seemed to have a good grip on the conflagration below. Once loaded, the platform swung through the air. *I've done some daft things in my life, thought Bert, but rescuing a top hat beats them all.* Newbridge looked so beautiful from up here, the sun gleaming on the river and the clock-tower of the new supermarket. He would get an earful from his superiors when they touched down, but actually he was enjoying himself. *So he rescued Charles Lamb's marmalade, did he? Who the Dickens was Charles Lamb?*

Barbara's reprimand came later, as she was sitting up in her hospital bed. She had been admitted for smoke inhalation, shock and concussion. With four stitches in her scalp, she was told she must be monitored for the afternoon before her friends could reclaim her. Now the police arrived.

"You do realize, Miss Rainbird, that what you did was extremely foolish and dangerous and could have lost others their lives?"

"Oh, yes I *do*," she replied penitently. "And I am *truly* sorry. I can't *think* how it happened. Must have been hysteria. After I bumped my head I wasn't myself." She smiled so demurely beneath her lopsided bandage, the policeman conducting the interview had to hide his amusement behind his clipboard.

"I was delirious, and I want you to make sure that the Fire Brigade know that. That nice guy who rescued me, I don't want him to get into trouble. I take full responsibility about the books."

"Well, you'd had a traumatic experience, and actually, you were lucky to wake up at all. Did you know that none of your smoke alarms were working? You say you think you know the cause of the fire?"

"A dry rot fumigator that someone sent me, for the cellar. I'll swear it was that. As for the smoke alarms – I don't know. I guess I've been too busy to check them recently."

"On the upper floors, the batteries had been removed..."

Barbara stared.

"...of course that will make a problem for you with the insurance company."

"Look here, officer, I'm dotty, but not that dotty. Somebody sent me a state-of-the-art dry rot fumigator the day before – Swedish guy. Obviously, it was faulty. He fixed my computer back in the winter. He ran through my whole stock check. Went over everything in the shop..." She sat suddenly to attention. "You don't think *he* stole my batteries, do you?"

"I think you need to rest," said the policeman, patting the side of the bed. "We'll talk again when you feel more up to it." *Barmy as a fruit cake,* he noted, *the Fire Brigade were quite right.*

Kirsten assumed the same thing, when she came with new clothes at five o'clock.

"No buts, you're coming home with us. Sven and the children have just arrived back from Kingsbury. We'll all have tea together."

Part Four.

Antiphon. Midsummer

Chapter Twenty-Five

Return to Humbug Cottage

At the end of June came news that Pedro's second operation had been a success.

Frustrated at losing the thread of her Kingsbury story, Trudi had returned to school with an air of defeat. School felt boring and impersonal and she resented the hours spent there, but she had to admit that she scarcely preferred being at home, for the once easy-going Larsson house had become a strange, uncomfortable place.

That all-consuming work on the Tranquillity Project pooled in a spreading tide until every room downstairs was littered with plans and pins and fabrics and there was simply nowhere safe to sit. Kirsten would surface from her labours only to ward off interruptions: "Don't move that, darling! Don't touch! Can't you see I'm busy?" Sven, hot on the trail of 'Sudden Oak Death', and wary of the haberdashery, decamped daily to the University Library and when he wasn't there, buried himself in his study, emerging only to forage for biscuits, or sign for the parcels of research papers which arrived by express delivery. And Jurgen, wavering between enthusiasm for his new cello and his old obsession with Zub, was no company at all. Parties and outings seemed a distant memory.

As for Barbara, once she had recovered from her black eye, she baked a cake and took herself off to Kingsbury to reassure herself that Corky was on the mend. One could argue that she was not yet really fit to travel and that her nerves, in their hypercritical state, gave her a somewhat jaundiced view, but she found the trip an ordeal.

Corky seemed so consumed by the attentions of the nuns, he hardly noticed she was there. And in truth there was little she could do to help. Though everyone treated her kindly, she felt out of place. In her opinion, Corky needed shaking up a bit, not coddling. He looked stronger, but had let his mind go dreadfully. He drifted – he muddled things... She was not entirely sure that he knew who she was. He actually called her Bernardina! She worried about

Pedro, but she could not get near him, either. The Sisters had him equally firmly tucked beneath their wing.

Disappointed and upset, she returned to Sussex and commenced a legal battle with her insurers. No company, it seemed, answered to the name of *E.magic Dry Rot Solutions*. Experts agreed that fumigation was not, in any case, the correct treatment for the fungus. Olaf Stromberg had simply vanished without trace and the fire investigators decided, to her dismay, that hair tongs had been the cause of the blaze. The implication? That Barbara had instigated the whole affair by negligence or worse.

She could rant as long as she pleased about not being seen dead with her hair straightened, about Corky testing all the fire alarms at Christmas, about her insomnia because of the blind boy, but she could not make anyone believe her. She had to admit to the hateful underwriters that financially, her business was in crisis. Yes, insurance fraud *might* have appealed to anyone less passionate and dedicated. *They* threatened to take steps. She replied hotly that her conscience was clear, but inwardly she knew she was in deep water and paddling for dear life. There were moments when she wondered if she had actually gone off her head and *imagined* the dry rot fumigator.

Two weeks later, a new Book Department opened its doors at BioDawn and Barbara knew that she was sane. "Somebody stole my shop," she explained to Woodridge of Woodridge and Barking. "If you want to see it, go to BioDawn. It's all there. Even the Sherlock Holmes display." Mr. Woodridge put the receiver down with a smile. "She's really lost it now. She's got a conspiracy theory!" Barbara withdrew to her room and fumed alone.

Nobody had time to attend to Trudi and her concerns. Though there were occasional updates from the Missing Persons Department in Litven, the family now generally avoided speaking of Grandfather Larsson. It was all too upsetting. Corky and Pedro barely got a mention either and the question of the Bookshop was certainly taboo. Every subject of interest, it seemed, lay in a forbidden place and it was unsafe to go there. Conversation foundered. Trudi's head teamed with questions but she could find no one who even wanted to hear them, let alone provide the answers. She felt herself iced in, becalmed in a sea of doubts. Perhaps, she thought, in her bleaker moments, her adventure would never have a proper plot, never reach a climax, or resolution, and events would simply peter out before she could discover any meaning or purpose in them.

She was therefore joyfully surprised to answer the phone one day and hear Sister Bianca's voice on the line.

"Trudi, good news," she said, and it was so like her to confide it straight and not play that horrid trick of telling important things to adults first. "Pedro is home already and he's fine. The bandages come off tomorrow, but they are hopeful that this time he will really see."

A surge of excitement swept over her. Of course Trudi was glad for Pedro. But the excitement – that was for herself. It was her fair wind. It meant things were moving again: "That's wonderful," she yelled.

"Sister Matilda has taken charge of him," Bianca went on. "She has devised a programme of exercises and vitamins and heaven knows what and of course he has to go back for check-ups and Sister Emilia has made a special page about it all on our new website. You can look us up, if you like."

"And what about Corky?" At last, glimpsing the Kingsbury world again, she felt free to speak.

"Corky is well." This time, Bianca's optimism sounded guarded. "They say he is suffering from stress. Mr. Brambling has brought him seedlings and tried to encourage him to grow radishes and lettuces in the garden. But he doesn't have a lot of energy yet. Perhaps when Pedro is running about again, he will pick up too."

"And Mrs. Sparks?" Trudi wanted to picture the whole house.

"Mrs. Sparks has hurt her knee, but she is just the same as ever. Oh, and we've got some new house guests. A nice minister from York, here for a sabbatical and a young research scientist called Marina."

Trudi knew what a sabbatical was. It was a kind of working holiday academics took when they wanted time to develop their ideas. She knew about Marina too, remembering vividly the girl Hamish had teased at St. Gregory's. She wanted to ask if they were still at war, but didn't quite dare.

"Do you want to speak to Daddy?" she offered dutifully, instead.

205

"Better," replied Bianca. "But how are you Trudi, and that brother of yours? You know we think of you a lot. All of you."

How reassuring that was to hear! It transported Trudi momentarily out of herself, so that she felt she stood, not here in the hall at home, but over there, with friends in the convent office, seeing what life looked like from the other side and reaching out to those distant folk, the Larssons, who were having such a difficult summer. There might even be a little bit of paper on the prayer board behind them with her name on it. Trudi didn't believe in prayers, but she found the thought a comfort.

"We're fine," she lied. "Except for History. I've got a horrid teacher with pimples."

Sister Bianca laughed. "Oh Trudi, what a breath of fresh air you are! Always honest. You can be relied on to call a spade a spade! Yes, I'd better speak to your father. You look after yourself now. See if you can persuade him to bring you back to Kingsbury. I know it would mean a lot to Pedro."

Yes, the fair wind was blowing again. Pedro would be cured. And Sven would take Trudi and Jurgen with him when he gave his lecture. He could not possibly say no. Suddenly the way ahead opened like an arctic flaw-lead and she went sailing through.

This time they did not have to stay at an impersonal hotel. The ever-thoughtful Mr. Brambling had offered to put them up at Humbug Cottage. This would be a stay of only a couple of days, so while Sven delivered his lecture and attended meetings at St. Gregory's, the children could visit Pedro and Corky at the convent. Sister Emilia insisted.

Mr. Brambling welcomed them, beaming at the gate.

"Ah, my friends! My friends! Come in, come in and bring your bags. Can you manage? I'll hold the door. You can put your things down there for now, while I show you to your rooms. Trudi, I've put you at the back. Bathroom is just down there. Mind your head, young Sven, the ceiling is rather low. You are all together at this end of the cottage. Jurgen, you're in here, with my boxing trophies. Yes! I was quite a sportsman in my day. Boxed for Cambridge after the War. Sven, you have got the bigger room. That door there doesn't go anywhere, but I keep it locked. Death watch beetle in the floorboards! No television, I'm afraid. But there are games in here," a tiny cupboard room full of lumber, "chess and backgammon, that sort of thing, and of course you can use the wireless."

"I've got plenty of games on my phone," said Jurgen, tactless to the last.

"Ah, yes, I forget those things," Mr. Brambling chortled. "Marvellous what they can do."

Trudi found the cottage more delightful than ever. Her own little room, tucked up, like a martin's nest under the thatch, looked out over the orchard and the honey-coloured wall where the bees lived. Mr. Brambling had put lavender on her pillow. Wide oak floorboards sloped drunkenly to a window-seat just large enough for a child. There were old embroidered texts in frames on the walls, and a chest of drawers with a mirror and wash jug on top. Heaven!

How tempting it would be to take refuge here forever! Sitting on the pink coverlet, she felt the weight of worry suddenly fall from her shoulders. It had been so hard, all these months, carrying the secrets that Per had given her, fretting over impossible problems and mysteries, feeling alone and somehow responsible for every catastrophe: the bees and Mincke and then Per and Corky and now the Bookshop, and the poor dying oak trees... How could she possibly solve all their troubles?

As her mind settled, she recalled the room that Per had prepared for her at Christmas. She had thought it magical then, with its narrow wooden bed, and jug of bitter juniper, ice patterns etched on the window. But the magic had a poignancy close to pain. It seemed very far from Pinkney. Here she felt safe and warm. Nothing was asked of her. What, beyond the antics of a mad cockerel, could disturb her here?

Per's world, the world in which a man might freeze and starve, haunted her thoughts like a disquieting dream. But this space, cosy as a honey cell, where everything was sweet, offered sanctuary. If she had to choose between the two, she was, for the moment, not sure she would choose the Swedish room. Actually to forget Mincke and his troubles, to set aside the worries about Laser Wag and BioDawn and whatever evil lurked in the Beedome and to accept the trustful optimism that saturated life here, would be to take a blissful holiday. One could imagine that all was well, and always would be. The bees and the oak trees were thriving. The lettuces were real.

If only Per and Mr. Brambling could meet. They would have so much to say to one another, so many interests in common. Perhaps, Trudi reasoned complacently, the atmosphere of Humbug Cottage would do Per good, soften his rough edges and soothe his mind. Perhaps she could arrange it... She pictured him, in his great boots and belted coat, stomping ahead of her, once more. He turned, appealing to her to follow. But the sight of his beloved face knocked such wishful-thinking out of her.

Nothing would domesticate Per! He was as wild as a wolf. And wasn't that why she loved him so? Her own heart unerringly chose his path above all others. She belonged with him. She didn't *want* him to change. She dashed the tears out of her eyes. She would hold fast to her promises. Remember the Nail Star! No wavering! Mr. Brambling was a dear, kind man, but he would never understand the immensity of the venture she was on. One day, he and his paradise garden might need her protection, but they would not distract her from her purpose.

First, she determined, make a plan of action. See Pedro and Corky. Then find out about Marina and her links with Sir Maximus Bligh.

They arrived at St. Lucy's in time for tea and received an effusive welcome from the Sisters.

"Come in! Come in, you dear people! Pedro has been so looking forward to your visit – a little bit shy – a little bit apprehensive – but very excited. He's doing so well with the exercises. You'll see the change."

Trudi felt nervous herself. Would they still be able to talk in the old, easy way? She thought of their games of blind man's buff. All that would be over now. Pedro could no longer be indulged as a pet. Suddenly he had grown up and they would have to begin again – find new grounds for friendship.

The afternoon sun streamed through a fringe of leaves at the common room window, picking out reds in the well-worn carpet, and the scattered browns of the furniture. Trudi recognized it all with pleasure. Particles of dust were dancing in the sunbeams and the light played on the broad mirror over the fireplace, where reflections of familiar faces smiled above their tea. There was

Corky, sitting passive in a corner, his hand toying with a half-eaten bun. And Sister Matilda, very animated, talking to a girl whose back was turned. And raven-haired, Pedro, fiddling with a set of beads.

Sven strode forward and wrapped him in his arms. "How are you, chico? You look well!"

"Si, si, I good. I very good. I can see you now." He shrugged and gave a self-conscious smile.

"Can you really? That's so cool!" Jurgen *would* say something silly, wouldn't he? "How many fingers am I holding up?"

"Everybody sends their love!" roared Sven, letting Pedro go. "And you too, Corky. How are you feeling, old chap?" He grasped the invalid's hand. "No, don't get up. We have presents from Sussex. Biscuits, of course, and books and ..."

Trudi let her attention wander. She did not know how to talk to Pedro and she felt embarrassed when he looked at her, while Corky seemed an utter stranger. His eyes swam about, avoiding everyone...

The door flung open and in marched Hamish.

"Ah, princess!" he exclaimed. "Back again?"

"We've come to see Pedro."

"It's a miracle. He really can see, you know. And he takes it all as cool as a cucumber! How's the princess?"

Trudi knew he was laughing at her, but she didn't care. "We're staying with Mr. Brambling, at Humbug Cottage. Daddy's giving his oak lecture tomorrow."

"*Doctor* Brambling, you mean," interposed the girl whose back was turned.

Hamish made a gesture with his hand. "Princess, ye'll remember Marina, won't you? You met, I think, at that St. Gregory's Dinner at the beginning of term. The lovely Marina is staying at St. Lucy's while she is doing a special assignment. Marina, you know, is a food scientist and just at the moment she has left the hallowed halls of the String Kitchen to plan the catering arrangements for the new BioDawn Supermarket at Pinkney."

Marina flashed him a look of contempt.

"At *Pinkney?*" cried Trudi, unable to disguise her concern. "Why Pinkney? It's just a tiny village." The ghost of Auntie

Barbara put in an appearance: *Whatever would happen to the funny little post office and the old-fashioned grocer if a supermarket moved in?*

"There's an out-of-town store going up at Pinkney roundabout. You must have gone past it if you're staying there with the doctor," said Marina loftily.

Trudi, resenting her tone, retorted in kind:

"We're *not* staying with a doctor. We're staying with Mr. Brambling, the old man who keeps the bees."

Marina smiled. She could soon out-trump this little upstart. "And do you know who he is? That 'old man who keeps bees'? Only one of the world's most respected academics. He's got honorary doctorates from five universities; multiple degrees in different disciplines. He's the patron of countless institutes and academies, not to mention charities and research programmes. He is simply very modest. You mustn't judge just by appearances, little girl." She shot a triumphant look at Hamish. "Ask the Sisters if you don't believe me. Ask them who is Chairman of the Board at the nursing home next door. Who got permission for your friend Corky to go and stay there to convalesce? Ask them..."

"About Sir Maximus Bligh? And why he has donated £20,000 to the St. Lucy's Pedro Miracle website?" This thrust from Hamish took Marina by surprise and she paused to catch her breath.

Trudi turned in bewilderment from one to the other, but Hamish pressed on.

"Could it be to stop the Sisters at Pinkney from complaining about their new neighbours? I mean it is one thing to have a supermarket next door. But the Beedome is in a different class altogether. Who knows what goes on in that curious edifice?"

Marina blighted him with her eye. "I'm sorry for you, really I am!" But she had been beaten and she knew it. She was not at liberty to say, or perhaps she really did not know anything about the Beedome. She turned on her heel and walked out.

Hamish chuckled, unrepentant.

"One to me, I think!" He piled some cake onto a plate and handed it to Trudi. "Don't take any notice. She's highly strung, poor thing. Oh, I say!" he held on to the plate while he savoured the joke. "That's rather funny: *'String Kitchen scientist highly strung'*. Do you get it?"

210

But Trudi wasn't listening. "She's wrong, isn't she?" she pleaded. "Corky's *not* going next door. That's a bad place next door. I've seen what they do to people in there!"

"There was some rumour about it," Hamish dropped his voice and then raised it again. "Probably nothing will come of it. It costs a fortune to stay there, and then there's Pedro. Those two are inseparable, and Sister Emilia needs Pedro *here* for her website. Don't worry your wee noddle! Marina is just using you to score points against me. Do you understand?"

Trudi shook her head, so he continued: "Well, that's just as well. We're all crazy, Trudi. All scientists. Look at me. I've got an exam tomorrow. I need every hour possible to revise in. And what am I doing? I'm setting off on a midnight hike with Archie to look for his aliens on Drayholt Hill."

Trudi's eyes widened.

"There is an eclipse of the moon tonight, and Archie reckons the cosmic influences will be at their best. Me, I just want the walk. I love walking at night. It's good training for a mountaineer!"

"Are you going to read the stars?"

"Read them, listen to them, *talk* to them! Who knows what messages they have for us? But I'm also told," he added in a less mocking undertone, "that you can see the lights on the Beedome mast at night from Drayholt. And I'm curious. I have to know what is going on there, one way or another."

Trudi was thinking fast now. She wanted to talk to Hamish. She wanted to understand what he knew. This Beedome, for instance. What was it? And why was it so secret? If only she and Hamish could share their evidence, they might get a clearer picture. But every time she thought she had found an ally, something terrible happened to them. Per and Mincke had disappeared. Corky survived only as a shadow of himself. Barbara had become impossible since the bookshop burnt down. And now Pedro, who might have helped, shied away, distant as a stranger.

They were all stuck on their own paths, like planets trapped in orbit, or voices in a fugue... For Beery O'Leary, Bach's music embodied eternal truths - held a key to cosmic mysteries... It sounded far-fetched to her, but Archie believed it too.

In a fugue, he said, the music circled round just like the stars at night. The voices took up the musical themes and ran with them,

211

chasing one another, snatching the melodies, answering and reinventing as they went. Sometimes the top part would set off first; sometimes the bass or the middle lines, but whichever way it was, the parts joined in one by one, tumbling along their individual paths till they were all playing together. Then just when you thought the harmonies were so involved they must trip over one another, they would calmly untangle themselves and step back into the silence from which they had come. You could picture a fugue as a skein of sound, winding in and out of existence. New, old. Old, new. Bach's great cycle of preludes and fugues progressed through every key till all the notes were ringing. Resonance... the music of the spheres!

Trudi's ideas themselves went round and round, urged on by their own imperative. BioDawn and Laser Wag, The Beedome and the asylum next door – they were all linked in some invisible way, she was sure. Then there was Pachakuti... If she was to make sense of it all she would need more information. Perhaps seeing the Milky Way would help?

"Can *I* come with you?" she asked.

"Good heavens, no!" laughed Hamish. "We've drowned you up there once already. Whatever would your father say?"

"Daddy wouldn't mind," she replied without hesitation. "He could come too."

Hamish was adamant. "Princess, NO! This is strictly for physicists and violin-makers. Besides which, you are going back to Pinkney." He watched her face fall. "The Sisters have got something lined up for you tomorrow. Don't worry, you won't be bored."

"It's not that." Trudi felt her cheeks stinging – how she hated to be put down. "*I* need to know about the Beedome too. What is it? What does it do?"

Her words had a sobering effect. Beneath her innocent candour, he spotted a steely determination. Here she was, her blond hair gleaming in the sun, her big round hazel eyes, pink cheeks, a kid to be quizzed... and yet, spinning below the surface, he saw uncompromising particles of a soul that was not childish at all. Splinters of pure passion. She might be capable of doing something desperate.

"You really *do* want to know!" he said, as much to himself as to her. "Well, I wish I could tell you. It's a secret building buried in the Pinkney woods. We saw the perimeter wire when we drove out to Brambling's in the spring. It's something to do with laser research. And it was funded by Sir Maximus Bligh. It is shaped like a traditional beehive and it won awards at the time for innovative design. But what goes on in there, nobody will tell. I can't take you there because the place is patrolled by security guards on three sides, and on the fourth is the Convent of the Assumption, the mother house of St. Lucy's here, and they don't allow men inside!"

"I'm going to find out," said Trudi, no longer concerned with Hamish.

"Be careful, princess," he cautioned, now looking grave. "I make jokes about it, but it's not really funny. The laser crowd are dangerous people. Better forget all about it. *You* don't want to get mixed up in something bad."

'Something bad' - those were Per's very words and her next rejoinder sounded like a challenge: "Do they frighten you?"

"Well, I don't want to be turned into a lettuce, do I? Eat your cake. I think Bianca made it, so it's okay!"

He sloped off leaving her to crumble her slice alone and it was not long before Sven took his place.

"Aren't you going to talk to the boys, Trudi? They've gone into the garden."

She shot him a calculating look. "Daddy, Hamish and Archie are going on a midnight hike to watch the eclipse of the moon on Drayholt Hill."

"*Are* they indeed!" He grinned, though she thought she detected a shadow of envy in his eyes. Beside young Hamish, Sven looked older, grizzled even. This was just the sort of caper he would have organised himself in days gone by. Now he would be an onlooker. He had bigger responsibilities. Since Per's disappearance, he had developed a habit of sucking in his cheeks and biting them and it gave him a hungry look. Trudi persevered.

"Have *you* seen an eclipse of the moon?"

"Oh yes. Very strange. Beautiful, in an eerie way."

"Would it be fun to see it from the Worm?"

"Great fun, Trudi. One day, when we are less busy, we'll go."

213

"We could go tonight!"

"I have a lecture to give tomorrow."

"Hamish has got an exam!"

Sven laughed. "You have an answer for everything, but perhaps you can't always have all your sweeties *just when you want them!*" and Trudi buttoned her lips the way she always did when she meant to be stubborn.

In the garden, the boys sat huddled over Jurgen's Laser Wag. Pedro had never seen a miniature screen before and this was his first introduction to Zub. They looked up with distant eyes as Trudi approached.

"Archie and Hamish are going on a midnight hike to see the eclipse of the moon tonight." She waited to see their reaction.

"I seen the moon," said Pedro. "From my window. Very nice."

Jurgen shrugged. "You can get all that kind of stuff on here. It will tell you when all the eclipses are going to happen. There are star maps for every month with zodiac pictures. Tell me any constellation and I'll find it straightaway. Ask me anything! Anything at all!"

"All right, if you're so clever, look up Beedome."

Jurgen's fingers played across the screen. "What star is that? There's nothing called that here. There's a Beehive Cluster. Star cluster in Cancer. Distance: 520-610 light years away. Nothing interesting about it."

"*You* could ask," Trudi went on, ignoring Jurgen and appealing to Pedro instead. "You could ask if we could go too. Hamish might listen to you."

Pedro hunched his shoulders and wriggled. "I don' want to go. I have to be here. Is safer here."

Trudi stared. "Safer! But you can go anywhere in the dark!" She was remembering his blindman's hide-and-seek and his capers on rooftops.

"Mm." Pedro put his head on one side. "That was before. Now is not so easy."

Could that be true? Could the gift of sight actually take away your confidence? Where was the fearless Pedro who used to talk to bees and who slid down all the banisters at St. Lucy's without a thought?

214

Trudi turned from one boy to the other without success. "When I see better maybe we can go," Pedro apologised. "Just now is problem, but Sister Matilda says 'be patient'. Even Virgin Mary have to wait to get to heaven. She can't just do Assumption any time. She have to wait to be called. So I try."

Trudi had seen the word 'Assumption' written on a box by the pigeon holes in the hall. And when she asked Bianca what it meant, she had explained that it was the name of the big convent. Any post for the Sisters there, went into the box and was taken next time someone visited. Of course that was not enough to answer Trudi's question, so Bianca sent her to Matilda and Sister Matilda gave her a full account. According to the church, she said, the Virgin Mary didn't die like other people. Indeed some people thought she didn't die at all. She was translated directly to heaven on a cloud, sometime towards the end of August.

The feast of the Assumption was a special day for the Sisters, because they were also hoping to get to heaven, only they could not take a short cut. They would have to wait till their lives were over and pass some other tests first. All the same, they had dedicated themselves to the Virgin Mary and her miracle.

People in the Bible did quite a lot of flying. Did that mean they were shamans too, Trudi wondered? But shamans always wanted to come back from their journeys. Trudi could not imagine wanting to leave the earth forever.

She thought of the souls of the Inca who lost their pathway home, and the bees, which Archie claimed had been stolen and hidden amidst the stars. Suppose they were in that Beehive Cluster 600 light years away... Wouldn't they miss the warmth of the sun on their fur? No, the more she thought about it the less she liked the idea of the Assumption, but she could not say so to Pedro. Stripped of his protective blackout, he suddenly looked vulnerable and she realized she could press the matter no further. "You'll get better, I know you will," she said instead. "Don't worry!"

She would have to give up. The little bell rang for Vespers and the Sisters shuffled off. Corky slipped away to rest in his room. Hamish gave Sven a farewell clap on the shoulder, and stuffing a sheaf of revision notes under his arm, strode upstairs, his long legs straddling three treads at a time. When she next caught her father's

215

eye, he had such a sad, far-away look she thought he had given up too.

But of course she was wrong. That was the thing about Larssons. Larssons never gave up.

Chapter Twenty-Six

Midnight Hike

Sven seemed particularly anxious to hustle the children to bed that night. Trudi heard him talking to Mr. Brambling at the foot of the stairs, and though she could not catch exactly what was said, she guessed he was asking a favour, for the conversation ended on a louder note, with Mr. Brambling laughing and saying gaily: "Any time, my dear fellow. Only too delighted to help. I hope you enjoy every minute. It will do you good."

At that they parted. Sven retired to his room, doubtless to consult his notes for the morning, and a few moments later the plaintive sound of Mr. Brambling's cello issued from the parlour. He was practising his part for the orchestra tomorrow. His strings were out of tune.

Frustrated in her wishes, Trudi found it impossible to go to sleep. She had tried to see the moon from her squint-eyed window, but the thatch eaves came down too low and the cottage walls stuck out too far and the midsummer sky between them still glowed too pale to show any stars. There seemed no hope at all of observing the eclipse from here!

Then she fell to wondering about Mr. Brambling. Was he really an important person? Hamish had dismissed the matter with a laugh, saying you should never judge a sausage by its skin. Sister Matilda, for instance, she was a doctor too. She had been one of the few women to take a medical degree at Kingsbury just after the War. Her interest in Pedro's recovery was partly professional.

Trudi summoned her likeness now, with her leathery-weathered face, plain, tortoiseshell glasses and paper-skin hands, so clever at sewing; and then added her walking stick, her pointy, black shoes with the toes just curling up and the capacious cloak which she wore on windy days. The image of Mr. Brambling, leaning a little to the left because of his deafness in that ear, joined her, and together they took off up the Pinkney Road in a quaint hobble-step. Dear old pets, so humble and self-effacing. Were they truly powerful intellectuals? And if so, why did they hide it?

Marina didn't hide her cleverness. She used it like a weapon. Did that mean that she wasn't really clever? And how could you find your way in a world where every sausage wore a disguise?

A car with a faulty exhaust drew up on the other side of the cottage and two doors slammed. Trudi shot out of bed and crossed the landing to the bathroom which overlooked the road. Below her, on the doorstep, illumined by the light from the hall she made out two figures, one long and lanky, the other, stockier, dark, with glasses. Hamish and Archie! There could be no mistaking them. And now the door opened and another figure came out and joined them, cautioning them to keep their voices down before ushering them inside. But they did not close the door. From the landing now, Trudi could hear them in the hall, shuffling about and in a moment she guessed exactly what was happening.

Her father was fetching his things: boots, magnifying lens, a flask of coffee, perhaps. He was sneaking off to watch the moon on Drayholt Hill. And worse, he was leaving her behind! The deceit made her wrinkle her face in fury. Of all the rotten, unsporting tricks... How *could* he? Well, Trudi had no intention of missing out. Two could play that game! She would secretly smuggle herself along and see it too.

With no time to lose, she dived back to her room, pulled a pair of jeans over her pyjamas, grabbed some trainers and a dressing gown and pattered across to the boxroom with the dormer window. At this end of the cottage, the thatch swept down almost to the ground - a smooth run, nicely finished off with chicken wire to stop birds nesting in the reeds. All Trudi had to do was open the window catch, stand on a chair and wriggle through. And straightaway she began to roly-poly down, landing gently in some hollyhocks by the water butt.

The light from the hall still streamed out into the garden, but there was as yet no sign of the lunar expedition. And Trudi knew why. A Larsson could not embark without proper provisions: torch, compass, biscuits, scientific log book. How many times in her childhood, had she been left hopping up and down, impatient to set off, while the grown-ups checked their supplies!

She wriggled her feet into her shoes, and creeping along the dark side of the garden, reached the car, its old engine still gargling, sputtering exhaust. Hamish had left his driver's door

218

wide open and for a moment Trudi primly considered switching off the ignition, but she decided against it and turned instead to the boot, with its broken lock. What if it was already full? What if she couldn't squeeze inside amidst all the clutter Hamish usually carried? Doubtful, she hesitated. Suppose the lock came to life again and jammed, trapping her inside? Suppose the back filled up with fumes and choked her to death? But she had no time to delay. Voices were approaching. Sven had filled his flask and at any moment he and his companions would be setting off.

She grasped the latch and slipped inside, pulling the lid down after her and landing on an assortment of tools, very lumpy to lie on. Luckily for her, the car was roomy and accommodated her with ease. But she needed to be more comfortable. Fumbling in the dark, she found a holdall for a pillow and a groundsheet, which she used to cover herself. Seconds later, the lid went up again.

"Sling your boots in there!" said Hamish easily. "It's all junk."

Sven didn't 'sling' things - he was a proper, careful Swede – but he wedged his boots firmly into the small of Trudi's back, tucked his knapsack, with the unmistakeable aroma of Auntie Barbara's gingerbread, in beside them, closed the boot and then climbed over a pile of Archie's radio equipment, onto the back seat. The car rocked darkly as Archie got in and Hamish ground his gears, swore an amiable oath and lurched out into the night.

Success! They were off and they hadn't found her!

From her hiding place, Trudi could hear little above the roar of the exhaust. Occasionally, the other passengers raised their voices in laughter or exclamation. They were excited as schoolboys on a prank, or soldiers slipping out of camp and Hamish and Sven certainly had good reason to feel guilty. She fought the temptation to sit up. The boot was musty and claustrophobic. It would be nice to get some air, make a little gap from which to survey the road, but the risks outweighed the need. Mile after mile they bumped, till the journey seemed wearisome and her euphoria faded away. Would they ever arrive? She began to wonder whether she had done such a clever thing after all. What if the eclipse wasn't really worth it? What if she had gone too far?

'Watch and listen,' Grandfather Larsson had said. Well, she was doing that. Per had been a hunter all his life. Last summer he had told her how he tracked creatures deep in the forest. These days he

might take no more than a rabbit for the pot, but years ago the foresters hunted deer, and in the far north the Sami once tackled bears and wolves. With such powerful animals it was easy for the hunter to end up as prey. Their days were fraught with danger.

The amulet that Per's mother had given him was made of deer bone. Trudi felt for it now, instinctively. It had been polished smooth by Per's thumb over the years, and she imagined him feeling for it, whenever his life was in peril. *'To be successful you must study your quarry, anticipate his every move. You must know where he finds his water, where he takes his afternoon nap, who are his friends and who his enemies. Animals listen to one another. If you disturb a squirrel, the squirrel will alarm the deer.'* Tracking the Sneevelings was a still more difficult business, for they could not be seen. It would be comforting to conclude that they therefore didn't exist, but Trudi knew better. She knew they existed because of the tell-tale trails they left behind. And she knew that they were deadly.

Though it felt wrong to be spying on her own father, she persuaded herself he would one day thank her for it. Just now he stood in a precarious place. She could not dismiss the possibility that he and Hamish had become 'pooties', unwitting puppets for the likes of Olaf. Olaf was bad, she knew. He worked for Laser Wag, the spy-phone company. But Waggle Phones were actually made at the Toy Forge which belonged to Sir Maximus. And Sir Maximus, dabbling in all his manifold enterprises, was an even greater cause of concern. Both the Global Science Institute and St. Gregory's now owed their success to the Maximus millions, which meant that Hamish and her father were indirectly indebted to them, too. Everyone laughed about Bligh's dictatorial manner, as if it was a joke. But they couldn't see the dangers. Suppose, with all his power and influence, Sir Maximus turned out to be the real Sneeveling? Had decided to use Sven and Hamish for his own purposes? Or to destroy them? She *had* to know.

Lying low, Trudi plotted nervously in the dark. She would follow the moon-spotters, like a Sami hunter. She would eavesdrop in the shadows and find out just what they knew and where their loyalties lay. And they would never suspect a thing. How could they? They all thought she was sound asleep in bed!

When the car finally jerked to a halt and its occupants got out, groaning and stretching their legs, she sat tight and held her breath.

Up went the boot-lid once more and Sven retrieved his belongings.

"I don't like the look of all those other cars," said Hamish. "I hoped it might be nice and quiet down here on this side of the hill."

"Not a chance, old boy," Archie was heaving his receiver onto his back. "Not these days, with the internet."

"Did *you* put it on the internet?" Hamish sounded appalled.

"Good heavens, no! But something like a lunar eclipse attracts attention. As you know, I'm not the only person who believes this is a 'special' place. Every eccentric in the county thinks so too. They are all 'tweeting' to one another on their mobiles from dawn to dusk and if one of them has a good idea, they'll all come along and make a party of it."

"Well I don't want to go to a party."

"Calm down, man! You'll get your wilderness walk. They'll have come in sandals and they'll give up when they tread on their first thistle."

Sven gave a loud guffaw. It was so long since Trudi had heard him laugh aloud, she felt happy and sad at the same time. He didn't laugh like that with her any more. Oh, but her knees were aching. If only they would get going, she could creep out of her hiding place and straighten up. That would at least distract her from other thoughts. The smell of that gingerbread had made her tummy rumble!

At length, after more argument about whether they should use a torch and who should lead the way, they set off and Trudi could shake herself free.

Now she understood Hamish's remarks, for there were cars parked all along the lane: camper vans with ribbons tied to their aerials, and smart looking sports cars left higgledy-piggledy, half in the ditch. All abandoned. The people must have gone ahead to the party. Was this what they called a 'flash rave', Trudi wondered. Hamish turned in at a wooden gate and then struck left and followed the bridle-track up the hill. The land opened out, just as it did at Corky's nursery, offering scant cover for a stalker. But Trudi need not have worried. The three ahead were so engrossed in their own adventure they had eyes for nothing else.

High overhead sailed the full moon, casting its brittle light and painting grey shadows on the grass. Trudi's heart pounded so hard with fear and excitement and the effort of keeping up, she thought it would burst inside her. Her senses thrilled at every step. Euphoria returned. Now I am a mountaineer, like Hamish, she thought; now I am an explorer, like that fearless Viking woman who took her spindle to Newfoundland. I can't put a foot wrong. I am walking with wings. I am walking under the great tent of the ancestors and at the centre of the tent will be the tent-pole and at the top of the pole, the Nail Star. And on midsummer's eve you can fly there...

Why did people make so many excuses to stay indoors when they could be out here in this clear, scintillating air? Pedro would have loved it. Just the night scent of the elder-flowers, yeasty like wine, and a glimpse of the tiny rosebuds on the wildbriars, these were worth any fear and discomfort. Their memories would remain to brighten times when life was dull again. Was that why Hamish climbed his mountains? And why Archie did what he did? Trying to reach something impossibly secret and far away?

"What was that?" Hamish wheeled round, peering back down the hill. "I could have sworn I heard something behind us."

"One of Archie's aliens, I expect! That bush there, doesn't that look just like a little girl, crouching down?" Sven laughed and strode on.

"Moonlight plays funny tricks," said Archie, readjusting his load. "But I'm not falling for your practical jokes. I'll tell you that now!"

At the top of the hill, the 'rave' was in full swing. Shadowy groups of figures had gathered round little impromptu bonfires, some in fancy dress, some barefoot, in hardly any dress at all. There were parties of astrologers carrying hazel wands and star-gazers, setting up their telescopes and sitting expectantly in garden chairs, laptops at the ready. People had popcorn and programmes, just as if they were at the cinema, waiting for a film to start. Some had brought their dogs and the dogs were happily nosing around for food.

"This is a disaster!" groaned Hamish, shouldering his way through the crowd. Archie and Sven followed and Trudi had to tread almost on their heels to keep up.

"Hey, folks!" An elderly, blond lady, whose flat chest and wasted thighs gleamed beneath a scanty negligée, clapped Trudi on the shoulder. "Here's one of our group. Young girl in a dressing gown, looking lost. Anybody own her?"

"I'm not lost, thank you!" hissed Trudi, plucking herself free. "And I'm not with you!" But she had lost valuable time. Which way had the men gone?

Hurrying on, she almost missed them, holding council by the light of the torch. Hamish, of course, had a map. Their words were swallowed up by the nearby sounds of revelry, but she caught enough to guess the drift.

"...ten minutes left..."

"...not staying here... insufferable..."

"...strike out... forget the Worm... that way..."

"...down the hillside... away from the people... weaver..."

They must be heading for the hidden valley they had found before. There would be peace there and proper darkness for Hamish, but it would be more scary, dropping down off the hill top. Trudi glanced back regretfully at the glowing campfires and the picnic atmosphere of the 'rave' and wished they wouldn't go. She felt cold and rather silly in her dressing gown. Yet she knew she must see this thing through. *Come on,* she scolded, *You're a Larsson, aren't you? Hearts of Oak. Mind the anthills!*

Already they were slipping and stumbling on the scarp. Half way down, Hamish turned and peered behind him once again. "I could swear there's someone there!" he growled.

"Will you come on, man? There's barely five minutes before the eclipse begins. Who's going to want to snoop on us?"

"That's what I want to know." returned the Scot. "*Who?*"

"Sit yourself down, for goodness sake. It's a good place, this. Nice vibes." Archie loosened his knapsack and pulled out a camp stool.

Sven squatted down easily on the turf and began, with the help of the torch, to investigate the myriad tiny plants embedded in it.

"Real proper downland, this," he commented in approval. "Look at all the snail shells – these amphora-shaped snails are quite rare now, but this place is littered with them. Is it too soon for coffee?"

"Much too soon. And bring that light over here! Can't find the lead for my headphones."

Hamish wandered off a little, savouring the dark in solitude and all but stumbled into another figure coming up the hill.

"I'm so sorry, did I make you jump?" The voice belonged to a woman.

"Well, yes, you did," bluffed Hamish, vexed that even this place had been bagged by someone else.

"I didn't expect to find people on my hill." explained the newcomer. "Are you here for the eclipse? But of course you are."

"*Your* hill, is it?"

"Well I live just down there, so, naturally, I claim ownership of the valley."

"You're not the weaving lady, are you?"

"You've heard of me?"

"You gave us sanctuary in your house a few weeks back – my friend and I and a bunch of young kids."

"Of *course!* The Scottish explorer! How delightful to meet you again. Are you all here now?"

"No – no. The pleasure's mine." Trudi knew that they were shaking hands. "There's just myself and Archie here and Sven, a runaway from the University."

"And the little girl up on the hill, then?" asked Mrs. Partridge calmly. "Is she not with you?"

"Little girl?" Hamish wheeled round.

"There – surely you can see her? She has been watching you for some time."

So the hunt was up. And to be honest, Trudi felt glad. She had not exactly given in – her surrender was honourable - but now she could feel safe. She knew that once he saw her, Sven would almost certainly give her a piece of cake. And it would be so much more companionable to see the eclipse with friends around her. The arrival of Mrs. Partridge had changed everything. Hamish allowed himself to relax and reverted to making gallant puns. A picnic seemed inevitable.

But Sven's first reaction was one of horror.

"What the devil!" he roared, and his dear face looked so black and furious, Trudi actually quailed in fright. Surely he should be *pleased* to see her. Did he really not want her come and share what

224

they were up to? Suspicion shot through her mind like a sparrow-hawk. *Could* he be involved in something wrong? She didn't mean playing truant – of course that was understandable – but the whole business of watching on the hill with torches and radios and aerials... binoculars trained on the distant lights? Did a dark motive lurk somewhere?

Then his eyebrows went up and she knew that all was well. "Trudi Larsson! You *bad* girl!" Straightaway she was in his arms, his curly beard crushed against her cheek, his big hands smoothing her hair. "You could have got lost... you could have been... Those lunatics up there ... *anyone* could have kidnapped you! How did you do it? No don't answer." He held her at arm's length, marvelling at the way the moonlight glittered, silver, in her eyes. "You are your grandfather all over again. Wild and unreasonable. My bad, wicked girl! You must be frozen. Here, come and have some gingerbread and coffee. Put your hands in my pockets.

Mrs. Partridge gently interrupted: "No time for that, just now. See, the eclipse is starting ..." and she turned them round to look.

The moon above had contracted a strange, lopsided appearance and some of its brightness had fallen away. You could see the shadow engorging on one side, clinging fast, like a deflated bag. As the eclipse progressed, they watched in silence, motionless, enthralled.

Of course, Trudi knew what an eclipse was. It meant that, for a random moment, earth, sun and moon had all lined up in a row. The sun was shining, way over there on one side and on the other the moon was sailing through Earth's shadow - a mystery that was otherwise lost in the invisible shadows of space. They had done a lesson on it at school. Folk in the past thought such an event was an omen. But scientists had disproved all that. They knew exactly when an eclipse would happen now and why. There was nothing supernatural about it. Those people, with their wands and bonfires on the Worm, were an anachronism like the Swedish Tomte porridge. Their party, a superstitious indulgence!

And yet... and yet something astonishing was underway here, something that made her twitch, deep in her innermost core. She felt a curious pain as though a hook-line was attached to her heart. One tug on that line, she thought, and she would be up, up, soaring skywards, just like Per's noaïdis.

225

Gradually, inexorably, the shadow ate up the moon, extinguishing its familiar light, until nothing but the deflated bag remained. Shape-shifting! For the first and perhaps the last time, Trudi glimpsed a new perspective: a heavenly body shorn of radiance - something cold, solid, and very old - a reddish lump, like an old potato or shrivelled puffball, mere brick dust suspended in space. Dead rock. Then a little slip of light returned, like a brightening fingernail, ousting the shadow until, inch by inch, the brilliance returned. A banal round of applause sounded from the hill above.

Sven gave Trudi a squeeze and reached for his thermos. Hamish got up and stretched his legs. Nobody knew how to break the silence. Perhaps they had all felt that twitch of pain that troubled Trudi. Did they also wonder for a moment which was real? The silver disk, or the old potato? The mask, or the face behind the mask? Luscious lettuce, or jumble of isotopes?

The scent of coffee broke the spell, and everyone began to speak at once.

"Well, Arch, what did you get? Any messages from little green men? Any celestial codes? Landing instructions? Astral music?" Hamish felt particularly sardonic.

"Nothing," replied the older man, packing up his headphones in a defeated way. "It's quite odd. Somebody was jamming the airwaves. Must have been a very powerful signal. I couldn't get satellite or anything. Why would someone want to do that? Unless it was a release of magnetic forces from here on the hill..."

"Those warlocks up there!" laughed Sven.

"Or the Beedome?"

"Who knows?"

"The Beedome is right over there, in Pinkney Forest. I reckon it's *there* where the red lights are winking. Perhaps the bees inside were buzzing too loud!"

"Could just as well be the military doing something at the Frogdyke airbase." Archie ignored the joke. "Well whatever, they've spoilt our chances."

Trudi felt they were missing the point. They hadn't sailed up into the sky, after all.

"What about the Beehive Cluster?" she asked, picking up a cue. Perhaps if he found some stars instead, Archie would feel better. "Can you detect that?"

"The Beehive Cluster, eh?" He stopped his fiddling and looked up. "The gateway to eternity! You know that's what Ptolemy and Plato thought. Somewhere in the Crab constellation is a secret gate, through which the souls of the newborn descend to earth. It's a bit late in the year to see it, but you might be lucky!" He was concentrating now. "Can you find the Pole Star? And the Great Bear? Now go across to Castor and Pollux the twins, those two bright stars, just above the horizon. The Beehive is a little smudge to the left. Here, look with the binoculars."

Trudi could not see anything through the binoculars, but with the naked eye she scanned the dark spaces of Cancer.

Somewhere, there, lay the mysterious mass – a nest, where new stars were being born, where the souls of the bees lay trapped. When she strained to look, it vanished. But when she focused somewhere nearby, she became aware of it, glimmering like a thumbprint in her optical field. Stars too far away for Sami-lore.

Also too far away for Laser Wag, who reported nothing special. If Pedro was right and his premature birth had cheated him of a soul, perhaps *that* was where his spirit lay stranded. It might explain his unearthly temperament, so unlike ordinary folk.

"Gingerbread," urged Sven. "Take a middle bit, it's squidgier. I put your coffee there beside you. Don't knock it over."

Snuggled up now in her father's jacket, Trudi wedged her warm cup between her knees and applied herself to the cake. Here was Auntie Barbara at her best. The honeyed crumbs melted in her mouth, bringing back memories of sunny days. For whenever things went wrong in the past, it was always Barbara with her cake and her raw American humour that saved the day. Trudi could just see her now, laughing in her apron, her ample frame filling a doorway; Barbara with her arms full of books, letting off steam about something quite incomprehensible and reducing everyone to fits of giggles; Barbara with her incense and her hairspray, giving hugs all round – outrageous, unfashionable, irresistible.

With a twinge of guilt, Trudi realized that she had been so engrossed with her own interests lately, she had hardly given Barbara a thought. Barbara, like Corky and Kirsten, had become a distant wraith, eaten up with cares she could not share. As she licked her fingers, she wondered what had become of her. The cake still spoke volumes, but Barbara herself was silent.

Meanwhile Hamish was talking on another matter: "Suppose the aliens are there, and do contact us, and suppose they decide to take us over. What then? You could have engineered the end of the world, Archie. Does that not bother you?"

"They would be so far superior to us – like angels, Hamish – we would think it an honour. Would you resist being taken over by an angel?"

"Probably. I don't want to be taken over by anyone. I'm quite happy as I am!"

"Not even if they brought peace and harmony on earth?"

"Hasn't every despot tried that line? What peace and harmony did conquerors ever bring, except the peace of the grave?"

"Friends, friends, there is no point in arguing," interposed Mrs. Partridge. "Let me *show* you a miracle instead, some characters as strange as any aliens, and tucked away here on our own earth so quietly we walk past them without ever knowing they are there. I make just one proviso..." She turned as she stood up. "Before we go, you must promise not to tell a living soul. This is my great secret. I trust you, but no one else must know what is here. These creatures are under my protection and it could be the end of them if collectors found them."

Intrigued, they scrambled to their feet, brushed off the last of the cake and followed her down the grassy slope. As they pushed forward, they huddled closer together, hands outstretched to steady one another. Once or twice, Hamish stopped in his tracks and looked behind, still somehow convinced that they were being watched.

Turning right, Mrs. Partridge led the way into the heart of the combe.

"Now," she stopped. "Up there – What can you see?"

Above them, on the hill, they detected a pin-point of light; one, no two, no three – there was a third a little higher. They were unwinking and needle bright. Now, Trudi spotted a whole cluster of them where the shadows lay deepest and a straggling trail, high against the horizon. Overhead, the stars sailed on. What were they?

"Give up?" asked Mrs. Partridge, breaking the silence.

228

But Sven was already grinning. Of course he knew. "Now this *is* a miracle! There must be more than a hundred here."

"The season is nearly over but they are still plentiful. I've counted nearly two hundred on a good night. So many snails, you see..."

"*Are* they snails?" asked Trudi incredulously.

"No, my dear, they are glow worms. They live on the snails. For just a few weeks of the year the females come out in search of a husband and their tails shine luminous and bright. They sit themselves down on a blade of grass and hold up their tails and wait for a partner to find them. They are slow-witted little beetles, and they sit very still, till the right mate comes along. For the rest of the year they are dull and negligible. In fact these adults won't live terribly long. But they create a marvel on a summer night. Dearer than angels to me!"

"I wonder if Mincke drew them."

"You what, darling?" asked Sven.

"I was just thinking – why do all the best things have to be secret?"

"Trudi, you're a philosopher! Why do stolen moments taste sweeter? We are all renegades here and should be tucked up sensibly at home. But this has been a rare treat, Mrs. Partridge."

"Oh, Eleanor, *please*! I'm so glad we met."

"We're firm friends now. We'll meet again soon, I'm sure. Thank you for trusting us."

Thanks and good wishes were murmured all round. Hands shaken. Trudi found herself briefly in Mrs. Partridge's arms.

"If you want the quickest way back, just follow this path down to the road and continue along the foot of the hill. I'll come with you. I'm getting cold myself."

Trudi cast one farewell look behind her. Already trees blocked most of the valley, and the magical vision was lost. Only a couple of lights remained, glinting, for all the world, like a pair of spectacles in the moonlight.

Chapter Twenty-Seven

A Collector and a Thief

The next day, Hamish, resplendent in gown and mortar board, set off for the Graduation Hall to sit the last of his exams.

"Think of me," he groaned. "I shall be in torment for the next three hours!"

Sister Bianca made the sign of the cross over him and clenched a fist in the air: "Sock it to 'em!" she laughed. "You can do it!"

Sven ferried the children to Pinkney Road and then drove on to St. Gregory's to face his own ordeal. He had been going over his notes since sunrise, anxiously cramming like a schoolboy, for the future of the Fellowship depended on this lecture. But Trudi was not worried for him. She knew that no one could bring the subject alive as enthusiastically, or as memorably as he. They would *have* to love him.

Jurgen seemed oblivious to it all.

Unaware of the night's goings on, he slept late and spent an inordinate length of time writing up his diary for Zub. He had to be propelled into the car, still glued to his screen, a piece of toast in one hand, the ever-demanding Laser Wag in the other. As soon as he arrived at St. Lucy's, he collared Pedro and the two boys immersed themselves straightaway in one of Zub's interminable games. Trudi was not invited to play. Pedro threw her an apologetic glance. He knew she was scornful of the Waggle Phone, but after struggling through his exercises with Sister Matilda, he felt he had earned the right to a little relaxation, and Trudi had become so odd recently. She seemed to disapprove of everything. She, for her part, knew he was avoiding her and wandered out into the garden, alone.

On the back step she met Mrs. Sparks beating the doormats and the old lady gave a kindly smile as she sidled past. *Poor little lamb,* she thought, *she looks fair worn out.* Normally, Trudi would have stopped and told her all about the trip to Drayholt. Did Mrs. Sparks know about glow worms? But the midnight hike and the glow-worms were a sworn secret, and in any case, she did not feel like chatting, today. Her spirits laboured under a cloud, depressed that Zub monopolised the boys and made them boring. There were no Sisters about. Perhaps they were at their tasks, or in retreat. They took it in turns to have quiet days when they sat alone in the garden with a book and ate their meals in their rooms. Today though, Sister Emilia's office door stood firmly shut, a fact signifying that some sort of crisis was in progress.

When Bianca arrived, her face showed signs of strain.

"We've got two hours," she announced, pulling off the elasticated cuffs she wore to protect her sleeves while working. "Let's do something that's fun, for a change."

She had been wringing out altar linen at the mangle in the wash-house. Trudi had watched her do it before, fascinated by the heavy cog-and-roller mechanism and the cavernous double sink over which it presided. Sister Emilia had ordered a new tumble-dryer with some of her website donations, but Bianca preferred the mangle. She appeared progressive and practical and yet she always chose the hard way of doing things, laughing that it was better for her soul. This made no sense to Trudi, who disliked chores, but she was attracted by the smell of the wash-house, and the solid feel of the wringer handle. And she admired Sister Bianca. She recognized a flinty core of determination and passion at the heart of her that resonated with her own. *Larsson's forever! Do or die!* Sven used to joke. But Bianca had discipline too. She never talked about her feelings so you could be tempted to think she did not have them. Rubbish, of course!

"Let's go to the Wallace-Aardhof Museum, and then have tea at the German Café," she said, rounding up the boys as if that was settled.

Trudi and Jurgen knew all about Wallace Aardhof, for Professor Saxmund had told them amusing tales about him in the old days.

Wallace Aardhof was a Victorian explorer and collector who travelled the world, studying remote civilisations. A hybrid antiquarian, archaeologist and ethnologist, he returned from every trip with great packing cases full of souvenirs. Just about everything you could imagine went into those cases, from statues, pillars and kneading troughs, to hair-pins, arrows and shrunken heads! Back in England, he turned his Kingsbury residence into a museum, planting the garden full of palm trees and building special

231

arcades to house his finds. And as time went on and he immersed himself more deeply in his project, he began to look like one of the exhibits himself! Friends would call to find him dressed in buckskin and feathers, smoking a peace pipe in the conservatory, or discover, to their consternation, that dinner was to be served on banana leaves on the floor.

Gradually, acquaintances fell away. Rumours circulated that the old man had eaten his cook; that he kept a crocodile in the bath. He was certainly a crackpot! After his death, he decreed, his remains were to be burnt on a funeral pyre on Kingsbury Beacon and he left his house to the nation. But by then the estate was bankrupt. He had spent every last penny on his collection. His watch and silver-tipped walking stick were all that remained of his once vast wealth and his household effects had to be repurchased from creditors by public subscription.

This time Bianca and the children took the bus to save time. Wallace Aardhof's house sat in a leafy street leading to the Warren, a maze of lanes at the heart of the city. Grey and stately, it looked unexceptional in the sun. None of the children really cared about the man, but it was nice being with Sister Bianca. People turned in the street at the sight of a nun in full habit, and being stared at made them feel important. Better still, Bianca knew the young assistant on the desk, who waved them through as though they were official guests.

Inside, blinds dimmed the broad windows and it took a while for Trudi's eyes to adjust to the gloom. When her sight returned, she saw for herself the strange amalgam Aardhof had created. Part Victorian, part aboriginal, the domestic and exotic elements of his life were as mixed up as the batters in a marble-cake. There were African ritual masks and tufted spears peeking out between the lace curtains and oil lamps of the drawing room and a stuffed wildebeest standing to attention at the library desk. Jumbled amongst the slippers and letters and medicine glasses common to any home of the time, were artefacts from the farthest corners of the earth.

In this authentic 'visitor experience', the exhibits lay about quite casually, just as their owner might have left them. *He* had never bothered with cases and labels and 'do not touch' signs. An audio guide explained, if you had patience to listen, that throughout the house you could do as you pleased. The award-winning 'hands-on' displays had been created using pioneering restoration techniques, all funded by a local research establishment. You were invited to make yourself at home, sit down in a chair and put your feet up!

Here were spinning tools from the Urals, carved with animal figures. Here, a pair of snowshoes, a Maori necklace, a honey pot, a shaman's belt... Trudi stopped. A Sami belt, just like the one she had carried in her pocket at Christmas. Familiar turquoise beads decorated the ends... She knew the feel of them... She could remember how they rubbed together between her fingers! Next to the belt, with a distinctive T-shaped hammer for a beater, sat a noaïdi's drum, identical to the one Per had made and given, last summer, to Jurgen. There were symbols painted on the hide in red. Had she not known better, she could have sworn they were *the very ones* he had drawn. The sight of them hurt like a knife in her heart.

Oh, Grandfather! Where are you? For a moment she wanted to cry, longing for certainties. If only he would return. If only everything could go back to how it had been last year: her father working for Professor Saxmund; Barbara happy in her bookshop and Corky digging his vegetables and playing his saxophone in the market-place. Just now, she thought, she would give up being rebellious and difficult; she would almost welcome the routines of school and tennis lessons, just to know that people, *her* people, were safe. She understood why Pedro had offered up his chance to see... But time would not turn around. It would take magic beyond imagining to unwind the clock. And wishing, as she had found on Drayholt Hill, achieved nothing. It merely showed her how unhappy she was.

Pedro didn't believe in going back. He had more faith in the future. She recalled how he had pushed ahead, so certain of the way, when she was lost in the maze. *'You must go through; then ju can go out...'* Was life itself a maze? And if she kept going would things come right again? Midsummer had come to Kingsbury but her heart was still in winter...

As if she read her thoughts, Sister Bianca came up behind, slipped an arm round her and gave her a squeeze.

"Ready for a hot chocolate?" she said. "It's too nice outside to stay in here. I'll go and find the boys."

Trudi stayed gazing at the Sami relics. Did her grandfather know that she was here? Could she call to him through them? The idea had no sooner suggested itself, than a familiar voice whispered in her ear.

"You find them irresistible, don't you, Trudi? But they are beautiful and intriguing, are they not? And they so remind us of home and the lovely things of long ago..."

She wheeled round and found herself staring into a pair of spectacle lenses. The owner had bent down to speak at her level and his breath touched her cheek. With horror she recoiled, recognizing both the voice and the pale eyes that peered expectantly at her. Olaf Stromberg, in his shiny, tailored suit, smiled intimately back.

"And here are the others," he straightened up and gave a wink to the boys.

"Boss!" cried Jurgen enthusiastically. "Pedro this is my contact, my Laser Wag man. You remember him don't you?"

Pedro shrugged. "Sure," he said, but he took Olaf's handshake with indifference and Trudi was gratified to see that he avoided his eye.

"So, Pedro," continued the Swede, unconcerned. "What a marvellous thing to see clearly, huh? And you look so well."

Sister Bianca stood protectively, with a hand on the shoulder of either boy.

"I don't think I've had the pleasure," she said.

And immediately he was all hers.

He actually clicked his heels and gave a little bow: "Olaf Stromberg. Delighted to meet you. The children and I know one another well. Sven, their father, is one of my closest associates. Indeed, you might say I am a friend of the whole family. We have spent some very special times together in Sussex. What a wonderful surprise to meet by chance, this way!"

Bianca nodded. "Well Trudi and Jurgen are here just for a couple of days. Pedro is staying at our hostel until he is discharged by the specialist. I'm Sister Bianca."

Her handshake suggested farewell, but Olaf had no intention of letting them go so easily.

"I know, I *know*," he continued, smiling to reveal a mouthful of narrow teeth. "I know all about you. *All* about you *all*. Sven has

234

told me so much." He glanced at his watch. "Well, the lecture must be almost over now. Perhaps we could have tea together and meet him afterwards. He is expecting to see me, but it would be such a pleasure for him to find you with me."

Bianca demurred.

Trudi's face had turned to stone, but Jurgen was jumping up and down.

"Oh, go on, Sister Bianca. Daddy would like it. Olaf is a technical wizard. He fixed our computer. He can fix anything. Anything in the world!"

"Is that true?"

"It's a knack," said Olaf modestly. "I don't charge. I just do it for friends. My real work is with mobile phones." He produced one of his familiar business cards.

Sister Bianca turned the ticket over in her hand, making an inward calculation. "And you can cure computer viruses and such like?"

"Oh, viruses!" Olaf loosely waved his hands. "Nothing to it!"

"We have a problem at the convent just now. Sister Emilia's website has crashed and the estimate from the software company seems excessively high. Sister Emilia has come to rely rather heavily on her website. She is very distraught... She hasn't set foot outside her office since it happened."

"Dear lady, I would consider it an honour to help, if I can."

"You *can't!*" said Trudi rudely, gripping hold of Bianca's habit.

Stromberg gave her an indulgent smile and continued to talk above her head.

"All I need are my computer, and a couple of things from my flat and the matter can be resolved before Vespers! You know, a convent – how fascinating! I have always had a deep interest in the religious life. It would be a positive pleasure."

Bianca detached Trudi's hand firmly but quietly.

"Perhaps a drink and meet Sven first. We were just going to the German Café."

"No need! No need! My flat is only moments away. I can offer you tea, squash, fresh-fruit-smoothies – even cinnamon buns from BioDawn! Jurgen, don't you want to see where Zub lives? I can show you the very terminal you send your reports to!"

"Please Sister Bianca!" Trudi tugged once more in vain. Olaf's charm had taken hold and now there would be no stopping him.

"I'll telephone Sven and tell him where you are..."

"Thank you," smiled Bianca. "I'm sorry if I seem hesitant. One can't be too careful these days."

"My dear lady, call him yourself. Then we can all be happy!"

Sven sounded excited on the phone. The lecture had ended with a standing ovation and he was just off to drinks at the Master's Lodgings. He would be free in about an hour, and couldn't wait to see them all. Another call, this time to St. Lucy's, secured an exemption from attending chapel at noon. Indeed, the promise of a cure for the website brought an unaccustomed warmth to Sister Emilia's voice. "Sister, you have done well," she enthused. "Surely your good angel has been watching over us today!"

Outside, the sun dazzled between the plane leaves. Olaf's party made their way from Wallace-Aardhof's house, along the dappled pavement to the Market Cross. From here, roads departed into the labyrinth of the Warren and to the Great Library, with its pinnacled tower, but Olaf took a different way, past the back gate of St. Gregory's and down a narrow lane which divided the college from its richer neighbours. There must have been gardens on the right hand side. Treetops nodded over the wall. Further on, the buildings resumed and there were practice rooms. Trudi could hear music from the upper windows: a snatch of piano scales – someone blowing a horn. For one desperate moment she imagined that it was Hamish; that she could call out to him and he would come down and rescue her. But Hamish could not help, she remembered, her heart sinking. He was taking an exam.

Every nerve in her body told her that they were walking into a trap, yet no one else could see it. So much for going foward! She had watched one person after another accept help from Olaf. And all had so far come to grief. Mincke and Barbara and Corky, all had paid the price. Now it was to be the turn of her own father and the innocent Sisters at St. Lucy's.

Olaf would no sooner get into their computer, she felt sure, than some catastrophe would befall them. She did not believe for one moment that he had a genuine interest in the religious life, any more than he had cared about beetles or bookshops. He merely camouflaged himself so that he could work unseen. *Parasite,* she

236

thought. *Carrion fly.* He would wait till they were off their guard and then strike! After that it would be too late to resist – they would be as helpless as babes.

All around them, the world carried on, regardless: the birds singing, the bells chiming, Jurgen, full of excited chatter, Sister Bianca making polite conversation. And Trudi's mind raced ahead, trying, trying to work it all out. Why did Olaf want them to visit his flat? Would he lock them up? Like Per? Was that what had happened to Per? The thought increased her desperation. She began to take note of markers along the street, memorising her route, just as Per had taught her to do in the forest. Here a broken paving slab, there a gate with a dragon's head, a bicycle minus its wheels, chained to a lamp-post... She tried to catch Pedro's eye. Perhaps he would back her up. But he was walking, head down, silent and withdrawn.

At the end of the lane they emerged into the bustle of Bacon Street. Olaf spun on his heel and slipped down an entry beside a stationery shop. Narrow, dirty stairs led to a landing above.

"Just a temporary home, you know," he laughed, turning his key in the lock. "Though a good observatory. From here you can see all the life of Kingsbury go by. Perfect place for a spy!"

Trudi hung back, making one last attempt to stall, but Bianca rounded on her this time and hissed a definitive warning: "No, Trudi. I don't particularly want to do this any more than you, but sometimes we have to consider others. Think of your father, and of Sister Emilia. They may really need the friendship of this man and it is our duty to be supportive. I'm relying on you now."

So in they went.

The room beyond had a bare and functional appearance, but, as Olaf said, enjoyed a spectacular view of the city. Stretching away on either side were the shops and pubs and gateways to the colleges which lined the street below, while across the road stood the Graduation Building where poor Hamish was sweating out his exam. Rows of computer monitors lined one wall, a tangle of wires and terminals such as Trudi had never seen before. And the rest of the space was filled with maps, filing cabinets, printers, black swivel-chairs... all the trappings of a military command.

"Of course, this is only one little outpost of the Laser Wag organization, but it's not unimportant. The reception is simply marvellous here." Olaf noted their astonishment with satisfaction. "The Astronomy Faculty lies just over there and we can piggy back on their receivers to pick up almost anything in the world. Can you see the dishes, poking up above the roof? That's how we contact Zub, Jurgen. We can speak straight to outer space!" He seemed full of excitement.

Jurgen's face beamed back. This was his moment. Wouldn't Trudi, wouldn't all his friends at school be sick to know he had such powerful friends. "If Archie could only see this," he crowed, "he'd die of envy!"

"Archie?"

"You know, the man I told Zub about, who makes the violins." He ignored the warning poke that Trudi gave him. "He tries to talk to aliens in space with his radio. He's a bit of a weirdo, but he's all right, really."

"All the best people are weirdos, Jurgen!" smiled Olaf. "I'd like to meet your Archie. I think we must have a lot in common! And I could give him some advice perhaps. But I promised you refreshments. Please, make yourselves at home." He gestured towards two vinyl-covered sofas and opened a fridge in the corner. "Blueberry Vitamin Torpedo, or Sparkling Peach and Passion Fruit?"

A feeling of nausea swept over Trudi - the effect of the sun, and fear perhaps, and the sickly smell of the drinks as Olaf poured them.

"Which way is the bathroom?" she gasped.

"Why, just through there. Second door on the..." She had gone already. "I hope nothing is wrong." He turned to the others.

"Nothing at all," Bianca assured him. "Please don't concern yourself. She's a little overtired today."

Once out of the room Trudi put her face in her hands, took some gulps of air and tried to get her bearings. Second door, Olaf had said, but was it right or left? She found herself in a lobby with openings on either side. Her head was spinning, her mouth felt dry. Perhaps she would not be sick, perhaps she would merely faint. She grabbed a door handle and stumbled through, but this was no bathroom.

It looked more like an interrogation cell. Trudi had just long enough to take in a desk, littered with papers and a blanketed divan tucked up against the wall, before everything went black and she slumped down, her head upon her knees. How long she was unconscious she could not tell, but gradually the ringing in her ears subsided and she started to revive. Her thoughts were whirling now. If Jurgen's messages to Zub went straight to Olaf, then that meant that Olaf had effectively been spying on them all along! He would have known everything about the fire at the bookshop, and Corky's illness, and by now he knew about Hamish and Archie and poor Mr. Brambling, doubtless, at Humbug Cottage. Perhaps Jurgen had even, in all innocence, tipped him off about the trip to the Wallace Aardhof Museum that morning, so that their meeting by the shaman's belt was not an accident at all, but part of a deliberate plan. But *why?* What did they all know that could be of such interest? What did *she* know?

Well, for one thing, she knew that Olaf was a fraud. If only she could find the proof, then perhaps she could convince others and that would be a start. But time, time was against her. At any moment now, Bianca might come looking for her, and then she would have to go back. Dear Bianca, what if she should fall ill, like Corky, or like Mincke's bees? She could not bear the thought.

She jumped to her feet, her mind now clear and began to sift through the documents on the desk. Many were indecipherable - scribbles of scientific formulae, and mathematical proofs, mixed up with pages of music manuscript, letters, recipes, and architectural plans. A waste paper basket overflowed with more of the same. Nearby, hummed a scanner and a large shredding machine. Suddenly Trudi understood. The papers here were being processed, scanned and destroyed. Two sackfuls had already been discarded. All these papers had come from a folder marked 'India'. And numerous files for other countries bulged nearby. Trudi tipped them out, searching frantically for something, anything familiar. 'Japan', 'Portugal', 'Russia'. Nothing there. Her hands shook. Her temples throbbed. 'Sweden'... At last! A decorative border caught her eye, painted in those vibrant colours which characterised all of Mincke's work. She had uncovered a page of the 'Ny Saga'. There could be no mistaking that European hand.

So Olaf had actually stolen the manuscript before setting fire to Mincke's cottage...

Hearing someone at the door, she hurriedly stuffed the page inside her tee shirt. Bianca must not see this yet. But when she turned around she found that the figure on the threshold was not Bianca, but Olaf himself.

He smiled, displaying his rodent teeth and licked his lips:

"Curiosity killed the cat?" he enquired.

"I opened the wrong door," gabbled Trudi.

"Ah, yes. Easy to do, even though you're such a sharp, clever girl!"

"They all looked alike ..."

"And there are such interesting things in here, aren't there?" Olaf approached and stroked the papers with his hand. "Find anything good?"

Trudi froze. If she dodged under his arm she might reach the door before him. But he seemed to read her thoughts.

"No need for that. You and I are too alike not to be friends. You know some things and I know some things, and together we could do such interesting work. I know that interesting things appeal to you. For instance, together we could find your grandfather. You do want to find him, don't you, and I could help you."

"Never!" hissed Trudi, backing away.

"Perhaps I know where he is."

"I won't talk to you. I will tell everyone what you are!"

"Pity." Olaf smiled again, but his irritation clearly showed. "Because no one would want to hear you and you could do your friends and family a deal of harm."

Was he threatening her?

"They don't need you!" said Trudi.

"Oh, but Trudi, they do. Who do you think secured that Fellowship for your father and proposed the lecture today? Who arranged a visa for Pedro? Who has persuaded the police, *just at present,* not to prosecute Barbara for arson? They need me *very* much. And many others, who do not yet even know it, need me. That young Hamish, I hear, is about to fluff his exam. Then there's poor Mr. O'Leary. He's not really fit to teach, is he? Even Jurgen..."

"I won't listen!" Trudi put her hands over her ears.

"Then help me," urged Olaf, coming closer still. "Help me to contact Per. You are the only one who can do it. It would be so

240

easy for you. And in return I could protect all these people you love. I could make all their dreams come true!"

But he seemed to know that he had underestimated her and his menace had a brittle edge.

Now she ducked. As she evaded him and darted from the room, she felt a sudden flush of triumph. He had gained nothing from the encounter, but she... had her proof! Granted, the danger was nearer and more deadly than before, but now, at last, she had drawn her enemy into the open and with Mincke's manuscript in her possession, she had a proper case to lay against him. Best of all, he had as good as admitted that Per was still free. The Sneevelings had not captured him and they did not know where he was. Wily old wolf, he would be hiding up somewhere, perhaps right under their noses, disguised as only he knew how, which meant that he had been faithful to his word. He had not abandoned her. He would help her to the end.

Without looking to right or left, she wrenched open the door of the flat and hurled herself down the stairs.

"Trudi – wait!" she heard Bianca's voice behind her, but she would not stop. She was flying now, back along the passageway, past the mutilated bicycle, past the practising pianist, and in through the gateway that led to St. Gregory's Quad.

"Hey! You can't just go in there like that!" expostulated the porter behind his little window. "College members only!"

But she was flying. Past the new building works and the students playing croquet, down the secret passage Hamish had used as an escape from his tutor and out into the street, beneath that figure in fresh-hewn stone.

Now which way? She had come from the Warren with Hamish before...

Someone caught hold of her and lifted her off the ground.

"Hey, scamp, where are you running to?"

"Oh Daddy!" she stammered. "I came... I came to see you! I couldn't wait for all the others!"

Chapter Twenty-Eight

Pachakuti and the March of Time

After lunch, while Olaf toyed with Sister Emilia's computer, the children de-camped to their corner of the garden. Pedro flopped onto the bench, elbows on knees, and covered his eyes with his hands. He felt tired, for the sun had given him a headache. Jurgen plumped down beside him, feeling equally glum. He had been so looking forward to seeing Olaf's flat and showing off his knowledge of Zub and all his hopes seemed to have collapsed in a heap. When Trudi fled, Bianca gathered up her things and dashed after her, dragging Jurgen and Pedro along behind. Olaf, expostulating, hurried at their heels, but his demeanour had visibly changed.

"Whatever happened?" gasped Bianca.

"She was feeling sick!"

"But to run off like that! She doesn't know where she is going."

"Please don't panic." Olaf had a moment's inspiration. "She is going to meet her father. She just wanted to get there before us."

"She really *isn't* herself today!"

"Oh yes she is. She's always like this," panted Jurgen, his legs striving to keep up. "She always has a turn and messes things up." He knew exactly why she had run out. She was jealous of Zub. She couldn't bear to see that Jurgen knew something she didn't and, since Olaf had promised to demonstrate his latest satellite programme, she would have had to sit through it all, feeling mortified that she didn't understand because she had given her Laser Wag away. Now she had not only spoilt the morning, but far worse, she had damaged Jurgen's special relationship with Olaf. You could see that the Swede was furious, and though he tried hard to conciliate Sister Bianca, he cut Jurgen as if he simply did not exist. After all that he had done for him, too! When they reached the gate of St. Gregory's, he greeted Sven and Trudi with apparent effusions of joy, and promised to follow on to the convent as soon as he had collected his things. But he would not give his 'special agent' so much as a glance of farewell.

Well, Trudi needed taking down a peg. As a girl, she could hardly be expected to understand the value of cyber-science - hive minds, media clouds - all the promises of the future, but Jurgen was not afraid of her and he would tell her straight what he thought. He might be younger, but he was a boy and in time she would realize that boys counted for more.

Meanwhile, Trudi had devised a plan of her own. She walked up and down the little cinder path by the bench and then knelt on the grass and lifted a face full of artful innocence.

"Jurgen, if I could prove to you, beyond doubt, that Olaf Stromberg was a thief, would you give up your Laser Wag?"

"Certainly not! And you can't anyway."

"I can." She sounded more animated.

Pedro raised his head.

But Jurgen was ready for her and his bitterness bubbled over: "You've got it in for him because you're mad. Everybody knows it! The school psychiatrist says so. They are just afraid to tell you. But I'm not. Trudi, the world has moved on. You can't turn your nose up at everything. Technology is here to stay and you have just got to live with it. You'd like us all to be living in caves with flints and stone axes. But you can't stop time moving on. Businesses like Laser Wag are going to run the world and people *want* them to. The future belongs to Olaf and his friends because they are the clever ones who can make people happy. We don't want the Black Death and famine any more. Laser Wag makes life better. You hate it because it's bigger and brainier than you. But you are a fossil, Trudi! You are living in a dream. Wake up!"

Trudi teased out a lock of hair and watched it shine in the sun.

"Tell him," she said quietly to Pedro. "Tell him what happens when Time really moves on."

"It can be upside-down time – the end of the world." Pedro rubbed his face.

"You are *both* mad!" cried Jurgen.

"No, no it's the stars, you see, Jurgen. The stars really make time move on. Of course they go round and round each day, or seem to, because the earth is turning. But every year they shift a little bit across the sky as well, so it looks as if the universe has slipped. It's got a special name. That's how ancient people knew that time existed. They studied the stars for everything - for telling the time, for recording history, even for predicting the future and for medicine. That's how their doctors and priests contacted spirit-helpers, following secret paths that took them out of this world. Lose those paths, they thought, and you lose the meaning of life itself."

"Is true," said Pedro.

"Why do you listen to her?"

"In Peru," continued Trudi, "the stars began to slip out of line with the ancient pathways, so the Inca people thought that pachakuti was coming and they lost their will to live."

"Is not *her*," confirmed Pedro. "Is history. Inca history. When they think they will lose the way to the ancestors they try to make magic to stop time. But they couldn't do it so they believe the world was finished. Then when the Spanish soldiers came, they didn't even try to fight. They just die."

"So what does that have to do with Laser Wag?"

Trudi cut in. "People believe that our world is doomed, don't they? Nature is dying. The ice caps are melting. Time is running out. Only technology can take us into the future. Everyone gives up without a fight. They think only technology will save them. Laser Wag makes you feel powerful for the moment. You can do anything, find anything, know anything at the touch of a button. And meanwhile, you believe the company is making everything better. They are looking after you and they are looking after the planet. But you don't really know what they are doing in your name. The Aztec priests murdered thousands of victims, thinking that that would feed the sun and save the earth from destruction. Not all magic is good."

"In Peru, too, even before the Inca. In the old culture, they kill people to please their gods. Kind of Black Magic."

"You can't call Laser Wag Black Magic!" cried Jurgen.

"I think Laser Wag is doing something similar – a kind of human sacrifice. But that doesn't matter for now – I just want you to believe me about Olaf. Jurgen, do you remember my old pink phone? The phone died, but the memory card survived. There are only twelve pictures on it, but some are of stories that Mincke wrote. Do you remember the old man in Sweden...?"

"Another nutter!"

"He looked a crank, Jurgen, but he was a very brave man – your kind of hero. He escaped from the Nazis, you know. He was a writer and an artist and his work was so beautiful. He showed me, on Christmas Day. I went with Grandfather Larsson to his house – he showed me the stories he wanted to publish. He wasn't mad then – just old and ill and unhappy. He was a genius. Like Bach."

"Yeah! Another nutter with nits...."

"No, *you* are the nit, Jurgen! Listen to me. I had my phone-camera with me and I photographed some of the manuscript. I thought perhaps Mummy or Daddy could show it to a publisher here and we could get the stories printed. But then Olaf Stromberg came. Mincke had had a visitor who fixed his television, just as Olaf fixed Barbara's computer, just as he is doing the sisters' computer now, and guess what happened? His house burnt down, just like the bookshop. And Mincke lost his memory, just like Corky. Wherever Olaf goes, there's trouble. Grandfather Larsson disappeared. Corky's bees vanished."

"But you don't know that Mincke's visitor was Olaf..."

Trudi produced her page of drawings.

"I found this in Olaf's flat today. It's part of Mincke's story. I can prove it because I have still got the memory card with my Christmas photos on it. You could view them on your Waggle Phone, but Olaf can read everything on Laser Wag and he must not know that we are on to him. Jurgen, you have been feeding him all the information he needs to spy on us through your ridiculous texts to Zub. Now all the people we know might be in danger: the Sisters here and Archie and Mr. Brambling. Who else have you betrayed?"

Jurgen sat looking pale, but defiant.

"You still don't know any of this for sure. Olaf might have found the manuscript after the fire at Mincke's and kept it as a memento. Mummy and Daddy are all right. And we are all right. *Why* should he want to spy on us, anyway? Why are we so special? He can't spy on the whole world from that little room."

He had a point. Trudi filed it for later consideration.

"Today at the flat Olaf threatened me. He's looking for Grandfather Larsson, and he wanted me to help him. If I don't, Jurgen, he has threatened to step in and hurt people. Daddy might lose his job. Pedro might lose his visa. Barbara could go to prison.

Believe me, Olaf is a blood-sucker. That's why I ran away! You saw how he changed towards you today. He tries to hide his ugly side, but sometimes it shows through anyway.

"Jurgen help me! Help us! You are the clever, technical one. You can understand more than us. I *don't* say all progress is bad. Daddy is a scientist, isn't he, and so is Hamish and they're not bad. But there is something very wrong with Laser Wag. It's like a fungus. You see pretty mushrooms here and there, but the real business lies underground and no-one knows how far the network spreads or what its real purpose is. Laser Wag feeds off knowledge. They take clever people, like Daddy, and Corky and Archie and somehow suck them dry. We have to warn them. Who else did you describe to Olaf? Think!"

Jurgen bit his lip. "Well, Beery... Beery O'Leary. Zub wanted to know about the mead he made. He wanted the recipe. He was quite insistent about it. He said we could make it in the String Kitchen. It sounded funny."

"Oh, Jurgen!"

"And Sister Emilia... and..."

"And Mrs. Partridge?"

"I don't know."

"And Scarp?"

"No. Scarp's gone," said Jurgen. "Anyhow, what does he know that's special?"

"He knows lots of things, like how to pick locks, and how to mend machines." For a moment the gypsy wandered into her thoughts, lean and wary, with his crooked teeth and tattoos. "Besides, Auntie Barbara's in love with him. He'll turn up one day. You'll see."

"What about the old man?" asked Pedro.

"Brambling? He already knew who he was. But I had to tell him anyway, about the bees and especially the mad cockerel. And which room did you have and which way did it face – all that kind of rubbish. Boring really."

"We have to warn Beery! We can't ask Mummy. She wouldn't believe us. But Barbara might. She's furious about the fire. I think she half suspects Olaf anyway. Barbara would warn Beery if we explained it all to her! But we can't use text or e-mail – they are not safe.

"Olaf has the passwords to our computer at home and I'm sure he can hack into our phones too. I'll write her a good, old-fashioned letter. Sister Bianca would find me a stamp - I know she would - and there's a post box right outside St. Lucy's. Barbara will like that and in the mean time we'll tell Daddy everything. Daddy will go to the police and they will arrest Olaf and sort it all out. You, Jurgen, text Zub and tell him... tell him you don't feel very well and you may not be able to write for a while. You are with me, aren't you?"

Trudi blazed, once more triumphant, while Jurgen's brief rebellion lay in ruins. Pedro gave him a nudge.

"'S okay," he commiserated. "You better just say 'yes'. If she's right, maybe it will be crazy adventure. We'll take on a real bad guy, just like Spider Goddess in the game. Maybe then Corky can get better." He spoke only half in jest.

But the plan got off to a bad start. When they returned to the house, they discovered that Sven had been recalled to the Institute. Sir Maximus had sent his chauffeur-driven limousine with urgent instructions to fetch him right away. No time for good-byes. Sister Bianca, bearing coffee and biscuits for Olaf, waved him off.

"Don't worry about the children," she called. "They're safe with us!"

Chapter Twenty-Nine

The Mayfly

Hamish passed him as he cruised into the drive on his bicycle. He had swung one leg over the saddle, ready to hop off and was balancing on the nearside pedal at a drunken angle. He looked weary after sitting his paper but his spirits were high.

"Go well?" called Bianca, holding the door.

"Not bad. This is the first year they are doing exams on computers. I just hope they don't delete it all by mistake!" A lasting grin implied that he had been lucky with his questions.

"You'll need some lunch."

"Had lunch, thank you, with a bunch of ravenous physicists in town. Now I'm going to enjoy a well-earned rest."

"I see." Bianca smiled in an ominously sympathetic way and dropped her voice. "Hamish... I was wondering if you could help us out?"

Oh, no. Not the children again! He braced himself but the blow did not come right away. Bianca jerked her thumb indoors and plucking him by the sleeve, led him through the hall, past the open door of the office where Olaf sat in a sea of papers, and into the student kitchen. Once there, she threw her weight behind the door, closed her eyes and put her finger to her lips.

"What's going on?" laughed Hamish. "And who's that out there?"

"Olaf Stromberg, some friend of... well it doesn't matter too much. He's fixing the website for Sister Emilia, and adapting it to do something online... webcams in the chapel, I think he said. Anyhow the point is, as you saw, Sven has gone off. He has been summoned to see Sir Maximus again, and the children are *here*. I've looked after them all morning, but I have my work to do. We can't leave them running round the place while we're busy, and I have already missed chapel once today. *Are* you booked up? I know you must be tired, but I wondered if you could keep an eye on them until Mr. Brambling comes to fetch them at six. I have no idea when their father will be back."

She took a deep breath and leant forward in confidence, dropping her voice lower still: "I'm worried about Trudi. She was behaving very oddly this morning. You know she has had problems before. Sven did once admit to me that she sometimes suffers from delusions and irrational impulses. Today she reacted in a most disturbing way when we met this Olaf. It was all very embarrassing. He was trying to be friendly and she actually ran off in the middle of our visit. When I asked if everything was alright she insisted she was fine, just needed some air. *Could* you, perhaps, take her and the boys to the Park, or somewhere where they can play and be children and forget all about the grown-up world?"

Perfect! Hamish nodded stoically back, bidding goodbye to his carefree afternoon. "We can go to the river. She can't escape if she's on a boat. By the way," he gave her a straight look, "are you happy about having a webcam in your chapel?"

"No. Not really. But Sister Emilia is sold on the idea. This Olaf is an expert at installing such things and he's doing it for free. It means anyone in the world can join us for prayers online. It's hard to argue with that."

Hamish smiled as if he would be willing to try, winked and turned on his heel.

"Also," Sister Bianca cautioned. "I haven't told them yet about Corky..."

If the afternoon promised to be a fruit sundae, that was the cherry on the top!

"What do you *mean?*" shrieked an incandescent Trudi when she heard the news. "He *can't*. He can't possibly have gone there. No one can have let him go."

"Trudi, it was *his* idea. He wants to get well, and the house next door is a proper convalescent home, where they can really care for him. And he's so close by, you can all go and visit him whenever you like."

"It's a mental asylum! It's a prison! I've seen them in there!"

"He would not go without me," said Pedro undercutting her hysterics.

"It's for a few days only. They've got a bed vacant and Corky wants to try the cure. You wouldn't want him not to try."

"They'll lock him up and he'll never get out." Trudi struck a tragic tone. "Like that girl in the dressing gown."

"Nonsense," replied Hamish. "I'll climb in with my climbing ropes and rescue him, if that's the case. But let's be reasonable first. It's Mr. Brambling who has arranged all this, and you know he wouldn't suggest anything that wasn't for the best. Sister Matilda wouldn't stand for it, for one thing! You are all surrounded by good friends who love and care for you. How can anything bad happen here?"

Trudi scowled and bit her lip.

"Mr. Brambling doesn't understand. Nobody does." Her voice became choked with tears.

"Come on, princess!" coaxed Hamish. "This isn't like you. You're my second in command. What's going to happen to the expedition if you crack up? I'll personally make sure you get to see Corky as soon as possible, to put your mind at rest. But for his sake, and for everybody else as well, you need to be brave and patient and put up with me for this afternoon. Besides, I want to show you the river. Is that a deal?"

Trudi glanced at him, and then at her shoes and nodded, subdued. Things were moving so fast now she could hardly take them in. At this rate there would be no time to write to Barbara. She might have to trust to a land line call instead.

"Is that a deal?" he chucked Pedro under the chin.

But Pedro still shook his head. "He would not go without me," he repeated.

"*Is* it?"

The boy looked away and shrugged: "Is okay. No problem. I coming."

The river lay east of the city gardens. At this time of year, three rival boathouses did a bustling trade in punts for hire and the University Reach thronged with picnic parties of students who had finished their exams. Young lovers sought out the shallows under overhanging willows, enjoying a quiet canoodle, while the day trippers splashed about noisily, shouting warnings and advice as they tried to figure out how to steer. But there were smaller craft also available.

College punts had to be booked in advance, so Hamish chose a neat little rowing boat for the children.

"Sorry mate!" said the boathouse attendant. "One child per adult only on the river. It's the new Health and Safety rules."

"What?"

"Don't knock me. It's not my idea. It's losing me money." He gave a lopsided grin, then picked up his boat-hook and sauntered to the water's edge where a returning party had wedged themselves, wrong end first. A dexterous prod pushed them off again.

"Right oar, *right* oar!" he commanded, turning his back on Hamish, as though that was that. But he had not entirely finished. Catching the boat by its stern, he guided it once more ashore. "Try the canal if you want an outing," he called over his shoulder. "They're doing pleasure trips over there."

Trudi eyed the river with regret. How lovely it looked, with its glassy reflections and its oh-so-green banks.

"Thanks!" shouted Hamish and redirected his troupe. "Come on then. We'll find the canal. It's only a few streets away, the other side of the Infirmary. *Everybody* goes on the river. It's a bit common, so this will be better. I should have thought of it before."

"I come this way for my eye exam," observed Pedro, as they left the park behind and, dodging the traffic, passed the Infirmary building. Ahead lay a quieter district. Here the grand city architecture gave way to small, brick, residential terraces with privet hedges and sleepy cats on window-sills. An antiquated charm pervaded. There were still the ubiquitous bicycles chained to every gate and railing, but the place seemed deserted. Weeds grew between slabs. Notices for dances and lunch-time concerts, long gone, faded gently on sunny walls.

"Look!" said Trudi with sudden excitement. "There's an old-fashioned phone box!"

Sure enough, a quaint, red-painted kiosk, completed the vintage look.

Hamish marched on. "It's part of the conservation scheme I expect."

"But I haven't seen one for ages!" This was not strictly true, for Pinkney had retained one on its village green, but Trudi dropped to a dawdle, then stopped altogether and coolly announced.

"I'd like to make a call."

"What? *Why?* You've got a phone, haven't you?"

251

"But I'd like to make a call from there, for old time's sake." She was squinting against the sun, trying to read his face. The boys kept quiet.

What was it Sister Bianca had said about behaving strangely? And what ought he to do? Indulge her? Or try to be firm? If they arrived too late they would miss the canal trip, so this delaying tactic made no sense. Trudi *wanted* to go on the water. Perhaps it was best to play her along. In a couple of hours she would be back with her father and then safely home in Sussex and Hamish could wash his hands forever of the charge.

He had set his sights on the Dolomites for the summer and promised himself long, blue days, climbing alone. In solitary evenings, when he should have been revising, he had been perfecting his rock-climber's grappling-iron harpoon and the Dolomites would be the perfect place to test his invention. It might even bring him much-needed money if he could patent the idea before some thieving competitor stole it...

"I can't imagine it will work," he grumbled, returning to the present. "They never do, you know. It may not even take money."

"What do I need? A pound?"

"Are you going to speak for *ages?*"

"Maybe."

She held out her hand, this time with a smile. "Daddy will pay you back. I'll explain it all to him."

Hamish shook his head and gave her a selection of coins, then made a speechless sign to the boys and they all crossed the road together. "Don't..." he faltered. "Don't do anything rash, will you Trudi, like phoning the Fire Brigade."

Trudi gave an incredulous laugh. "Why would I want to do that?" But she was acting a part and it showed. "Don't stand where you can hear me," she commanded, and slipped through the door.

Please, Barbara, please, please, please pick up the receiver! I know Mummy will be at the Tranquillity Clinic, but you must be there, you must! And how does this horrible contraption work?

Inside the box the air smelt of grease and worse. People had scratched graffiti on the steel panels which once contained instructions. Trudi lifted the receiver, and followed the directions on the pay-phone screen instead: Insert Coins. They all promptly fell out at the bottom. From where she stood she could see

Hamish's long legs stamping up and down outside. *Please, please work!* She posted her money again and this time got a dialling tone. *Hurrah! Oh, heavens! What was the number? 01213 748462... ringing... ringing... Please, Auntie Barbara, hurry!*

"Hullo?"

"Auntie Barbara?"

"Hey, Trudi! How are *you?*" No mistaking those juicy American vowels.

"Auntie Barbara, listen, I haven't got much time,"

"Are you okay, honey?"

"I'm fine. But I've discovered something terrible going on here. Auntie Barbara, there's a huge plot to destroy us. That's why Grandfather Larsson disappeared. He told me, but it was a secret. I can't tell you everything now, but Olaf Stromberg is at the bottom of it and they steal people's ideas - that's why Mincke's house burnt down and you lost the bookshop and now they've kidnapped Corky and Daddy and they're going to set fire to the convent. Olaf was here, messing about with the computers and Jurgen has been giving him information on his Laser Wag phone so Beery O'Leary is in danger - Auntie Barbara you must go and see him and warn him not to let them into his house because they want his mead and when they want something they will do anything to get it. It's deadly serious, but I can't tell anyone but you..."

"Hold it, girl, hold it!" cried Barbara.

"There isn't time, because the money's running out..."

"Well give me your number!"

"I can't. I'm in a phone box and it's all scratched off."

"Is somebody with you?"

"The boys and Hamish. The boys know, but I'm not sure about Hamish. He might be a spy. I don't think he is, but you can't tell. I trusted Sister Bianca but then she brought Olaf back to the Convent..."

"First, listen to me," Barbara decided to be firm. "Corky and your father are fine. I've spoken to them both on the phone this afternoon. Corky has got a lovely room in the convalescent home and you are going to visit him tomorrow. And your father has had some very good news. They were so pleased with his lecture this morning, this Maximus Blight person has offered him an extra research post studying environmental stress in Pinkney Forest.

253

They've gone out there right away to see the site. He's not kidnapped at all. He's coming back tomorrow and in the mean time you are all going to stay with that nice Mr. Brambling. So honey," she raised the pitch of her voice, "You have got to stop panicking and calm down. No one is going to hurt you. I know it's confusing to be in a strange place when you don't quite understand what is going on, but you have to trust the people who care for you."

Trudi replied with a horrified silence.

"Honey?"

"You don't believe me!"

"I didn't say that."

"You're like all the others, you don't believe me!"

"Trudi!"

The line abruptly failed. Barbara tried to trace the number, but in vain. Then she sat down on the stairs and thought hard. For the moment she felt infected by Trudi's urgency. Should she contact Sven, or Kirsten, or the convent, or the police? When a child makes a call for help one has to act immediately. But she did not know where Trudi was exactly, and the danger she spoke of, vague and suspect as it sounded, concerned others not herself. Barbara's reassurances regarding Sven and Corky were, by contrast, perfectly valid. She had indeed heard from both of them within the hour and both had seemed happy and optimistic about their news.

No, the danger for Trudi might be her own over-active imagination. Hamish would take good care of her, but he might not appreciate the depths of grief her little mind was suffering over the loss of her grandfather, or the capacity for rage and mutiny her spirit harboured over the simplest of injustices. She did not for one moment consider Trudi mad, as she feared her own mother did. She would not for worlds put the authorities on her trail. But her heart yearned for the child. She wanted to enfold her in her buxom arms and reassure her.

By the time she had sat long enough to feel stiff, she had come to a decision. She would leave a note for Kirsten, and she would pack an overnight bag and take the coach for Kingsbury. Then she could see for herself, under pretext of visiting Corky, just what was going on. She could bring the children home with her, out of danger. There! She was beginning to sound like a conspirator already! Yet the longer she considered Trudi's ramblings, the more she found a sympathetic logic in them.

She herself felt distinctly uneasy to learn that Olaf Stromberg had resurfaced. In her own mind the man remained a villain. She was quite certain that he had destroyed her bookshop and his interest in the Larssons seemed both dubious and repellent. The thought that he had some hand in Corky's fate only added to her misgivings. If Olaf Stromberg meant to harm anyone dear to Barbara, he would certainly regret it. Barbara pushed up her sleeves as though relishing the thought of a fight. There were outstanding scores to settle and if she could run that fox to earth she would give him such a drubbing he wouldn't sit down for a week!

As for Beery O'Leery, she knew of the man and his house. She had several times seen a reluctant Jurgen being carted there for music lessons. Perhaps she would, just out of curiosity, pay him a visit and see if there was any truth in Trudi's claims. Then to Kingsbury – and her vowed retribution!

Meanwhile Trudi, her heart pounding with the conviction that now even Barbara had failed her, hung up the receiver and redoubled her determination. She would build a wall of bricks around her heart, so that no one could touch her. She would fight on to the last breath in her body. When she emerged from the telephone box, her voice was steady, her eyes gave nothing away.

"Well?" If Hamish hoped for an explanation, he did not get one.

Trudi tipped the change back into his palm. "My friend wasn't there," she lied. "She'd gone out, so I left a message. Everything is fine now." She shot a loaded glance at Jurgen and Pedro.

"So are you satisfied about the phone box?"

"Yes thank you," Trudi could be utterly infuriating. "I don't think they're really worth preserving. It was very smelly in there." She would never tell anyone that she had been fobbed off so shamefully. In any case, it was better by far for the boys to believe Barbara was on their side. Otherwise they might back out. "Which way is the canal now?" She put the matter behind her.

"Due west," replied Hamish. "Follow the setting sun in the afternoon and keep the pole star on your right at night. Watch the sky. That way you can navigate, even if something happens to your compass!"

"My Grandfather can do it – *could* do it," Trudi corrected herself.

"For all their scientific progress that's how mariners still steer a course at sea. Using the stars to work out their position. But you don't have to be at sea to do it."

"What you do when is cloudy?" asked Pedro.

"Use a Laser Wag, of course," joked Jurgen. "Satellite navigation! You find it. It finds you!" He had spoken without thinking and caught Trudi's eye too late.

"But you haven't got your Laser Wag on *now,* have you, Jurgen?"

Jurgen shrugged.

"We don't want it on *now,* because we're going on a secret adventure. It will spoil it all if *everyone* knows where we are going!"

Jurgen fumbled in his pocket and produced the offending device. There were three missed messages from Zub. *"Where are you? Text me! Are you okay?"* He reluctantly turned the power off.

"If we get lost, you can save us, Jurgen," promised Hamish. Thank God, he could see the gate to the towpath ahead.

'CANAL TRIPS ON A GENUINE GLOUCESTER NARROW BOAT' read the sign in bold lettering. 'DEPARTURE TIMES: *View the Splendours of Kingsbury: every hour, 10a.m.-4p.m. Round Trips to Pinkney: 11 a.m., 1 p.m. and 3 p.m.*"

Foxgloves nodded by the booking office door.

"'Fraid you've just missed that one," said the man at the window. "And the *Splendours of Kingsbury* is off today. Albert's got the 'flu."

"Damn! Is there nothing else at all?"

The ticket-vendor shook his head. "They're the only two licensed craft. I'm packing up now anyway." He peered out at the disappointed faces of the children and suddenly took pity. "You could try walking up to the moorings," he muttered. "Don't say I sent you, but some bloke turned up there the other day, offering unofficial trips. It's really not allowed. More than my job's worth to tell you. But if you ask up there, you might be lucky. He's a genuine sort - take you on as private guests, maybe. There's nothing the company can do about that. Look for a foreign boat, nicely done up, with a roof garden and all. German I think... You

256

want the old boy in the fisherman's cap!" This last was called from the doorway. Funny little party they looked, trotting solemnly away.

The moorings lay about fifty metres upstream, beyond the lock. The land opened out into meadows on either side with a lagoon large enough for boating; a picture-book scene, dotted with pollard willows and toy cattle grazing. Diminutive figures strolled about exercising their dogs. It all felt very Dutch. To the south, the spires of Kingsbury shimmered blue on the horizon. In a shallow basin, about twenty five boats of all descriptions lay docked in separate berths and here sailors and boaters briefly mixed together. Behind the towpath, a channel fed into the lagoon. Members of the sailing club had their own chalet clubhouse there with a landing beach, and their white sails blinked out on the water. Larger vessels were confined to the canal side, where a sign warned overnight visitors to register and pay their mooring fee. Trudi counted off rich, fibre-glass pleasure-cruisers, one or two decorated barges, a wherry with a red sail, house-boats, characterised by their old garden chairs and washing on deck and last of all, a green-painted hulk with flower pots, and a smoking chimney. A figure in a shapeless jacket stooped over a cooking pot, peeling potatoes.

"You wanted an adventure." said Hamish. "Well here we go. *He* won't quote us health and safety!" He cleared his throat and called out casually: "Afternoon! Lovely place to stop." Just like Sven, he had the ability to talk to anyone, anywhere, and get off immediately on the right foot. The old man put down his potato and blinked.

"Ay," he nodded. "That it is!"

"We heard you offered trips on the canal. We've missed the last run to Pinkney."

"Not me, governor. That wouldn't be allowed. You need a permit for trips. You're welcome to come aboard though and have a look around. I'm off to Pinkney myself shortly. I could give you a lift..." his weather-beaten face creased in a smile, "...if that's the way you want to go."

"And back again?"

"Soon as I've got what I need."

"Would we be back for five? I have to get the children home for tea."

"Wouldn't want to miss yer tea now, would you?"

That seemed to settle the formalities. "How would we pay you?"

"No payment between friends. I'm here any time for those who need me." He gave a long look at Trudi, seeking out her eye. "Know what I mean?"

She didn't, but she took a liking to him. He had brown, leathery hands and dust-covered shoes. He belonged to the unofficial world of people like Scarp, who took life as they found it – far from the soap and polish of Stromberg's sort. He pulled up a broad gangplank, one end of which he passed across to Hamish on the shore.

"Come aboard and welcome. Welcome to the *Mayfly*."

"Is that its name?"

"*Her* name, young miss. Boats like to be treated with their due deference. Otherwise it hurts their feelings, see?"

Pedro giggled.

"Why *'Mayfly'*? What is mayfly?"

"Little creature you find on the rivers in May. They're never around very long. They dance over the water for a while, and then they're gone. That's me and my boat. Here today, gone tomorrow."

"Like a gypsy," mused Trudi, still thinking of Scarp.

"It's the best of lives. Canals take the flattest route you see, so there's always a sunrise or a sunset coming or going and time is slow. You can't hurry a narrow boat and you can't hurry a lock. You have dinner when you're hungry and you go to bed when you're tired."

"Don't you get bored?" asked Jurgen

"No, because the world's always changing. You've always got new neighbours, new folk to meet. Like you now. Who would have guessed you would turn up just when you did? Now we're off to Pinkney. Another day there'll be another adventure. Mind your heads now."

Putting a hand on the cabin roof, he ducked and disappeared down some wooden steps.

"Come on in. There's not much room."

They piled in after him, dazed at first by the change in light, for the cabin, panelled in dark wood, had the feel of a refuge-hole. This was a place to sleep and hide-up during a storm. It had a sleek, black stove on legs, a narrow bunk and a table built in under the window. Pictures of sea ships and fancy rope knots adorned the walls. The curtains were made of gingham and an array of brilliantly polished brass fittings and pots winked from every shelf and rail.

"It *is* like a gypsy caravan!" marvelled Trudi, remembering Scarp's old home in the woods.

"The new barges are different," continued the old man. "They've got sitting rooms, wardrobes, kitchens, televisions... We're just basic, see? But my engine is just as good as theirs – better even – makes a nicer sound, and I have all I need. Herbs growing up there. Geraniums. I've even got tomatoes in tubs."

"It's beautiful!"

"She!" he insisted. "She's a beauty, all right. What about you? You from these parts?"

"We're from all over," laughed Hamish. "Pedro is from Peru, Trudi and Jurgen are from Sussex, but they're also Swedish and I'm a Scot, as you can tell by my accent. Yourself?"

"I'm from far away." A wistful note entered his voice and his eyes, hidden beneath their bushy brows, grew moist.

A wolf note! thought Trudi, *he is like Mincke, like all who have lived long and seen much, a man with hidden resonances.*

"You can call me, Old Tom, if you like. Now we'll go back on deck and I'll start her up. You can sit on the roof and watch the view. No running mind. I don't want to end up in the canal, fishing one of you out!"

Old Tom stood at the helm then, watching the length of the boat before him, and the children scrambled up amongst the geraniums and lavender and sat with their legs dangling. Hamish squeezed himself alongside and as the engine whirred into life and began its rhythmic thrumming, they gave one another excited smiles. How fortunate that all their plans had gone wrong, for this was immeasurably better than hiring a silly rowing boat! The *Mayfly* offered an entirely new way to see the world, with upside-down trees in the water, floating cows on the banks and a travelling garden which visited its bees. Like an old fashioned snuff box, its plain exterior concealed treasures within. A place for surprises. An idyll.

Trudi quietly surrendered to the moment. She forgot about Olaf and Barbara and the computer at St. Lucy's. With a sigh of relief, she found she had left all her anxieties on shore. They would have to be taken up again of course on her return, but just now nothing practical could be done about them and the thought made her glad. The air surrounding the Mayfly had grains of magic in it and they were to be savoured long and slow.

"This is paradise!" she called back, over the murmur of the engine. "It's perfect. Just *perfect.*"

"I hope not," replied Old Tom.

"Hope *not? Why?*"

"Because I like things natural. And nothing in nature is perfect. Look at any flower, any leaf, any fly, look at your hand even. They are living things. And how do you know? Because they are never the same from one moment to the next and they are never perfect. Every petal has a little scratch on it, or a little bite out of it, every fly, if you look close enough, has some crumple in its wing. Your own young body will be scarred in some way." (Funny he should say that.) "That's the signature of life. You'll never find a perfect snowflake in nature. Beware of anyone who says you can."

"What about a lettuce?" asked Trudi.

"Couldn't be no such thing. It would be an aberration."

"Even if it could feed the starving?"

"If a lettuce can't feed a slug, how can it feed you?"

"Magic!" said Jurgen

Old Tom tutted with such vehemence he might as well have spat. "Something that is truly *perfect* can't change, can't die. And if it can't die, it can't live neither. You are right about this being paradise. But paradise was never perfect. Or perhaps we don't use the right words. Paradise is a place that is simply more alive than anywhere else."

"What about stones then," said Jurgen. "They can't die. Can they be perfect?"

"No one truly knows if a stone can live. Them as built Stone Henge probably thought they could. And what about the trolls in Norway? We hardly know what happens in the heart of a stone, and even a scientist would struggle to tell you. But they know that stones don't stand still. They are a mass of dancing atoms, with their own secret laws and reasons. They are as alive as the stars over your head, the great spiralling galaxies we all come from."

"That's true," Hamish agreed. "I'm a scientist. I'll second that."

"In old culture of my country they believe that stones have special power to help us here on earth. Wiraqocha, god of fire could send magic stones, called *thunderstones* from the sky. For the Inca, they were the most sacred thing you could imagine. They would not give them to the Spanish - not for anything..." Pedro was sitting up, taking note, his high, flat cheek bones clear cut in the sun. For the first time he seemed to want to participate in what was going on.

Suddenly they were all talking, all arguing, just like the old days in the Larsson kitchen back home, with Corky spouting philosophy and Barbara chipping in as she served up some irresistible confection.

"Oh darn!" Trudi could almost hear her say. *"The pavlova's gone soggy. Why would that happen?"*

"I'll eat it anyway," murmurs Scarp from the corner where he is slouched, one plimsolled foot crossed over on his knee.

"We'll all eat it anyway!" decrees Professor Saxmund, tugging his beard. *"Won't we, Per?"*

And there is Grandfather Larsson, quietly nodding and winking, accepting a glass of aquavit from Sven. And Kirsten, her lovely mother, shaking her head at all the mess and smiling, as only she could smile when she was happy...

The phantoms faded as quickly as they came, but grains of pleasure, fine as pollen, lingered in the air, and quickened the senses and Trudi closed her eyes, rolling a sample on her tongue like a wine taster, separating the notes: sweetness, and a bittersweet undertone; something rough and woody, smelling of earth and a salty, pungent body note, reminiscent of tears. Dear ghosts, don't go...

They had left the flood meadows behind and now passed through farmland with little copses here and there. The red roofs of new houses peeped across the cornfields, where lines of lorries on the Pinkney road trundled along like ants. Busy life, coming from nowhere, going to nowhere... The afternoon drifted idly by. One or two holiday barges passed them, but otherwise they had the canal to themselves. They slipped along, quiet as fugitives.

When a rim of woodland appeared, Trudi began to recover her bearings.

"Does the canal pass Pinkney Forest?" she asked.

"Cuts straight through," said Old Tom. "But you can't see it from the boat."

"Can't?"

"They've put up that high boarding they use on motorways to keep people out. There's a lock, just before the Forest begins. Most people turn around there."

"Will we turn around there?"

"Most probably. You don't feel welcome further on."

"My Daddy's going to work there," said Trudi carelessly, her mind temporarily distracted.

Hamish shot up from his sprawling position.

"What?"

Now she had to think fast. "Sister Bianca told me. They've offered him a job as a researcher there. He's gone to look at it now. He's in there, somewhere."

The mysterious, blue line had spread and now blanketed most of the distant view. A lot of pine, Trudi thought, and oak. Perhaps they had oak disease in there – that's why they asked him.

"I wish I had known," murmured Hamish. "I could have told him some things."

"Is it really dangerous there?"

Hamish laughed. "Of course not! Just a bit creepy for the likes of me. Nothing to frighten your father!"

"Do people die in there?" asked Jurgen, ghoulish to the last.

"No, they don't! They look at insects. You can learn almost everything about the state of the world from insects."

Yes, thought Trudi, Mincke knew that.

The *Mayfly* slowed to a crawl as they entered busier water. On the right stood a cottage with a red, painted door, and tubs of daisies and petunias dotted along the front. The towpath widened at this point like a railway platform, with benches and litter bins provided. Across the water, a pub, nestling between the trees, advertised home-made lemonade and 'free meals for kids'. The place felt like a terminus. Ahead lay the machinery of the lock and figures were scrambling about, turning wheels and calling directions to a vessel that must lie on the other side.

Old Tom leapt neatly off the boat and inspected the nearest gate. Then he pulled a pair of binoculars from his pocket and scanned the scene. It all looked very jolly and intriguing. Hard to turn back without knowing what lay beyond.

"Funny," murmured Hamish. "I thought this place was closed up."

But Old Tom returned, ready to get back to his supper and his solitude. He steered deftly into a loop of water that served as a turning space and re-emerged facing south.

"Pinkney lot," he muttered. "Think they can improve nature. Super-moths, bionic bees, unicycle worms... It will come to no good. Mark my words."

"Sounds cool!" said Jurgen, imagining a performing maggot. "I'd like a unicycle worm."

"What is it?" Pedro leant forward.

"Don't rightly know," Old Tom began backing off, but Hamish had heard of them too.

"Well, it's a worm that is genetically programmed to die."

"We all are!" objected Trudi

"No, but this worm can't breed. It is quite partial to eating ordinary worms, but that doesn't seem to matter too much because this worm is better. It is very strong and powerful and it can dig tremendous tunnels. It is immune to sprays and pesticides and a ton or two of these worms can plough a field in a couple of days. All organic, see. Marvellous. All the farmer has to do is buy in his worms at ploughing time and sit back and relax. They do all the work."

"But that is fantastic," admitted Trudi. "Corky could have used them on his nursery."

"Ah, but after a few days, the worms begin to die. In fact they all die. Not one survives. They can't lay eggs, you see. Their bodies make perfect fertiliser."

"So?"

"So next time the farmer wants to plough his field he has to buy more worms and they are very expensive."

"But if there are no eggs, how does the company make more worms?"

"*That* is the question, Trudi. How do they do it? How do they keep on producing identical things by the thousand and the million?"

"How?"

"If we knew that we would be as rich as Croesus."

For a moment she felt tempted to suggest the Toy Forge. Sir Maximus had said they could create anything there. If they could manufacture lettuces they could surely make worms. And a fleeting vision of Marina in her white coat, churning out worms from a giant pasta-machine, passed through her mind.

"Maybe Daddy will find out," said Jurgen optimistically.

"He'll find out something, assuredly."

The conversation lapsed and they completed the journey in thoughtful silence. Once back at the moorings, Old Tom bade them an affectionate goodbye.

"Keep your money, lad! As I said, I don't do anything for money. You look after those little ones, now. They're lucky to have you."

Down went the gangplank and he and Hamish helped the children ashore. Taking Trudi's hand in his, he guided her over the geranium troughs, and she noted with interest that his fist was disfigured by a ragged scar. A dog bite, maybe? What he said was true, then: *Time wrote its name on everything.* "That's it, darling. You jump down now and follow the others. And remember what I said. I'm here any time for friends that need me." His kindly eyes twinkled as Trudi descended and, on a whim, she reached up and kissed his cheek.

"Thank you for our taste of heaven," she whispered.

"What's the time? I'm afraid we've missed tea," Hamish strode ahead, retracing the route into town.

Jurgen automatically whipped out his phone. "Five thirty!" he shouted from the rear. There were missed calls from Olaf and more texts waiting from Zub:

"Jurgen, why won't you talk to me? You know, if you don't write to me, I will get ill and die. You don't want me to die, do you? Jurgen, please don't kill me! Please Jurgen, you're my only friend!"

For a moment his heart ached. Zub had been his constant companion and comfort for so long, it felt callous and cruel to abandon him. But he had to confess that Trudi's warnings worried him. Clearly she knew more than he did about the mysterious comings and goings of Olaf Stromberg. And Olaf had influence with Sir Maximus and between them they had his father at their beck and call. Jurgen tried to imagine Sven doing their bidding, battling through a forest of cyber insects. He didn't like it. No, Zub would have to go.

"Die, alien!" he pronounced as he hit the delete button and closed the mobile down.

When he caught up with the others they had joined a sightseeing crowd in Longmarket Street. Huge lorries and painted vehicles with cranes and trailers were rumbling into the city from the north. One after another, they trailed past, arresting every eye with their decorated panels. Now came a convoy of caravans, mostly chrome campers with satellite dishes, but one or two in the vardo-style, pulled by hefty four-by-fours.

"What's going on?" asked Trudi, mouth agape.

"Of course! It's the Fair," said Hamish. "Third week of June. My exams have been so late this year, I forgot all about term being over."

"What Fair?"

"Well... the Gooseberry Fair. They don't sell gooseberries any more. It's a fun fair now. But it has been going on here, June 22nd, every year since fourteen hundred and something. I think they set it up right here in the Longmarket. I've never seen it before. Well, you must visit and find out for yourselves. You must get someone to take you!"

Chapter Thirty

Two Kinds of Gold

Standing in the sun-blistered porch in Acacia Drive, Barbara wasted no time beating about the bush. "Are you Beery?" she asked as soon as the door opened an inch.

Fergus O'Leary took in with horror, the plump, over-heated figure on his doorstep.

"If you're from the Parents' Association..." he began, but Barbara cut him off.

"I'm *not* from the Parents' Association. Are you Beery?"

The cello master emerged to fill the doorway and drew himself up to his full, if insignificant height; then began again more formally, as if that would inject the necessary authority into his voice: "I can assure you, that if it is a matter of 'Health and Safety', I have got all my papers in order. The back step is being attended to, and I'm having the front paving fixed next week..."

"Beery, it's about the booze!" said Barbara.

Now he blustered: "It is purely for my own consumption. Sure a man can cook and prepare things in the privacy of his own home, or what's the world coming to! "

"*Did* you have a visit from a helpful Swedish gentleman, any time in the last month?"

"I have many visitors - and I must say -" Beery began to collect his thoughts, "that even if you are from the police, or the council drains department, I am not bound to answer questions from unidentified strangers on the doorstep!"

"Okay," Barbara backed off a little. "Okay, I'm sorry. I didn't introduce myself. I'm a well-wisher and here is my ID." She reached in her handbag and pulled out a sheaf of singed papers, the crumbling remains of a book. "*I* was visited by the said helpful Swedish gentleman a short while ago, and this is now what remains of my bookshop after the incendiary device he sent me reduced it all to ashes."

Beery shook his head dismissively, so she went on:

"Prospero's at Newbridge? You might have heard of it?"

"Yes, but…"

"Listen, I understand you have a passion. *I* had a passion. A great idea. Olaf Stromberg stole my idea, and destroyed every trace of it. My shop is now a gleaming new department of the BioDawn Supermarket and rumour in town has it that I burnt my own premises down because I couldn't face the competition! That man is a commercial spy, Beery, and very dangerous."

"Dear lady, you should go to the police," the Irishman faltered, feeling suddenly overwhelmed.

"The police?" Barbara laughed. "On what evidence? A dodgy dry rot cure for which I have no provenance? The deductions of an eleven year old schoolgirl who can't tell fact from fiction and is already under surveillance by a shrink! Oh yes. And I nearly forgot - the testimony of two elderly and forgetful gentlemen in Sweden, both of whom have vanished off the face of the earth!"

"I can't see how I can help you." Beery still considered denial his best line of defence.

"Listen, dunderhead," Barbara threw up her hands and a sprinkling of cinders showered the step, like confetti. "I'm here to help *you!* The girl in question is sister to Jurgen Larsson. Remember Jurgen, your star pupil? Bright little Jurgen, who saw your private brewery in there, and then spilled the beans about your enterprise to the BioDawn company? Now *did* you receive a visit from Olaf Stromberg?"

That hit home. Clutching the door-post, Beery turned an ashen colour himself. "I need a drink," he whimpered.

"So do I." Barbara pushed him firmly into the hall and marched through after him, shutting the door behind her with a bang. "And you'd better pour out something good, Beery. You're going to need it!"

∞∞∞∞∞∞∞∞∞∞∞

Back at St. Lucy's the nuns were saying Vespers, but they had left tea in the dining room, so Hamish and his party found mugs, kettle, bread and jam, all waiting in welcome on their return. Mr. Brambling, who had installed himself in one of the common room armchairs with a copy of *The Times*, now put in an appearance, eager to hear all about the afternoon's adventures.

267

"Well, I say!" he chuckled. "You could almost have walked to my cottage and saved me the trouble of coming to fetch you. And to think that your father was working so close by! It seems as though little Pinkney really does live up to its claims to be a place of *'global significance'*. I've always thought that was a whim of our more pretentious villagers. But of course, with all these new things happening, strangers arriving, the place is bound to change and it certainly seems to become busier every day. Pity really. I rather like it quiet. Of course I don't include *you,* dear friends, when I speak of strangers. *You* must always think of Pinkney as your home."

He beamed goodwill, adding: "Did you go through the lock?"

"No, no. It didn't seem worth the bother. And not too inviting on the other side."

"Very wise. I always find locks rather sinister places for all that they look so jolly. Such a force of water! I'm always afraid there will be an accident. But then I'm not a good swimmer ..."

"Can we see Corky today?" asked Trudi, rudely breaking the train of conversation.

"Today, my dear, he's resting. I visited after lunch and he's very comfortable. He has got a room overlooking the garden. He can see right out across the rooftops to the water meadows from that room. But the move has tired him and he has been advised to keep quiet today. Tomorrow I will take you and you shall see for yourselves how pleasant everything is."

"Can we go any time?"

"Best to make an appointment. The nurses are very busy. And rest is so much part of the cure." As usual the grown-ups had an answer for everything, but none of the children felt particularly reassured.

For this evening, with Sven away, it had been decided that the three of them would stay at Humbug Cottage together. Sister Emilia, even now giving thanks online for her deliverance from the computer virus, had left overnight things packed ready for Pedro and a slip of paper, warning Mr. Brambling to take special care of Trudi and they all climbed into his vintage motor as soon as tea was over.

Winding down her window, Trudi held out a formal hand: "Thank you, Hamish. It was a lovely afternoon."

268

"Ah, you daft lassie. My pleasure. My pleasure," he replied.

"Hamish," she held onto his fingers a moment longer and lowered her voice. "You will make sure that the fire doors are closed tonight, won't you? I don't want anyone to get hurt."

"You be a good girl now." He eyed her carefully. "I'll see you when you're back tomorrow. I'd like to visit Corky myself!"

"Bye!"

"Adios!"

"Adios!"

Their faces appeared fleetingly in the back window as they pulled out of the drive. Then they were lost to view.

Talk to Sister Bianca, Hamish determined, before packing up to go home.

∞∞∞∞∞∞∞

Rambler roses and honeysuckle sweetened the early evening air as the car drew up at Humbug Cottage. Trudi noted with some concern the hollyhocks she had flattened in her descent the night before. *Could it really have been only the night before? So much seemed to have happened in the last twenty-four hours and she could feel her lack of sleep catching up with her.* Perhaps he had not spotted the damage. Mr. Brambling made no comment. He was too busy, fumbling with his keys and fussing to put on the lights. The rooms were so dark indoors. And would they like him to light a fire, for the cottage felt cool? And were they hungry enough for supper yet?

He ushered them into the back parlour, where he had set up an antique magic lantern with slides for their amusement. He seemed excited with the toy himself and paused to demonstrate it before tying on an apron and bustling off to the kitchen to fry eggs.

"This one has been fitted with an electric lamp, you see. It's like an early film projector. You put the plates in here and – hey presto! – an image appears on the wall! You know, this was invented nearly four hundred years ago and perfected by a scholar-priest called Athanasius Kircher?"

"I know him," said Pedro. "Jesuit. Father Hieronimo tell about him."

Mr. Brambling clapped his hands. "Astonishing boy! Well, I am talking too much. I must let you play. But I can't help wishing I could have met your Father Hieronimo – We shared so many interests. There's a new statue to Kircher in Kingsbury, just outside St. Gregory's college. Well you might even have seen it! The poor man was ridiculed as a fraud for centuries and only now are people realizing just how brilliant he was. He wanted to gather all the knowledge in the world and save it. A global compendium! He wrote books on every subject from music to magnetism. Of course, he didn't always get things right – that's a lot to ask. But what an endeavour! He was an astronomer, mathematician, linguist, biochemist. And such a sense of humour. He built a special museum in Rome where he could frighten the visitors with hidden voices and ghostly apparitions from lanterns just like this. Yes, one of the giants. A collector's collector! Three eggs, did you say?"

Once he was gone, Pedro inspected every corner of the room, testing his new impressions against those he had formed when he was blind.

"Is smaller than I thought," he mused. "And very low roof. Like little cave. These floors I know, I could feel them before and over here is the museum, yes, where we look at Inca treasures. *He* is mad collector, too, right? Like Wallace Aardhof man in Kingsbury!" Since the trip on the canal, Pedro had found his tongue. Trudi gladly encouraged him - she hated to see him silent and dejected.

"Can you remember what they were?" It became a challenge, like the party game with things on a tray.

"Si, si, easy. Pottery from Peru. A little statue of Inca Sun God. And big, heavy bowl. Here on this shelf."

The three children crowded close to see. Trudi was surprised to find new additions to the display, including a honey pot exactly like the one she had seen that morning. The door of the cabinet stood ajar, and Pedro, who had already located Wiraqocha, opened it gently and reached inside, but before he touched the figure, his hand rested on the ceramic dish.

"Is this the one we saw before?"

Trudi and Jurgen nodded.

"Ju didn't say it was like this." His lip curled.

"I didn't like to," whispered Trudi. "I didn't want to think about it. What is it?"

"This," Pedro lifted the bowl and turned it so that they could see the rim of skulls more plainly. "This is something not good."

"But what?"

His voice dropped to a whisper. "This a Wari bowl. Wari people live before the Inca. Cruel, people. They build stone cities, like, how you say, like the lab... the laver... that herb thing in the garden here."

"The maze?"

"Si, si laverinth. No windows. Just prison walls and slaves work in the prison, doing all things for the rich people. They believe in the sun but they live in the dark. They live with the dead. And the dead sit in big tombs with open lids. This is the Black Magic I talk about before. They kill and no one knows why. They make magic wine and then they burn down the wine house. Why they want people's heads? To take what they know? They kill and they make bowls for blood. They are like bad bees. Working. Working. Building bigger and bigger, roads and cities. But bees love the sun and the Wari love the dark and death and gold only."

"Did Father Hieronimo tell you this too? What happened to them?" asked Jurgen.

"No one knows. They just disappear one day. But why does anybody want to keep *this*?"

They were so intent they did not hear the parlour door open again, so it was not until Mr. Brambling was almost upon them that they realized they had been observed. Startled, Trudi wheeled around and as she did so, she knocked the bowl from Pedro's hands. It fell to the floor, hit the corner of the hearth and shattered into a hundred pieces. All froze.

"Oh, Mr. Brambling. I very sorry!" stammered Pedro.

"No, *I* did it. It's *my* fault," said Trudi. "But we didn't mean any harm..."

Mr. Brambling stooped to pick up a couple of fragments. "Of course you didn't," he clucked, quite unperturbed. "It's good to be curious when you are young."

"But the bowl - it must be worth a fortune."

"Well yes. But money is not everything, you know. And if you like, I'll let you into a little secret. This is no ordinary bowl. It was given to me as a present and it has a very special, magic property. No matter how many times you break it, you can reconstruct it

271

again, if you have only the tiniest little bit left. Every part of it has a code inside, a blueprint a bit like DNA, which contains all the information you could ever need to recreate the whole."

Pedro had said that the Wari practised magic, but this seemed like real sorcery.

Mr. Brambling looked at their disbelieving faces and smiled. "I'll prove it to you, if you like! I'll have this bowl mended by tomorrow."

"How can you do it?" asked Trudi.

"Holograms. Holograms!" Mr. Brambling was laughing outright now, rubbing his hands on his apron. "A hologram is like the spectre of something real. It has all the secrets of the original stored inside it, yet it is proof against the ravages of time!"

"But this is not a hologram, Mr. Brambling," Trudi objected gravely. "You can't touch a hologram. And it has to be in a special tank, like the pianist at the Toy Factory, otherwise it can't work."

The old man beamed in delight. "I see you've done your homework. No, no this is, or rather *was* a real bowl, but the hologram of the original bowl is stored in a secret place and from that recipe you can make a thousand, or a million bowls and no one could ever tell which is the original! This one was not the original. Merely a copy. My friend who gave it to me will doubtless give me another if I ask him nicely. Now, toast." He banished the levity from his voice. "Do you prefer one or two slices?"

"And the honey jar?" persisted Trudi. "Is that a copy too?"

Mr. Brambling shot her a dark look, as if she tried his patience and then relented. He clearly was not used to the tenaciousness of children. "No, my dear, *that* is an original. So please don't try dropping that one! Now, let us leave all this and go into the kitchen where it is warmer. I'll clear things up later, while you have your baths. You must be tired after such a long day." Attentive as a mother hen, he ushered the children out of the parlour. And in truth he was right. After the first few mouthfuls of supper, they began to yawn and rub their eyes and they hardly remembered how they got to bed.

Some hours later, Jurgen was roused from sleep by the familiar tinkle of his Laser Wag, playing its little tune. Heavens! He must have pressed the 'start' button by accident during the evening. In a rush of guilt, he tumbled out from under his duvet and began

272

groping around in the dark. Normally he kept his phone just by his pillow, but tonight he had forgotten all about it. Where on earth had he left it? Somewhere in the jumble of clothes he had discarded the night before? *Dear God, if you really want me to grow up and play the cello, please don't let Trudi hear this. She will certainly kill me!* By the time he located the offending device the ringing had stopped. An on-screen update announced another voicemail from Olaf. But Jurgen felt too tired to deal with that. Whatever could the man want to say at this hour? Besides, Olaf had been so unfriendly, he did not deserve an answer. He tossed the thing aside and slept till morning.

Chapter Thirty-One

Missed Call

Before breakfast however, his curiosity got the better of him, and he opened his message.

It wasn't at all what he expected. For one thing, there were *two* voices: Olaf and somebody else. And they were in the middle of a private conversation, clearly unaware that they were being recorded. Jurgen soon worked out what had happened. Olaf must have been busy talking to a friend and unintentionally pressed the re-dial button on his phone. It was easy enough to do if you forgot to lock your keypad. Jurgen himself had made a similar mistake only yesterday. Once activated, the Laser Wag had automatically called its last contact number, which happened to be Jurgen's. The voicemail recorder had done the rest. By the muffled quality of the sound, he guessed that the phone was tucked inside a pocket, but the anxiety and urgency in Olaf's voice came through loud and clear:

"I'm going to have to move faster than that. This last case didn't go well and I've got a black eye to show for it. If I don't mop up the rest of them in the next twenty-four hours the whole scheme could be blown apart."

"Olaf, my dear chap, calm yourself, please."

"I assure you I was never calmer. Twenty-four hours, Brambling. You must give me the girl or I can't answer for the consequences. Bring them all, by force, if necessary."

The second speaker gave an unmistakable chuckle: "You know how I deplore the use of force. I couldn't possibly violate the trust those children have put in me, so you can bluster all you like. There are more important things at stake here and my heart is set on those. You *must* be patient."

"Then come alone. Meet me at the Beedome, tomorrow. There is no time now for preferences and principles. The entire *Beehive Cluster* is at stake. And I won't let you jeopardize the project over a private matter like this. Do you understand? "

"And what shall I do with the children?"

"Leave them at the convent for now, if need be. There are plenty there to take care of them. But I *will* have them and soon. They can't be left at large. And nor, for your safety, can you."

"You are a very harsh and insensitive man, Olaf. I might almost say a bully," Mr. Brambling complained.

The other steadied his voice: "Tomorrow, St. John. Get rid of the children and come tomorrow afternoon. I'll have emptied the flat by then. I'll be waiting for you."

At this point the mailbox ran out of memory. Jurgen sat a moment, stunned in disbelief, then leapt up and, collecting Pedro from his room, took the phone to Trudi. And Trudi, enthroned on her pillows, like Boudicca in her chariot, heard the news with an imperious air.

"I *told* you! I *told* you!" she crowed. "Well now we must save Mr. Brambling. He's trying to defend us, but he has no idea of the danger he's in himself. If he goes to the Beedome alone, he will be lost, like Mincke and Corky, for whatever they do there, I'm sure it's something very bad, or why is it all so secret? We can't tell him we've heard this. He would be too shocked if he thought we had been eavesdropping, but we *must* try to ward him off!" They would need to act swiftly. She spread her hands on the coverlet, gravely considering the pattern, as if it was a plan of campaign. The boys, impressed, looked on. "We'll play Olaf along - be good, be clever, but keep watch" she said at length, "...and I will devise something." Then she added for effect: "He won't take us alive!"

Mr. Brambling had risen early and, donning his bee-suit and gloves, pottered out into the garden to inspect the hives. When anything troubled him he resorted to the time-honoured custom of confiding in his bees and just now he felt a little anxious and the scent of the dew-laden herbs and the contented hum of the colonies within their skeps acted as a soothing tonic. The workers busied in and out, trusting him, as they trusted that each day would bring them sunshine and flowers. Their chambers would soon be full of fragrant honey and in a week or two the harvest could begin. What a wonderful thing it was, this partnership between man and nature! He went on caring for his hives and they went on toiling for him until all their labours were complete, never doubting or suspecting for a moment the one secret they could not be told. For, of course, it would not do at all for them to understand what 'harvest' really meant. Harvest, for them, would signify something quite momentous. It would mean the end of all striving forever more. Eternal rest…

Death.

This year, Mr. Brambling felt a sense of finality for himself, as well. As he got older, the delight he took in his garden increased until it swallowed up nearly all his attention and he had to bully himself into fulfilling his duties and obligations elsewhere. If paradise was already here, what could all the other fuss signify? But such solitary pleasure promoted a selfish frame of mind. And Mr. Brambling took a larger view. If the bees had anything to teach him, it was the principle of self-sacrifice. Community first! They would always lay down their lives in the defence of their hive. And for Mr. Brambling 'the hive' meant the whole world. Yes. One must serve that, whatever the personal cost. So these sunny days amongst his herbs held the poignant bitter-sweetness of last things. If all went as he anticipated, this would be the last summer not only for the bees, but for himself as well, and who knew what would become of the house and the flowers then?

For a moment his sentiments made him blink and he caressed the shining skeps with the back of his hand. Then he turned away, forcing his mind to more practical concerns.

Trudi met him on the terrace.

"Up early! Up early!" he beamed, lifting off his hat and veil and shaking his head free.

"Mr. Brambling," Trudi pitched her voice rather high, trying to sound spontaneous. "We wondered if we could go on a picnic today with you."

"My dear child, what a wonderful idea! But I am afraid I have tedious things to do today. Not at all interesting for children. Besides, you are going to visit Corky." He slipped his hands out of his clumsy gloves.

"But *after* that. Oh do please say you'd come. I'm sure…"

"No, no, alas, I have already given my word. One can't go back on that, you know! You children must stay at St. Lucy's until I get back for you. I have business here in Pinkney today."

"*Not* at the Beedome!" Trudi dropped all artifice.

Mr. Brambling stood astonished. "The Beedome?"

"Don't go, Mr. Brambling. It's too dangerous. If only you knew! If only you knew what I know about Olaf Stromberg, you wouldn't trust him any more!"

The old man put up his hand and stroked Trudi's shining hair.

"Why, my dear, you're all upset! We can't have that, can we? And whoever told you I am going to the Beedome?" He paused a moment and his eyes narrowed as he tried to work it out.

"Well, *nobody* told me," Trudi stammered. "Sometimes I just know things."

Mr. Brambling, resting his hand now on her shoulder, searched her upturned face. "Yes. I know you do. That is a gift from your family."

"From my grandfath...er..." Trudi began and then bit the words back.

"Exactly." The grey eyes smiled. "What a wonderful man. If only we knew where he was... He would be so proud of you. But you know, Trudi, we people who know things sometimes have to keep quiet about what we know. Ordinary people do not always understand. Most people do not understand about the Beedome. How could they? It is a great secret. No need for others to know. We can keep that to ourselves." Now he was speaking in riddles and she lost his drift.

"Mr. Brambling," Trudi tried a different tack. "The pottery bowl that we broke last night. You said it was a gift."

"So I did."

"Was *that* from Olaf? Olaf Stromberg?"

"Do I know this man?"

"He was looking at things in the Wallace Aardhof house when we went there yesterday. The honey jar in the museum was *just like* your honey jar. He's a thief, Mr. Brambling. He stole Auntie Barbara's bookshop. And he stole Mincke's stories. He's a bad man. You can't, you *mustn't* trust him."

She wanted to take hold of his hands and make him promise, as she would have done with Per. But something prevented her. Some reserve chilled the air between them. Perhaps she had caused offence.

"Oh, child, you are so young and bright and full of loving intentions. That is your beauty, dear Trudi. And you are perfect just as you are. In fact it would be a crime for you to grow old and

277

change. But I *am* old and I can see and understand a little further than you. You must not worry your pretty head about such matters. Leave the Beedome and the bunglers who meddle with it to crusty creatures like me. Do not fear. I am well able to deal with them. *Trust the day*."

He propelled her firmly back towards the cottage. "And let us return to the safety of the kitchen before Mordred wakes up and chases us." As they reached the door he shook off the last of his solemnity. "Now breakfast. Orange juice? And would you like a pancake?"

He has made up his mind, thought Trudi, *and he leaves us no alternative. We shall simply have to follow and save him in spite of himself!*

Chapter Thirty-Two

A Rebel on the Loose

When you are a child, you are not supposed to follow your own nose. Others are there to plan for you, make decisions, oversee your games and activities, in short, to keep you out of mischief. For when you are a child, mischief means whatever you think up for yourself and do without asking. Even the simplest, most innocent things - experimenting with the bathroom soap, say, or picking off the wallpaper, digging mines in the strawberry bed... writing secret messages in books... taking the wrong way home to spy on a creepy house... *all* will surely meet with dismay and disapproval. And the more attentive your elders and betters, the more they will strive to protect you from such enterprises.

In the past, Trudi had taken a positive pleasure in the way her life was organized for her. She loved to have her clean socks ready at the end of her bed in the morning and her packed lunch waiting in its little pink case. She relished going to extra dancing lessons and swimming coaching after school and she even enjoyed her homework, ticking off her tasks and collecting her grades. Despite the odd prank with friends, she hardly knew the meaning of disobedience – a girl without detentions... All until last summer, when she had discovered a hidden dimension to life. This secret life did not feature on her weekly wallchart; had no place in the school curriculum; seemed to be frowned upon by all and sundry. But it beckoned all the sweeter for that and dragged Trudi into a whirlpool of subversive thoughts.

Even before Per talked to her about the stars at Christmas, she had begun to listen with longing to the whispers of this withinside world. It had a far-off hum - what Beery O'Leery would have called a resonance, a note - and this 'note', humming away like an inner tuning fork, gave her the pitch of other things around her. When they jarred, out of tune, she lost interest in them, regardless of whether the world approved or not. She began to question the ready-made assumptions of life. She delved instead into ancient mysteries. She cultivated an independent spirit. People thought her crazy, but the habit stuck.

As time went on, she cleared a secret corner in her head, a kind of priest's hole. And here she collected whatever hints or clues might bring that 'other' reality closer. For of one thing she was certain. Out there, somewhere just the other side of knowing, lay a magical homeland, a Great Beyond. Her grandfather called it Nowhere. He had lived there all his life. But she wanted to see it too. Of course the World did not recognize the sanctity of any priest's hole and threatened to swamp it every day with all the débris that was routinely brought in on the tide. Trudi exhausted herself with tossing this rubbish out. No doubt she made mistakes. Sometimes she cleared out things she needed. Sometimes she clung too literally to advice she had been given: *"follow this"*, *"hold on to that"*. But what else could one expect? She was alone and had no one to remind her of the wisdom she had forgotten in her cradle: *There is no fixed route to freedom.* She had been searching for a literal path, with signposts and stiles to help her on her way, but of course visionaries, real freedom-seekers like the noaïdis Per spoke of, they found pathways everywhere.

How else did the Sami shamans walk out of prison? They did not have a ladder to the starry sky. They made themselves small, so small they could ride to liberty on a grain of dust, and so quiet they could hear the wolves calling from beyond the ends of the earth. That reindeer with the faraway eyes at the Christmas Fair, doubtless she could hear them. That was why she had looked so sad.

When the wolf-song fell silent in the Swedish forest, did that mean the wolves had truly vanished? Or simply that Per could no longer hear them? *He* did not wait to seek advice. He set off straightaway to find the answer.

Now it was Trudi's turn. The time had come for her to strike out too and never mind about the rules. All she knew was that she must keep Mr. Brambling in sight. He believed he could take on Olaf alone, but he clearly did not understand the danger he was in. He was going to need help. And if providing that help meant absconding from the safe, protective circle of carers and helpers who had always surrounded her, Trudi was ready. Jurgen and

Pedro would come if she led the way. And it would be a true adventure, better even than the lunar eclipse.

She tidied her room with particular care before she left, locking her box of treasures, along with the page of Mincke's manuscript, in her suitcase. But at the last minute she stuffed Per's special stone, for good luck, into her pocket. She would not take the shaman's belt. Per had told her that that was useless. Instead she picked out Mambo-Hambo's string, and wound it, like a bracelet round her wrist. If Corky seemed better, she would give it to him today.

After breakfast, Mr. Brambling selected a book of crossword puzzles and a jar of lemon curd for the invalid and drove the children to St. Lucy's, where Mrs. Sparks greeted them, duster in hand.

"Sisters are at prayers, but you come in, my loves. It's nice and sunny in the common room, or you can go through into the garden."

"Thank you, Mrs. Sparks." Mr. Brambling clutched his hat to his chest. "We've brought some gifts for Corky. Is young Hamish about? I believe he wanted to tag along."

"Oh, Sister Bianca too. She's made him a cake. Hamish is buzzing about somewhere, loading up to go home, I think."

Trudi felt a stab of disappointment at the news. Though she had never really confided in him, she still regarded Hamish as an ally and his presence gave her courage. Besides which, he wanted, more than anyone, to see the Beedome. It would be sad to have to go without him.

When he breezed in, it was clear that his mind was half-packed too.

"A well-earned vacation?" Mr. Brambling smiled.

"Dolomites!" came the reply.

"Que? What's Dolmites?" giggled Pedro.

"Mountains, Pedro. Like the Andes, only not quite so high. I'm practising for when I do the Himalayas with Trudi!" he winked in an off-hand way that Trudi found particularly hurtful. He knew very well that he would never take her to the Himalayas. But he could hardly understand how much she would like to go.

A shuffle of feet in the passage brought the Sisters out of chapel and back to their morning tasks. They looked, as always, solemn

281

and unapproachable until their sanctity wore off and they remembered how to laugh. They were like turtles: chapel made them chilly, but in the garden sun they soon warmed up again. Trudi wondered, looking at their clumsy feet and coarse summer habits, did they also ride to heaven on grains of dust? They certainly knew about silence.

Sister Bianca tucked back the forelock that escaped from her wimple and swung into the common room.

"All fit, are we?" She might have been leading them out to hockey.

"All fit!" Mr. Brambling struggled out of his armchair and drawing his gifts from his leather shopping bag, placed them in her hands. "Oh and these are for the house, somewhere here?" Shyly, he produced a bunch of roses.

"I'll put them by Sister Matilda's sewing table," she said without hesitation. "Then we'll all get the benefit. *Thank* you."

"Well, I must go. I have an appointment. More bees to attend to! Give my regards to Corky, won't you, and tell him I'm sure it won't be long now. And Trudi dear, no worrying. Remember our little talk. I'm trusting you to be a good girl and do the right thing! And then we can all look forward to being together again very soon, what?" His face shone and with this blessing he shuffled out into the hall, past Mrs. Sparks's mops and buckets and on to the waiting day.

Sister Bianca's eyes rested brightly on him till he was gone.

"He brings them every time, you know," she smiled, shaking her head. "Just for Sister Matilda really. Has done it for years."

"Does he *love* her, then?" asked Jurgen.

"He loves everyone," replied Bianca. "Everyone and everything!"

"Are we going?" Hamish sounded abrasive. He could not help thinking that eulogies were best saved for funerals. All this shilly-shallying about jarred on his nerves. If he was going somewhere he liked to get on, not stand dithering on the doorstep. Besides, he felt a sudden unease about his packing. Underneath his bluster, he had developed a real affection for his young friends and it bothered him to be leaving them at such short notice. Nothing in their lives had been satisfactorily resolved and by next term they would be gone forever and he would only hear at third hand, say, that Pedro had gone back to Peru and that Corky had got a pension.

As for Trudi, whatever would become of her?

The little band of well-wishers, deflated by his asperity, filed quietly out of the door.

At the entrance to Corky's nursing home they paused and rang the bell. Now they all felt jumpy. Even Sister Bianca, normally so plucky, quailed before the forbidding whiteness of the door. The Carmelite Convent nearby had a door just like this, which admitted people and then shut them in forever. That was an enclosed order.

How long, she wondered, before they got out of here?

The door opened and an iron-faced nurse in grey gave a peremptory nod. She had been warned to expect them. She admitted them to the hall, gesturing with her hands as if to say: *'Please don't touch the surfaces'*. An aseptic chill pervaded the place. They took in more pristine paintwork, and more doors, mostly closed, bearing shiny labels: *'Reception. Consulting Room. Clinical Waste'*. A tightly-stuffed, black-buttoned sofa kept guard beneath a sign which read *'Wait here'*, as if challenging anyone to dare.

The air reeked of disinfectant and - from somewhere deep within the house – the smell of boiled cabbage.

"We can go straight up," said the nurse. "Doctor has seen him already this morning."

They duly mounted a flight of stairs. Sunlight streamed in through high windows, hurting Pedro's eyes. Then came a corridor; gleaming grey linoleum and still more doors (all closed) with numbers and alarm bulbs overhead. And fire extinguishers. And voices from innumerable television sets, playing inside the rooms. A tiny Philippino girl struggled past, pushing a washing trolley twice her size.

"The patients use the garden in the afternoons."

They peered from a landing window at lawns previously glimpsed from the garden gate below.

"That's nice." Bianca winced at herself. What a dreadfully trite thing to say, but she could think of nothing better.

"And your friend is in here. Twenty minutes. He's not to be tired."

"Gulag matron!" hissed Hamish as the woman receded and turned a corner. Bianca met his eyes with a despairing smile.

"He *can't* stay here!" she whispered.

But Hamish, for once, seemed lost for words and gave a hapless shrug.

Corky's emaciated figure sat slumped in an armchair, facing the window. He wore pyjamas and a white fluffy bathrobe. His hair had been neatly plaited and he smelt of talcum powder. Such cleanliness seemed offensive to Trudi, who remembered him in his happy, dirty days. She could picture him now, as of old, his dungarees torn and patched, arms encrusted with soil, digging a pond or fussing over his bike, an oil-can and an old rag to hand. Dust and mess were his native elements. Why, even when they went fishing, it was Corky who ended up in the water! There he was again, fixing the central heating, his head popping up through the floorboards all covered in cobwebs… lighting fires with home-cured charcoal. Jack-in-the-Box Corky, with his limp and his schoolboy grin and his endless fund of knowledge.

This pale, torpid person… who was he?

Pedro lunged at him and plumped down on his lap. And Corky, wincing a little under his weight, put out a friendly hand.

"We've brought a delegation," said Hamish, "to see how you are."

"Oh fine, I'm fine." Empty eyes smiled back.

"Are they treating you well?" Bianca's face, all concern, came close as if she was going to kiss him, but she stroked his forehead instead and laid her cake on Pedro's knees. "That's Sister Matilda's recipe, so I take no blame if it is heavy! Everyone sends their love, Corky."

The patient scratched his head, momentarily overcome. "So kind," he murmured. "So kind."

"And Mr. Brambling sent these," Trudi pushed forward.

"Ah, yes. Perfect."

"You *do* know who I am, don't you!"

"You're the little girl from next door. I'm sorry." He snorted apologetically. "That's me all over. No head for names. But don't tell me, it will come to me!"

"Are they keeping you busy?" asked Hamish.

284

"Oh, yes. But I'm very lazy, I'm afraid. Had a bath… and lots of injections…"

His words suddenly broke Trudi's dream about the clinic and the bee-sting. A wave of fear swept over her and she glanced over her shoulder, half-expecting to see Olaf's hateful face at the door.

When the nurse returned, she actually felt relieved. At least that meant they would soon escape from this place, and everything in it, even from Corky, who had been effectively assimilated into it. The very idea of rescuing him seemed impossible now. She saw no point in giving him her string. Hamish had already said goodbye. And in any case, what use was he? The only man who could climb up and break down a door, would soon be knee-deep in Italian snow. And Bianca was a nun. What could a nun in a habit do? No. Corky was lost as surely as a soul that had died.

As they traipsed back along the corridor, she felt they were leaving behind a living corpse. Her heart sank lower and her footsteps lagged. They were all stuck fast – helpless and alone - doomed by indifferent destinies. Poor Mincke. No doubt, he lay trapped in an institution just like this one. And Per? Perhaps the Tranquillity Centre, which her mother was designing, would be another…

At that moment, quite without warning, an icy hand gripped her arm and pulled her into a doorway. Trudi had time only to notice the label overhead, *'Extraction Room'* before she found herself in the dark, another hand clapped over her mouth.

"Don't speak or I'll kill yer!" The voice belonged to someone young, female and desperate.

Trudi, convinced that Olaf waited in the shadows, bit the hand and kicked out for all she was worth, but her strength could not match her assailant.

"It's okay, stupid. You don't have to go mad. I just don't want you shouting for help. I gotta talk to you. See?"

The bitten hand let go and opened the door enough to reveal a figure in industrial overalls. She was short, dark and shapeless. Her black eyes glittered like the buttons on the face of a toy. Trudi instantly recognized the girl who had written her the note at St. Gregory's. She spoke with the same Cotswold burr as Mrs. Sparks. Every vowel had a curly cadence.

"You gotta help me get out!"

"What?"

"Listen! You gotta help me get out!"

"How can I? There's no time. They'll come back and if they find me here, they'll lock me up too."

"Be at your garden gate this afternoon. I'll come there somehow when the others are exercising. Find a way of opening that gate, if you ever want to see your friend here again. Otherwise we've all had it. Two o'clock. Don't let me down. Promise me!"

"All right, I promise. Now let me go!"

The door opened further and the same hand pushed Trudi back into the corridor. She heard the latch click behind her and flew along the lino and down the stairs till she caught up with the others.

"Where did you go?" whispered Jurgen.

"I took a wrong turning."

Jurgen gawped in disbelief.

"Tell you later."

As the realisation of what had just happened sank in, Trudi's depression began to lift and a tremor of excitement appeared in its place. She had a fleeting presentiment that everything might now come right. As if by magic, she could feel the currents of hidden forces stirring beneath them, driving things forward. They were no longer stuck – they were moving again. Perhaps Grandpa was right, after all. She would not have to do everything herself. A little bubble formed inside her, like the first bubble of something fermenting. She had not known this feeling since she leant her cheek on the rail of the Christmas ferry all those months ago and peered out into the dark. Now, it seemed, she had something to encourage her. Hope! Hope was not dead after all. Its bubble expanded and trembled beneath her rib cage and she bit her lip, waiting for it to burst.

But the rest of the party left in low spirits, Pedro silent and sullen, Bianca and Hamish exchanging uneasy looks.

At St. Lucy's, they faced a quizzing from Mrs. Sparks. "Well?"

Bianca put on a brave face: "Well, he's very comfortable," she said.

"I don't care for the place, not I." Mrs. Sparks wiped her forehead, and adjusted her curls with her sleeve, her hands being wet. "Not after what happened to poor Edmund."

286

"Edmund?"

"He was there right enough when he first had his breakdown. But they never done him no good."

"You mean Edmund who comes for sandwiches?"

"Told me, once. After he left the Honey Farm place. I wonder he comes back this close, to be honest. They done him no good in there, poor lamb."

"I haven't seen him all week, now you come to mention it."

"I seen him, this marnin', while you were all over there. He wanted a coat. Which warn't like him. And he were asking after the children too. Where were they staying, like. I told him, Mr. Brambling's. Took himself off in a right storm, he did. He don't like the mention of that place next door and I for one don't blame him!"

Bianca wished she had not spoken so in front of the children. People thought they didn't hear or understand - that it was safe to talk over their heads, but she was young enough to remember what nonsense that was. Children often listen most when they seem least interested. She hurried them away.

"Look here, chaps, I have more laundry to do, so until we hear from your father, or Mr. Brambling, I'm afraid you must try to keep out of mischief here. Can you do that?"

"Don't worry about us, Sister Bianca. We've got lots to do. We'll play quietly in the garden." Trudi led the boys away with suspicious alacrity.

What, she wondered, was the little minx up to now?

Once out of earshot, Trudi almost dragged Jurgen and Pedro down to the hidden bench.

"I no doing nothing," said Pedro flatly. "I don' want play games any more."

"Pedro this is not a game! This is saving Corky."

"Stupid girl talk," Pedro hunched forward on the bench and stared at his sun-browned feet. "Why ju make up things? Always you pretend you know a secret. Like now ju put that thing on your hand. That is Inca weapon – not toy. Ju don' to know nothing."

"What do you mean 'Inca weapon'? It's the wampum I bought from the busker in Kingsbury."

"Is a sling. Ju can see. Inca weaving. Here hole for the finger. Here knot. Here place to put the stone."

"I bought it for Corky. I thought it was a friendship bracelet."

Pedro was no longer listening. "Same with what happen now. Ju think you can save Corky. But he is dying. And is all my fault!"

"What?"

"Is all because of my eyes that we come here and Corky get ill. I wish I was in Peru."

"Pedro I promise you, you're wrong. I may not know exactly what is going on yet, but every day I learn a bit more. The Laser Wag Company tracks down people who know things, people like Mincke and Corky, and Daddy and Edmund (he knew about bees, you know, he told me) and they *make* them ill. I think they make them ill to get the knowledge out of them. That's why they are after Mr. Brambling."

"You think Daddy is ill too?" gasped Jurgen.

"We haven't heard from him, have we? And we haven't heard from Mummy either. They are normally always on the phone, aren't they?"

"But you made me turn my phone off!"

"It's too late to worry about that now. I'm sure that that house next door is something to do with the Laser Wag plot. Just before we left I saw a place called *'Extraction Room'*. Sounds like a dentist's room doesn't it? And there was a chair in there, just like a dentist's chair, but over the top, a helmet thing like one of the funny hair-dryers they used to have in hairdresser's shops. And there were rows of computers."

"How did you see?"

"Someone pulled me in there. It was dark, but when the door opened a crack, I saw enough. It was the girl I've seen before. She is trying to escape. I saw her at the St. Gregory's dinner and the other day she was out in the drive. They use her as a servant. She was wearing their cleaning overalls. She must have stolen the keys from somewhere. She has information about Corky, I'm sure of it." Trudi then told the story of her abduction and her promise to help.

They examined the garden door. There were two massive rusted hinges and a keyhole, but no key. It could not have been opened for decades.

"Impossible!" said Pedro "Better put over a rope, so she can climb."

"You haven't seen her," Trudi snorted. "She's short and fat. I don't think she could climb anything."

"Chop it down," suggested Jurgen.

"With what? And then how do we explain that to Sister Emilia? And wouldn't the whole world notice? She needs to slip through and put it back just as before."

Jurgen smarted under her sarcasm. Clever pants! If only Scarp the gypsy was here he would have been able to pick the lock, or stick a jemmy in the hinge and put Trudi in her place...

"What about Hamish, then," he said. "He's got climbing ropes and axes and special boots with spikes in his car. And the back is never locked. We could borrow some tools and return them before he realizes."

"Jurgen, you're a genius!" To his surprise and alarm, Trudi flung her arms around him.

"What are you doing? Get *off!*"

Trudi recovered herself. "We'll offer to help him pack and borrow one or two things at a time and hide them here under the bench. Only we must smuggle them back before he leaves."

And that is precisely what they did.

There never were three such helpful children. It positively irked Hamish, whose room lay in an unruly muddle and who needed time to order his thoughts, but he had not the heart to send them away. While he parcelled his books, Trudi washed up the last of his dirty mugs and wrapped them in newspaper. Jurgen fished out some old socks from under the bed and re-folded his shirts. Pedro took down the wall posters of precipices and gaping glacier holes. Clearly Hamish's mother had made a poor stab at training her son in the homely arts, whereas the Scandinavians and the Peruvian nuns had taught their charges well.

When the clothes and crockery were sorted, there remained the rest of his personal effects: files full of notes, maps, National Geographic magazines, cards from admiring girls, a bottle of port and the computer, all of which were stowed into a metal trunk. A rather shameful pile of unreturned library books would have to be dropped off once he was on his way.

After lunch the help melted away. Doubtless the kids had got bored. Just as well, thought Hamish, readjusting and muddling things once more to his liking.

But the children had not finished their work. They had managed to filch a good selection of tools and, having laid them out on the bench by the gate, were now considering their best course of action.

"We can't just bash the gate down. It will make too much noise and draw attention."

"Unscrew it," said Jurgen showing his practical side. But the screw heads on the hinges had rusted beyond recognition. They abandoned that idea.

"Use this," Pedro picked up a hacksaw and turned it in his hand.

"How?"

"To cut the lock!"

The tool slipped easily between door and frame.

"Do it quietly!"

"And quickly. We've only got five minutes."

The saw made a horrible scraping sound. "Is no working."

"You're not doing it fast enough. It should make sparks. When Scarp does it, it makes sparks."

"Si, but Scarp not here. And my arms bigger than your arms - see? So I am the most strong one here."

"Just get on with it!" hissed Trudi.

"Is no working."

"Perhaps we can cut away the frame…"

A voice from the other side startled them all.

"Have yer done it yet?"

"Nearly," stammered Trudi. "Two more minutes."

"Gawd help us – what kind of wimps are you? There's three of you and one measly, pathetic door. I haven't got two minutes... Someone will see me."

The voice went quiet, then ordered: "Stand back. Let me try."

Moments later, the structure shuddered under a heavy impact and the top hinge fell away from its fastening.

"Don't just stand there. Pull! It's stuck at the bottom now."

They all heaved till the second hinge sheared off, creating a ragged gap. With some difficulty the fat girl squeezed herself through and forcing the door shut once more, hurled herself against it, hands behind her back, face upturned, breathing hard.

When she revived, she surveyed her rescue team with undisguised contempt.

290

"I suppose I could have done that any time in the last year!" she muttered.

"We were trying to help." Trudi felt rightfully aggrieved.

"Yea, yea, you were."

"And we didn't have to. We don't know who you are, or anything."

The fat girl snorted by way of acknowledgement and nodded. "I know. I am grateful really. But we haven't done this properly yet, have we? I mean we've got to mend the gate now, so *they* don't know. And then we've got to talk."

She was seventeen or perhaps eighteen years old, with black hair, roughly cropped. Her face had an unhealthy pallor, livid around the eyes that Trudi had likened to buttons hours before, and her white arms, bare to the elbow of her polyamide, stain-proof top, looked as if they had once been strong. You would not want to argue with her.

"What other tools have you got there?" She scanned the heap on the bench.

"Nothing very useful – a screwdriver – a saw… they've got to go back."

"Have to jam it then." Her eyes lit on a nearby lilac stump. "Saw out a bit of that and make a wedge."

"We can't damage the garden…"

"Oh give the saw here and *you* lean on the gate. This is an emergency, isn't it? That's dead anyway!"

Grabbing the tool, she hacked and broke off part of the stump and thrust it into the rotten hinge-hole. The original screw slotted neatly between old wood and new, and held. As for the bottom, she merely dragged the bench across and left it there to take the weight.

"It's not very good," she said. "But it will do until they miss me. And by then I'll be away."

"Who *are* you?" asked Trudi.

The fat girl turned round and fumbled in her trouser pocket.

"I'm Sophie," she replied. "Know what that is?"

She held out a crumpled piece of newsprint and they crowded forward to look. The already yellowing paper depicted what looked like a round window, similar to a rose window in a cathedral, but smaller. Trudi had seen the great rose window at Chartres; the diminutive figures suspended in their wheels of glass above the labyrinth pavement below. This window held just one emblem, a form straddling the space from rim to rim, like a spider, or like one of those Indian dancing gods with arms and legs fine as tendrils. They must have had the picture upside down for the creature before them was standing almost on its head. A bright light flooded in from behind.

"Know what it is?" Sophie urged.

And when they shook their heads, she closed in, pointing her finger.

"It's ME!" Her face crumpled like the cutting and her voice suddenly broke. "It's me! That's who I was a year ago. I was a living legend. Sophie Startail. That's seven metres up that is, on a circus stage. I could turn round in that wheel, like a little hamster, with a great fire burning underneath. I was a show-stopper! I was beautiful!"

Trudi looked incredulously at the filigree figure in the picture.

"What *happened?*" she found her heart racing.

"*They* got me. Same as they got your friend in there now. Same as they got all the poor devils they use for their research."

"We can't talk here, Sophie. Someone might find us. Come down to the gardener's shed. Pedro has made a seat at the back of the compost."

Trudi led the way past the daisies and campanulas, Sophie now gulping back great sobs of self-pity.

"You can be okay now," said Pedro, patting her on the back. "Trudi is boss in charge, so everything okay! And if ju can get out, so can Corky get out! We will help together."

Squeezed in behind the rhubarb and piles of old potsherds, Sophie began to tell her tale: "I was a bad kid, right from the start. I grew up here, on the Kitehill Estate. No Dad. My mum always had a new boyfriend and most of them hit me. Sometimes they'd shut me out for hours, with just a box to play with in the garden. When it rained I'd bang on the door, but they never heard. I hated school. I hated everyone. I was always in trouble." She stopped to eye her audience. "Kids like you wouldn't understand. Your mums take you everywhere."

Pedro shrugged.

Trudi pushed the hair out of her eyes and watched her, unblinking, willing the story to go on.

"I tell you I was 'orrible. Lying, stealing, fighting. But there was one thing I was good at and that was climbing. I could run alright. I had plenty of practice at that! And I could climb like a monkey. The big kids on the estate used to use me to break into places for them. They gave me cigarettes, or other stuff. And I knew the police station as well as my own home. I think I spent more time there, probably. All them social work people had a go at straightening me out. I had counselling – the lot. They was talking about taking me away, putting me into care, like. And then this bloke come round the school and saw me playing rounders. Someone socked the ball over the boundary fence and out onto the road and I done like I always did, shinned up a post and hopped over the top to get it back. He couldn't believe his eyes! Next thing I knew he put me in for a gymnastics competition. And that's when I met the people from the "Mudlarks Circus.""

She spoke hurriedly, as if anxious that she might lose her thread before she had got the whole story out.

"That saved my life. I'd have been dead from drink and dope, but they give me something to live for. The Circus was full of people like me, street kids they'd rescued and we could all do something and none of us had anything to lose, so we was happy to dice with death every day. Don't get me wrong, they done all the proper health and safety stuff, but it was the big stunts the audiences liked best. They got all the papers signed for me to leave home and go on the road with them and I made friends for the first time in my life. Haven't you ever 'eard of it?"

She stared in disbelief. "Where've you *bin?* Well it's famous, right. I mean, really famous! We toured all round the country and abroad – places you couldn't imagine. We even went to South America. And my act was the best. I'm not just boasting, like. I was on all the posters, crawling round that ring, while they belted out street music and the public went wild! You dunno what that feels like – to be on top of the world after being nothing. I quit all the drugs and the drink and everything. And I worked like the devil. No one was ever gonno catch up with me again! And then *they* found me... This Swedish guy turns up..."

"Go on."

"Says he's got this mobile phone company that wants to sponsor me. He can get me the biggest agent, ever. World contract. Blah, blah. I said I wasn't interested. I was happy in the circus, right. But then he says: 'what you gonno do when you're not a kid any more?' The circus is just for up to eighteen, see. 'Where are you gonno go, then?' I never thought nothing about it before. I didn't want to leave my friends. So I said 'I'll make my own circus then, and you push off!' only I said it a bit stronger – he was a 'orrible slimy bloke. It was like water off a duck's back with him. He said that was just what this 'agent' would help me do and he give me a digital stop-watch, pedometer thing, like, as a present, to help me with my training. It looked like silver. It was good too. I tried it out. That's when I had my fall. I was timing myself in a rehearsal and suddenly my mind went blank – I couldn't remember where to put my feet. Next thing I knew I was in 'ospital. But the worst thing was, that slimy Swede done a deal behind my back with the management, to buy me, like. And when I come out of hospital, I was out of the circus, too.

"'Never mind', they said, 'we've got a convalescent home. You've had a breakdown – too much publicity. You can rest and take it easy and then we'll make you the biggest star, ever.' *Liars!*"

"Was it next door?"

"I've bin there a year."

"Couldn't you tell someone?"

"I didn't even know who I was at the beginning. They suck your brains out!"

"The Extraction Room!"

"That watch done something to me."

"Same with Corky!" shouted Pedro. "He help time us, remember? In the maze. And next day, he don't know where he is!"

"They scan your mind and steal whatever they want out of it. They took away the only thing I had to live for – my agility. I tried, over and over to remember how I did even a simple handstand. But it was gone."

"But Sophie, you *do* know who you are," said Trudi. "You haven't forgotten. You're a rebel and a fighter still and now you've got away. How come you've held out so long?"

"When you train," said Sophie. "It hurts like hell. I mean *really* hurts. If you thought about it, you'd give up. So you don't think. You send your mind to a secret place where the pain can't hurt you any more. I suppose that's what I done when they put me in the Extraction Room. I was so terrified, I escaped there and maybe they couldn't find all of me. I found the cutting just by chance. A visitor brought some newspapers for another patient and I always looked, in case I could find something about my life before. There was an article about the Mudlarks and they still used my picture because it was kind of iconic. I hid it in a plastic bag in the hinge of the gate here, in case they found it."

"But what do they do with all the knowledge?"

"God knows. Build some bloody great computer. It's not just knowledge they want, they could scan books for that. It's the way people think. They want people who think in a different way. In there," she jerked a thumb towards the wall "there's pianists and artists and conjurors and writers and they're all zombies now. When they've finished with them, they let them go again. They get a pension and go into care or just wander the streets ... Human junk. No one wants them any more."

"Like Edmund!"

"I pretend I'm more dumb than I am, hoping they'll let me go, but I'm too useful to 'em, doing the cleaning for nothing, and 'working in the community' to get them government funding!"

"Wouldn't anyone at St. Gregory's help you?" asked Trudi.

"They've bin warned, haven't they? Not to talk to the mad girl."

"But Mr. Brambling gave Corky the watch," Trudi backtracked, struggling to piece it all together. "And he's okay. How come Corky got ill and not Mr. Brambling? Surely he'd be affected too, wouldn't he? And what about us? We've met Olaf lots of times and we're okay."

"I think they use some people as bait for others. Like, maybe they used you to get at your friend. And then this other guy, maybe they'll pick him up later."

"Pooties," said Trudi. "Perhaps we've all been pooties all along. Perhaps we still are. That's why they've let you escape now, hoping you'll lead us to something bigger."

"If the device is linked to a satellite," suggested Jurgen, still considering the watch, "then it could be operated by remote control. Perhaps there was a hidden webcam. The control centre would know who was holding it and could start it up whenever they wanted. Perhaps the watch was a present to Mr. Brambling…"

"Like Wari vase," put in Pedro.

"So we know where it came from!" cried Trudi. "Everything leads back to Olaf and Laser Wag."

"I reckon this operation is coming to an end." Sophie, as ever, ignored what she did not understand. "I heard two of them last night talking in the stores. Something about 'mopping up before the final transfer'. I think they might be going to torch the place. Perhaps it's getting too hot for them. The media want to know what goes on at that Beedome building of theirs. I've heard people talk about it at St. Gregory's. I don't see how they can keep things quiet forever. But they're trying for a big fish first."

"A big fish?"

"That's what they said. They reckon they've almost got him. Once he's in the bag, they'll have the means to start going independent: building special intelligence without humans."

"Listen to our side now," said Trudi, and she recounted from the beginning, all the evidence she had amassed, from the first warning of trouble to her fateful visit to Mincke, Per's disappearance, Corky's collapse, the burning of the bookshop, Sven's appointment, the incident at the Wallace Aardhof House, Olaf's threats, the Wari vase, the webcam at the convent and Mr. Brambling's ominous rendez-vous at the Beedome."

"Looks like they want him next, then," nodded Sophie. "Maybe he's the big fish. It might be too late for him already."

"We need to go to the police. With your evidence too they'll *have* to listen to us!"

"Police?" Sophie burst out laughing. "I in't got no friends in the police! Send me there and they'll bang me up right away!"

"What then?"

"I got a plan." Sophie leant forward and a dark fire burned in her eyes. "The Summer Fair's on, down in the town, in't it? I 'eard the lorries driving through last night. One of my mates from my early days is in the Fair – great big, strapping bloke. I'll talk to him. He'll believe me. He'll help us. He's got friends. If we can get out of this place and down into Kingsbury, we'll find him and organize a raid. Get our revenge."

296

"A raid?"

"On that Beedome. That's what you want, isn't it?"

This sounded wilder than anything Trudi had in mind. After all, they didn't know if they could trust Sophie yet and Sid and his mates might be little more than thugs, but Pedro jumped at the idea. "Si, si. Knock out the bad guys."

Trudi tried hedging her bets. "We'll have to tell the Sisters," she said, "or they'll call Mummy and she'll be worried..."

"*'Call Mummy'?*" Sophie jeered. "You tell anyone, right, and I'll leave you all here and go on my own. I don't want no nuns coming after us. It's not *The Sound of bloody Music!*"

"How do we know we'll find your friend at the Fair?"

"Can't miss him. He'll be the biggest bloke there. Trust me, eh? I might be an escaped loony, but I know my way round the world. You show me how to get out of this convent and I'll show you how to stand up for yourselves for the rest of your lives. You want to find your Dad, don't you? So are you coming, or not?"

"I coming!" said Pedro.

Jurgen threw in his lot. "I'm coming too."

"Give me your overall, Sophie and I'll wrap up the tools and slip them back to Hamish's car." Trudi devised another plan. "We can meet up at the post box. You go out by the bicycle shelter and I'll nip through the laundry."

No one objected to this.

The laundry stood empty. Bianca had finished her work and hoisted the damp linen up on the big wooden airer that hung from the ceiling. Trudi tiptoed across the duckboards, and then darted into the student kitchen. No one here either. Hamish's food cupboard stood empty and ajar, his half-finished pots of pickle and peanut butter ranged as parting gifts on the table, his melamine memo pad forlornly wiped clean. In a moment of inspiration, she grabbed the felt pen that dangled by a string and wrote a message:

"Gone to the Fair to get help for Daddy and Mr. Brambling. Don't worry about us. And Goodbye. Love Trudi." Hearing someone coming, she abandoned the temptation to write more, drew a hasty sketch of a beehive and ran.

Part Five.

Vigil. Feast of St. John

Chapter Thirty-Three

Lost at the Fair

One hour later Sister Emilia stood intractable at her desk. Like a *châtelaine* under siege, she had retreated behind walls of flint and dropped the portcullis. And here she was now, making her speech from the battlements. Her voluminous habit had become chainmail. Her heart was steeled; flesh, hard as stone. She had folded her arms across her breast, thinking of the Church's saints and martyrs and how they had suffered through the ages. She did not lack their courage! Fate may have decided to bring mayhem to St. Lucy's, but she was not going to let it disrupt the order of the Order! That was her duty.

As far as she could see, the precious routines of prayer and reflection that held the Community together, had simply gone to pot during the past twenty-four hours, plagued by distractions of a most lamentable kind. And things were threatening to get worse...

First there were the three children, who, though not exactly noisy or naughty in themselves, might as well have been thirty-three, for all their ability to get underfoot and create disruption. *If they didn't need feeding, they needed entertaining, or transporting somewhere, and then there was the mother, forever ringing up for reassurance that they were well...*

On top of that, came all bother of the end of term: *Hamish and Corky leaving and a missionary from Uganda coming for a conference; rooms to clean; bills to settle. Then the computer virus. Not to mention the unrest amongst the Sisters about the new chapel webcam. Nothing had been said, but she knew perfectly well that they were whispering in corners.*

Now, to make everything complete - a fresh crisis: the children had run off. A white-faced Bianca stood wringing her hands in the office.

"I am most certainly *not* going to contact the police!" Emilia rocked on her toes. "How ridiculous would that look? They have *not* been abducted. They have simply done what children always

301

do in Fair Week. And of *course* they won't answer their mobile phones while they are playing truant! That would spoil all the fun."

She could remember, not half a century ago, a certain diminutive Emily Wilkins, aged nine, who lived at the house next to the corner shop, and who had organized just such a spree for the urchins in her street when the Circus came to Wigan, sparking reports of lions in cages behind the gasworks. "They will be easy enough to find. Go to the candy floss stall." (She almost added: *"That's where I always went!"* but bit the confession back in time.) "Take Hamish with you, if he is willing. Go now and fetch them home and I will telephone the father and tell him they cannot stay here any longer. The whole situation has become quite intolerable. I might as well be running a zoo!"

Marina let fly with scornful remarks over tea: "That child wants correction. She has been spoilt and indulged all her life and thinks she is queen bee of everything. Well now she's on her wedding flight and she'll lead the lot of you a merry dance. I'd leave her to it, if I were you. She'll soon come home if she thinks nobody cares. She only does it for attention. First she's mad, then she's sad. What she really needs is an old-fashioned spanking and off to bed without her supper. That might calm her down a bit!"

"Marina *dear!*" Sister Matilda shot her a penetrating look. "A little charity for the vulnerable, please! All the children are in a very difficult position, through no fault of their own."

"All I'm saying is she exploits it to the full. She squeaks and you all jump. There's nothing very special about her except that she looks the part."

Sister Matilda let it go. Poor Marina cut a plain figure beside Trudi. With her heavy glasses and lank hair, she did *not* look the part and one could detect more than a little painful envy in her venom. Charity for the vulnerable had to include Marina too!

Hamish had already loaded his car to the roof, so there was no way he could squeeze Bianca onto the front seat without wasting valuable time. They decided instead to go on bicycles - in any case it would be easier to park a bike. Bianca tucked her veil into her jacket collar and they set off at a sprint. The day had clouded over and a dry wind blew from the north, turning over the leaves of the trees and whipping dust out of the gutters. As they reached the end of Pinkney Road, they could see the gilded masts of the Fair towering above Longmarket Street, banners flying.

"Let's split up," suggested Hamish. "You take the left hand side and I'll do the right and I'll meet you back at the Helter-Skelter here in half an hour. If only you had a mobile phone we could be more efficient, but at least it will be easy for me to find you! There aren't too many nuns here!" He grinned and strode off into the crowd.

Bianca sighed as she watched him go. The day had seemed oppressive from the start. At Matins, in chapel, the knowledge that that little computer camera was spying on her had knocked any sense of peace quite out of her head. The visit to Corky had proved a most dispiriting affair, and though she cheered up briefly afterwards, posting her communion napkins through the wringer, she had then found herself facing utter blankness at Sext.

Now the children were in trouble. Poor little souls they were, passed from pillar to post like bits of lost property – and none of them what you would call children with their feet on the ground, conversant with the rough and tumble of life. Added to that, even the nicest people, and here she included Hamish, seemed to think that because she was a nun she must be simple in the head, unpractical and naïve, when in fact she was a match for anyone. She almost said it out loud for comfort. It was a homely cure, like rubbing your elbow when you banged it. But it took away the pain: "I'm a match for anyone, in mind or body. Just see if I'm not!"

Yet her troubles paled beside those of her convent Superior. Sister Emilia had scarcely recovered her equanimity after dismissing Hamish and Bianca, when the doorbell rang and someone admitted a furious whirlwind of a woman in a purple dress.

"Are the Larsson children here? Trudi? Trudi Larsson? Long, blond hair? Little Swedish kids and the Peruvian boy? I'm their aunt. I've come to take them home."

"You need to see Sister Emilia. She's in there, if you knock." Marina turned unhelpfully on her heel.

Barbara paused to secure her topknot, patted and smoothed her sides, picked up her capacious bag and launched forth.

"'Scuse me, I'm looking for Sister Emilia."

Emilia was ready for her.

"I am she." She would be gracious, stately, chilly and impenetrable.

The purple whirlwind, red-faced from her walk, and temporarily out of breath, brazened a smile.

"I'm Barbara. I'm sure you remember. We met before." *(A not entirely happy occasion).* "I've come for the children – I think it's time they went home."

"Well there we are in perfect agreement. But I'm afraid they are out – just at the moment." Emilia fenced on a knife-edge. She could not actually tell a lie, nor could she admit that she had lost them – certainly not to this American plum! "Yes, they have gone to the Fair. I expect you saw the Fair on your journey here. And Sister Bianca and Hamish, one of our most dependable students, have gone too – while the children's father is detained with his work." All true, so far as it went.

Barbara frowned. "Too right. All the buses are up the creek because they've closed the road. I had to walk the last twenty miles!"

Emilia missed the joke. "Twenty miles?"

"Two miles, twenty miles, whatever it is from the station!"

"Well, they won't be back for a little while," Emilia began some rapid calculations. "Perhaps you would like a rest…"

"Oh no, thank you. I've got things to do. If the children are busy, perhaps that's as well. Perhaps better. Because there's someone else I need to see first and I believe you can put me on to him. His name is Olaf Stromberg. He's a computer specialist. He did some work for you recently? Slippery looking guy with a shiny suit and pink hands, like a mole?"

Emilia stiffened, feeling another onslaught coming. "I really cannot give out confidential information."

"*Sure* you can! I need his address, see. I know he was here."

"He called in merely as a friend of your friends…"

"But he did work for you, right? I need to see him, Sister. If you don't help me, you'll regret it all the rest of your life - that is - assuming you have a life left to regret it in."

"Are you threatening me, Miss Rainbird?"

"You got it! If you don't help me, I am going straight to the newspapers with my story and the people of Kingsbury won't believe their ears. How come a respectable house of prayer like this was found helping one of the worst crooks that ever snooped on decent folk? *Criminals* – that's what I'm talking about. Gangsters in industrial espionage! You've got to help me stop him, Sister Emilia, or I can't answer for the consequences. You were selected, you see, like me."

The whole family must be stark, raving mad! Emilia turned to the letter rack where she filed recent papers. *Get rid of the woman, as quickly as possible!*

"This is his business card," she held it just out of reach. "But I want no unpleasantness. The man came to us in friendship and good faith…"

"Yeah, yeah. I know. Don't worry, I shan't use violence, Sister. I've another way of making him talk." Barbara plucked the card from Emilia's fingers. "This is the most Christian thing you've done today! Hold on to those children for me when they come home. Oh, and turn off any devices Olaf might have installed here. Just to be on the safe side! I shall be back as soon as I've got to the bottom of this… Bacon Street. Where would I find that?"

"Back in the town, I'm afraid. Perhaps I can call you a taxi."

Emilia sank down in her chair, as the sound of the car receded. Never had troubles crowded in so thick and fast! And prayer, the one solace for her difficulties, seemed utterly remote and cut off. She could no more talk to God than she could turn the clock back to happier, tranquil times. Perhaps at Vespers they could all pray together for a resolution. Then if no good came of that she would sink her pride and call the police.

∞∞∞∞∞∞∞∞

All this time, the children had been looking in vain for Big Sid at the Fair.

"He'll be on the roundabouts," said Sophie to begin with. "They have to get them up by hand and the parts are so heavy they need strong blokes to help."

But the woman on the Merry-Go-Round couldn't remember when she last saw Sid. She leant out, one arm anchored to a barley-twist pole and gave a sympathetic smile. In the old days, before her hair turned grey and her lips grew thin, she would have done such a stunt to the admiration of all the lads about, her dark eyes and

305

tiny waist a legend. Now, neither she nor the gilded horses were enough to tempt the punters aboard. These were hard times for fairground people, what with the road taxes and the safety regulations, and the public looking for better gimmicks every year; then the long hours, setting up, dismantling, waiting for custom in the rain, and the new rides always breaking down and there being nowhere to park their caravans at night. Even the eco-friendly paint they used for their hoardings wouldn't stay on and blistered in a season.

"Come up dearies, and I'll give yer a ride half price. Sid'll turn up. He's wore himself out this morning I expect. He'll be having a pint in the pub, if I know him."

"Thanks, Auntie Linda," called Sophie. "Next time."

Trudi cast a wistful glance as the Merry-Go-Round speeded up and the lettering on the golden crown dissolved into a blur: *"Fun Fun Amusement Carousel 6d a Ride"*. Old times. Old pleasures. The glassy-eyed horses gazed yearningly back.

Next time…

But Sophie's plan didn't really allow for consolations.

"C'mon. This way. Keep together!" Struggling along through the desultory crowd proved arduous and frustrating. Half the rides were closed.

"Picks up in the evening, I expect," she called, forging ahead. Such optimism seemed out of place to her followers, but after two more failed enquiries she began to lose heart herself.

"Well *someone* must have seen him. We could be stuck like this for hours."

Women with pushchairs and groups of aimless teenagers clogged the pavements. Being short, all four had difficulty peering past them, so Pedro's suggestion, when he made it, had an instant appeal.

"We could go on that," he pointed to a Big Wheel which had been erected at the gates of Gloucester-Deakin College and now towered above that institution's crenellated roofline. "Then we can see all the Fair from up high."

"Brilliant! Who's got six quid? I in't got nothing. Haven't seen money for ages …"

Trudi and Jurgen emptied their pockets and pooled £8.78 between them and Sophie imperiously took charge of the funds and

306

approached the operator, a swarthy youth with an earring who was lurking at the back. He had slunk off duty for a moment and, taking cover behind the jumble of vehicles, was eyeing something of interest nearby. He held one hand cupped behind him, sheltering a fag from the wind.

"All right to get on?" Sophie shouted and he slowly turned and took stock. *Four passengers. That wasn't enough to warrant starting up the Wheel. His ride had rails set up to accommodate a queue. But where was the crowd? No one seemed interested today. On the other hand, if he got four on, others might follow… He supposed it was worth a try.* He dropped the cigarette under his heel, ambled across and waved them up to the barrier. *Might as well take their money now.* He had done it so many times he could run this ride blindfold. He lowered the chain and helped them up the steps with a practised indifference. Trudi watched in awe. His hands were covered in silver jewellery. Handsome eyes, unresponsive. When it came to her turn, she felt suddenly anxious. This attendant had a gypsy look like Scarp, but his manner was distant, unsmiling, perhaps even a little hostile. Did he despise them, or was he simply shy? It didn't bother Sophie. "Get a move on!" she called. Maybe she could see the girl he was showing off to on the Hoopla Stall.

Trudi swallowed her nervousness and accepted his hand. And immediately her fears melted away. It was as easy as getting into a ski lift. Nothing to it! When they were all seated and locked in, Sophie stuck her head over the bar.

"Is Big Sid about?" she asked.

"He *was*," replied the youth. "Went off to meet someone."

"Can you tell him Sophie's looking for him?"

She got her answer with a cursory nod. And he slipped the cage forward so the next party could board.

It seemed an age, waiting for other customers, so when at last the ride jolted into action, it caught them unprepared. The wind whipped in behind them and their hearts leapt as they swung up and away. Within moments they were moving amongst the branches of the nearby trees and then floating above them. They could peer in at the college windows on their left, and to the right survey the panorama of the fair.

307

Over there was the Carousel, pumping out its organ tunes and whirling at speed, a handful of riders clinging on. Here were rooftops and fancy, brick chimney pots, normally concealed from view. Down below, the figures on the ground receded, shrinking to the size of puppets in a cardboard theatre. And still they went on up. Other spires and domes of the city came into view. They spotted a champagne reception in one of the gardens. The trees of Longmarket Street, blending with those of Pinkney Road, formed a green ribbon that led out of town – and in the distance, way beyond the spires, lay the shining expanses of the flood meadows, the river flats and a widening circle of hills.

"It's magical!" cried Trudi.

"Are you helping me, or what?" Sophie took umbrage. "Have you forgotten we're supposed to be here for a purpose?"

"I don't know what your friend even looks like," Trudi objected. "I might see him and not realize. But if you look over there, you can see the satellite dishes on the Astronomy faculty. That's where Olaf has his flat. And way over there, in the middle of that wood, almost on the horizon, there's a strange hive-shaped building, like a mosque."

"There *is* mosque here somewhere," said Pedro.

"No, no, out *there*. Look! Really big."

Pedro whistled.

"Beedome!" pronounced Jurgen.

"Where? Let's see!" But already the wheel was going down and the spectacle slid into reverse: meadows, then spires retracting behind one another, till the figures on the ground resumed their natural size.

"We get a second go," said Sophie. "Look out properly this time."

As the wheel clanked and juddered forward, they sat to attention.

"There's a big man!" cried Trudi pointing towards a Hot Dog Stand. They were frying onions and the smell filled the lower air.

Sophie let out a derisive grunt. "What, that bald old turnip? He's gonna be a lot of use, isn't he? I mean a *big* bloke! Like a body-builder – young. Ginger hair. Got a neck like a bull."

"There's a dog the same as Bella!" said Jurgen. He obviously wasn't going to be any use.

"Shut up and concentrate!"

"And there's a nun," he persisted. "Like Sister Bianca. Do you think she's come after us? She's talking to someone. The attendant man? – no - he's got a black top on."

Jurgen narrowed his eyes as the ground sped away once more.

"Trudi, *look* at that man in the cargo shorts! He's got a snake tattoo on his arm. That's Scarp, isn't it? It *is!*"

Trudi threw herself forward to see. If only it *could* be! Scarp would know how to put paid to the Sneevelings all right. If only Scarp had been there at the beginning none of all this might ever have happened.

But the frame of the cage now hid the ground from view, hoisting them higher and higher and Sophie sat glaring disapproval. "You call out to anyone," she threatened, "and this whole thing's off. I'll just save my own skin and you and your friends can shift for yourselves."

"But Scarp a good guy," reasoned Pedro. "No problem, Scarp."

"I said, *'no nuns'*, all right?"

In the end it made no difference. By the time they left the ride, both figures had vanished into the crowd and the little dog was nowhere to be seen.

"Okay," Sophie rallied her troupe on the pavement. "You still with me, then? We'll check the pubs for Sid and if that's no good we'll set off on our own. We haven't got time to mess around."

The children exchanged doubtful looks and fidgeted. Going back for tea seemed more appealing.

"You *wanna* help your friend, don't you?"

"We can't go into pubs," said Trudi. "And even if we could, how do we know we can find him?"

"*I* can go." Sophie had more stamina. "You gotta *trust* me! Just do it and see. If you don't do it, you'll never know, will you?"

'Trust'. That was Mr. Brambling's word. His advice resounded still in Trudi's ears: *'Trust the day'*. And again: *'I'm trusting you to be a good girl and do the right thing.'* Whatever would she feel if anything happened to him? And what about poor Sister Matilda? There would be no more flowers and crossword puzzles for her! And then it wasn't just Mr. Brambling whose future was at stake, but dear Corky, too, and her own father…

'Hearts of Larsson!' she thought. *'Do or die!'* She rose at once to the challenge: "It's all right, we're coming! We're not afraid."

Sophie gave her an approving thumbs up. All the same, she slipped back and whistled to the traveller boy: "If Big Sid comes back... If you see him... tell him Sophie from Kitehill needs him. Tell him she's in big trouble. She's with the foreign kids from the convent and she's going to Pinkney – to the Beedome thing. Tell him to come and bring some help. We're gonna need him. Can you do it, Alfie?"

Alfie frowned. "What big trouble?"

"It's life and death, Alfie. Them or us. You got that?"

He nodded.

"And if anyone else asks, you haven't seen us!" Then, an after-thought. "Don't suppose you've got any money for bus-fare? Naow... Didn't 'spect so. Cheers!"

Chapter Thirty-Four

The Man with the Snake Tattoo

Scarp, the gypsy, stood at the foot of the Helter-Skelter, rubbing his grease-blackened hands on his vest and pushing a discarded Coke can about with the toe of his boot. To one side, in private conference, stood a long-limbed Scot and a nun. Scarp eyed them both with deep suspicion.

It was the nun who had picked him up. *Had he seen three children? A girl with flaxen hair and a boy, her brother? Also a South American lad? The girl, slim, tall for her age, wearing blue, cropped jeans and a funny, bone pendant on a string?*

She belonged to an old-fashioned order, of the sort you hardly see these days, all rigged out in black: wimple, and long habit, with a silver cross, almost the size of your hand, hanging by a thong on her chest.

Scarp had never spoken to a nun in his life and felt painfully embarrassed, but mention of the necklace struck a chord. Yes, he had known a girl just like that once. "Not the Larssons?" The words slipped out casually, but they had an electrifying effect, and quite forgetting the reticence befitting her calling, this holy sister had seized his arm and literally dragged him here, deaf to objections. Now, absent from his post at the Shooting Range and with Bella, his terrier, audibly whining for him, he had to wait while she consulted her companion.

He had passed a steady, uneventful year since taking off from Newbridge in the autumn, for the Fair had kept him busy most of the time. They needed a mechanic. He needed money and a place to rest his head, out of reach of the authorities. And though he didn't much care for dealing with the public, the travelling life suited him perfectly. They worked all the big historic fairs at towns across the Midlands, never a week in the same place, never time to get into trouble and he felt easy in the company of the fairground folk, who were sound and reliable and didn't ask too many questions.

Naturally, there were days when he missed his old life. He'd had good friends in Sussex and a real, proper, red-painted vardo of his own to live in. Every morning he'd wake to the sound of the birds. And at night, he'd sit up by his camp fire, listening to the late combines working the fields nearby, or catch himself a rabbit or two for supper. And he missed the children in particular, those funny little Larsson kids and their quiet Grandpa, who knew just about every wise thing there was to know - and plump, crazy Barbara, with her fiery temper and her cakes and kindness... A little too fond of Scarp, she was, and perhaps another reason for his 'bunk' into oblivion. But there was more to it than that. He didn't really mind about the truck. A stolen truck was not the end of the world. Such things could be put right. No, the problem was his wood. The wood where he lived had changed. Late last summer, the Conservation people had found rare things in it and once they arrived and put up all their fences, he could no longer come and go as he pleased. Before, he had been just another fox or badger, sneaking through. Now there were regulations and it no longer felt like home...

Well, he would go back, he thought, perhaps later in the summer, and surprise his old friends with a visit. Maybe old Per Larsson would be there again and he would resume the life he had abandoned, mending cars. In the mean time he preferred to be footloose here. No commitments. No problems...

Out of the corner of his eye, he spotted a queue forming at the Shooting Range. *'Hit three ducks and win a life-size leopard. Genuine fake fur'*. If this couple didn't get a move on, he *would* have problems... He'd be lynched by that Big Sid, for one thing. And Scarp wanted no quarrels. Beside the likes of Sid, Scarp was just a puny chap and his best skill in combat had always been his ability to duck a blow. Not that he exactly lacked courage. He'd stand his ground if he had to, but he was better at cunning. Skinny legs run fast and he usually found it quicker to slip off through the back door than to fight it out at the front. Hence his nickname: Scarper! Scarp! He kicked the can into the gutter. *Hurry up! Hurry up!* Ah, she was coming back now...

"May we confide in you?" she asked trying to engage his eye.

"Yeah? Yeah, if you like," he kept his gaze firmly fixed on the ground.

"These children – the Larssons – You say that they are known to you…"

"I know the family like – and some of their friends."

"Yet you did not know that they were in Kingsbury?"

"Might have known it. You hear bits and pieces by word of mouth. But I can't exactly walk into a college now, can I, and ask where they are?"

"Did you know they would come to the Fair?"

"Might have thought they could. What's the problem? They're good kids."

"But you didn't see them?"

"No, I didn't. I told you. What are you accusing me of?"

"Woah! Woah!" Hamish stepped in. "No accusation! It's just that they have run off on their own. And we've been sent to look for them. You understand it's a very delicate situation."

Scarp conjured up a mental picture of Trudi, with her plaits and her butter-wouldn't-melt-in-my-mouth, innocent, wide eyes. Secretive as a quicksand.

"She's up to something isn't she?"

"I'm afraid so, but she doesn't realize what a dangerous place the world is. Ever since her Grandfather disappeared, she has lived in her own fantasy dream." Bianca found relief in speaking out. "She looks smart, but..."

"What do you mean, 'Grandfather disappeared'?"

"You don't know?"

"Course not! I'd have gone back if I'd known there was trouble."

"There's been nothing but trouble since they went to Sweden, and every day it seems to get worse… I'm not allowed to say all this. I've been forbidden by my Sister Superior and you know it's a serious thing for me to go against the rules, especially speaking to a stranger like yourself. After all, you might be one of *them…*"

Scarp darted a look: "*Them?* If anything has happened to the Larssons there will be hell to pay. I promise you that. Give me two minutes to get a bloke for my stand and I'll be back. Don't move from here!" He gave a nod, then nipped between the bystanders and crossed the street.

"What help is he going to be?" Bianca felt herself frustratingly close to tears.

"He's got another pair of eyes, and he knows the people here…
Perhaps his little dog can sniff them out."

Scarp returned a few moments later. "Woman on the
Roundabout saw them an hour ago. With a friend. Looking for Big
Sid. They could be in any of those indoor rides and you wouldn't
know." He pointed to the pop-up hoardings which towered above
the college facades: *'Journey to the Underworld; The Ice Palace;
Rainforest Survival Adventure'.* Paintings of sultry girls in bodices
beckoned alluringly at the doorways, promising adventure and
excitement within.

"Let's sit where we can watch the street for a moment,"
suggested Bianca. "They'd have to come this way to go home. In
the mean time, please, Mr. Scarp, tell us your story we will explain
to you what we know."

"Scarp," he replied as a matter of fact. "I don't do 'Mr'. I got to
know the Larssons last year. They were kind of neighbours of mine
and they helped me out of a spot of bother. Good people. Clever,
but normal like – not snobs, if you know what I mean."

"And the Peruvian boy – did you know him?"

"Knew *of* him. He was the lad Corky rescued. Blind boy in an
orphanage, somewhere. There was talk of him coming over."

"So nobody told you he was here?"

"Like I said, I left in the autumn. Haven't been back since. I'm
not very good at keeping in touch." With a twinge of guilt he
thought of the texts from Barbara he had left unread. Finally, she
stopped sending them and in any case, he lost his phone. "Is the
'trouble' to do with Pedro?"

"Partly."

"Keep talking," said Hamish. "I'll walk round again, just in case
and come back."

Sister Bianca sat with her back to the wind, her hands folded in
her lap, and confessed all the accumulated anxieties in her heart.

Scarp, close beside her, rubbed his eyes from time to time, or
leant forward, elbows on knees, his unkempt hair falling over his
ears, listening.

"Do you have a mobile phone?"

"Just this cheap thing. Can't afford a snazzy one. I had one
once, but too many people tried to get hold of me. Anyway, like I
said, I lost it. Hardly ever turn this on."

"Well it's no use ringing the children. They're not answering. The thing is, I'm afraid they won't just stay here at the Fair, but try to get out to Pinkney, looking for Mr. Brambling."

"I could take you," said Scarp. "I could borrow a fairground van. *They* wouldn't mind, not for something like this."

"Perhaps you could go with Hamish. He knows the way. And I'll carry on looking here. You say this Big Sid likes a pint. Perhaps they've followed him to a pub. I could ask around."

Scarp grinned. "You're going round the pubs? A nun?"

Bianca frowned. "I don't have to drink!"

But her indignation only enhanced the joke and Scarp's grin broadened to reveal a set of broken teeth.

"A nun who's lost her children, looking for a fairground geezer in a pub!"

"All right it sounds funny. But who cares, if it works?"

"And what does Mother Superior say if she gets to hear of it?"

"She *doesn't* get to hear of it! Will you help?"

Scarp sobered up and nodded. "*Trudi Larsson, you're going to be in such trouble when I catch up with you.* Don't worry, we'll find them." He almost convinced himself. "And if not, we'll go to the police, and Sister Emilia can lump it. They're probably at this Brambling's cottage already."

Sister Bianca gripped his hands. "I'm so glad to have found you," she effused, with an earnestness that made him blush. "Nobody else would listen to me but Hamish, and he's going home."

"Well I'm not going anywhere," Scarp looked her in the eye and took in for the first time how pretty she was – a stunner really - fair hair and a slender neck, half hidden by her veil. Momentarily, he caught himself wondering what she looked like when she took it off. Then he pushed the thought away. "I'm with you till we sort this out. I mean the whole lot – Corky, Sven – this Swedish nut – Grandfather Larsson and all. Ned will look after my dog, I'm sure. You do your pubs and we'll try this Humbug Cottage. Take my phone and if we have any luck we'll call you."

"Bless you!" said Bianca, releasing his hands and wiping the oil she had picked up from them on her knees.

Blessed by a nun! Who would have thought it!

The plan sounded simple. Bianca made her way to the *The Tapster* and the men set off for Pinkney. And the wind from the north swept all the summer warmth out of Kingsbury, ripping the petals off the flowers in the quads and scattering loose papers on windowsills. There was a change coming. The fairground people reluctantly read it in the sky. There would be rain and a storm brewing up somewhere. Perhaps this was just the tail of it. But when the good weather returned, there would be a harvest bite to the air. That sappy sweetness of early summer would be gone for good.

At Humbug Cottage the story was the same. The rambler roses, swaying in the gale, had shed pink snow all over the grass. Hollyhocks and delphiniums lay prone. It looked, at first glance, as if there had been a scuffle.

Hamish had planned to break in if his knock brought no reply. He reckoned it would be a small matter to shin up the thatch and loosen that dormer window on the side, just in case the old boy had collapsed inside, or somehow come to harm.

Scarp's mind worked a different way. He had been fingering in his pocket the bent wire picks, used only that morning to do a job at the Fair. The moving belt that carried the Shooting-Range ducks round their pond had jammed, just as the booth was about to open and no one had such patience, or nimble fingers for fixing things, as Scarp. That was how he had got lumbered with manning the stall, and how his hands came to be covered in grease. Now the picks would be useful for breaking in, if no one was at home.

As it turned out, neither scheme was needed, for the door already stood ajar. They wavered a moment on the step and then went in.

"Hulloa!" called Hamish. "Anyone about? Mr. Brambling? It's Hamish. Hamish Wall!"

Silence.

He stepped back outside. "He might be in the garden. I'll go round the back. You look here."

Scarp blinked at the dark within, and fumbled his way to the kitchen. Everything tidy there. Then back to the parlour. All as you would expect, except that the wind had loosened the window catch and done some damage. An ornament lay in pieces in the hearth. It must have taken quite a gust to shift that – and there were letters strewn about. Someone ought to secure the catch, but he knew better. All it needed was a nice set of finger-prints to pin a charge of burglary on him! He climbed the stairs instead. Bedrooms all in apple-pie order. Bathroom. Box-room. And then the last… A shadowy door, tucked away on the other side of the landing, with the thumb-latch all but wrenched off. And inside, an office, with computers, a lot of them… absolutely trashed!

"Oh Gawd! Scarp!" muttered the gipsy. "What have you walked into now?"

When Hamish arrived, he was still in the doorway, shaking his head.

"Oho! Getting warmer!" Hamish rubbed his hands. "Perhaps Trudi was on to something, after all!"

"I don't like it," said Scarp. "This looks like a proper police job now. And I don't get on with the police. There's probably a body round the corner."

"Shall we look?"

Hamish marched inside, and peered behind the door. "All clear! You can come on in!" Since Scarp made no move to join him, he proceeded alone, wrapping his hand in his sleeve when he touched any evidence. The desk had been ransacked and books and files pulled from the shelves, their contents rifled and discarded at random.

As for the computers, they lay in pieces, wires ripped from sockets, monitor screens smashed, printers dismembered, as if bludgeoned with a heavy implement. Traces of blood suggested that the intruder had cut himself in his frenzy. But something else, amidst the scattered papers, made Hamish stare.

There were typescripts and manuscripts, some looking, at first glance, like talks for the local Horticultural Society: notes on bee-lore, herbal cures, lunar planting and all sorts of astrological nonsense. But other jottings, which could not reasonably have interested the gardeners of Pinkney, discussed archaeology, necrology and ritual sacrifice, with detailed plans of burials and funerary monuments. Sometimes the subjects were mixed up together. There were drawings of ziggurats, with bee-nests superimposed upon them and subtexts, all in algebraic mumbo-jumbo! Brilliant scholar? This stuff made Mr. Brambling look more like a crank. Hamish shook his head. But what really caught

317

his eye were the great ledgers, bound in Morocco leather, which lay discarded on the floor. They had been drawn up in longhand - fine copperplate - using an old-fashioned fountain pen and they contained shopping lists of subjects, in columns, like a plantsman's catalogue. The headings gave general classifications, highlighted in italics... and sub-categories, to be ticked off in red: *found, cultivated, harvested*. Hamish gingerly turned the pages.

Some volumes were filled with the names of plants and animals, giving species and genus - exhaustive directories, carefully annotated. Some listed human professions. There were dancers and bookbinders, clockmakers and magicians. One whole section detailed the members of a tribe in Borneo. They had been harvested in March. In another book, entitled 'Spiritual Interest' were plans of brain types, showing the nerve centres which were stimulated by music or prayer. A Hindu Mystic had been located in Birmingham. A Dervish from Morocco was found to have a particularly fine frontal lobe. From St. Lucy's Convent, in Kingsbury, Sisters Caroline, Morwenna, Teresa-Benedict, Emilia, Matilda, Roberta and Bianca had all been contacted and were undergoing cultivation. *Sister Bianca!*

Forgetting all about fingerprints, Hamish fell to his knees and began to thumb through the index. 'S' for Scientist. So many names! Here were astronomers, biochemists... ecologists... Yes! Each name had a number, like a convict.

And here, the latest entry: *'Larsson, Sven. No.56,620. Harvested June 22nd'*. That was yesterday!

At the beginning of the book, under letter 'B', several pages were torn out.

But who had ransacked the room? Surely not the children!

Who had torn up these architectural plans? Scraps covered the carpet, depicting what seemed to be the lay-out of a vast, complex building with chambers resembling prison cells. Hamish began to reassemble the pieces until he could make sense of them... Compact, hexagonal, like honeycomb, the units formed a spatial labyrinth with connecting alleys running in all directions. The artist, Escher, had once made drawings of fantastic buildings, but nothing on this scale. Each numbered cell, here, held an occupant and the whole added up to a great dome-shaped edifice, similar in

318

appearance to a beehive. Other charts plotted a general site with areas of forest and research facilities.

"My God, Scarp, I've got it!" Hamish cried. "This is the key to it all. Brambling had the key to it all. He must have been researching the whole project in secret. These are the plans to the Beedome. No wonder the children thought he was in danger!"

A gloomy Scarp folded his arms. "Like I said," he repeated. "Police job."

"This could go right to the top."

At that moment Hamish's mobile rang.

"Praise the Lord," cried Sister Emilia's disembodied voice. "God has answered our prayers! I've just spoken to Sven. He rang only a minute ago to say the children are safe with *him*. They are all together at Pinkney. Isn't it wonderful? Tell Sister Bianca to come home right away. I shan't be angry about her missing Vespers. We'll have a special celebration supper tonight!"

"Sister Emilia…"

"No buts, my dear boy!" she insisted in her imperious way. "This is a true miracle and, please God, it will be the end of the affair!"

With that she cut him off. Hamish practically choked. *The end?* He felt that things had hardly begun! How could he leave matters here in such confusion? Yet Sister Bianca must be fetched and all he could do now was take some snapshots, for evidence, on his phone. That would at least give the police a start. Before he left, however, he could not resist pocketing some fragments of the Beedome plans and charts. They must not fall into the wrong hands and they might prove useful in the future. He felt sure he had not heard the last of the Beedome.

As they made their way back to the van, Scarp tripped over something half-buried in the grass. It was a knobstick, a vicious-looking club with a worn and polished handle. "Murder weapon?" he suggested. He was still convinced that there must be a body.

"Very likely!" Hamish took it from him. "But I know it from somewhere… I've seen someone brandishing it recently. Of course! It belongs to Edmund, the tramp who calls at Lucy's! Whyever should he want to come and do damage here? He's not normally a violent chap and Mr. Brambling has always been very kind to him. Do you think he interrupted someone else? Or did he himself have an interest in something beginning with 'B'?" There was no way of knowing. The missing pages might have covered anything from Bell Ringers to Bicycle Thieves... unless 'B' stood for Brambling himself... or Beekeepers...

Chapter Thirty-Five

Barbara's Honey Trap

When Barbara alighted from the taxi, she thought there must have been some mistake. No 38, Bacon Street appeared to be empty. The shop below, whose sign still read, 'Wilkins and Co. Quality Stationers', presented blank, whitewashed windows to the street and a large 'To Let' board, nailed above, announced its permanent closure.

As for the flat itself, Barbara heaved herself up the narrow stairway that led to it with a sinking heart. It looked very much as if the bird had flown. Then, as she reached the final step, the door flew open and Olaf himself, loaded to the chin with technical equipment, a large plaster affixed to his right temple, burst forth. Seeing his passage blocked he stopped, staggered and beat a hasty retreat, but his arms being full, he was not quite quick enough to prevent Barbara's foot in the door and when he finally managed to close it, the two of them stood inside, like a pair of hostile cats, eyeing one another at close range.

"So, this is where you hide up, is it?" Barbara allowed herself a survey of the room. Now stripped bare, it looked like any ordinary room. In fact, with that wonderful window bay, it had a certain gracious charm. Another tenant would have made much of that and provided a seat and a pile of books. Of the Laser Wag furnishing, nothing remained but the vinyl sofas and stacks of documents in files.

Olaf put down his burden and squinted from intruder to window as though briefly considering escape that way. But he could not leave without his luggage, and being a coward - he had always shrunk from risks of a physical nature - he tried bluffing his way out instead.

"I can't stop now. As you can see, I'm very busy. Come to my new office. I'll give you my card ..."

"Olaf Stromberg ..." Barbara intoned in a low, slow murmur. "How I have waited for this moment."

"You – you won't, you can't hurt me! Not here! Why? Wh-What have I done?" Panic gleamed in his eyes.

"I don't know, exactly," Barbara, set down her bag. "But I sure as hell am going to find out! Now you and I are going to have a little talk, just cosy like, on that nice sofa of yours, and you are going to tell me... *everything!*"

"No, no! There are laws in this country that protect an individual in his own property..."

"Unless of course, that property happens to have burnt down?" she kept up the same quiet, purring tone. But Olaf knew that the screeching and swearing would follow soon enough. This was how cats fought. He could see Barbara now as a great tabby creature with fur in spikes, green eyes blazing... Magnificent in a deadly sort of way.

"What do you want? What do you want from me? Money? I can give you money, if that's it."

"Oh, Olaf, it's *you* I want! No use dashing for the door. You're going to sit down there and see what I've got for you. Brought it all the way from Sussex, as a gift. You see, *I'm* the one who's giving."

"I'll do no such thing! If you don't go I'll call the police. I'm a very busy man."

"Oh yes, a good idea! Let's call the police because they have been looking for you for months and didn't know where to find you."

"I don't know what you're talking about. I've done nothing wrong. I won't be bullied in this way..."

"Bullied? By a poor helpless woman who has come to see you as a friend? Olaf! Shame on you! I've come to learn from you. You know such a lot. And I know a little, in my way. Together we could make a great team."

Olaf gave a brittle laugh. "You? Preposterous!"

"Just try a taste of this and then tell me if I'm preposterous. You see, you knew about my special bookshop, but you didn't know about my special cakes. Now these would put BioDawn, well, in a class entirely of its own. Have you ever had a BioDawn cake, Olaf? It's not a pleasant experience. But *this* cake is to die for. If you had the recipe for this cake, you would be the darling of the nation. No, don't reach for your gun, or your phone, or whatever it is you've got in your pocket. Sit down and try a bit. It's the only way you'll ever know for sure."

Barbara backed him up to a sofa and he sank down, white and trembling.

"Mrs. Rainbow…"

"Bird, Miss," she corrected.

"I'm a very busy man. I have a terribly important appointment…"

"Sooner you eat, sooner you go," Barbara sounded like a nanny with the medicine spoon.

"One tiny bit, thank you. Then you must let me leave."

"Sure," purred Barbara. "You shall leave whenever you want."

She delved into her bag and brought forth a bundle, wrapped in a white cloth, two china plates, tea forks and glasses of the kind they use for drinking schnapps.

"We must have something to drink. Even good cake is too dry without."

A warm, spicy aroma tickled Olaf's nostrils, making his mouth water as she unwound the cloth. "This is a recipe for summer evenings. It's not very nice today, cold and windy. So we'll make our own sunshine." Her knife slid through the crust, and prized free a slice, light, moist and golden. There was a marzipan topping, dusted with sugar spangles. "Can you guess what's in it?"

Sweet and heady, the cake melted on the tongue.

Olaf shook his head, but after one bite he wanted more.

"Try again," cooed Barbara, cutting another slice. "Now, what's in it?"

"Sherry?" asked Olaf.

Barbara laughed. "You'll want a little of this to wash it down." She brought out a bottle of amber brew. "Just a little, mind. It's quite strong." She filled his glass and poured some for herself, which she did not touch.

"This!" Olaf sat up with a sudden smile. "I've had this before. It's mead, isn't it? *Wonderful stuff."*

"And the cake?"

"Mead cake. Pure genius! And you'll let me have the recipe?"

"Oh yes, but you must try this one too." Out came another parcel. "This is the chocolate version. Try a sip with that!"

323

Olaf popped a sample into his mouth. "This is gold. Pure gold! Sir Maximus will be beside himself."

"Of course he will," said Barbara, refilling his glass. "You're going to be head boy, Olaf."

"I am head boy, already!" Olaf expostulated. Then he giggled. "That's the joke. Nobody realizes how powerful I am."

"Course they don't," Barbara carved another slice. "You're so modest Olaf. I expect they treat you bad, take you for granted."

"You're right! They do. It's 'Olaf do this, go there, fetch that.' Nobody recognizes that without me…"

"Everything would fall apart. You're the one with the brain, Olaf. Who else would have thought of burning all the evidence so conveniently, to keep the police off your trail?"

"It was *my* idea. And my technical skill."

"It was genius, Olaf. Drink up!"

"*I* was the butterfly hunter. They merely stuck the specimens on a board."

"Ah, you did it all, didn't you? Sniffing out the people who had something special to collect…"

"Collect! That's the word. I was like a truffle-hunter."

"You sure sniffed them out! So why are you packing up?"

Olaf, dazed by the vision of his own magnificence, had to stop to consider. Holding out his plate automatically, he seemed suddenly deflated, depressed.

"It's all coming to an end."

"What, BioDawn? Surely not!"

"BioDawn is only part of it. Laser Wag – they are all subsidiaries of the big project."

"Which is?"

"To create a new world. A totally new world. A paradise of all the best things in this world - but perfect and eternal - in cyberspace."

"Surely you're joking! Here, have some more."

"Never more serious. Of course it's top secret. It will be a bank, like a seed bank, but on computer, of everything we need to preserve on earth. With global warming and fuel shortages and wars, well, we might lose everything. This way there is a future. Eventually the computers will be able to carry on the work without us. They will have enough knowledge and expertise and of course they can work so much faster and more efficiently than we can. They don't get ill and die. They don't fall in love, or quarrel. Imagine it! No more disease. No more disasters. We won't need the earth any more."

"So Sir Maximus…"

"…is merely a caterpillar on the vine. He's making a profit now and providing the money. He paid for the Beedome. He funds the research."

"And Laser Wag…"

"…is the technology. The laser technology encodes all the information and stores it in holograms. I could make a hologram of your cake, just like that, and save it in the Beedome. And every crumb of your cake would contain the code for the whole cake. We could make millions at the touch of a button. All protected by international patents."

"And people?"

"Just the same!"

"Is that what happened to Corky?"

"Corky... Do I know Corky? I meet so many people."

"The guy who's just gone into the sanatorium, here in Kingsbury. I think you stole his bees back in the spring."

"Oh yes, the hunchback. Yes we harvested him some months ago."

"Harvested?"

"It doesn't hurt." Olaf assured her.

With a supreme effort, Barbara sat on her fury, and squeezed out another smile.

"Show me," she coaxed. "Prove it. Who's next on the list?" She plied his glass again.

"Next is an instrument maker – very fine. Local."

"Doesn't make cellos by any chance?"

"That young lad Jurgen has one! Now Archie, we'll use his first name, he is a UFO fanatic. What could be easier? We both love radios. He's forever listening for a message from outer space. I can send them. But his equipment is a little out of date. Imagine, one day - such a pity - it fuses out and starts a fire. A fire in a workshop full of woodchips! You can imagine. Skål! Of course, we need to collect all those instruments first and the maker too. I can call him in whenever I want. He'll come like a moth to a candle. All I have to do is perform a little modification to his radio, attach my miniature laser scanner and… Bingo! Fortunately, he's a smoker… Everyone will think it was an old cigar…"

"Do it," commanded Barbara.

"What?"

"Call him in now. Prove to me you can do it. Otherwise I shall think you're just a bragger who's had too much to drink!"

Olaf stood up indignantly and then plopped back in his seat. His legs had gone and his brain was spinning.

"That's indimtimation!" he complained.

"Do it!" Barbara insisted. "I'll help you."

"Mr. Brambling won't like it. He won't like it at all."

"*The* Mr. Brambling? The old guy?"

"Who else?"

"*He's* in this?"

Olaf giggled again. "*In* it?" He laughed till the tears rolled down his face. "He *is* it. The whole thing is his brain-child. Don't be deceived by appearances. St. John Brambling is as lethal as cyanide."

"Olaf," said Barbara, "We've got to stop this thing. You and me. Before they turn on you too."

"Ah, but they can't," Olaf wiped his eyes. "I know the codes, you see. They don't think I do, but I do. I could send the whole thing up, boom! whenever I liked. I know the bee codes - everything!"

"And could you undo what has been done?"

The Swede looked askance.

"Could you bring back the people who have been 'harvested'?"

"Turn back the clock?"

"Yes. Could you do that?" She watched him closely.

"Can't get at the computer. It's all locked up in the Beedome."

Barbara tried a different tack. "Well, I don't believe any of it. I think you're drunk and raving. If you're so clever, why didn't you harvest me when you had the chance?"

Olaf wriggled in his seat. "Don't take this the wrong way – I just didn't think you were special enough to make it worthwhile. Of course I didn't know then about the cake…"

"But Corky was special."

"Yes."

"And who else is special? Are the Sisters special? And Sven?"

"Yes, yes."

"And my lamb, Trudi, is she special?" *Say you've taken her, Barbara pledged, and I'll brain you!*

"No, for the moment she's safe, unless she does something foolish," said Olaf. "We're saving her till she brings in someone else."

Barbara frowned and then beckoned as though Olaf was a dog who had picked up something he shouldn't.

"Tell, Olaf!"

"No. Can't. I'll plobly already be excrutiated already for saying what I've said."

"Tell!"

"You won't get it out of me. I'm uncorpupt... inpercrup... uncorrprubtiple."

"You don't even know!"

"Don't know? I've been trying to track him down for six months. But where has he gone? Vanished up like smoke – poof! I can't bear it!" Olaf put his head in his hands.

"We'll find him together,"

"Yes."

"Have another drink. You'll feel better."

"Yes."

"And a piece more cake."

"I *never* failed before!"

"Course you didn't. Let's see if we can catch him now. We'll call Archie, first, and then we'll go and look. What's his name?"

"Per Larsson, stupid!" Olaf rubbed his face. "You're trying to trick me, but I'm smarter than you think. I'm not going to confess under torture – not to any Mother Superior – Anyhow I've got them covered. Every word they say goes straight to the Beedome. I put a camera in the chapel..."

"Call Archie now," wheedled Barbara.

"I have my dignity to respect!"

"Course you do. How do we call Archie?"

"'S on the radio... My radio. Which way up does it go?"

"Let's try this way. You put on the headphones?"

"Tickles!" objected the Swede. "What do I say?"

"Say the aliens have landed – whatever you like. Do you have a code for it? Tell him to come and bring his radio."

"Oh yes. Where *are* we?"

Barbara shook her head. *Oh Boy, Beery. That sure is some liquor!*

By the time Archie arrived, Olaf was rambling, inarticulate. But Barbara had enough information to give a plausible account of his doings.

"The question is what to do with him next? Do we hand him over to the nuns? Or to the police? Or do we get him to take us to this Beedome?"

"I don't see what we can do, alone. It all sounds so far-fetched. We need evidence."

"And before the effects of the mead wear off."

Barbara sidled up to the somnolent Swede. "Olaf, we are going for a little drive in your car. Can you manage that? Have you got the keys?"

"Keys in my pocket."

"Can we have them?"

"Certainly not! *My* keys, *my* car!"

"Olaf, honey, you're too drunk to drive."

"My car very clever car. Can't crash. Computer brain. All sensors everywhere. Don't you see the adverts? Stupid people!"

"Let's go then. Perhaps Archie can help you."

"Don't need help, thank you! I want to go home anyway. Tired now."

They stumbled together down the stairs and across the street to the bay where the white convertible waited. Olaf's hasty packing had left hardly any room inside, but Barbara scrambled into the back and said a quick prayer, while Archie and Olaf tussled over the keys.

"*My* keys!" Olaf wrenched them free with surprising strength, and launched himself behind the wheel. "Nobody drives my car but me. I got sasellite navi - navitation, see. That tells me where we're going! Whoops! No problem!"

With a screech of tyres and a smell of burnt rubber they careered out into the traffic.

"Call someone for help," Barbara tapped on Archie's shoulder.

But Archie shrugged helplessly back. "I'm a radio man!" he shouted. "No phone!"

Shooting the lights at Market Square they narrowly missed a removal lorry, took a shortcut up the bus lane and sped out towards the ring road and the open countryside. The sat-nav system seemed to have been preset for the west and gave out directions, frequently interspersed with scoldings about incorrect procedures and re-routing schedules. The sign-posts they passed pointed to Drayholt. Olaf sat upright as an Egyptian mummy, staring blindly ahead.

"You been this way, recently, Olaf?" called Barbara.

"Shut up!" he replied. "Can't you see, I'm busy?"

Wherever they went they were met with flashing lights and angry horn-blasts from other drivers. At least one cyclist chose the safety of the ditch and careered off the road as they approached. Two speed cameras caught them doing seventy miles an hour through residential areas and they knocked over a painter's ladder at a level crossing.

The roads got smaller as they left Kingsbury behind. Country lanes now took them between pastures with high hedges where ox-eye daisies and yellow hawkweed waved. *Any minute now we are going to meet a tractor coming the other way – and that will be the end of us!* thought Barbara. But miraculously they survived. At the foot of Drayholt Hill they veered left, down what seemed no more than a holloway, a tunnel of dusty thorn trees. And at the end of the tunnel, where Barbara first became aware of the helicopter overhead, and where Olaf violently slammed on his brakes, they came to rest at the entrance to a hidden valley. By the roadside reeked the remains of what had once been a cottage; its naked roof-timbers charred; its windows, empty sockets with smoke-stained lintels above. The fire brigade, who had clearly arrived too late to save the building, had barricaded the site with candy-striped tape. Boards bearing 'Danger - Keep Out' signs were nailed across all lower points of access. At the rear, a sorry cluster of beech trees stood scorch-blackened on their hithermost side.

"Mrs. Partridge!" gasped Archie. "You villain! What have you done to her!"

"Wasn't really her I wanted," Olaf mused, fingering his plaster. "It was the worms. The glow worms. But she interfered. Quite a virago. I had no choice actually. It became a question of self-defence."

"She was the sweetest, kindest woman you can imagine. And *you* are the only worm around here!" Archie flung out of the car and, marching round to the driver's side, pulled Olaf from his seat, his big chest heaving, his face sweating with rage.

"Don't kill him, Archie," cried Barbara. "We need to save him for later..."

∞∞∞∞∞∞∞∞

"...Those were her precise words," announced the Special Constable who made the arrests and brought the miscreants in for questioning at Kingsbury Police Station.

Directed by the police helicopter, three cars, with sirens blaring, had followed Olaf's trail of destruction and caught up with him just in time to interrupt the fray. Within an hour, all suspects were sitting, kicking their heels in an interview room. Not only the *Gloucester Gazette*, but the *Kingsbury Chronicle* had got wind of the affair and were already pestering for details for their morning editions.

"...They were just about to start a punch up!" He was new to the job and proud of his catch.

Sergeant Peach, the officer on duty, gave a weary grunt. A glance at the station clock satisfied him that it was almost time to go home. Six p.m. already and he was looking forward the end of his shift. He had bought one of those BioDawn steak and kidney pies for his supper, for since his wife left home, he had, thanks to the 'Organic Home Gourmet Range', become a dab hand with the microwave. He had also set up his satellite digi-recorder to tape the Kingsbury Ranger's qualifying match. He fancied a nice, lazy evening with his feet up. The last thing he needed now was a scene with a bunch of goofs.

"You realize that you have committed very serious offences, I suppose," he began.

"I was drugged and kidnapped," whined Olaf, who had entered a phase of self-pity.

"He took off in the car before we could do anything about it." Archie's defence sounded hardly more convincing.

330

"Oh, what the hell," said Barbara, dispensing with excuses. "We were coming here anyway to hand him in. The road thing is really neither here nor there."

"Reckless driving. Drunken driving. Speeding. Threatening a police officer. And attempted assault, I've got written here," said the Officer in Charge.

"Yes, yes, I know, but that's not the point."

"Would you like to suggest another one?"

"Mass murder!" she replied, as though it was the most obvious thing in the world. "This man is an arsonist, a spy, a kidnapper and a thief. He is plotting the overthrow of the world as we know it."

Oh Lord!

"If you don't believe me then make some phone calls. Ask the nuns at St. Lucy's. Ask for the missing persons register in Litven, Sweden. Oh, and there's a cello teacher in Tilchester who will vouch for me."

Not tonight, prayed Sergeant Peach. *Please Lord, not tonight. Let me just watch my football and eat my pie!*

But she hadn't finished yet. "I'll more than gladly write it all out in a statement…"

Perfect.

"And Archie will too, I'm sure. He was there at the scene of that fire, only two days ago, looking for glow-worms and UFO's during the lunar eclipse. And everything was fine then!"

UFO's… glow-worms… whatever had these people been drinking?

"You have a car full of valuable equipment, Mr. Stromberg. Can I ask how you came to be in possession of that?"

"It's perfectly letigimate!" he expostulated. "I work for Laser Wag. Call them. Call my solicitor. Call Sir Magnimus Bligh. I insist!"

Thank heavens. Here's the coffee.

"And you say you know nothing about the fire?"

"Oh no, the fires are mine. I specialize…"

That's enough. They're all out of their tinies! I can't sit listening to this - I'm off!

"Hargreaves, see if we can find accommodation for these people until they have sobered up. They can write their statements and then sleep on it. I'll talk to them again in the morning. And tell

Constable Truman to take no nonsense from them or any of their friends. If the Laser Wag thing is true, they can go as soon as assurances are made that they will appear for charges, when summoned." In an undertone he added: "No need to bother with the woman's stories. She's obviously nuts. Just let them write what they want and give them a warning about wasting police time. That should do it."

However, Olaf would not submit quietly. Having worked himself up, he made an enormous fuss about his rights until the requisite phone calls were made. The solicitor finally contacted Sir Maximus, and he came blustering on the line at seven.

"I never heard such a farrago of nonsense. Stromberg is the soundest man alive. What proof do you have that he was at the wheel?"

Constable Truman had been given the facts rather late.

"Precisely. None!" continued Sir Maximus without pause. He was trying to fasten his bow tie in the mirror and had the telephone receiver tucked askew beneath his ear. Such a delicate operation always put him in a ticklish mood and he found this interruption, when his limousine was waiting at the door and the canapés were probably already circulating at the Chamber of Commerce Evening Do, simply too provoking.

"They were all out of the car when your men arrived. Could have been any of them and by your own admission the other two were sober. Now stop making a nuisance of yourself and harassing my man. He's on special work, you know. If you value your job or any chances of promotion," he coughed, "you'll forget this whole business and let the fellow go. Hush it up. He's been under a lot of pressure. I'm seeing the Chief Constable at dinner tonight. I'll explain things then. Got it! Good chap!"

However, by the time the order for Olaf's release came through, he had fallen into an impenetrable slumber. Determined not to leave his side, Barbara and Archie hung on till the early hours, reasoning that if all else failed, they could blackmail him to take them to the Beedome.

And by order of Sir Maximus, Barbara's appeal for help slipped quietly into the waste paper basket.

Chapter Thirty-Six

On the Trail

By seven o'clock the children had scoured every inch of the Fair, but found no trace of Sid or Scarp. Sid, it turned out, had gone to visit his mother at Copsley, and Scarp had last been seen driving away in a borrowed van. Tired, cold and hungry, they took stock of their situation with sinking hearts.

"Perhaps we should go home," suggested Jurgen.

"Fine for you!" snapped Sophie. "I in't got a home. They'll all be out looking for me! If only we had the bus fare, we could get ourselves to Pinkney easy. Now we got a long walk."

"Wait a minute." Trudi swung round. "We can get to Pinkney an easy way! Old Tom would take us on his boat. He as good as offered to when we said goodbye yesterday. *'I'm here any time for friends that need me.'* That's what he said."

"Who's this, then?"

"Old Tom, he got a boat. Might give us dinner too!" said Pedro, remembering the potatoes.

The sun, like a ghost in a shroud, was sliding towards the west. And still that wind, that promised bad weather somewhere, worried at the college flags and stirred up 'devils' of dust in eddies along the pavements.

"Come on," cried Trudi. "Follow the sun – that's what Hamish said. We need to pass the hospital, that's the big building with the angel on top, and then the phone box and... we'll remember when we get there."

"*I* know the way to the canal! I've lived here more than half my life, haven't I? Yer want Cromwell Street. Then cut through Elysium."

"Elysium? Where the dead go?" Pedro pricked up his ears.

"It's just the name of the district."

"Because of the meadows!" said Trudi, feeling rather pleased with herself. "Elysian Fields! I've heard of them."

"Not today, thank you! Come on, cross here!"

They scampered along after Sophie, re-passing the streets, and geranium pots they had seen the day before. Soon the canal wharf appeared, the ticket office now boarded up, the water prickling beneath the wind.

"Up here!" Jurgen ran ahead along the towpath. He too was thinking of potatoes.

At the moorings, only two barges remained. The fibreglass craft had departed, while the little yachts huddled together, secured on their beach, for everyone knew that rain was coming and the sunshine sailors had headed home. A general air of desertion was intensified by the roar of the wind in the poplars and the pink-pink of the yacht riggings tapping their metal masts.

If Trudi shut her eyes she could imagine herself a thousand miles away. Nowhere… And who could say which was more real? The mad momentum of this present here-and-now, or the suspended stillness of a land which knew no time? In the blink of an eye, the pink-pink of the rigging halyards could become the 'tink' of innumerable reindeer bells as the snowbound landscape of her imagination unrolled beneath a sky sequined with stars. And which was really home? This instant world, that offered no comfortable place to rest, and reproached everyone for not keeping up, not staying abreast, racing ahead? This glorified fairground ride? Or that place, elsewhere, just over there on the shadow-side of things, where time did not need to hurry, but pooled and waited while new worlds were born?

"He's here!" cried Jurgen. "He's still here. Look, the chimney's smoking!"

No time to go there now. Trudi opened her eyes and hurried to the landing stage.

"Mr. Tom!" She called. "Mr. Tom, can we come aboard? It's the Larssons again…"

Old Tom stuck his head out of the cabin door and nodded as if he had been expecting them. Trudi did not think to question why.

"…We need to get to Pinkney. You did say you could help us."

"Who's this then?"

"Sophie. She's coming with us. To look after us," she added, thinking there might be an objection.

But Tom was not concerned. He slid the gangplank ashore with a welcoming grin.

334

"You on an adventure then?"

"Sort of."

"'Spect you'll be hungry then. Take my hand, young Sophie and step up. Welcome to the *Mayfly*."

Ungainly as she seemed, Sophie lumbered aboard without help and the children hopped on after her.

"Get yourselves down in the cabin, now. Mind your heads. Supper's almost ready."

Tucked down, out of the wind, the cabin felt cosy and warm. A pot of meatballs and dumplings simmered on the stove, giving off tempting aromas, and while the children arranged themselves along the corner bench, Old Tom threw a blue-check cloth on the table and set five places.

"Food first. Then leave. We've got an hour or two of daylight easy, I reckon. Plenty of time to get you to Pinkney before dusk."

"What will you do? Will you come back here?" asked Jurgen.

"How long you going to be?"

Trudi shook her head. "We don't know. We might be some time." She had given no thought to the future, beyond finding Mr. Brambling and her father. She was not entirely sure that they would even be coming back. All of them shared an unspoken understanding that if they failed it would be the end of them and everything they knew. There would be no future to worry about then.

Old Tom let the matter pass. "Two dumplings? Three? A growing boy, like you should have three!"

The barge clock ticked languidly on.

After dumplings came a lemon pudding with hot sauce. The wind whistled in the tarpaulin outside and Old Tom debated whether or not to bring in his geraniums.

"You're going to need coats if you wander out in this. There are some waterproofs there, in the cupboard by the door. And caps, in case it rains. Can't have you catching a chill now, can we? Well, if you're all done, I'll go and start her up. You rest youselves, best you can, and I'll call you when we get there."

He lurched up the steps and the wind slammed the door shut behind him. His barge shuddered to life moments later. They heard the heavy mooring rope flop down on deck and the thump of the gangplank as it scraped over the gunwhale. Then the propellers whipped up a froth and the *Mayfly* eased forward.

No one spoke. They felt tense as a raiding party, their differences suddenly put aside. *Trust the day*, said Mr. Brambling. Well, they were certainly doing that now! They were out in uncharted waters and who knew where they would finish up?

When they arrived at Pinkney Lock, Old Tom pulled into the side and let his engine idle.

"You going to be all right now?" he said with fatherly concern. "Someone meeting you?"

"Oh yes," Trudi gave a confident smile. "Mr. Brambling. He's looking after us while Daddy is busy."

"You know which way you are going?"

"*I* know the way." Sophie could match anyone when it came to lying. "We'll be just fine!"

"Good luck, then!" he handed them tenderly ashore.

"How can we thank you, Mr. Tom?" Trudi gushed. It felt like a last goodbye.

"No need for thanks. It's my pleasure. Just keep your wits about you!" his leathery grip intensified. "I wish I could come with you, but I can't." He considered for a moment the charm round Trudi's neck and touched it with his finger. "Take care, now! I do believe if anyone can find their way tonight it will be you. You have come a long way but you have done well. Not much further now. You hold on tight, my darling, and all shall be well." He dropped his hand and turned to go. "I'll wait here a while. If you need me, you know where to find me. Call and I will come."

It never occurred to Trudi to wonder why he cared. Or why, since he cared, he did not try to take charge as grown-ups invariably did. Contrary to waterway regulations, he had resolved to moor up where he was and the last time Trudi looked back she saw him already fumbling with a lamp.

Ahead, lay the black waters of the lock, with its sinister drop and winding equipment. Behind them, the darkening meadows. A path, musky with camomile, set off through open country to the right.

"This is it," said Sophie. "This leads to the woods over there. That's Pinkney Forest, that is, and the Beedome is somewhere inside. If we can hide up there overnight, we might be able to break in before the morning staff arrive. God, I hate the countryside! Do you think there's bats in there?"

A five minute tramp brought them to the field-edge. Here the path doubled back on itself and dog-legged away through the corn, but it had brought them to the beginning of the wood, and a wall of trees now reared up before them, blotting out the sky. With dilated eyes and pounding hearts, they tiptoed closer and peered in... Nothing to be seen. Not a signpost, a boulder, a fern even, showed between the foremost trunks and everything beyond was lost in impenetrable gloom.

There was a perimeter fence made of thick chain-link, finished off with barbed-wire... The rim sloped outwards to deter intruders and in the waning light it looked ominously high. Sophie gauged it with a critical eye.

"In the old days I could've bin over that before you could spit. Look at me now! Couldn't get one lousy leg up!"

"Perhaps *we* can climb over and then find an opening from the other side," suggested Jurgen, whose blood was up.

Pedro began to scout about. He still had a better sense of direction when the light was dim. "Is sunthing here. Bad news, I think!" He had found a notice nailed to one of the poles. Of course he could not read the text, but the message was clear enough.

"Warning. Electrified fence. Guard dogs patrolling at all times," read Jurgen. A drawing of an Alsation's head made a decorative footnote.

"Oh no! Not dogs," Trudi recoiled. "I can't go in if there are dogs." Instinctively she hugged the shoulder which Beor had bitten almost a year before.

"Dogs no problem," grinned Pedro. "I can talk to dogs, like I talk to bees. Sure, really. No problem. Come on – we're saving Corky. We can get in somewhere." He felt his way along the fence. "This not electric anyway."

Jurgen spotted what looked like cables overhead. "Up there it is. We need to go under or *through.*"

No sooner had he spoken than Pedro began to laugh. "Like I said. No problem. Someone cut it already. Look."

Sure enough, the wire had been had clipped and wrenched apart to admit a person of medium height. The nettles inside had been trampled.

"Looks as if someone was expecting us," Sophie squeezed through.

"I can't do it," cried Trudi, hanging back. "Not with dogs. Not without Grandfather to protect me."

"But you *are* protected, silly!" said Jurgen, suddenly inspired. "You've got your amulet. And so have I. That's like *two* Grandfathers."

"And I got the Virgin Mary," beamed Pedro shaking his medallion.

"And I in't got nothing," said Sophie. "So the dogs'll eat me first, while you lot run away!"

Their bravado put Trudi to shame. How that cold feeling at her heart made her tremble! But she could not be left behind. She could not be the one to disgrace herself as a scare-baby. She took refuge in humour.

"We are going to die, you know," she pronounced from the rear.

But Sophie was standing for no half-heartedness.

"You get cold feet now and you'll die sooner than you think, 'cos I'm gonna kill you first. Okay?" This was how it had been in the old days. At the circus, with the chain saws whirring down in the ring, the young acrobats would queue in the darkened wings, waiting for the big trapeze to swing out towards them. And someone – she had done it often enough herself - would suddenly feel sick and want to go down, but you couldn't let them. You had to conquer fear or you would fall. So they made crazy threats and jokes to one another. She had forgotten the exhilaration and terror of it and this unexpected reminder fired her spirit up. She was ready to go out and face death again. She almost willed a dog to appear. But the woods, groaning under the gale, seemed empty. The only difficulty now was deciding which way to head.

A little further in, they found a clearing with pheromone traps for insects in the trees. Here the under-storey made a barrier, blocking the wind, and there was an eerie calm.

"This way," said Pedro. "This the path – and there, look! A hut. Maybe is where your father staying, Jurgen."

At a distance of perhaps twenty metres, stood an octagonal kiosk with a neatly mown lawn in front. The whole effect was quaintly rustic: walls constructed of wooden ship-lap, and a conical roof topped with a CCTV camera. Situated nearby was a metal structure - a kind of watch-tower with a platform - and on the platform, perched high above the trees and accessed by a metal ladder, a white-painted weather station. Down below, on a washing line, stretching from wall to post, dangled a ghostly pair of socks.

Lamplight ran down the sides of the window frames and spilled out in crude splashes on the grass. The windows themselves glowed like open eyes.

"Isn't that just perfect?" Anything seemed better to Sophie than the prospect of bedding down on the forest floor. "Looks like a proper welcome!"

"I don't like it!" said Trudi pulling back. "We're safer in the dark."

"Let's just *look*, first." Sophie crept forward and flattening herself as best she could against the wall of the hut, peered in, like a movie cop.

Shortly, she was beckoning wildly. "Come on! It's okay! The place is empty!"

Better still, it was unlocked. Inside, they found a couple of bunks with pillows and army blankets, a reclining arm-chair and seated desk-room for two. A calendar on the wall displayed large, glossy pictures of moths of the world. The room was otherwise bare and functional, typical of the research stations Trudi had heard her father talk of in the past. An unwashed tin mug and plate stood abandoned on the desk. Had he been here? Had he drunk from that mug? If only he had scribbled his name somewhere!

"This will do till morning, and by then Big Sid will be here and he'll help us sort things out," Sophie now seemed buoyant. "One of us can keep watch, while the others sleep. At least it's not cold here and we can see out on all sides. I'll watch first, if you like. You lot must be dead beat. If anyone comes, I'll wake yer and we'll hide in the woods."

Her optimism inspired confidence and, in spite of her fears, Trudi fell asleep the moment her head touched the pillow.

Meanwhile, Scarp and Hamish, having telephoned ahead to break the joyful news about the children, drove back to Kingsbury to collect Sister Bianca. They loaded the bicycles into the back of the van, and with the young nun crammed in behind them on what looked like a re-cycled Chair-o-Plane seat, set off together for St Lucy's.

An uneasy hush descended. Scarp was suffering from another fit of awkwardness and Hamish did not know how to describe what he had seen without inflicting new distress. His information clearly put paid to Emilia's theory that all was now well with the Larssons. And that left a stark alternative. In the end it fell to Bianca to break the silence.

"I can't say I think Sister Emilia is actually lying," she reasoned, leaning her elbows against the head-rests in front, and staring in a preoccupied way through the windscreen. "But it just doesn't add up."

"How do you mean?" Scarp whipped round to find his cheek almost touching hers.

"She says that she had the phone call immediately after Vespers. Vespers ends at five-thirty, so let's say it was five-thirty-five. At a quarter past five I was still hot on the children's trail at the Fair. The landlord at the *Yard of Ale* confirmed they were there asking questions only minutes before I arrived and they were seen by the candy-floss man, ten minutes later, cutting back towards the swing-boats. At the swing-boats I drew a blank. But I know that they weren't alone at any time. They were accompanied by an older girl. And they were looking for someone called Sid."

"Big Sid," nodded Scarp.

"That's right. Well he'd gone to see his mother. His mate Charlie told me that. But some of the fairground people wouldn't talk – they must have been primed. After five-thirty my trail went cold. Then you telephoned. But don't you see? There wasn't time for them to get to Pinkney and be with Sven by then? Even if he picked them up. And why should he take them back to Pinkney?"

"Perhaps Sister Emilia misheard."

"Perhaps someone else was lying... That's the house. Turn in here."

This seemed as good an opening as any. Scarp pulled into the drive and braked.

"Tell her," he said to Hamish.

So Hamish recounted their adventure at Humbug Cottage and they all sat in silence some minutes more. Then Bianca spoke again:

"I'm still sure they were trying to get to Pinkney. A couple of people said they asked them for the bus fare. And they knew that Mr. Brambling was in trouble. Trudi drew a beehive on the notice-board. I should have put two and two together."

"I'm afraid we've all been very stupid," said Hamish. "And I blame myself particularly. I allowed myself to infect the children with my own morbid misgivings about what was going on in Pinkney Forest. Only yesterday I took them on a boat trip to the edge of it. I was so busy with my own concerns I did not see that they were truly worried about their father being there."

"Are *you?*" asked Bianca.

"Well, yes, I suppose I am."

"Then your misgivings were genuine, not morbid. This other girl, whoever she is, may have known something that acted as a spur. The Fair was only a stepping stone to what they really intended. Now I think the stupidity was mine. Trudi's reaction to that Swedish friend of Sven's was so extreme, I should have known there was some serious cause. Instead, I blamed the poor child for being unreasonable."

"And yesterday she made that bizarre phone call, as I told you – insisted on using a public telephone box – not a mobile."

"It all comes back to Laser Wag. Trudi felt violently opposed to the idea of that man coming to fix Sister Emilia's computer. Laser Wag have always been associated with the research that goes on at Pinkney, so perhaps they think the company has stolen their father. And of course they couldn't confide in us because they didn't think we would believe them. Trudi's mother was complaining this morning that she couldn't get through to her son on his phone. I think they've simply cut themselves off."

"Well I reckon you'll *have* to call the police now," said Scarp.

"What was it Mr. Brambling said this morning?" mused Hamish. "'*More bees to attend to.*' I assumed he meant at home, but he might equally well have been talking about the Forest. Isn't there a Bee Farm somewhere there? Part of the insect project?"

"The BioDawn honey place? According to Mrs. Sparks, Edmund worked there once."

"Edmund, the tramp! – *That's* what I wanted to say. He has gone missing, hasn't he?

"Mrs. Sparks just said he 'went off in a storm'…"

"...When he heard where the children were staying! We forgot to tell you we found his stick at the cottage. *He* might have smashed up the computer, though I can't think why. More likely, he went to help. Brambling – Brambling... Marina said he was clever, cleverer than anyone possibly suspected, but whatever could have made him rash enough to take on the likes of Laser Wag, alone? At least *he* could have gone to the proper authorities!"

"Well I'm going out to this Beedome myself," muttered Scarp. "I'm not leaving those kids there on their own. While we're sitting here talking, they could all be having their throats cut."

"You'll never get in, Scarp. There's security everywhere. Razor wire. Dogs. Sentry Guards..."

"I know a way in," said Sister Bianca quietly.

The men stared.

"Pinkney Forest lies just the other side of our main convent grounds. Of course, *we* are their security on the western side. No lay person can get through the garden there unspotted and we nuns are not exactly dressed for shinning up walls, but there are a couple of disused gates. All locked up of course. They date back to the old days before the Beedome project began. We came across them when I was helping Sister Friedel clear the 'wilderness' last year."

"Could you get us in?"

Bianca suppressed a smile. "Could you disguise yourselves in habits?"

Scarp threw himself back in his seat. "Trudi and Jurgen are being butchered in the woods and we're dressing up as nuns!"

"Just to cross the grounds. You don't want to be caught, do you? Listen, we must try the police first. They should organize a proper search. If that's no use, meet me here at ten, after Compline. We'll borrow Sister Emilia's car - it will be less conspicuous at The Assumption. The Sisters observe what we call the Great Silence after the last office of the day. Nobody speaks then until morning, after Lauds. It's a very important part of the contemplative life. They all go directly to bed. God willing, we'll slip out unnoticed and return the car before it's missed tomorrow. If we can only find the children, we'll bring them straight back here and hope the rest will resolve itself."

Scarp clamped his hand on her arm, an admiring warmth in his eyes:

342

"Good girl!"

"See? Nuns *can* be useful sometimes!" she winked. "Now let's see what Sister Emilia has to say."

Sister Emilia was not to be swayed. She had spoken with Sven – there could be no mistaking his voice and why should he lie about his own children? Someone had also called from the convalescent home next door with news that a patient, answering to the description of the girl at the Fair, had escaped. It seemed most likely that she had lured the children away and that Trudi and Jurgen had called Sven to come and rescue them.

"Sven, realizing that we must be worried here, rang immediately to reassure us."

"But then, where is he? Why did he not call in, if he was so close by? The children's clothes are here and all their things... Mr. Brambling must have known he would not return tonight. He brought their pyjamas..." Bianca's voice suddenly wavered and she felt a knot rise in her throat.

Emilia sternly adjusted her veil, took a deep breath and spread her hands on her knees.

"There must be no hysteria here. On that point I am adamant, sister. If you two young gentlemen wish to talk to the police, by all means feel free to do so. I cannot prevent you, though *I* am confident in a rational explanation. We are taught here to trust in God's mercy, and wisdom and that is what I intend to do. Now we have supper to get. The work of this house must go on."

With that she rose and swept from the room. An icy draught followed her.

Bianca, rebuked, fled to the kitchen and Scarp and Hamish exchanged looks and filed out under the inscrutable eye of the office crucifix.

"Police station. Where is it?" said Scarp.

"Back of Utopia Street. I'll direct you."

∞◌◌◌◌◌◌◌◌◌◌∞

Poor Constable Truman had no sooner rid himself of the dangerous driving trio, than in walked Hamish and Scarp.

"We'd like to report a disappearance..."

"And a burglary..."

"Well, not exactly a burglary... more a break-in..."

"But with criminal damage and maybe assault as well ..."

"Or kidnap. Or both. Oh, and there's a convicted lunatic at large..."

The Officer looked them up and down and fetched the forms with an air of resignation.

"Philkins," he asked in the back office. "It's not Hallowe'en is it? I've got a toothless gipsy and a Scot in hiking boots out there, talking about a plot to do away with some children. It's another Laser Wag story, complete with mocked-up photographs. And it's more than my job's worth to bother Sir Maximus again."

"Tell them you're looking into it," said Philkins, who had more experience of Kingsbury affairs. "And just to be on the safe side, put out an alert for anybody spotting youngsters on the run. Oh, and you could ring the sanatorium. See if they confirm the story. Nothing has come in on it so far – could be a University prank. End of term... Rag Week... you know."

"Oh I hate these complicated things," groaned Truman. "Give me a decent pub brawl any day!"

The sanatorium had changed its tune and denied any knowledge of the affair. And Hamish and Scarp signed their statements and re-emerged into the street, feeling hungry and depressed.

"You didn't show the plans..."

"What would have been the point? You could see he didn't believe us. Besides, it would have made me look dubious, removing evidence, and all that. Supper at St. Lucy's?"

Scarp shook his head. "I'll get a hot dog at the Fair. Talking of dogs, I'd better make sure Bella's all right too. Perhaps Sid will have come back by now and I can learn some more. I'll meet you, like we agreed, at ten."

∞∞∞∞∞∞∞∞

The bell for Compline always rang a minute or two before the service, giving the Sisters time to arrive in a state of quiet reflection. Of all the hours of the Holy Office, Sister Bianca loved Compline best. It seemed such a beautiful way to end the day, praying for sleep and the comforts of divine forgiveness and love. The high wavering plainsong rose from the chapel stalls, now on this side, now on that, as the Sisters sang their alternating

344

responses. Pitched above them, the silvery sound of the altar-bell resonated in the air, reminding them of the sacred Spirit that dwelt in their midst, before fading into the evening shadows. Bianca loved the way the older Sisters' voices trembled, she loved the sound of their robes as they knelt and stood. Above all she loved the silence in between. All the irritations and petty differences of the day melted away during Compline.

"I will lay me down in peace.

"And take my rest…"

Only, of course, tonight Bianca was not going to lie down in peace at all. She was going to be very wicked and steal Sister Emilia's car. She tried to concentrate on the words in her leather-covered book:

"From all ill dreams defend our eyes,

From nightly fears and fantasies:

Tread underfoot our ghostly foe…"

She had never felt so much in need of special protection, and so little able to ask for it. She was quite sure that God was going to be very cross with her. She didn't want Him, or anyone else to see what was in her heart just at the moment, so she forced herself to think of something quite irrelevant and she imagined she was washing the stairs, like Mrs. Sparks, till the final words were over.

The Sisters left chapel looking drawn and troubled, as though they all had undergone some spiritual crisis and departed to their cells in silence.

Bianca let herself into her room and sat down on the bed. She had hidden the car keys in her anorak pocket after supper so as not to have to return to the main part of house and risk arousing suspicion. Two spare veils and habits lay neatly folded on the blankets. They had been lifted from the laundry. She rather frightened herself with her aptitude for deception. All that remained now was to wait until the last lights were extinguished in the Sisters' wing and then let herself out into the corridor, open the emergency door and slip down the fire escape into the garden. From there she could cut through the bicycle shed to her rendez-vous. Scarp and Hamish should be able to push the car out into the road to avoid starting the engine in the drive. And they would just have to pray that they did not meet the Ugandan Missionary or Marina while they were doing it.

In one capacious pocket she had a flask of warm ribena for the children. In the other, some socks and extra tee shirts, pilfered from their luggage. They were sure to be cold on this windy night. There was also a much-thumbed teddy bear which she had found in Trudi's bag. He might be handy for consolation.

She took off her silver cross and laid it with her Bible, by her pillow. It would be a heavy impediment if she had to run, later. She felt as if she was going to fight a duel. Should she scribble a will?

If she failed, she would face terrible castigation, perhaps expulsion from the convent. But then if she failed, it would mean that the children were lost and if that were so, nothing on earth would matter any more. Such motherly feelings astonished her, but here she was, fluffed out like a broody hen, ready to peck the first hand that approached her chicks. She felt glad that the night was dark. Perhaps it would hide her renegade thoughts.

At ten, the clock of St. Ignatius, two streets away, tolled the hour. Sister Bianca grabbed her things, and effected her escape. Just as planned, Scarp and Hamish eased the car out of the drive, hopped in and within seconds they were speeding north. Relief put them in a holiday mood.

"I brought these just in case you needed them," Bianca tossed the habits over her shoulder. "If the gates are closed and I have to rouse someone to let us in, you may have to crouch down, pretend to be elderly or ill - we'll think of something - until I can park somewhere quietly at the back."

"And I brought these," Hamish indicated a heap of rope beside him on the seat, belays and crampons, even the grappling harpoon, the showpiece of his climbing gear. "Might be handy for getting in somewhere."

Scarp nodded darkly. He had packed his picks, wires and croppers, for dealing with locks, but at his side he carried a more secret and deadly tool. His return to the Fair had allowed him not only to gather more information about Sid, but also to visit the caravan where his private belongings were stored. And there, amidst a jumble of clothes and shoes, some old horse bells and photos of his Nan, he unwrapped the hunting knife which Per had given him last summer. This was the weapon that had killed the beast, Beor. The tempered blade gleamed as it slid from its sheath. He had put the thing away, vowing never to use it, for it was a friendship gift and Scarp's bad old days with knives and fisticuffs lay behind him. But the thought of the Larsson children in peril, brought back his fighting spirit. He slipped his hand around the haft, feeling the polished reindeer bone, snug beneath his fingers. A good grip. He would test it if he had to. He improvised a belt for it, re-sheathed it, concealed it beneath his clothes, then set out with tight-lipped determination.

Now in the car, he adopted a lighter air. "By the way, it *is* the Beedome they're heading for. I still couldn't find Sid, but I managed to get something out of one of his friends. The girl is called Sophie, or Little Sophie, and grew up on one of the estates here, near Sid's family."

"And were the children all right?"

"Went for a ride on the Big Wheel."

"Is that all?"

"Sid rushed off again when he got the message."

"The message?"

"To bring help and meet them at the Beedome."

"It gets worse and worse!" lamented Bianca.

"Sid's all right as long as you're on his side," said Scarp. "I'm *glad* someone else is coming. This Sophie was a star in a children's circus, then she disappeared. Hardly anyone at the Fair recognized her – said she had changed so much." They passed the outlying villages of Copsley and Sallowmarsh and took a narrower, left-hand turning. After a mile or two, Sister Bianca slowed down.

"Are you ready?" she warned. "The Convent gate is just here… and it's closed."

"Well, I'm not wearing one of these," Scarp dug in his heels. "*I* can fix a gate."

"Impossible. It's a security gate. Probably all wired up to alarms. Sister Emilia normally presses a button on her key ring and points it like that and it opens automatically…" she mimicked the action and to her astonishment, the solid oak shuddered and yielded before her, first on one side and then the other.

"Bravo!" cheered Hamish. "In we go!"

Dipping their headlamps, they crawled past acres of neatly clipped lawns, and skirted the dark hulk of the house, the chapel with its dainty cupola, outbuildings, then the guest wing, infirmary and old stable block.

"I'll park here, by the gardener's shed. This is where guests stop when they come on retreat. We might avoid detection here for a while."

The car crunched to a halt, tripping some security lights and Bianca hurriedly turned off the engine and looked back to see if there was any response. But all remained quiet. Almost anything could trigger these bulbs - foxes, sniffing nearby, or the wind in the trees. This time they were lucky. They tumbled out of the car and made for the shrubs where the shadows lay deepest.

"No torch, I suppose."

"Och I have one, but is it wise?"

"Well just hold on then and I'll guide you. There's a tunnel of pleached apple trees through the middle of the vegetable plot. We'll head for that, then through the garth ..."

"The what?" Scarp, at the back, missed most of her words.

"...Where the sisters are buried..."

He gave a shudder of revulsion. *"Brilliant."*

"...then along the prayer-way to the Garden of Our Lady and down to the 'wilderness'. There are sheep pastures that way and the community farm. Sister Winifreda's hermitage is over on the right. We mustn't wake her up."

"What will they do to us if they catch us here?"

Bianca gave a withering look.

"*You* will be fine. You're just a prowler. You'll probably get off with a criminal record. *I* am the one who will really have to face the music, so spare any sympathy for me!"

Admonished, Scarp fell into line. Better not mention that he had been arrested innumerable times before. All the same, he felt that violating a convent sanctuary was both ridiculous and somehow especially wicked and a rebellious, piratical humour welled up inside him. For the moment he bit his tongue and, thanks to Bianca's prior knowledge and Hamish's nocturnal navigation skills they got along pretty well.

At the 'wilderness' they stumbled through undergrowth reminiscent of the woods Scarp had left behind in Sussex. Here they had to negotiate fallen logs and brambles and high stinging nettles and the gipsy began to regret his naked shins, but eventually they reached a brick wall, the outer boundary of the convent.

"There's a door, somewhere here, I'm sure. Sister Friedel found it."

"Looking for a way out, no doubt!" Scarp quipped.

"Recording the wildlife, if you must know! This is a site of special scientific interest. We have natterjack toads…"

"Kissing a toad wouldn't get you out." In the dark it was easier to be irreverent.

Sister Bianca pushed past him. "You know, one can get tired of cloister jokes!"

"Sorry sister! It's just I never thought I'd find myself in a place like this before."

"Might do you some good!" she flushed angrily.

Scarp grinned. *So they were real people, after all. And feisty ones too!* His next words sounded more respectful.

"Don't let's fight. Save the fighting for later eh?"

Bianca bit her lip. She also felt ridiculous and frightened and her heart pounded, full of fury. She laid a hand on Scarp's sleeve and mastered her thoughts, as she had been long-trained to do.

"Pax!" she replied.

"Here's the door!" Hamish had gone ahead and found it. By the light of the torch, which they now deemed safe to use, they examined the locks and Scarp diligently set to work, like a sapper, easing them one by one. There was a big new padlock on the other side but Hamish hopped over and unscrewed the hasp fixings with his Swiss Army Knife, so, cheered by success, they filed through, relieved to have got *out* of the convent and *into* the forest in one simple step. Hamish replaced the padlock to cover their tracks. It would be easy enough to undo it all again if necessary. But any complacency ended there. The gate, it seemed, was just a first line of defence.

"Now the hard bit."

Scarp surveyed the woods on the Pinkney side. Here the undergrowth had been cleared in a wide, peaty path leading to a moat. Long ago, this might have been a separate tributary of the Kingsbury canal, for there had been sand quarries at Pinkney until the 1950s. The cutting consisted of a four metre chasm, lined with brick and weltering, half full of water. Ink black it looked in the gathering gloom. A good place for drowning. A bridge spanned the dyke, but that was barred by a heavy-gauge, metal gate, flaunting spikes at top and sides. Reminiscent of the deterrents that still existed in Kingsbury to stop intruders climbing into colleges, it presented a formidable challenge. Scarp's croppers were no match for the fastenings here and a search for an alternative way across proved fruitless. You would need long arms and impeccable footing to clamber past.

"I reckon I can do it," said Hamish and eased himself gingerly round.

Scarp devised a way of standing on one of the spikes and holding on to another while swinging his body out over the water. He landed on the bridge with a thump and then came back for Bianca. But she stood shaking her head.

"In this?" she held out her long skirts. "I don't think so."

"You could... you could hold on here maybe."

"And straight in the ditch! In slippery sandals! No thanks!"

"What about underneath? Could you climb along there?"

"I'm not a sloth!"

"*Try it.* You can probably do more than you think."

"Perhaps, you need to wait here for us, Sister Bianca. We'll have a look round and report back." Hamish, the more gentlemanly, had less faith in her.

Bianca glared through the bars.

"You *can't* go without me!"

"I can't carry you over. And the ropes won't help here. If you can't do what we've done, maybe you'll *have* to wait. Remember, we haven't much time ..."

"Oh, go ahead and do what you like!" she snapped, finally losing her temper. This was a serious lapse. Nuns were not supposed to give in to impetuous feelings, but Sister Emilia wasn't watching and she had already cooked her goose with God, so what did it matter! "At least take these things with you. The children will need them!" She passed through the heavy flask, the tee-shirts and the teddy and flounced off into the shadows. *Men! Patronising, ignorant, stupid... She'd show them...*

"Where has she gone now?" said Scarp. "We can't afford to lose her as well."

Hamish shrugged. "It always happens when you take a woman. They can't help it. They usually have to go back. I love Sister Bianca dearly, but we might get on better with just the two of us."

At that moment they heard a sudden rushing sound and something dark came flying out of the trees. A flash of white, a vision of shapely legs, momentarily suspended in the air and Sister Bianca made a graceful landing on the Pinkney side of the cut.

"What the *devil…?*"

"Language!" She bent down to adjust her habit, untying the scapula that she had looped up for ease of movement and slipping her sandals back on her feet.

"*How* did you do that?" Hamish stared open-mouthed.

But now Bianca was smiling. "All Surrey Senior Girls Long-Jump Champion 2004! I can still do it, it seems, when the occasion demands." Triumph gleamed in her eye. "Now I'll have my flask back, *thank* you. Where do we go from here?"

From that moment, Scarp was her slave. He had never seen anything to match her for sheer nerve, and he did not forget the shapely legs, either!

"Straight into the woods, my lady. Perhaps you should lead the way!"

Hamish whipped out his navigation tools. He still had the fragments of map he had lifted from Brambling's cottage and now he began to study them by torchlight, compass laid on one palm:

"This here is the perimeter fence. Here are research huts. Here and here outbuildings, laboratories? *'Extraction chamber'*… whatever that is… I reckon we are here, west of the Great Wood. There's our little canal, looping back to Pinkney Lock. There should be a Forester's Lodge, a former habitation that must have been swallowed up by the development, over to the left. Looks derelict on the map. Perhaps we could use that as our base camp and mark off the site in sections, searching each in turn. That way we'll know we haven't missed parts out. If that is north, then that is our path."

"Shouldn't we just head for the Dome?" asked Bianca.

"Too risky. Let's see what we're up against first. If the children are still in the wood we might not have to trespass that far. I reckon we've got four hours before daybreak. But it's a huge compound. There are dozens of these satellite stations dotted amongst the trees and if they are manned, it could prove tricky checking them out. Sven must be in one somewhere. Finding him would be a help."

"Can't you phone him?"

351

"Och, there's no reception. This place is so hush-hush, it's quite cut off from the outside world. Though the official receivers on the mast must work, I think they jam the airwaves down here, just as if it was a prison. It's all very sinister. We must not lose each other here."

They stumbled on till they reached the Forester's Lodge, a Victorian cottage, as Hamish predicted, abandoned and virtually reclaimed by nature. Young trees had grown up and burst through the roof, giving it a gothic appearance.

"Good," said Hamish. "This front parlour looks the soundest part. There's even some furniture." He ducked under the gaping sash and swung his legs over the window sill. "This is perfect. You two make yourselves as comfortable as you can here. I'll do a wee bit of spying and report back. If I haven't returned in an hour," he added ominously, "don't come after me. Go for help. Go to your Mother Superior!"

So Scarp and Sister Bianca did as they were bid, and sat themselves on an old divan frame, whispering to pass the time. They compared likes and dislikes, favourite puddings and games they had played when they were children. Then films, scrapes, misdemeanours at school (Scarp never spent much time at school so he had fewer to report!). Without warning he suddenly changed his tone:

"Why d'ya do it then?"

"Sorry?"

"What did yer go and become a nun for? You were just a normal kid, like me."

Bianca hit straight back.

"Why did you become a drop-out?"

He shrugged the question off, but she persisted.

"Why did you leave your family? I thought gypsy families were always really close. Yet you even dumped the Larssons when they had accepted you as one of them. You'll never have a real job, will you?"

What she said was true yet Scarp could not openly admit the reason. How could you explain that perhaps you just couldn't face people when you felt you had let them down? He gave a defensive reply:

"I like my freedom, I suppose. I need time to think."

Bianca smiled. "Well perhaps *I* like time to think. And the contemplative life gives me freedom too."

"Washing old sisters' socks, till you end up in that garth thing, along with them?" he shivered and rubbed his tattoo.

"There is *inner* freedom, you know."

"Why don't you get out while you're still young and warm? You could have a good life. Find…"

"… a husband? And wash *his* socks?"

"Have kids …"

That hurt.

Sister Bianca wrapped herself up in the pain and gave an affronted laugh.

"We don't choose our destiny, you know. It finds us. And sometimes it is hard. If we could have just what we wanted all the time we'd never grow. And if you stop growing you begin to die. Some things are stronger than human desire."

"Really?"

"Really! So stop poking!"

Scarp accepted the reproof and changed the subject. And the summer night wore on.

∞∞∞∞∞∞∞∞∞∞

At two o'clock in the morning, there came a knock at Sister Emilia's door. She was not asleep. She had lain awake, tossing and fretting for hours, but she jumped up in alarm nonetheless, for she knew that nothing but a genuine emergency would justify disturbing the peace of the night.

"Is there a fire?" she called as she freed herself from the bedclothes.

At the door stood the diminutive Sister Matilda, her hair let down in a plait, her naked feet peeping from under her nightgown. How ancient and frail she looked without her customary dress!

"What is it, Sister? Are you ill?"

"Forgive me for breaking the Silence. You know I would not do it lightly. But I am afraid I *must* speak to you. I am in great trouble in my spirit, Sister, and I fear already that I may have left things too late."

"Come in, come in." She knew her pastoral duties. Sister Matilda had age and experience beyond her own - she could not be

353

sent packing, like a novice, till the morning. Besides which, Emilia felt in need of company herself.

"It is the chapel, Sister. Something is very wrong in the chapel. It began as soon as that camera was installed. From that moment I have felt all my powers of prayer and concentration simply melt away. I cannot think. There are times when I can hardly remember who I am. The notes of the plainchant might as well be Egyptian hieroglyphs. I am afraid I am losing my mind."

"Are you alone in this feeling, Sister?"

"Everyone seems depressed. And I know for a fact that Sister Bianca has not slept a wink tonight. Her bed has not been touched and I confess I cannot tell you where she is."

"Gone after *them*. She has gone after those children. I *know* it."

"Sister Emilia, I beg you, something must be done."

Emilia's bosom heaved under its ponderous weight of cares. First the money. Then the fire regulations. Then the blind boy. Corky, the website, the missing children. The father and Mr. Brambling, vanished without trace. And now this, this dreadful vacuum of the heart that she had felt herself all day. The Sisters in mutiny. Lunatics at large. And no solace whatsoever from on High.

She was a proud woman. She had worked her way up from the backstreets, fought for her degree, challenged her family, won respect from her peers, and every step had stiffened her back and confirmed her moral rectitude. But now she felt the tide sweeping all her achievements away like the sand-castles she once made as a child, on Morecambe Bay. She had felt touched and humiliated by Bianca's loving concern over the children. Her pride had not allowed *her* feelings to speak so truthfully. And now she felt humbled by Sister Matilda who could confess that she had lost God, when Emilia could not.

She folded Matilda's fingers in her own and led her quietly from the room and the two of them together made their way along the corridor in their nightshifts and down the stairs to the chapel. In the dark, the sanctuary lamp kept vigil beside the new winking light of the webcam. A trace of smoke tainted the air. Sister Emilia, bald and trembling, marched up to the altar, plucked the wires of Olaf Stromberg's device neatly out of the wall, wrenched the smouldering camera from its bracket and dropped it into a stoup of holy water.

At the chapel door she turned, crossed herself and made a low obeisance, before taking Matilda once more by the hand.

"And now," she braced herself, "we shall phone the police..."

Truman was just nearing the end of his shift when the call came through.

"There's a Sister Superior on the line, sir, insists on speaking to the officer in charge. Something about a Swede and a webcam?"

Heaven preserve us! Not another one! He picked up the receiver, to catch the end of her monologue:

"...not to mention attempted arson. Three children, a Senior Research Fellow, a tramp named Edmund, and an elderly resident from Pinkney have all gone missing, together with an inmate of the asylum next door."

"Not to worry, madam. It's all in hand."

"I have reason to believe that they have gone to this Beedome place. They may *all* have been abducted."

"I've got officers on the case already."

"Brainwashed, I mean. They do it with mobile phones. Even my own Sisters here have been affected."

"I can assure you that we are doing all we can to resolve the situation."

"Have you searched the Beedome?"

"Well even the police can't simply go in *there,* madam. It's top security. Needs clearance from the Home Office and it just happens that the Minister has been out at a function all night. Now as soon as we can make arrangements, we'll pursue the matter further. Meanwhile, we have spoken to several suspects already."

"Are you arresting the man from Laser Wag, or not?"

"We are following all relevant lines of enquiry..."

Emilia swept such obfuscation aside.

"I must say," she warned, "that if the police drag their heels on this, I shall turn to others who are more willing to act and, Home Office or no, *they* will gain entry, by whatever means they can find. A 'line of enquiry' is for weary, old pen-pushers. Do you have no passion for your work? When young lives are at stake, one needs people with courage and conviction! And *I* know where to find them, even if you do not!"

Chapter Thirty-Seven

The Beedome

The birds in Pinkney Forest began their dawn chorus at four-thirty. You could hear the wave of song approaching in a crescendo from the East, a faint, bell-like frisson - then a pedal note against which the middle-distant voices played in harmony - finally, the soloists close at hand, though it would have been hard to tell whether it was the dawn itself which set them off, or simply the noisy twitterings of their bedfellows.

Trudi recognized the shrill descant of the wren, the syncopated warning cries of blackbird and robin and the long canto fermo of the rooks and pigeons. When the crescendo had reached quite deafening proportions, it passed overhead, and moved westwards, gently dying away. The birds, having once had their say, applied themselves to the more urgent business of finding breakfast, while their neighbours took up the challenge of waking the world. The wave of sound pulsed on towards the mountains of Wales, like a ghost flock on the wing.

Per had taught her last summer how to listen to the birds, distinguishing the separate voices, picking up the cries that meant a predator was close, and the silences too that might signal a change in the weather, or mark a summer siesta. Trudi was glad to have their company as her night watch drew to a close. When she thought about her adventure – for it *was* an adventure now, no mistake! - she could see similar wave patterns eddying through it all, building up to something momentous. Surely she felt, the crisis was coming soon and she would need all her resourcefulness to deal with it.

She wished she could understand what the birds were saying, as her Grandfather would have done. She was sure that they could tell her many of the secrets of Forest, for daylight itself showed little. Uniform trees stretched in every direction. To get any idea of the geography, one would have to climb up to that weather station and try for a bird's eye view. Even that wouldn't disclose where Mr. Brambling was, or how to find him without being caught. She roused her companions and ventured outside to test the air. Still cold. And she was hungry. The pair of socks flapped uselessly on their line.

Jurgen joined her, rubbing the sleep out of his eyes, but the socks caught his attention first.

"Who tied that ribbon there?"

In her eagerness to explore, Trudi had been too preoccupied to notice, but Jurgen was right, a tag of red tape now marked the spot.

"Trudi, someone was here!" On closer inspection they discovered that the socks were old and full of holes.

Perhaps Sven had left his signature after all! How like him to have given an academic lecture, the most important in his life, with his toes poking out in his shoes! His methodical preparations always fell apart when he was truly engrossed in his work. And then to have wandered off without even bothering to dress properly! Little acts of boyish spontaneity! Typical! No doubt some plant had caught his eye and he had simply pulled on his boots and gone exploring...

"He *was* here, then," Trudi annexed the idea as if it was fact. "I thought he must have been. Perhaps Daddy left the ribbon as a sign for us to follow him. Jurgen, come up there with me and help me see where we are. He can't have gone far, surely."

Jurgen rejected the ribbon theory. He didn't believe his father would have visited the hut and left without waking them up and giving them a hug and telling them stories of all he had been doing. But he was curious to find out more, so together they scrambled up the ladder, while Pedro and Sophie watched from the ground.

"Anything?" called Pedro.

No reply.

"What happen?"

"Are you okay?"

Yes, they were okay.

But brother and sister had been struck dumb by the view at the top. The whole site unfolded before them in its symmetry and grandeur, like the grounds of some great formal palace or temple from ancient times. The land had been laid out in concentric rings: this outer flank of forest, giving way to rainbow-coloured meadows and these, in turn, to orchards - acres of fruit, planted with mathematical precision. The fields radiated in strips, neat as

Dutch tulip beds and were dotted all over with structures resembling up-ended bales of hay. There were thousands of them. All identical.

At the heart, rose the Beedome itself, coil upon coil of it, diminishing skywards, its giant camber now gilded by the rising sun. There were neither windows, nor doors, nor balconies, nor ornaments to break the monumental simplicity of its form. To the east, stood what looked like a large electricity sub-station with grey transformers and a soaring metal pylon, decked with satellite dishes. Around this, a scatter of buildings. The whole scene gleamed with an unnatural brilliance, for the sun's appearance would be brief today. Already a mattress of cloud was massing overhead. It seemed that the wind of yesterday had not yet finished its work.

"That must be the mast Hamish was looking for on Drayholt Hill," murmured Trudi. "Do you think the dome is an observatory?"

"I think it's creepy. Where do the people go?"

"In these hut things, I suppose. There's something over there that could be a factory, beyond the meadow. And there are other lookout places like this one – see, in the trees. Perhaps they have units attached to them."

"Trudi, it's really scary. How will we ever get out again?"

"Mr. Brambling and Daddy will know the way!" How easy it was to fib when you had no choice! Trudi knew that Jurgen might bolt if he felt too frightened. "We just have to find them. And if Olaf catches us, well, we are four to one. We should be able to call for help, or knock him on the head, or something! If we walk towards the sun, we'll reach the meadows and then we'll be able to see where we're going... We'll have to be like explorers and remember our route."

This plan met with approval and they set off through the wood, guiding themselves by the shadows on the trees and cheering one another with flippant remarks about what they would have for breakfast and how they would spend the afternoon when they got back to St. Lucy's. Before they set out, however, Jurgen doubled back, slipped his talisman over his head and strung it on the line beside the socks, as a marker of his own. If Sven *did* come by, he would know they had been there and perhaps he would come to find them... Fifty metres further on, the girls came across a second tape, tied to a branch, and then a third. So they proceeded from sign to sign, as though they were guests on a treasure-hunt.

Sophie's mood had mellowed overnight and she now entertained herself by imagining the punishments she would mete out to her enemies, once she caught up with them. Her reprisals sounded suitably appalling, so Trudi held her breath and tried not to think about it much.

At last, a fringe of emerald grass appeared between the trees. They had reached the edge of the forest and soon broke through into a dazzle of light. This, then, was the second circle. Here were the meadows and beyond, in the distance, rose the Dome. And now they could really begin to appreciate the scale of it. The structure seemed to dwarf everything for miles and its vast shadow stretched across the landscape like a bruise. As for the 'hay-bales', they turned out to beehives, stacked like city tenements, with colour codes and record sheets in plastic envelopes, attached. Despite the early hour, bees droned in and out, busying amongst the flowers which flourished in slabs of mono-crop as far as the eye could see. Every facet of the scene lay crudely pasted with light, the last the sun would shed before it buried itself in the coming storm.

So astonished were they by the strangeness of this vision, they did not notice the man in the bee-veil approaching, until he was almost on top of them.

"How wonderful! How wonderful!" he exclaimed, rubbing his hands. "My dear children, you *found* it!"

He removed his hat and there stood Mr. Brambling, smiling in welcome.

"Oh Mr. Brambling," Trudi rushed forward. "You're safe! We were so worried about you!"

"There, there, child," he cried, patting her on the head. "What possible harm could come to me here? But I'm so delighted that you have come. Now I can take you for a tour, and a proper honey-tasting. I'm afraid you've found out my little secret. I'm not really an amateur bee-keeper at all. All these thousands of hives are mine. A great project – perhaps the greatest that has ever been attempted in the history of the apiarist."

"Why didn't you tell us?" asked Trudi, her joy now matched by wonder. So Marina was right. Mr. Brambling did have an exceptional, hidden side.

"Well, in a sense I have, haven't I? I had to be sure that you were the right people to know. I can't just let anyone in here."

He shot a sharp glance at Sophie. "For instance, this friend you have brought with you. I'm trusting that she is a suitable person?"

"This is Sophie," said Trudi, pulling her forward and pinching her arm. "Sophie has done a lot of research."

Sophie glowered in response, at Trudi, at the old man and at the bees. Her distrust of Nature was no better by daylight and having steeled herself for a fight, she now felt unnerved by so courteous a reception.

"Exactly!" beamed Mr. Brambling. "I knew it! Well, Sophie, welcome, welcome! You won't regret your visit."

"Mr. Brambling, what about Daddy? We were worried about him too. Have you seen him?"

"Seen him? Why of course I've seen him. And you shall see him too. I'll take you to the spot. But there's no need to worry, my dears, he's doing the very thing he loves most, as you shall see for yourselves. I'll show you everything, since you've come so far. I promise there will be no more secrets now."

"And Corky, Mr. Brambling. What about Corky?" Pedro watched the bees with a distracted air.

"Trust me. You will have no more worries about Corky when you come with me. What?"

He anticipated, as usual, an answer which no one had made. Meanwhile, Trudi had been watching the bees and something about them began to trouble her. It soon became clear that they did not forage enquiringly from flower to flower, like ordinary bees, but flew with an undeviating sense of purpose, methodically stripping the meadow of its nectar, section by section.

"Ah, you observe their unique and tireless efficiency." Mr. Brambling read her thoughts. "These are rather special bees, not like my old friends at home. They are scientific bees, specially programmed for particular tasks. They are the core and substance of my research. And so extensive is that research now, no one quite knows where it will lead."

"Is that why this place is so secret?"

"Well, of course, my dears! Everyone wants to know how we achieve such a spectacular harvest. But let's start at the beginning... with the miraculous dance of the bee."

Jurgen pricked up his ears. Yes, he knew about that.

"As you will remember from your lessons with Corky, bees have a secret language and tell one another how to find food by performing a special dance in the hive. It is called a waggle dance. The bee which has found nectar, jigs round in a special figure of eight, trembling and shaking her body according to a secret code while all the other bees touch her with their antennae to find out what she has to tell them. They can then perform the dance for others. And soon they all know where to go.

"Well, here we have taught them to pass on very particular messages, so, for instance, the bees in these hives are trained to look for clover. They will only ever taste clover in their lives and their honey will be the purest clover honey ever sold on the shelves of the BioDawn supermarkets. Over there the bees harvest lavender, over there, heather. No need to box up and transport the hives. We have fields of continuous flowers here, thanks to some pioneering bio-techniques.

"The plan is to dispense with live bees altogether in time and programme little hologram laser drones to do the work. No need for all the messy business of breeding, inseminating the queens, protecting the hives, preventing swarms. No more anxiety about pesticides and chalkbrood disease. And we can teach them other things too."

Trudi looked in dismay at the creatures with their bulging pollen sacks. Fancy tasting nothing but clover! It didn't seem somehow right or fair.

"We could use them for surveillance – attach micro-cameras to their bodies and send them on reconnaissance flights. Once programmed to seek out a particular object they would be almost impossible to detect. They could even be deployed as assassins, using their stings as murder weapons. The same principal would apply. Out go the spies, looking for their target. When they locate him, they return and tell the hive. The hive can then attack in force.

"Or perhaps an individual can be equipped with a venom so lethal, just one sting will do the job... The world of espionage will never be the same again! Centuries ago, the Mexicans used bees to

361

defend their cities, so why should not we do the same and train them to act as soldiers? They possess such sophisticated communication networks. Every hive is like a living master-brain! And I have been experimenting already...

"These bees have learnt special instruction codes which they will accept only from a Bee-master such as myself. You know a proper shaman can induce a swarm to dance, to settle, to do whatever he directs, just like a circus-master. Of course, none of the people here know that! That is another little secret. But today I have told all the security guards to stay at home. The staff are taking a holiday and there is no one here but the two men on the gate. Today I can amuse myself as I please. Imagine for a moment how much time, expense and labour it would save, for example, if bees administered the injections, in hospitals..."

Mr. Brambling chortled just as he did at home, encouraging the daisies in his garden and Trudi searched in vain for some clue that he was jesting, but he had, as promised, now dropped all pretence. He spoke with natural fervour.

"Daddy wouldn't do this!" she objected.

"No, no, my dear, your father's skills were more botanical." That quiet use of the past tense sent Trudi's pulse racing, but Mr. Brambling was already moving on. He had a lot of ground to cover.

"Over here, the Extraction Chamber..." He reached the installation which Trudi and Jurgen had spotted at dawn.

"I'm not going in there!" warned Sophie, hanging back.

"It's quite safe!" Mr. Brambling began to scale a vertical ladder set into the wall. A viewing gallery ran around the top and he beckoned the children to join him and look down through the roof-lights upon a giant centrifuge. "I have left the lid off so you can see...The ripe honey-comb is fed in here and spun to separate the honey from the wax. You can see more combs there, ready to be treated today. And here is extracted honey waiting to go into jars. And over there, the vats of wax cappings... All the honey can be saved from those too. Through there is the packing room where the jars are labelled. Of course it is early in the year to be collecting honey. Currently, we can bring blossom times forward by a month or two. Once we are properly automated, there will be no end to the season."

362

"Who does the work?" asked Jurgen, looking out over the empty site. He thought, for a moment, that he caught sight of a figure clambering up a similar ladder, far over on the electricity plant. When he blinked the figure vanished, then reappeared higher up, as though making for the mast itself.

"Oh, wonderful young people," the old man enthused. He evidently noticed nothing unusual. "So bright. So enthusiastic! We recruit a lot from the University, you know. They normally come in later in the day."

"Marina?"

"Marina, yes, though she works mostly at the Laser Labs. *Very promising girl.*"

"And Edmund?"

"Alas, poor Edmund... too inquisitive for his own good." Mr. Brambling, sighed and shook his head, "but, he once did great work here." Then he roused himself. "However, all this is incidental to the real purpose of the place. You will want to see the Beedome itself. That is only natural."

Without offering the honey-tasting he had promised, he hustled his guests back down the ladder and along a radial path to the site of the main building. The Dome towered up directly before them.

"We must all stay close together now. No stepping out of line. No touching." His voice took on a nervous imperative. "Through here. Hurry now!"

A door of black basalt slid back at his bidding to reveal an inner atrium, thronged with milling figures. Mr. Brambling seized hold of a long-handled implement, like a spatula, and, wielding it with both hands, pushed the crowd gently back on either side to usher the children through. Almost at once the door began to close, and Sophie, suspecting some trick, made a dash for freedom. She did not get very far. The old man must have read her thoughts, for, flipping his pole over with surprising dexterity, he caught her by the curved end and shepherded her back into line.

"Don't want anyone to escape, do we?" he said with quiet menace. "It's such a nuisance to catch them again when they escape."

Trudi had seen a tool just like this before. Corky kept one to help him manage his bees at home, though his version was small by comparison - it sat neatly in the palm of the hand. You could

363

use it to separate the frames, or clear a space to inspect the brood chambers in the hive. It had dozens of uses, but Mr. Brambling's was so large, it could be brandished like a pikestaff.

"These are the new arrivals," the old man explained, "still waiting to be processed."

The figures clustered, silent as moths, pale-faced and glassy-eyed, as the children passed them by. There were people of all descriptions, thousands of them, all wearing the same lost expressions, with reference-number labels pinned to their clothing.

"We'll find them all a home in time," Brambling continued, as if that would be a comfort to them. "To be honest, we've had so many just recently, it's been a job to keep up with them all. But these won't really interest you. It's the ones you know that *you* will want to see!"

He paused a moment in thought. "Yes, fifth level. We'll take the lift, I think."

"I in't going nowhere!" growled Sophie. "You lying, murdering old devil. You're in with *them*, aren't you?"

"'*In with them?*' Ah, no, I promise you I'm not '*in*' with anyone. But you *will* come nonetheless, because you will be so very interested to see what I have to show you, and it would be a pity for you not to understand the procedure before it is your turn. Especially when you have made the effort to come here voluntarily."

He gave Sophie an unkind prod with the blade of his spatula. "I don't want to dispense with you here. You can be much more valuable if you come with us."

Sophie rushed forward once more and collapsed, winded by a blow beneath the ribs. Trudi screamed and Mr. Brambling turned to quell any mutiny.

"No point in it, children," he observed. "No more point than in that ridiculous cockerel that defies me at home. Pick yourself up, Sophie, and let's go quietly and enjoy the tour while we can."

Reader, have you ever seen pet lambs going to market? Have you ever witnessed that dazed look of panic, when they find that the hand they trust has suddenly turned against them? If so, you will know how the children entered that lift.

On the fifth floor one could get a better view of the Beedome structure. Narrow galleries ran between rows of glass-fronted cells, tessellated, for economy of space, in hexagons, like honey-comb. The building was brilliantly lit, with paths fanning out into a greater labyrinth beyond. Up and down went the paths, all looking just the same, and linked, through a series of stairwells, with further mazes on other floors, all equally indistinguishable from one another.

Within the cells sat vibrant exhibits of flora and fauna: striking-looking orchids, bromeliads, tree frogs -Trudi spotted a bristle cone pine - all things which she knew well enough to be endangered in the wild. Here was an oak tree, there a leopard, a cloud of butterflies, a wolf. They were bottled up, just like the specimens at the Vargsberg Gardens, but these appeared to be flourishing contentedly, positively brimming with vitality.

"How do you keep them all?" she could not help wondering aloud and Mr. Brambling grinned.

"Well, they're not alive, of course. They are very easy to keep."

"Not alive? But they are moving."

"Holograms, my dear. Like the pianist at the Toy Forge. They are exact in every detail, and in every detail of every detail. A perfect record for posterity of the miracles of evolutionary life on earth."

"But why?"

"Why?" He seemed surprised. "Because these things cannot be kept any longer in their native habitat. Even our beloved oak trees are under threat. One day there will be children like yourself who do not know what it is to stand or lie beneath a mighty oak. Who have never even seen an acorn. That fills my heart with sadness. Oak trees, like all rare and beautiful things, should be assured of eternal life."

"That's what Daddy says."

"And quite right he is too. But the world is a very imperfect place in which to establish a sanctuary. So many accidents occur - wars, droughts, diseases - the natural predation of one species upon another. None of these distressing things can exist in a proper Heaven. They would ruin the perfection of the scheme. But here I *have* created something perfect - a heavenly super-cosmos, where all can thrive in harmony together. Look about you. Every specification of the wonderful samples before you, has been recorded and stored in the memory of the vast computer I call my

BeeBrain. They belong already to the cybersphere. These phantoms that you see here are toys for our pleasure while we remain in this life. And they have their uses too. They can be replicated and manufactured as quickly as I can snap my fingers. The codes are all known. The patents applied for. Good business for the right people."

"So in the end you will be the only person to own an oak tree?" asked Jurgen.

"What a bright boy! Not quite. Copies will abound, at a price. But only the *finest*, you know. Imagine. These trees will be always magnificent, always healthy, always whole. I will simply retain the masterplan, the blueprint, in my celestial archive."

"And will there only be one tree, endlessly reproduced."

"Even the best schemes have their limitations," Brambling admitted. "If I could live long enough I could acquire more - young ones, old ones - but I have so many other things to collect too. The natural world can form only a part of my treasury, for the greatest triumphs of evolution belong to Man, and even Man may vanish if the planet gets too hot."

"You collected people too!"

"I told yer, didn't I?" Sophie snarled.

"Level ten, now. Come along. We haven't much time and I do want you to see everything."

Level ten was arranged in exactly the same way but on a slightly contracted scale. Here were the tribesmen from Borneo whose names had appeared in the ledger at Humbug Cottage. They were sharpening their spears and plaiting vines, just as they had been doing when they were 'harvested'. On every side, in identical chambers of their own, were representatives of other cultures: an Inuit drying fish; a Chinese fortune-teller, serving tea; a Berber, squatting in his dark blue cloak, telling a desert tale... Of course, you had to guess what he said, for the glass prevented any sound from escaping. Perhaps there was no sound, or perhaps it was recorded somewhere else. Nothing could be heard but the giant fans of the air conditioning system.

Level seventeen, at a dizzying height, had to be viewed from a special platform. The glass cells were stacked three high, like taxidermy tanks in a museum. But their occupants could still be seen, wriggling inside. "You can borrow these if you like. Opera glasses." Mr. Brambling produced a pair from his pocket. "The specimens on this floor will be of more interest to you. They have unique talents, which the world cannot afford to lose. Imagine if such people were to get sick and die and there were no way of calling them back? What a tragedy that would be! Here they are safe and they will shortly be immune from any earthly trouble.

"Do you see the pianist over there? That's Schnitzel. The greatest interpreter of Schubert, ever. And there, the chess-player, Korevich. Never beaten. Computer chess is such a bore, don't you think?"

Trudi scrutinized the distant subjects. There were conductors, footballers, explorers, chefs… She could not imagine how so many people had been abducted without somebody noticing and telling the authorities. The pianist looked familiar. Yes, they had seen him at the Toy Forge. But his antics, and those of his companions, appeared almost comical from here – like animated waxworks, doing a dance. One little Tomte in the far corner was particularly amusing. Dressed in a green jacket and gaiters, he flaunted red puppet cheeks, and pulled at his hair with an abstracted frenzy. Every few moments he jerked to his feet, marched around his desk, sat and scribbled a while, then tossed the papers on the floor, and jumped up again.

"It's Mincke!" Trudi cried in sudden horror. "It is. It's Mincke, writing his stories. *Mincke!*" she screamed above the hum of the fans.

"No use, my dear. He can't hear," said Mr. Brambling. "What about number 56189? Next to the ballerina, whirling on one leg?"

"Corky!"

"You see, they are quite safe. There's your dear father, cataloguing his plants. And there, my rebellious Sophie, are *you*. Do you remember what an extraordinary creature you were?"

Following the line of his finger, they located a cell furnished with a turning wheel and inside the wheel, high above the floor, they made out the figure of a girl, lithe as a lemur, rotating in a contrary direction as if gravity didn't exist at all. Now on her feet, now on her hands, she slipped effortlessly, wrist over toe, elbow under knee with faultless precision – her finest act…

This raised an uproar.

"Beast! You filthy beast! You'll pay!" shrieked Sophie.

"Let them go! Murderer!"

"I kill you!"

But what none of the youngsters noticed was that their guide had manoeuvred them neatly to the opening of an unoccupied cell. With a deft slice of his hive tool he toppled Pedro, Jurgen and Sophie inside and shut the door. No amount of fury would save them now. The solid glass repelled their blows and stifled all cries for help.

Mr. Brambling consulted his watch - the silver watch he had used to time the children in the herbs.

"Regrettable, but necessary," he observed. "They can cool off in there. Come along!" He took Trudi roughly by the arm and propelled her away and she had time only to note the number above the door before she was bundled into another lift and spirited up again.

This time they went to the top.

"The Queen Cell" announced the old man, proudly. "Nobody goes in here but me. Here are all the nerves, the cerebral coils of my miraculous creation, just as I began it, fifty years ago."

He pushed her into an ante-room with a window through which you could view the main chamber.

"What do you think?"

Trudi stared in stupefaction. Did he really mean her to believe that all the intelligence of the world lay captive here? Save in old films, she had never seen such cumbersome junk. Vast hulks of apparatus clogged the room – a mess of wires and steel casings, hardly resembling a brain! There were naked bulbs and levers, and reels of tape, like the spools on antique tape recorders, all spinning on their shafts at various speeds. Dials flashed. Screens flickered. It looked like Dr. Frankenstein's laboratory. But Mr. Brambling clasped his hands in rapture.

"I can call up any item in the collection at the mere flick of a switch," he boasted, then gave an indulgent smile.

"Of course it is not the kind of technology you are used to. Digital-this and Nano-that. They do all that, of course, in the other laboratories. But this - this secret nucleus is *my* baby and I am an old man. I have never lost my affection for the early machines that set me on my path.

"Magnetic tape! Well you can't have a bee-brain without magnets now, can you? Call me sentimental, if you like. They say it will be obsolete very soon, but I *love* magnetic tape – so versatile, so organic - if you see what I mean - rational. It fits the pattern of the universe, it equates with time. It can run backwards as well as forwards. And the modern format can hold so much information, an entire project will fit onto one reel. Sometimes I amuse myself here for hours, replaying the moment I collected a particular specimen. Shall I show you?"

"No!" cried Trudi, covering her face. "I don't want to see your cruelty any more!"

"Child! Child! You do not understand. There is no cruelty! I have done everything for the benefit of Creation. Imagine how sad it will be for God, if Man annihilates himself and everything else on the planet. Will He not be grateful for me for saving the best? All these souls here await translation to a heavenly existence where their perfection can remain untarnished forever. If only we could have preserved all the wisdom of the Ancient World so!

"In my little cabinet at home I have tiny fragments - pots from Egypt and Peru. But think, *think* what it would be like to have saved those civilisations entire! Suppose one could recover the *whole* of Leonardo da Vinci? Or of Bach? I could weep when I think of the things such men may not have written down. My project is a gift of homage to them and all that meant so much them. All the wonderful things in Nature...

"You can see, for instance, how the bees have been my inspiration. They were my first love. After them, I studied the human societies which modelled themselves on the wisdom of the hive: the Egyptians, the Babylonians and the Wari in Peru... I had planned a farewell party you know, in the Wari style, with honey-wine and a final conflagration. I even used Wari names in the secret codes I invented, as a private joke for myself. Yes, you look surprised, but I had to make codes, because it was all so secret. The codes are my signals to initiate the end of the world: - the End of this World, Trudi, that's what I have planned - *Wari One*, to launch the final 'Assumption'; *Wari Two* to destroy the Beedome; *Wari Three*, to mobilise the killer bees, if anyone tries to stop me. No use your saying the words, my dear. You are not a wizard or a bee-master and my subjects will not take orders from you. Not even Olaf can mouth or undo my spells."

He was talking at great speed now, as if he truly believed the end was near:

"I took my lessons from the best teachers. Scholars like Kircher, the trickster. You remember his magic lantern at the cottage? The man is a particular favourite of mine. Throughout all my endeavours, he has been my model and guide - you could almost say my hero! Why else do you think I insisted that they changed the statues at St. Gregory's? Wallis was a clever mathematician but Kircher had greatness - ambition beyond reckoning. Never mind the problem of infinity. Who needs infinity? Kircher didn't. In his great plan he would sit the universe in his hand and pluck out all its secrets.

"People used to say that he was mad! But he was a collector of knowledge after my own heart! He invented gadgets for translating languages and composing music. They were the first computers really! He called them 'arks' because words and notes could be preserved in them, just as the animals were preserved in Noah's Ark in the Bible. And now, look about you, here is my computer and all the holograms which *I* have saved, 'living' in *my* Ark! Nothing in the world can touch them now. They are destined to exist forever in my private paradise – I call it the *Beehive Cluster!* It is the new gateway to eternity! That's the beauty of tradition, Trudi. Reinventing the past!

"To cap it all, Kircher is the father of this magnetic clock that controls every other mechanism of the Beedome. See how beautiful it is! I improved the design, so this is now the only timepiece in the world which can run both forwards and backwards, according to the disposition of the magnets. It will enable me, at the critical moment, to become the Master of Time itself, and bring in the Age of Perfection."

Trudi peered through her fingers. Mr. Brambling was trembling visibly, swept away by his own excitement. He seemed genuinely moved by all that he said. But the words somehow left her cold. She could hear the voice of Old Tom, ringing in her ears: *"Nothing in nature is perfect... that is the signature of life. You'll never find a perfect snowflake in Nature. Beware of anyone who says you*

370

can." And then Sister Matilda: *"The Assumption was the moment when Our Lady was translated to Heaven..."*

"Do you mean 'translated', like the Virgin Mary?" she asked picking on the word at random.

"Why, *exactly* like the Virgin Mary! You really are a remarkably clever girl! Why else do you think I placed my research centre beside the Convent of the Assumption?"

"Because you were in love with Sister Matilda," she blurted rudely. She was past caring about manners.

"Ah. Matilda..." his eyes melted at the name.

"Yet you sent Olaf to St. Lucy's, didn't you, to spy on the Sisters with his cameras? How could you do that to someone you loved?"

"Don't you see, child, it is because of the love I have for all of you that you must be saved. Matilda will be with me at last when I call her. She may be here even now in the vestibule below!"

"And my Daddy..."

"I have the highest possible respect for him! As I do for you."

Trudi shrank from him. "Are you going to kill me too?"

Mr. Brambling shrugged. "That choice will be yours, my dear."

Whatever happened, she must keep her nerve. She must stay ahead of him if she could. Already she could see that he had told her too much to let her go.

"Mine?"

"Well, you see, with your quick wits and your insatiable curiosity, you have caused me quite a lot of trouble. I had allowed myself a few more years to complete my project, before submitting myself to the hologram process and then uploading everything together. I had certain gaps to fill. Important ones too. And a few scores to settle, perhaps. At the moment of the 'Assumption', this antiquated paraphernalia that you see here, will be consumed with fire and the files will go somewhere far away where the technology is advanced enough to carry on evolving all by itself, take on an independent life. Only of course it will be better than life, you see. Invulnerable! Immortal! No *matter*, then, if the human race destroys itself, and all other living species. I don't expect you to understand fully. But you can appreciate how tiresome it has been trying to head you off at every turn! I can't have people prying into what I do! Your meddling has forced me to bring my plans forward.

"Now, whether you wish to stay here with me, or forfeit your memory and return to your earthly life with your mother and your brother, is largely up to you. Poor Sophie, I am afraid, has gone too far to be released again. And Pedro? I am not sure. I *could* be lenient… But, as you well know, there is someone who must join me here first. As long as this person is at large, my whole scheme remains in jeopardy, for he alone, of all men alive has the power to undo my work. Therefore, I *must* have him, possess him, before I go."

Trudi dropped her hands.

"You alone can call him here. If you call him, he will not be able to resist coming to save you. And if you give him up to me, you can go back to whatever trivial life you choose to lead at home. It's not even as if you saw enough of him for it to matter very much …" the silvery voice wheedled on as Trudi listened, eyes wide in wonder. For a moment she floundered, wrestling with his riddles. Then she grasped the meaning.

Of course! The wizard who *could* mouth his words and undo his spells was Per! Her beloved Grandfather! If only he had been able to understand how the laser magic worked, he would surely have defeated it at Christmas. Jurgen could have taught him something. And she would have helped. Per guessed he was to be Olaf's next victim, after Mincke. Dear Grandpa! He had smelt the villains out all those months ago. He *knew* that something wicked was going on and he wanted to tackle it then. But lack of time prevented him, so he turned to cunning instead, playing dumb, playing dead. Well, in a sense he had won. He had thrown Olaf off his scent, hadn't he? He had nearly fooled *everyone* into thinking he was going soft - and then he had vanished altogether. He had not yielded up the wisdom that the Sami noaïdis taught him.

But Per was no coward. He would not abandon his loved ones, surely. He must have been busy all this time, doing something. Did he know that Trudi would ignore his warnings? Did he secretly hope that she would help him piece together the parts of the puzzle? Or had he merely put herself and everyone round her at risk by her obstinacy? Given her life over again, she knew that she would still follow the same path. She could not stand idly by while

Olaf played his tricks on all and sundry. And fate had seemed to encourage her on her way. There was that strange magician Pilliwig, and Mambo-Hambo, the Man of the Mountains. They accepted quite casually that she was on a special mission. And Old Tom, who never asked questions... They had all tacitly read her heart and wished her Godspeed.

She and Per belonged together. He had as good as said so that night beneath the stars, and certainly neither she nor he had any place in a paradise pleasure park. Where had he gone to? She must not even try to think! Looking afresh at Mr. Brambling, she felt a crushing sense of shame. How could she have been so blind as to class this villain with her own true kin? Well, one thing she knew now for sure. Let him do his worst, she *would* not submit to him or any of his wishes. She would defy him, unrepentant, to the last. And she would die rather than call Per to an ambush!

Blank-eyed she faced her foe.

"I *will* have him, nonetheless" he insisted, smiling. "Because you will not be able to help yourself. From here you can see the time quite clearly. I'll allow you half an hour to think it over. When Kircher's clock strikes nine, I shall give the command for the last 'translations' to take place. Then there will be no going back. The very clock itself will pass into the cybersphere.

"But if you call your Grandpa," he raised his eyebrows and cocked his head, "I know he will come for you. Then you and your friends, perhaps even the pugnacious Sophie, can return to the world you have left behind, and to the arms of those you love. They depend on you, Trudi. Don't let them down for an old man, past his prime. You are too smart for that.

"Imagine him, lonely and wondering where you are. How pleased he will be to receive even a wish from you. You have only to touch that little amulet at your throat... Just a wish will suffice to save you. And think how much pleasure it will give him to see you again?"

"Go away, Mr. Brambling! I won't listen to you!"

"Half, an hour Trudi. You can watch it all happen from here. Call him, or enjoy your last thoughts. They should be interesting!"

373

Chapter Thirty-Eight

Northern Iron

Clinging to the rungs of the access ladder, Edmund felt his boots cut into his naked heels and wished that he not left his socks behind. He had rashly panicked, hearing voices approaching in the dark, and abandoned the octagonal hut in the forest where he had planned to spend the night. No one must know he was here. And yet he remembered how difficult it was to find one's way about in this place, even in broad daylight. Each path, each clearing looked so exactly like every other. Even the research units were identical, so you could not tell if you had passed them before. That was why he had tied the strips of red tape to the trees, hoping that they would guide him on his return.

In the pocket of his borrowed coat, he fingered the plans he had stolen from Humbug Cottage. His heart still raced from the success of his recent raid. Now he was bent on revenge. He would put paid to the monstrous scheme which had stolen his youthful brilliance, his ability even to earn a living. If he could find Brambling, the perpetrator, he would finish him too. Brambling, who had professed such fatherly concern, showered him with gifts and praises and then stripped him of everything that gave life meaning and turned him out into a hostile world, a mere husk of a man. If the Sisters at St. Lucy's had not fed and clothed him, he might have died in the winter snow, or struck his own brains out in despair. And if that golden-haired child at the door had not asked him about the bees, he might never have begun to solder together the loose connections in his mind to figure out the injustice he had suffered.

Now Brambling would meet his nemesis. That symbol of his ambition, the great steel tower that transmitted all his secrets, was about to topple, and with it would fall the system of espionage and fraud on which his evil dreams depended.

Edmund still had gaping holes in his reason. He knew it, just as he knew that he looked a freak with his matted beard and sunken cheeks. Who wanted a man with a naked chest, and burning eyes?

He knew that people recoiled from him. That was why he had taken notice of the child. Children invariably cried when they saw him, but she had looked him calmly in the eye, unflinching. That was odd. It had sparked off a recollection of other happier days... What was it her tee-shirt said? 'I love honey'. Then she asked about the bees, and that really set things buzzing...

Even now fresh memories stabbed him, spurring him on. An infernal energy coursed through his veins, bringing strength beyond his natural ability. He had stolen tools from Brambling's shed and crammed them beneath his belt. He could feel them now, digging into his ribs: a hacksaw, and croppers and spanners and the insulating tape he had used to mark his route.

Swinging out above the treetops, he knew he must sever the cables that supplied power to the satellite sensors. But in his dizzy, dislocated state, he could not be certain which they were. Here was a copper rod, thick as his finger. Perhaps this was the one... It seemed to go straight to the top. He would cut out a section with his saw. He hooked one arm over a lattice beam and took stock. Strange how dark the sky was. The bees wouldn't like that. They always got funny before a storm.

Brambling! He'd string him up – right here on this mast, so that all the world could see what a charlatan he was!

His saw bit into the cable, warming, as he worked with the fury of ten men. Nothing would stop him now.

But only the ghost of Edmund's former genius could have seen that he was cutting the wrong link. This wire brought no power to the Beedome mast. It was merely the lightning conductor...

∞∞∞∞∞∞∞∞∞∞

For Trudi, alone in her cubicle, and consumed with her sense of failure, escape seemed impossible. Her fists rebounded from the window, ineffectual as kitten paws. No cry could pierce the walls. Of all dreadful places to end one's days, this seemed the worst. To be walled up in a ghostly mausoleum with not so much as a blade of grass for company!

At least Jurgen and Pedro and Sophie could reach out to one another in their prison cell below... For a moment she recalled Jurgen's frantic face at the window:

375

"Don't leave me, Trudi! Don't go and leave me here!"

Her own baby brother. However could he begin to understand? The thought of Jurgen brought the tears prickling into her eyes. And after Jurgen, came a whole procession of figures with dear faces, peering in upon her. They looked sad and distant, as though they stood at her graveside, but could not reach out with a human touch. Here was Barbara, her cheeks all flushed with weeping, and Kirsten, pale and bitter. *"Why Trudi, why have you done all this to us?"* There was Professor Saxmund, wearing a suit. It must be a funeral, then, for he never wore a suit. There stood Scarp, twisting something in his hands and vowing retribution. And Hamish, who wanted to throw her a line, but could not. How she longed to jump up and run to them and bury herself in their arms, but she dashed the tears away. She must not let herself think about such things in case Per somehow overheard.

She must focus her mind on something else... on the clock perhaps, behind its protective case? The timepiece was a marvel of engineering, but exquisite too: a painted model of the earth that pivoted, floating on its own ingenious axis. Lavish, in blue and gold, the globe was marked round the equator with the hours of the day and a gilded goldfish, suspended in space, nosed the minutes as they passed. Kircher must have had a whimsical mind. But he was a pragmatist too. A cylinder mechanism with magnets and weights drove the movement from beneath. This folly worked. Trudi traced the levers and pulleys as far as she could. Then gave it up. The whole thing was mounted high on a plinth. There was no way she could reach it, still less stop it. But her mind had settled a little.

In the time it took her to work the system out, the dial had turned ten minutes.

Turning, turning...

Kircher's clock revolved like one of those Viking spindle-whorls Mrs. Partridge had on her wall, spindles for teasing out lengths of yarn, yarns like tales on winter nights, tales told under the ever-circling stars. Trudi could see those cold Vikings of Greenland, shivering in their woollen cloaks, longing for the fires of Valhalla to warm them at a feast. They knew all about the turning of the earth, how to get from one continent to another and how to journey from this world to the afterworld perhaps, like the

376

Sami, their neighbours. The whole of the cosmos was turning. Sven had shown her how plants grew in spirals, one leaf at a tangent from another, and then there were pine cones and teasel heads and galaxies and storm-clouds, all patterned in whorls, like the snail shells on Drayholt Hill... *"All the secrets of the universe are locked up there..."*

If only she knew more. If only she knew where to hide from the machines that monitored everything through the glass of her tank, grinding out Mr. Brambling's demonic will as their reels spun round and round... The clock dial measured out ten minutes more...

Instinctively, she reached for one of her plaits and stuck the end in her mouth. She could hear her mother protesting:

"Trudi, don't suck your plaits. It looks so awful!"

But she carried on regardless. She needed the comfort of it just now. Her hair, tousled by yesterday's wind and her recent scramble through the trees, was sprigged with scraps of twig and woodland debris. By force of habit she began to comb stray wisps with her fingers, teasing out the tangles. As she did so, she dislodged a speck that she took at first sight to be a flower-bud or a seed, no larger than a pepper corn, but this speck let itself down further on an invisible thread, then halted and began to climb again. It was a tiny spider, pale, avocado green. She must have picked it up and carried it here, by chance. The spider, quite unaware of her, balanced itself a moment, then swung out sideways and, hanging on the air, began to fasten the rudiments of a web.

Trudi had long ago conquered her fear of insects. *"They are our teachers,"* Corky used to say. *"We can learn everything from them."* Mincke thought so too. Insects, spiders, creepy-crawlies... they were older than humans. They had seen worlds come and go. Now she held her breath and watched in fascination. She had never before seen a spider this colour, with such delicate creamy legs. Her father would have loved it! And together they would have studied the whole painstaking process as the creature worked out his design. But not here!

She felt a shiver of regret. The little spider had no idea that he was lost, so far from home. Busy spinning, he could not understand that he had stumbled into a greater trap: that in only a few minutes, his fantastic, cream-coloured legs and all the skill they embodied

377

would be reduced to mere computer code and then incinerated, sharing her own fate. Trudi would not willingly have brought him to such an end. If only she had spotted him earlier, she could have left him safe in the undergrowth... He hesitated, doubled back, secured his thread and busied onwards, defying gravity.

Now, when she looked again, she could see that the thread was not invisible after all, but iridescent where it caught the light, and that it was strong... strong enough to carry both the spider her thoughts. They were travelling together, embroidering emptiness. Her eye followed the line till it vanished on some untraceable thermal overhead. Oh! For a moment she felt lost. Where to go now? How could one climb up to nothing? Then she remembered the noaïdis. How, but by becoming small as nothing oneself...? Squeezing between the interstices of the wind, and hanging on a filament finer than a hair! Trust. That was the name of the filament. Up, up she went, like a climber being hauled to safety by an unseen hand...

The wind was cool. It cut between the needles of the fir forest, cut between the ice crystals on the needles and then between their filigree dendrites, bringing the scent of resin and the acrid tang of the dog fox to every creature far and near. And the frost on this spider's web trembled in the wind like the lace on a confirmation mantilla, collecting hoary splinters from the air. The creature which had made it was long gone - no more than a summer memory now - but this web, tucked between the bark fissures of a giant spruce, had weathered whole days and nights and winter storms. Trudi could not help marvelling at its tenacity. Her boots scuffed the forest litter, as she stood on tiptoe. Yes, just as she expected: cones, twigs, and fallen needles, all wearing the same white, winter crust and glinting as the afternoon light slanted in.

She knew this place. Not far away lay the blue line of the hills beyond Litven and behind her, the slope where Per had stopped to recover his breath at Christmas. If she carried on down this path for another mile she would reach his log pile and glimpse the smoke from his chimney. But she would not go there. The reindeer from the Isandeland Market was waiting for her nearby, and in any case she could not find Per there. She turned back towards the trees. She had never flown in a sledge before and she halted, momentarily unsure whether she should go.

378

When she looked up she could see the reindeer keeper sitting a little way off on a stump, his back turned, the blue smoke of his pipe curling above his head. *Forty euros for the ride.* There was a sign painted in red. She jingled the coins in her pocket and the reindeer man heard and turned around. And in a sudden deluge of joy, Trudi recognized him and flew into his arms and the smell of his hide jacket was straightaway in her nostrils and the firmness of his shoulder under her cheek.

"Grandpa! Grandpa! You're not dead!"

"Not dead! Not yet!"

"Don't ever go again. Don't leave me!"

Per gently brushed the hair out of her eyes and smiled. There was ice on his lips and on his eyebrows. He scattered the fire twigs with his foot and straightened up. His voice - *his* voice, that she had almost forgotten, in its sing-song, down-in-your-boots, bass-resonance - rang in her ears.

"You're coming with me. Can you hold on tight? Might be bumpy!"

Now he took her hand in his and led her to the sledge. So they would ride together, after all. She thought she had never been so happy. Too happy for this life. Was he dead? And was she dead too?

The Sami pulka looked for all the world like a little coffin or like a boat for one, the kind of boat that could cross a dark river. But she was no longer afraid.

She set her hands on the wooden sides and clambered aboard, tucking her feet under the seal-skin cover and Per hopped in behind her, took up his driving stick and tapped the reindeer's flank with his rein. Immediately the sled started forward, left the ground, skimmed the trees, touched down for a moment and took off again.

Now Trudi was able to look around her. She could hear the reindeer bell, sounding, as they passed over snow-bound settlements below: woods, churches, field clearings, the long snaking line of a river. Above her head, a frosting of stars. Soon they reached the coast. They must be travelling east and the unreflecting sea melted beneath them into a measureless void. Now land again, an island with trees and between this and the next landfall, a strait of frozen water which made a bridge. Rest here.

Then consult the wind and the lie of the stars and take off once more into the dark. This time, Trudi felt a rush of cold around her body. She was leaning into the air, wings outstretched, as the little island returned to view. In the lee of her companion's wing-strokes the flying was easy. She kept his shoulder on her right and his flightcall rang out over her head. They were skimming the shore already. Now they turned aside from the settlements and street-lights and headed for the unlit woods. At this height, blue star-shadows carved out the contours of the land and the cold cut to the bone. Above a circular clearing they banked and then, as if they had been shot, plummeted down amidst a welter of snowflakes - a honking flurry of feathers. Once more, she felt the ground firm beneath her feet.

Per brushed the snow off his coat, squinted behind him to make sure they had not been followed and held out his hand.

"Come, there's not much time."

Trudi, in her grey, furry boots, instantly forgot her goose-flight and stepped to the centre of the clearing.

"This space is a sacred lake," said Per, "important in the culture of the north. They call it the place where the sun died. When Louhi the evil wizard stole the sun, the sky god Ukko ordered a new one, so that mankind would not be left in the dark. But a spark of the new sun broke away and fell to earth blasting out this crater when it fell. So great was the impact, all the forest burned. And when the crater filled with water, it formed in its depths a mysterious passage to Tuonela, the land of the dead."

"Are we going there?" asked Trudi, suddenly afraid of drowning beneath the ice.

"Not today," smiled Per. "But you need to know that dark magic has been done before. And that the sky god cannot be quenched so easily. Ukko brought back the sun. And every atom of life contains sparks of that energy which are gateways to other worlds. Now listen, Trudi. This is the essence of good magic. If you want to have power, do not try to grab it or capture it, but let it lift you like a wave and hold you.

"Here!" Per stooped and picked up a burning brand. Others lay scattered, dark against the snow. "You remember the lump of iron I gave you in December?"

Trudi nodded.

"Did you keep it?"

"Yes, I promised." She pulled it from her pocket.

Per smiled slowly, his eyes, like damasked metal, glittering. "My clever Trudi. This little rock, has come from a fireball just like the one that landed here at Kaali. Northern iron. It has the mystery of a magnet. And here you can see traces of the furnace where it was born." He took the meteorite and stroked the uneven surface before handing it back. "See? These are the fingerprints of the forces which hurled it here; forces too great and too small to fit the shoe-size of our understanding. But open your mind and this same energy will take you anywhere, on a whisper of the wind. Then you can be truly free. The sparks from Ukko's sun will light up even the tiniest grain of sand till you can see new worlds within."

He tapped his brand and the sparks flew up into the sky.

"There are the bright stars of Favdna. See them between the trees? Favdna is the hunter of the heavens, and there, his chariot, Karlsvogna, chasing the celestial elk. Round and round they go. They too come from the fiery furnace but their destiny is to run to the end of time. Our lives follow the dance. And so does everything we know in this world. Beyond our life, lie the ghost-regions we are afraid to know – Neverness, where all that are unborn, unimagined and lost are held - but you and I need not be afraid of them. They are part of us too. The shadows of spirits can always come back, as long as we make room for them. Bear, elk, hunter, child. Do you understand me? There are ways of bringing souls back from the dead. The old medicine men learnt how. Legends are full of their stories.

"Only, if we break the dance, what will happen then? Will Life itself lose its meaning? That is what my ancestors always feared - that the magic could be lost. And if it was lost, could you or I restore it, find the meaning again? That is our quest, Trudi. *Our* hunt. And the last battles we have to fight will not be between man and man, or between man and nature, or even between Life and Death, but between longing and belonging. For real time is not the make-believe men invent with clocks, but an actual moment of the heart. When we find it, we become it. When we lose it, we and time both die together. Nothing then will matter any more. Hep! I talk too much. The horns of Favdna's elk point to the Nail Star and the Nail Star takes you home. Can you remember?"

"Yes, yes I remember."

"This meteorite is a stranger to earth. His real home is impossibly far away. And the noaïdis are strangers too. It is not an easy life, Trudi. No home will hold you if you choose to follow their way. No earthly loves will satisfy you. But you will have the stars and voices of the birds for company and the ecstasy of flight will be yours. Think on it hard, my darling girl. Keep your eye on the North Star. And good luck. *Lycka til!*"

His voice grew faint, and the burning sparks whirled Trudi up and away before she could say goodbye. Looking down, she saw his belted figure diminishing beneath her. Feet planted wide upon the encircling ice, his arms outstretched, he stood a moment with face upturned, his hair and beard a-stream in the wind, pale eyes burning...

"Grandpa!" The wind took her words and tossed them away and on she sped through the snow-clouds, far over the web of tundra lakes below.

Keep your eye on the North Star. That's where she was going! She felt she had left every living thing behind. From here one could commune only with the elements and their singing mysteries. When she was finally numb to the bone, and lost beyond all reckoning, she came to rest in the fork of a colossal tree. How to get down? How to find the friendly earth again? Her feet slipped on the polished bark. Terror gripped her heart. She scrambled part-way, fell and wrench her arm. The ground, so impossibly far away, lay out of sight. "Take an easier route," suggested a small voice at her ear; a spider, curled in a snag of leaf.

"I can't!" cried Trudi.

The spider laughed. "It's your adventure! You make the rules! Spiders follow their own devices. Why don't you do the same?"

Trudi reached out and grabbed a gossamer that hung from the stalk. Instantly she began to abseil, light as thistle-down, launching herself with a thrust of her toes from jutting spurs and bosses. This must be how Hamish feels, she thought, when he is mountaineering. No wonder he is addicted! This lovely buoyant feeling could go on forever and I would never get bored. I wonder if the Dolomites are as tall as this tree? She pictured them as

dragon's teeth, rocks like great molars, rising out of the snow. If I
was a climber, say, with Hamish on his Himalayan Expedition, I
would abseil down like this and he wouldn't laugh because I was a
girl. I wouldn't be afraid of anything and I should never be tired,
never...

∞∞∞∞∞∞∞∞

The thread snapped and she steadied herself against the glass
partition. Here she was, back in the Beedome, trapped like a bug in
a bug-box. She had the horrible feeling that Mr. Brambling was
watching her on one of his many television screens. The dial on
Kircher's timepiece had advanced another ten minutes. In a gesture
of sheer frustration she clenched her fists, felt the meteorite in her
pocket, and brought it out into the light of day.

Per had been right. Ukko's thumb-prints lay all over the surface.
It throbbed in her hand, still cold from its arctic flight. *Northern
Iron*, said Per. *A magnet.*

Perhaps she could escape again. Perhaps if she tried, she could
wish herself back to the treetop or the magic lake... She placed the
stone in her open palm and held it out before her... But nothing
happened. Nothing. And she would have so liked to prove some
justice in the world. A paltry two minutes remained until Favdna
captured his stag. She *must* do something. Tightening her grip once
more, she hurled the meteorite at the clock with all her might. She
was a good shot. All those junior rounders matches should have
paid off, but her missile bounced back and rattled to the floor.
Undaunted, she retrieved it. She would use her sling. What did
Scarp say about stopping an elephant? Now her hands were
shaking. She unwound the Inca braid from her wrist, and, fixing
Per's rock in the central split, slipped the loop end over and
pinched the knot between finger and thumb. Then she stood back.
She would give it six swings over her head, for good measure, and
let it fly... *This* time the glass case shattered and the shot landed on
the velvet cushion beneath the pendulum. But the movement still
ticked on. Useless! She closed her eyes and wished and wished...
If only Ukko could hear her in his sky kingdom. If only he could
spare one spark to save the world again...

He *couldn't* let the darkness win. Per had promised her: *The
sparks from Ukko's sun will light up even the tiniest grain of*

sand... She could see them like stars, fine particles of light, now visible, now melting out of focus, now a mere halo of memory and as she narrowed her sight and all her senses upon the point where they had been, she felt her mind glow with a sudden brightness. ... Was this the end? Had Mr. Brambling fulfilled his promise and pressed the final button?

A cannonade of thunder pealed as the storm, which had been threatening for two days, finally broke and released its fury overhead.

Cocooned in her cell, Trudi could not know how the lightning pounced upon the satellite mast nearby; or how, with its conductor severed, the structure itself took the impact of the charge, glowed like an incandescent string figure and buckled to the ground. She was not free, as others standing at the gate were free, to see the sparks fly the length of the connecting wires and lose themselves in the surrounding trees, nor could she imagine how the flaming manikin that was once the unfortunate Edmund, lit up an indigo sky as Fate reunited him with the cosmic elements. He blazed a moment and was gone. In that instant, the power supply to the Beedome failed and emergency generators whirred into action. Dozens of sirens across the complex began to wail and alarms rang at the Fire Headquarters in Kingsbury: "Send Pumps Six! Major incident at Pinkney Forest Research Laboratories!"

All Trudi knew was that the lights went out and that when they came back her meteorite had attached itself, like a limpet, to the magnets that drove Kircher's clock. She also realized that she was still alive.

And then she noticed more. The clock itself was gradually slowing down and stopped to undergo some mechanical realignment. When it started again, it was responding to a force beyond her understanding. *"Northern iron."* She heard Per's voice again. *"A loadstone. In Old Norse language that means a way-stone – it finds a path... just like a shaman..."*

As she watched, the time-piece began, slowly, almost imperceptibly, to move in the opposite direction. The action simply reversed so that first ten minutes remained until the deadline, then twenty, thirty, more... Gradually gaining momentum, the gilded dial started spinning on its axis and the spools of the Beedome computer juddered, stalled and obediently followed suit. Both now accelerated together till they were rewinding at the speed of light. Mr. Brambling's magnetic tape, inseparable from the clock which was its master and in defiance of its intended purpose, was deconstructing its own chronology, scrambling programmes as it went and unravelling all that it had done. The screens flickered wildly. Sparks flashed. And the infernal artificial brain that had threatened to end the world began to die. But *why?* Whatever had happened?

Trudi knew that storms were unpredictable. They had learnt about them briefly at school: how they were made and why you shouldn't take shelter under a tree... And then she had heard intriguing tales about travellers getting lost in them – aeroplane compasses going haywire - and ships foundering off course at sea... But electricity was a strange enigma and scientists still puzzled over it. No wonder if Trudi thought a miracle had happened! For this storm was no ordinary storm and the lightning, which had destroyed Edmund's mast, had bounced across the entire Beedome site changing its magnetic charge. Positive, negative, North and South had temporarily shifted places. The Beebrain, in its insulated tank, should have been safe, but Trudi had confounded the magnets of Kircher's clock with her meteorite and now the cogs and levers were whizzing out of control. Pachakuti! The mad, upside-down time that the Sneevelings had contrived was coming round right way up!

As the minutes and the hours flew back, the Beedome phantoms in their vitreous cells de-materialised one by one. The lights in turn shut off.

Mr. Brambling, in his master chair, awaiting apotheosis, with his silver watch before him, heard the thunder and assumed the end had come. So busy had he been, making sure all was in place for this moment, he had hardly considered what 'extraction' might feel like. Now, as darkness fell, he smiled expectantly. Perhaps this was the first sign. Perhaps he was already disembodied. He wanted to get out quickly now, before that execrable Swede caught up with him, for he would not be taking Olaf to the Beehive Cluster. And he would not really know until he got there, whether he had caught his 'big fish' or merely gathered in the girl and her confederates. Perhaps he would not even know when he got there. Knowing belonged to this life with all its anxieties and the pains of personal consciousness. In the Beehive there would be no pain, perhaps no knowing, just endless salvation…

Moments later he heard the fire alarm. The emergency lights flickered into life and by their dull glow Mr. Brambling read his watch: two minutes past nine. Damnation! Nothing had happened!

He leapt from his chair and started back towards the Queen Cell, but steel fire doors already blocked his passage. What to do now? If the 'Assumption' had somehow occurred without him, what would become of him? Thinking that all his earthly work was done, and that the contents of the Beedome had been safely uploaded to a secret lab in Puerto Rico, he had already given the final codes. Within moments the building would self-ignite and unless he could save himself, he would go up with it!

Fire escapes…

He remembered how he had argued with the planners, not wanting external ladders to mess up the design. His fire escapes took the form of hidden shoots, like the rubbish-shoots in skyscrapers. He would find one of those and get away. Nobody knew he was here except the children - and the children… well, it was unfortunate, but they would not be able to tell their tale, would they?

∞∞∞∞∞∞∞∞

Meanwhile Trudi had fled as soon as the alarm system released her from her cubicle. She had only one thought in her head. She must find Jurgen and the others and help them get out while there was still a chance. She dashed past the closing fire-doors and back towards the lift. 'Out of Order' read the display panel on the wall. Stairs then. The spiral flights made a tardy descent to the floors below, but Trudi, remembering Pedro's fearless feats at St. Lucy's, leapt onto the stair-rail and, steadying herself with her hands, flew backwards into the abyss. Level 17. Level 16. Level 15…

Here somewhere. They must be here somewhere… Gallery after gallery of abandoned cells greeted her on every side.

"Jurgen!" She yelled, suddenly terrified that she might be the only soul alive and as her lungs exploded in a scream, the lights went out again and someone grabbed her hand.

"*That's* done it! That's all we need!" said a familiar voice.

"Sophie?"

386

"We'll never get out now."

"Are you all here?"

"We've all had it now. We can't even see where the stairs start, or which way they go."

"*Jurgen!* Is Jurgen there?"

"Where's Mr. Brambling?"

"He went off on his own. Oh Jurgen, I didn't think I'd see you again. Where are you?"

"You in't going to see him again in this dark, are you? Listen, *you're* okay?"

"Yes, yes, I am now."

"Well, think of a plan, then. We haven't got long. Something is burning down there. I can smell smoke. And there's no exits, right?"

"What about Corky?"

"Corky's gone, Pedro. All the holograms have gone. They went out after the power failed."

"So we lost him!"

"I don't know. The computer started running backwards."

"You mean there's *nobody* left?"

"You heard her, didn't you? It's all breaking down here and we won't be left either, unless you find us an escape route pretty soon."

"The way out is always in the middle," said Pedro quietly.

"What?"

"This whole house like a maze, yes?"

"What do you know about it?"

"I know how to get out of maze."

"It's true, Sophie, he does. He's done it before, in Mr. Brambling's garden."

"How's he going to see to do that then?"

"He doesn't need to, *do* you?"

"No, I no need. Mr. Brambling he like tradition, si? So he will use traditional maze pattern here, like in the garden. I can do it blind – like in old days. Is easier in the dark!"

"If we go up," said Trudi, "maybe we can get onto the roof somehow."

"Si, si, *then* find the middle. Hold hands. I go first this way."

With fingers outstretched to the wall, Pedro felt the comforting darkness press once more against his eyes. This world he knew. He could see with his other senses.

"Stairs here," he cautioned. "Up again." They trooped along like climbers roped together.

"Here no more stairs. Turn right here, then feel on left. We take first left."

As Pedro's assurance grew, he began to cheer up.

"How we get off this roof? Is like giant slide. We no can slide to the bottom. We break our bums!"

"Shut up and get us there first," said Sophie, feeling his palm cool against her own. She was puffing and sweating, unused to the exertion. How long would it be before the fire reached these upper floors?

"'S okay. We nearly there. Left here. Then left. And now here is middle."

They found themselves in an open space with a central column. admitting slivers of light.

"That's the sky" cried Trudi. "Pedro, you've done it!"

"Not quite," Sophie raised one of the flaps that were attached to the frame. Heavy, clumsy, they were shaped like the wings of a propeller. Perhaps they swung out and turned when the building was working. Daylight flooded in. "It's some kind of vent – part of the air-conditioning, I think. Gawd help us. It goes right to the bottom." Pressing forward, the children peered down for themselves. Beneath them yawned the shaft, like a well, or chimney flue, sending up a delicate plume of smoke. Skywards, the walls rose sheer, three metres to the rim. One false move and they would tumble straight to their deaths.

"Finish!" said Pedro, throwing up his hands. "Mr. Brambling win!"

"Never!" cried Trudi, though it was clear they hadn't a hope.

But Sophie suddenly clapped her hands. "*I've* got it. I've *got* it! I can remember how to do it! I can bloody remember!" She grabbed hold of Trudi and hugged her. "You are a genius. I dunno what you done, but you just done something out of this world. You put me right! Look!" They drew back the shutter again and in the cloudy light made out her silhouette. She had kicked off her shoes and was walking about on her hands. Her legs swayed exuberantly in the air. "Look at me!" she shrieked. "I can remember what to do! I'll get you all out of here. Just watch me!"

Without a second's hesitation, she launched herself through the opening and across the smoking gulf. Arms eagle-spread, she flattened her palms against the furthermost wall. Now, gripping the bricks behind with her feet, and working herself round, she began to climb, hand over foot, elbow under knee, sure as a sloth, effortless as a lemur, defying gravity. She stopped once to cough and the children gasped in horror.

"Only joking!" she called over her shoulder and continued inching nearer to the rim.

Finally she slipped one leg over the parapet, and flipped herself over on her stomach, so that she lay, grinning down.

"Told ya, didn't I? Now you've seen the best!" Modesty was never her strong point.

"How do *we* do it?" cried Trudi.

Sophie looked round for inspiration and reeled at the view. It really was extremely high and slippery up here and she instantly realized that she had no useable plan. You would need a professional's head for heights not to feel giddy and fall. Couldn't risk it with the children. But way, way below, she could see tiny figures, like puppets, massing at the compound gates, crowds of them, with toy police cars... and a fairground lorry...

"It'll be all right!" she shouted back. "Hold on there. You'll be all right in a minute! I think Big Sid's arrived!"

Chapter Thirty-Nine

The Hunt Closes In

At six a.m. the telephones at Kingsbury Police Station began to go wild. First to ring were the Security Guards who manned the Beedome entrance: *Please would they send help. A mob of thirty or more ruffians and travellers, led by a ginger-haired giant named Sid, had turned up demanding the release of an unknown woman and were threatening to storm the site. Extra staff had been called in but had been engulfed by the crowd. The situation threatened to turn ugly.*

Sergeant Peach swallowed down the last of his peppermint tea, pulled a face, and winkled the sleep out of his eyes. Four hours kip. That's all he'd had. After a nightmarish, slow journey home, (police detours because of the Kingsbury Fair), he'd found that the football he had been looking forward to had been postponed because of flash-floods and thunder storms. Instead, his Free-Scan Memory-Box had saved him a programme on embarrassing diseases. As for the steak and kidney pie from BioDawn, that had looked all right, but had given him indigestion and he had spent half the night dosing himself for heart-burn. Returning to work for the early shift, therefore, had seemed a good idea until he looked at the computer log: three felons released without charge; two more jokers in fancy dress on the loose, spreading malicious rumours; a Sister Superior having a turn in the early hours… He sent young Truman off with a flea in his ear.

Now a riot.

Somebody must take charge before news of it all got upstairs.

At seven-thirty, Mother Constance of the Convent of the Assumption telephoned. She had reason to believe that a member of her order had been kidnapped and was being held hostage in Pinkney Forest. She also had it on good authority that there were children missing, and what was he going to do about it?

At eight, an enraged Sir Maximus came on, bellowing through his hangover that he was not having his staff at Pinkney bullied by threats from nuns or vagabonds. No one but authorized personnel were to enter the compound. Where was Olaf Stromberg? And what had happened to Professor Brambling? The land line had been cut off and nobody could get through on his mobile. With a mob like that at large, such important citizens surely needed police protection. Heads would roll if their lives were put at risk and they might be dead at present for all anyone seemed to care.

A 'crowd control' van was dispatched to Pinkney forthwith. Peach's superior set out for Humbug Cottage.

Then the Chief Constable put in his pennyworth and some hound from the Kingsbury Gazette got wind of trouble and mentioned it on his computer 'natter' blog. Before you could say 'anti-inflammatory', the whole world wanted to know what was going on at the Beedome. The Home Office said they were sending a man. MI5 issued instructions. The Army stood by. Speculation took wing and the nation consumed the breaking news from t.v.'s 'man on the spot' along with their breakfast cornflakes.

In fact, Big Sid's mob was soon outnumbered by media personalities, vying for a spot from which to cover the story. A police helicopter glimpsed a muster of nuns from the Convent of the Assumption, scaling the walls which formed their eastern boundary, some sitting atop, while others, brandishing picks and hammers, attacked the brickwork, determined to force a passage. "Keep at it Sisters!" cried their leader, with Amazonian zeal. "We're nearly through!"

Sister Emilia, finding that her car had been stolen, had roused her fellow Sisters at five and ordered taxi cabs for Pinkney. After filing into Lauds with the rest of the community, the Kingsbury delegation had then proceeded, in a body, to the office of the Reverend Mother and laid the whole matter before her. Mother Constance made enquiries and the abandoned car was soon discovered.

"Well, we can't wait for the police," she said with vigour. "It seems they are already busy with another matter. Something must be done here without delay. You, Sister Emilia, take tools and helpers and clear the way. I will try some higher diplomacy – see what the Bishop can do. Sister Bianca may be a wayward lamb, but she is one of my own and I will save her. As for the children, I feel for them as she has done. They must not come to harm. The older

Sisters and the infirm can stay here and pray and put on tea kettles."

∞∞∞∞∞∞∞∞∞

Meanwhile, it had taken Hamish the greater part of the night to search the northern end of Pinkney Forest. The paths on every side looked so similar, that, but for his trusty compass and map readings, he would long since have got in a muddle.

"All deserted," he reported back, time and again. The sun rose and vanished into cloud again. Time ticked on.

"*We* could be checking the other half," objected Scarp. Hanging about was getting on his nerves.

"We must stay together. And you'd be lost in two minutes."

Scarp snapped a twig and inwardly composed an unspeakable reply. His eyes flashed mutiny. There were other ways of finding your way about. You didn't *have* to have a compass and a map! His Great Uncle Ned was reputed to have smuggled himself across France during the war, just by using his nose and his gypsy intuition!

"Well, I'm with Scarp," said Sister Bianca, who also hated sitting idle. "I put my trust in the Old Man upstairs. He's our only hope. It's daylight now and all the researchers will be arriving for work and we will have achieved nothing. I vote we go that way and keep going till we find the Beedome itself."

"Amen!" Scarp stood up and brushed the pine needles out of his vest.

Hamish reluctantly bowed to pressure. And the three of them broke camp and retraced their steps to the south.

"These huts occur every couple of hundred yards. Beyond the inner edge of the wood are open fields – then the building itself. But there are watchtowers everywhere, and a large processing plant over there…"

"What's that?" asked Sister Bianca, who frankly wasn't listening.

"Well it's another hut."

"No *that*, on that washing line."

"That's *it!*" said Scarp. "That's our evidence. Somebody's socks, somebody's marker and… Trudi's little necklace. I know that. Her Grandpa made it for her. She'd never be parted from that.

392

She's dead isn't she? While you've been messing about with all your fancy gear, someone's gone and murdered her right under our noses!" His hand tightened round the knife at his thigh. He would just like to stick it into somebody now and Hamish looked a suitable victim.

But Bianca squeezed his elbow. "Why do you say that? There's no sign of violence here. Trudi and Jurgen both wore these things. I remember. They were for good luck, Trudi told me. *A hunter's bow to bring success in hunting.* Well, we're hunting aren't we? Perhaps it will bring us luck. Perhaps it was left here for us. As a sign. There are many ways to read the world and I think this is a sign from God."

Scarp curled his lip, but let the knife go. A further search revealed nothing in the hut, but then Hamish found the second marker, and they adopted Sophie's method, travelling from sign to sign until they reached the meadows.

"Now try the Beedome. You can see there's no one here."

Hamish stopped. "Did you hear that?"

"Thunder."

"No, no, something like police sirens, way over there."

"Whatever it is, I'm not interested!" Scarp meant business. "We are going to this here building thing. That's where *they* were going. And it's where we are going too. You got that?"

"Hamish, he's right. We can't allow ourselves to be distracted now."

Hamish sniffed, shouldered his rope, then folded his map and posted it carefully in his pocket.

"Why you bring all that Gawd only knows," muttered Scarp. "There must be a hundred metres there! It's not the bloody Alps, is it?" The tension was making him jumpy. "Why is there no one here? It's creepy, that's what it is. I don't like it."

"None of us *likes* it, man," snapped Hamish, hitting back at last. "We're not here for fun! We're here to do a job. So stop whingeing, will you, and let us get on."

Bianca, anticipating more trouble, gave Scarp a warning poke.

"No fighting. There'll be enough bloodshed when we get there!"

But some calamity was brewing anyway.

The sky had turned a filthy colour, clouds boiling up like volcanic ash. As the Dome drew nearer, its bulk seemed to consume the sky. The three figures in the meadow toiled along, small as ants, stopping and scolding and battling against the wind. They had crossed two thirds of the space when Bianca lifted her face and involuntarily uttered the words of the *Benedictus Dominus.* She had said them a thousand times before, but never with such feeling: *"Bow thy heavens, O Lord, and come down... Send down thine hand from above: deliver me..."*

Almost immediately, lightning struck and they saw the great mast before them blaze and crumple in a shower of sparks. Seconds later, smoke began to billow from the sub-station. Hamish glanced at his compass to get a bearing and found, to his astonishment, that the needle had swung off course. Magnetic north had skipped way out of line. That leader bolt must have galvanised the site!

"Come on!" he called, breaking into a sprint, "before the whole lot goes up!"

Running in a habit is not easy, even if you are the All-Surrey Senior Girls Long-Jump Champion, and Bianca was glad to have Scarp's hand to pull her along. Scarp, for his part, felt relieved to see some action at last. So they dashed on, ignoring the bees that clustered anxiously round their hives and the meadow blossoms, flattened by the wind. A stormy deluge was imminent, but that was the least of their worries.

Hamish, with his long stride, soon outstripped the others, yet even he felt it a frustrating distance to the Dome and when he arrived, he found all further access barred. The black basalt door stood resolutely closed. Shiny-smooth tiles rose in a precipitous curve from ground to sky, with nothing but ventilation grids to mar their surface. This looked more devilish than the Dolomites - not so much as a toe-hold in the form of sill or drainpipe - no fissure where you could secure a rope.

And here he faced a double challenge. With a mountain crag you had to climb *up*. Ascending was always tricky. But Hamish also needed to find a way of getting *inside* this monstrous rhubarb pot and heaven alone knew how that might be done. He scratched his head and peered aloft as the first fat drops of rain began to fall. High above, streaks of smoke billowed about the summit and dispersed in the wind. The whole thing resembled a kiln. Was it already alight? For the first time he faced the possibility of defeat, and he stepped back to get a completer view. That was when he heard a voice, a faint call from above:

"Hey you! Down there! Go and get help before we are all fried alive!"

Astride the apex rim sat a roly-poly, dark-haired girl, no bigger than a bean.

"Are you Sophie?" yelled Hamish.

"What? What the hell does it matter who I am? Just go and get help!" she shrieked.

"Eh? I mean, have you got the children with you?" Hamish could out-bawl just about anyone. "I *am* the help!"

"The kids are stuck inside, about three metres down. They're okay for the minute but you've gotta be quick." The wind took her words and blew them away.

Scarp and Bianca arrived, gasping for breath.

This, then, was the moment he had been waiting for. Time to test his grappling device. He slipped his ropes to the ground and began to buckle on the crampon overshoes. Round his thighs went the harness and the harpoon holder."

"How's this ever going to take your weight?" asked Scarp, handing him a bolt with a clawed head. The attached micro-filament cord looked flimsy as a clothes line.

"Och, it will." He slung the spare harness with its belay clasps across his chest. "No problem there. Nano-technology. The greater worry is whether I can aim straight."

"You weren't javelin champion *as well*, by any chance?" said Scarp in an aside, but Bianca had no appetite for jokes. Her eyes strained towards the heights where her darlings lay stranded. Hands in pockets, she clutched the ear of Sticky Bear.

Hamish steadied himself and fired his harpoon. It shattered the plastic of the lowest vent and the tempered steel claws tightened on the frame.

"That's it. I'm away." He tensioned his rope and swung into action, his legs suddenly sure of themselves as he hauled himself aloft. He should have been a pleasure to watch – not many climbers had this natural facility. But Bianca closed her eyes, feeling sick.

Way up at the top, Sophie lost sight of Hamish and her hopes vanished with him. He clearly wasn't going to make it. As for that skinny guy and the nun, she couldn't imagine them being any use at all. Losing patience, she began to scan the horizon for other assistance. Through the first spots of rain she made out a convoy of fire engines, now queuing at the entrance, but they must have got caught up in Sid's protest, or were waiting for clearance from security, or were still filling in their risk assessment forms, for the gates remained firmly shut. What help were they? She waved her arms, and screamed vengeance on the world in language that Trudi and Jurgen, (and Bianca too for that matter) had never heard before. But suddenly she sat to attention and pointed towards the trees.

"That's him! Look! *Brambling!* Don't let him get away. *He's* the devil that started all this. He's tried to kill us and just about everyone else as well and now he's escaping. For God's sake get after him one of you and stop him!"

Hamish, unable to hear, wiped the rain-streaks from his face, secured himself to his first belay, retrieved his harpoon, re-fitted it and fired again at a higher vent.

Down on the ground, Mr. Brambling had emerged from his chute, and now paused to get his bearings. He saw the climber swinging up above him, and other figures nervously looking on. Rescuers. Damn them! For a moment he considered summoning the bees. Should he make a final stand? But he quickly abandoned the idea. After all, what could be gained that way? The Beedome Adventure was finished, and the best he could hope for now was to evade capture. If the Beebrain went up in flames, at least the proof of his crimes would go up with it. No one else would have the codes – they were in his head - and one day, later, he might rebuild his dream. Already he was running for cover...

Just now he needed a refuge, away from publicity and the unwelcome attentions of the police. Persuading the world that he had perished back there would suit him well. Better to leave the site by a secret route and get away from Pinkney altogether. Then consider what to do with the rest of his life. He had a little boat down by the canal. If he could only reach that... If he could only reach the cover of the forest, he could slip away while everyone concentrated on the fire...

An ominous ache developed in his chest and his legs shook as he struggled along. Not much further to the trees. If only his heart would bear up, he would cast off Mr. Brambling as a snake sloughs its skin and emerge in a new place, with a new name. Thousands did it every day on the internet. He would reinvent himself. He still had his hungry mind and a thousand unfinished projects to pursue… Was there not once a piano-maker in Vienna who went on building instruments after he was dead…?

As the heavens opened, Scarp and Sister Bianca looked at one another and then at the distant fugitive.

"Is it true?" asked Scarp, suddenly seeing a vent for his rage.

"I think it must be. He has always appeared to help everybody, to be such a dear old man, but perhaps he had a darker plan. It's too awful to imagine. We trusted him absolutely."

"Well, he's had it then," the gypsy promised. "Old man or not. Here. Take this. I shan't need it and you'll get pneumonia standing there." He put his jacket over Bianca's head and set off in pursuit, his hair streaming in snakes, his sodden vest stuck to his ribs.

∞∞∞∞∞∞∞∞

By the time Hamish reached the summit of the Beedome both Scarp and Mr. Brambling had disappeared into the trees and the downpour was easing off.

Sophie greeted him wide-eyed.

"You're pretty good, aren't you? You ever thought of joining a circus?"

Hamish ignored the comment. "Are you okay? Where's Trudi?"

"Down there. But watch it. The drop goes straight to the bottom. One false move and you're a gonner."

"Can you hold on here?"

"Can I sit on a log?"

"You're not scared of heights?"

"One day I'll tell yer about me!"

"Listen Sophie, I'm going to see if I can bring the children up."

"In't yer gonna wait for the fire engines?"

"Can you see any?"

"Over there. They're coming in now."

397

"Keep waving. We really need a helicopter. Perhaps they'll send for one. But I can't sit by and do *nothing*. It's too dangerous, with a fire already taking hold down below." Re-tying the spare harness, he checked his clasps, then nodded. Everything hung on him getting this right. Two blows with the harpoon gun were enough to smash away some tiles and reveal the steel flue-liner underneath. This would hold. And once more the grappling hooks took his weight as he clambered over the edge and gingerly let himself down. Five minutes later he returned with a green-looking Jurgen in his arms.

"Hold onto him tight and for God's sake don't let him fall. Here. Clip yourselves to this. This is roped to the wall."

"I in't gonna slip!"

"Just do it, lassie!" commanded Hamish as he vanished once more...

∞∞∞∞∞∞∞∞∞

You can drink a whole bottle of good champagne without risking a hangover the following morning. Absinthe will leave you senseless in the gutter, and never give you a headache. But Beery O'Leary's Golden Mead could reduce the strongest body to a state of helpless prostration in a matter of hours.

When Olaf left the police station he was not sure whether either of his legs belonged to him or whether the hands which supported him under his armpits were his own, or someone else's. He tried to figure it out. These hands did not seem familiar, but if they were not his, then what had become of the ones he used to have? He could not feel them. And who were these strange characters who propelled him along the pavement at such speed and thrust him into the back of his own car? Perhaps they were doctors... Or dustmen.

For a frightening moment he thought he was being taken to the dump, before darkness closed over him once more and he dreamt he was at Buckingham Palace, queuing for a knighthood. He should have been feeling proud, but he had somehow lost his trousers. He knew he had left them at the Beedome, but there was no time to go and fetch them and the heralds could only offer him a flannel with which to hide his nakedness. *"Olaf, you are so careless!"* scolded his mother, rubbing his face with the flannel.

"One day you will get yourself into such a sticky mess, you will never get out again!" He woke in a sweat, head throbbing. He must have been eating sweets for his breath tasted of honey:

"Where am I, Mummy?"

Barbara frowned from the front seat.

"You're in your car, Olaf. And we're going to the Beedome, remember, to rescue all those poor souls you've locked up there."

Her voice, like a loud-hailer, echoed across the cavity where his brain once sat and drove pins into his eyeballs.

Ah yes! He remembered now. He remembered that he had to escape and warn Sir Maximus that his cover had been blown. He had to find Mr. Brambling, at all costs. He would play these thugs along and then make a dash for it when he saw his chance.

The night sky had cleared, bringing an early morning chill. Sprawling in the back seat of the car, he shivered and roused himself. At least the open top afforded a clear view. They were parked on a hill somewhere out of town and the violin-maker chap had taken out a pair of binoculars and was scanning the horizon. A hardened case, that one.

"Can't see it!" he was tutting.

"Pardon?" Barbara, busy looking for something, had not been listening.

"Can't see it. You know what that means? Bad weather coming."

"Sorry honey?"

"If you can't see the Beehive Cluster on a clear night, it means there's an almighty storm coming. That's what they say…"

The Beehive Cluster… How did this UFO freak come to know about that? Like a drowning man Olaf grappled with his thoughts, lost them and sank down into oblivion once more. How long he lay unconscious he did not know, but when he next surfaced it was broad daylight. The car now sat in a country lay-by. There were ugly clouds massing overhead.

"So, Olaf, do you feel able to drive again?" asked Barbara pouring coffee from a thermos. She had little Spanish breakfast rolls too, sweet dough dusted with icing sugar. "This will set you up."

Olaf blinked behind his glasses and meekly accepted mug and napkin. As his mind cleared, he weighed all that had happened,

399

gradually separating fact from fiction. Couldn't see the *Beehive Cluster,* could he? He nailed Archie with his eye. He'd help him find it all right! He pictured to himself the pleasure with which he would consign *both* his kidnappers to Brambling's hologram archive. Yes. They would fit in nicely. The Beedome would be the best place to take them, after all!

But when they arrived at Pinkney, they found the place in turmoil. Sid's rumpus at the entrance gates caught Olaf by surprise. Publicity was the very last thing he needed and yet here were reporters, special branch officers, fire engines and a crew of demonstrators wielding crowbars and coconuts and threatening death and destruction.

"Let me through, I'm an official," he said to the constable who blocked his way. "See – Laser Wag. My card."

The constable stopped to confer with a colleague.

"No one's going in till we get the okay from the Home Office, sir."

"Look, I *am* the Home Office," lied Olaf, in a flash of inspiration. "Sir Maximus sent me."

More conferring…

"Get back there, will you?"

A bottle bounced off the constable's helmet and shattered neatly in the road.

"What's going on here?" called Sergeant Peach, trying to impose some order.

"Just checking something sir."

A tin of fizzy lemon next exploded nearby, spattering everyone with citrus spume.

"Right! Get that big ginger one. He's the ring-leader!"

"They say you can go in now. Drive on."

Olaf smiled as the sea of bodies parted before him. Soon he would have revenge on them all. Up went the big white gates with the sentry boxes on either side and he cruised gently through. His mother would never scold him again! But he must get away quickly now.

He knew a secret way out of the compound for he had heard Brambling once let it slip. A private tunnel had been laid in, running from the Extraction Chamber, across the grounds, under the Pinkney roundabout and straight from an inspection vault in the

BioDawn car park to the cellar of Humbug Cottage. Construction engineers had been ordered to install it when they excavated the new road layout. Everyone thought they were digging drains. That way, Brambling could enter and leave when he liked without passing security or raising suspicions from his neighbours. If only Olaf could find that passage, he could lie low at Brambling's cottage till things had simmered down. Sir Maximus would arrange things for him.

As for his kidnappers, he had no doubt they would be dealt with appropriately. After 'extraction', they would make perfect inmates for Mr. Brambling's sanatorium and he would be glad to testify personally at their committal. They were practically unhinged already. The woman, sitting at his side, was even now threatening him with what looked like a broach pin, while the other, hunched in the back, sat twiddling the knobs of his radio, head-phones on ears, as though he were expecting an astral message. In this, of all places! With frequency jammers in operation twenty-four hours a day! Olaf allowed himself another smile but a cold sweat broke out on his forehead. His heart raced insanely.

Someone in the crowd shouted: "Get off me you idiots. *He's* the one you want! He's the kidnapper!"

No! No obstructions now!

He called and beckoned to the security guard.

"Andrew, has Mr. Brambling been this way?"

"Not today, sir."

"I've got a special message from the top."

"Sir?"

Olaf dropped his voice: "They… they want to know the serial number of your gun. Is it loaded?"

"Yes sir."

"Well, let's have a look anyway. Have you got a pencil?"

"Er, in the office. One moment."

"I'll hold this for you. Be quick. Mr. Brambling is waiting."

The guard gave him an agonized look. This was most irregular… Which was worse, to go against the rules, or to risk displeasure from above? No self-respecting guard ever gave up his firearm…

But Olaf had already plucked the pistol from his undecided hand and sprang to his feet. He was even now standing on the driver's seat, gesticulating wildly.

"Get down you fool!" cried Barbara, "Before you hurt someone!" and she jabbed her pin into his leg.

With that the gun went off. An ear-splitting report sent shock waves through the crowd and Olaf's arm, stunned by the recoil flew uncontrollably up. He instantly dropped his weapon and letting out a howl of panic and pain, leapt from the car and started to run.

Now a shot from a high calibre pistol can do a lot of damage and, as chance would have it, the bullet that Olaf fired veered off at a tangent and blew out the laser antenna of the radio jammer at the gate. The beam here was powerful enough to sweep the whole complex, which explained why nobody could get a satellite signal for miles. Not only did it protect the site from attack, but it stopped any snooping and prowling on the part of competitors and journalists and it kept the government suitably at bay. With a blue flash, the scanner exploded, sending débris into the crowd.

"Stop him!" called the Chief Constable. "Shoot him!" His blood was up.

"It's all right sir," replied the mortified Andrew. "He's unarmed now and the site is secure and empty at present. Nobody has been allowed in to work today and the other guards were all sent home last night. There's only me and William here on duty. He can't get far. We'll run him down."

The commotion was lost on Archie, however, who sat transfixed in a daze.

"Archie, are you all right?" For a moment Barbara thought he had been hit. She shook him by the arm, then lifted his ear phone and bellowed: "Are you okay?"

The rapture gradually faded from his eyes. "I can die now," he said.

"You'll do no such thing. Officer, a man over here has been hurt!"

"No, no, not hurt – just – touched." He took off his glasses and wiped them absently on his shirt.

"Where, honey?" asked Barbara, all concern.

"Everywhere. Barbara I *heard* it."

"He's delirious, poor soul."

"Oh shut up a minute and listen! I heard it. First of all there was that that jamming racket – you know, the white noise you get when someone is blocking the airwaves – and then without warning, the purest, most sublime sound ever ..."

"Angels?" asked Barbara. "He's dying!"

"The Music of the Spheres. I *heard* it. I actually got it on the radio!"

At that moment an explosion resounded from the Beedome.

"You fools!" said the Chief Inspector pushing rudely past them. "*'Nobody on the site'* - It's obvious that terrorists are already here!"

The detonation shook the fabric of the main building and some of the lower tiles flew off. Hamish, having assembled all the children on his chimney pot, decided he could wait for help no longer. Lord alone knew what was going on down below. He had clearly heard what sounded like a gun going off. If the dome caved in, then all their efforts so far would have been in vain. Better to chance a risky descent than perish for certain in the flames.

Sophie accepted the challenge with alacrity.

"Piece of cake!" she observed, considering the incline of the roof.

"It gets steeper as you go down," Hamish warned. "Have you abseiled before?"

"Have I ever had toast for breakfast?" came her mocking reply. "'Course I have!"

"Could you take Trudi with you and go first? I know this rope will reach the bottom because it got me here. I can drive more anchors into the structure. There are two harnesses and two sets of carabiners. You go down in tandem. This French knot here will hold you if you let go. Tie all the gear to the rope when you finish so I can haul it back up for us."

"*I* know what to do," declared Trudi, not to be outdone. "I've done it before. I've just come down the Tree of the World."

Jurgen winced. How could she talk such rubbish?

"Shut up and do what I tell you," commanded Sophie.

She and a partner used to slip head first down a rope in the Mudlarks Circus. Spider rappelling it was called. There wasn't much she didn't know about ropes.

403

The boys would be more of a problem. "I did a course once..." Jurgen volunteered.

"Good man."

Hamish tested Sophie's fixings and she and Trudi, fastened together, scrambled over the side. At the last minute Sophie winked. "Wish us luck! I'll yell when the rope is free."

Within seconds the girls had dropped out of sight and Hamish turned to Pedro.

"What about you. Do you think you can do it?"

Pedro had kept his eyes shut all this time and he grinned and shrugged. "If I don't see I no scared."

"You can't fall. The rope will hold you. But as soon as you reach the ground, get away from the building in case more things blow up."

"Si, si, no problem. At the convent in Lima I used to climb out of the windows, with the bedclothes. You tie in a knot. Is easy."

"This is a long way down Pedro."

"No problem. I fly like a bird when I can't look."

Hamish shook his head. "You use your feet, *slowly*. No jumping. This hand here. This one here. Feed the rope through like this."

Minutes later Pedro began his descent and there was another agonizing wait for the cheer that meant he had safely reached the ground.

Now Hamish retrieved his equipment one last time. He would rappel down with Jurgen, praying that the anchor pins would hold their weight. If they could survive this, he would send a report to the British Alpine Club. He would win his patent for sure.

Of all the children, Jurgen had shown most courage, for he could see with eyes wide open the terrible danger they were in, but he held his nerve as they inched gingerly down. When they finally felt the grass beneath their feet, he put his arms round Hamish's neck and rubbed his face against his shoulder so that no one would see his grateful tears. Hamish himself felt reduced to a jelly and had to blow his nose before recovering his composure. They now shared a secret which brave men know well, and neither would tell on the other.

Bianca clasped them all in her arms in turn and out came Sticky Bear, and the ribena. As they hurried away from the scene, they spotted a procession of vehicles trundling to meet them: Fire engines, police cars, ambulances and a lone figure running... A helicopter put in a late appearance.

"Fat lot of use they were!" said Sophie with unmerited contempt.

The rain having ceased, a ribbon of blue sky appeared on the horizon and shafts of sunlight began to burst through. The storm had rolled on to Drayholt and the Severn Vale beyond. Pedro opened his eyes and wandered away from the group. The world looked excessively beautiful in this wet light, every blade of grass, every petal gleaming, colours brilliant, edges clean. For the first time he rejoiced in his sight, and a great wave of thankfulness and joy welled up inside him. He was alive. He was free. He must tell someone.

He knelt down to rescue a bee that wallowed in the cup of a poppy. In this curious light the creature looked dark, almost black and Pedro lifted it onto his hand and stroked the water out of its fur.

"Estamos emancipados, amigo!" he whispered, laying his cheek close and gently fanning the wings with his breath. "Entende? Estamos emancipados. Jo y tu."

The bee, still dazed by the storm, lay damp and unresponsive, so Pedro tried again, coaxing: "Estamos libertados! Entende? No? Oh I see. English bee. English bee no understand espanish! Listen, bee. We are... We are – efree! Comprende? *W'are-e free!*"

As though electrified, the creature suddenly stiffened, every fibre alert, let out an angry buzz and flew off at great speed.

Pedro watched, intrigued, as an anxious swarm collected round the messenger. Bees do not like storms. They make them nervous. But Pedro had meant to calm and reassure, not madden the hive. Perhaps something else upset them. They say that bulls cannot see red and the same is true of bees. Red and black are all the same to bees, whose eyes are tuned to different aspects of the spectrum, but dark objects make easier targets for bulls and bees alike, which is perhaps why apiarists suits are always white. However, when it comes to scents, a bee can distinguish the minutest nuances and if there is one thing that infuriates a hive defender, it is the smell of stolen honey.

Now it was an unfortunate accident of fate that Pedro should utter Brambling's code to attack at precisely the moment that Olaf Stromberg panted by, conspicuous in his dark Armani suit, his breath fragrantly saturated with mead. The bees did not hesitate, but set off in deadly pursuit, and Pedro stood open mouthed, watching Olaf's legs redouble their speed and leap into the air as they were stung. He was making for the Extraction Chamber. Now he reached the door, tried it in vain, turned frantically and headed for the ladder. Up he went with the whole swarm buzzing at his heels, wrenched open one of the skylights and hurled himself through.

And that was the last anyone saw of Olaf Stromberg. He landed head first in the honey extractor and since some idiot carelessly started the motor shortly afterwards, his remains were processed beyond recovery, forcing the closure of the plant forthwith. Shops later blamed honey shortages on the weather, on the international markets, on a new bug from the Continent, for Sir Maximus had ordered an instant suppression of the facts.

"This is from Whitehall" he blustered to the Chief of Police. He was sitting, resplendent, in his bomb-proof limousine. "Drop all charges. Silence the media. We want a complete hush on this whole affair. Say an unfortunate fire broke out... blah, blah, blah... emergency services... exemplary whatevers... no significant casualties."

"I can't drop *all* charges," retorted the Chief, holding the receiver at arm's length. He could almost feel the spittle flying. "I've had a riot on my hands! I've got arson, vandalism, breaking and entering, grievous bodily harm, disturbing the peace and suspected kidnapping here... and that's just the beginning."

Sir Maximus blossomed one shade closer to purple. "From *Whitehall,* Bunty!" he insisted. "Just do as they say – there'll be a knighthood in it somewhere, if you cooperate. They don't want a scandal. There's a lot of security information at stake. That sort of thing! Find a nice piece of local gossip to feed to the papers instead. You know. Drunken student topples historic statue – something along those lines. There's a statue outside St. Gregory's I wouldn't mind toppling myself!"

"You mean, let them all go?"

"Let them *all* go. Even that big ginger chap. You could get them to sign something first to stop them blabbing, if you're worried. But nobody died, did they? I mean nobody important. These things happen in the business world. Boom and bust, Bunty. It's part of the spice of life. Move on. Move on."

∞∞∞∞∞∞∞∞

When Sister Emilia and her platoon of nuns arrived on the scene, they were greeted with ecstatic hugs.

"You all come back to the Assumption and have a bath and hot sweet tea!" she pronounced and her magisterial bearing seemed, for once, entirely fitting for the occasion. But the ambulance men strongly disagreed. This contravened all rules and procedures.

"You need to go straight to hospital."

Trudi glowered. Bianca wavered. Sophie swore. Hamish doubted. Barbara fussed. The ambulance men, tall and muscular in their green uniforms, insisted.

In the thick of the debate appeared two unfamiliar figures: Sven, who had staggered out of the woods, holding his head like a drunkard *("Can somebody tell me what's going on? I've been asleep for two days...")* and a slim, blond woman with grey eyes whom no one had noticed before. Making her way quietly through the crowd, she raised a hand and everyone turned to stare.

"I think," she announced, in a voice that made men's knee-caps tremble. "I think that for once we should ask Trudi and listen to what *she* wants."

"And who would you be?" asked Sergeant Peach.

"I'm the mother," replied Kirsten, "Kirsten Larsson. And you?" She put out her hand and Peach blushed and took it. God! What a marvellous woman!

So they all had tea at the convent - except for the firemen who stayed to contend with the fire. And that might have been the end of the matter, only of course it wasn't quite.

For one thing, there was Scarp. Nobody knew what had become of him, except that he had run slap into Sven in the forest and had stopped long enough to point him in the direction of the Beedome, telling him to hurry if he wanted to rescue the children. When Bianca hung back after the others and called for him, the forest

407

yielded no reply. Scarp had simply disappeared. Mr. Brambling knew the forest and Scarp did not. But the gypsy was the younger man and hell-bent on revenge... Sister Bianca feared dire consequences.

"There's something else," she said, tapping Sergeant Peach on the shoulder. "Two people are missing and they must be found."

The long-suffering policeman had been looking forward to tea and buns. He had never been inside a convent before. "I'll organize a search," he replied.

Emilia interrupted, waving from the bank. "...And tell the firemen to come across when their relief crews arrive. They will need a rest and we've got plenty of cake. It's a Feast Day today!"

"It might be *life and death*..." Bianca persisted and Peach gave a regretful sigh. *Just his blooming luck!* Abandoning the prospect of tea, he adjusted his hat.

"Not to worry, madam, I'll go myself."

∞∞∞∞∞∞∞∞

In the few moments it took for Scarp to speak to Sven, Mr. Brambling had scurried out of sight.

"Did you see him?" he gasped, shaking Sven by the shoulders, till the raindrops flew out of his hair.

"See who? Where are we? Are we at home?"

"You're in Pinkney Forest, you fool! Did an old man come by?"

"Can't get my bearings. Must have been knocked out. And whatever are *you* doing here? I haven't seen you for months."

"Get your bearings now!" demanded Scarp. "Your children are that way and they need you! I haven't time to explain. I've got to catch the old man."

"Which old man?" Sven pulled his beard. "My father?"

"Numskull!" Scarp dashed on. Explanations would come later. He ran straight to the end of a line of trees, scanned the rides on either side and doubled back. The old fox had vanished – slipped the chase and made off heaven knew where. Now he needed all Uncle Ned's tracking skills to pick up the scent again. He scrutinized the ground, the lower branches, the tufts of bramble and woodsage that lined the path. Nothing there. No footprints on the soft forest floor. No broken twigs... Then he saw it glinting - a

408

shred of silver paper – the wrapper of a pill, discarded in a crook of root: *'Angipan'*. Heart medicine. A flooded stretch of earth held clear footprints. Once more Scarp had his quarry in his sights.

At the end of the forest came the fence. Chain-link. With a metal gate swinging wide. Then a cornfield leading down to the canal and he could see clearly where someone had trampled the crop. Gone that way, had he? After the downpour, Scarp's toes squelched in his boots. Sunlight glanced on the distant water and dandled rainbows in the droplets that festooned every leaf and twig. Fat use being sunny now! He gave a violent shudder, wondering what had happened to the children. If the old man was on the canal, Scarp would collar him and beat the daylights out of him, *'Angipan'* or no. He ploughed on, his face like thunder.

But when he reached the lock he found the site deserted. A waiting boat bobbed, tethered to a bollard. Brambling was nowhere to be seen. The craft vaunted a dapper set of controls tucked under a canopy and a cabin below for shelter. She was painted white, neat as a toy and her name, *'Curlew'*, adorned the stern in fancy writing. On the floor of the deck lay a jacket, summer linen, sadly damp and soiled. The old devil must be hiding up then, in that cabin. He must be planning to pass the lock and lose himself among the pleasure boats at Kingsbury.

Scarp legged it over the iron barrier and hopped aboard, but before he had a chance to go further, he was arrested by a sound at his back. He should have anticipated trouble. Scarp was a magnet for trouble! But any such thoughts came too late. As he turned, a missile, aimed from some hidden vantage point, caught him neatly on the temple and promptly laid him out cold. In the few minutes that he was unconscious, his assailant hurried to the far paddles and furiously began to turn the windlass.

Now, anyone who knows about locks, knows that the lower sluice lets the water out and that it is extremely dangerous to leave a boat tethered while the water level is changing. It is one of the first rules of the canal. But Scarp knew nothing about boats and in any case he was dead to the world. He woke to feel warm blood coursing down his face and dimly made out a shiny, silver object just inches from his nose. He lifted his head, saw that it was a rather fine stop-watch and blacked out again. The next time he came round, someone was calling his name.

"Hey! You there! Wake up, for God's sake! Unhitch your rope!"

He thought at first he must be drunk or concussed, for the deck beneath him slanted down at a dangerous angle, but when he staggered to his feet he realized what was happening. The *'Curlew'* was straining against her mooring as the lock waters drained away. Already, her bow dipped crazily down. The weight of the craft was tearing her apart. He could hear the timbers splitting.

"Unhitch your rope. You'll drown!" called the voice. The walls of the lock inched higher above his head every second, coated with a slime of matted weed. "You'll *drown!*"

His head was spinning. His feet slipping. He seemed to have lost all power to move. But he knew he was in a fix, right enough. There would be no way out for him if the flimsy boat ripped in two. He could not swim and in any case the under-current here would drag him down beneath the gates. Death would be horrible - dank and dark.

With a supreme effort he recovered his senses, whipped out Per's knife and severed the line. The boat groaned and slipped down into the water. Way above him, on the balance beam and silhouetted against the narrow window of sky, he could see two figures wrestling. Now it seemed that they would topple in upon him. Now they lurched the other way, first one and then the other gaining a better footing. One he took to be the man who had called him, a bluff fellow in a nautical cap; the other seemed older, shorter. Yes, more like the character he had pursued. Could this be Brambling? The swine! Instinctively, he picked up the stop-watch and hurled it at the old villain's head. Bull's eye! Still clutching one another, the veterans staggered and plunged down into the canal and the rest of their struggle continued out of sight. Down in his basin, Scarp strained his ears till the cries and splashes died away and he was distracted by a scraping noise at his feet. His keel was letting in water and had grounded on the base of the lock.

When Peach's rescue party arrived, they found a shocking scene: a shipwrecked ruffian covered in blood and signs of misadventure ashore - more blood and shreds of clothing. A naval cap lay on the towpath, where it had fallen.

But Scarp's story cut little ice with the police.

"*I* don't know who the bloke was. He just called out to me. I assumed he was the lock keeper."

"Old Tom?" P.C. Hawke had been a copper a long time and knew this run of customer. "There isn't no lock-keeper at Pinkney. Hasn't been for a long while now. Old Tom went off his head and disappeared more than a year ago. The cottage is derelict, you can see for yourself!"

However, the Chief Inspector had said 'no arrests' so for the moment they let the gypsy go with a caution and ordered the canal to be dredged.

Chapter Forty

Trudi's Choice

One week later, a visitor to Humbug Cottage would hardly have guessed there had been a storm. The garden delphiniums and canterbury bells stood proud in drifts of white and blue, while all around bloomed other flowers: larkspur, candy-tuft, love-in-a-mist, the very names conjuring metaphor out of nature in a tangle of sweet sounds. And sweet sounds were plentiful in the garden this sunny afternoon: first the strains of Corky's saxophone, which set toes tapping across the lawn to a medley of ragtime tunes and then the genial popping of corks as Sven and Hamish served up pink, fizzy glasses of wine and lemonade infused with strawberries, not to mention the excited barking of Bella, Scarp's little terrier, who crouched down on her elbows, bottom up, tail wagging furiously, waiting for Jurgen to throw her another stick.

A tutored ear would also have noted the counterpoint between laughter and sober debate, as guests savoured, questioned and teased over the events of the previous months... the tinkling of forks on plates, and the hum of contented bees.

Yet one week on, the world wore a different face.

Attempts to trace the bodies of Mr. Brambling and his wrestling partner had regrettably failed. A silk cravat and a leather wallet had been retrieved from the canal, but Mr. Brambling was now assumed officially 'missing'. Searchers with dogs had combed the area for miles. Secret watches had been put on ports and airports. But media postings had been quashed. All tacitly agreed it would be better if Mr. Brambling were simply allowed to 'pass away'. The executors of his estate, a firm of solicitors named Burnett and Blott, read his will and discovered that he had left his considerable wealth, including his cottage, and his antiquary's collection to the Sisters of the Assumption. If ever he was absent and unable to look after his home, he had requested, the Order should appoint a caretaker to do it for him.

"It is entirely keeping with his charitable nature," noted Mr. Burnett.

"Rubbish!" said Bianca. "It's his gift to Matilda! They were students together, you know, after the war. He left England to travel, in pursuit of his studies. His appetite for knowledge was voracious. And he had a special interest in arcane matters. They say he scoured the globe, hunting out shamans and medicine men, trying to put together a workable theory of magic.

"For four years he didn't write and Matilda, broken-hearted, finished her degree and took up the post of infirmarian at an orphanage in Bangalore. That's when she decided to give her life to God. By the time the adventurer returned, ready to marry, she had taken the veil. He never quite recovered from the shock, but hovered on the fringes of Community affairs, just for the chance to glimpse her now and then and he poured his disappointed energy into a frenzy of new research. Matilda's calling was entirely genuine, however. Though she cherished his friendship, she never regretted her vows."

"Wasn't she shocked when she learnt what he was really up to?" Hamish glanced across to where the tiny figure in black held court. She was telling one of her music hall jokes and her eyes shone mischievously behind their spectacles.

"Nothing shocks a person like Matilda," replied Bianca. "She long ago took the measure of the world. She says she had always known that Mr. Brambling was a little too intense. Many of the evils of mankind come from an over-zealous desire to make things better. But that's not to say all passion is bad. Actually we couldn't live without it. Matilda feels as passionately with her heart as any soul alive. It was *her* idea that the Convent should assign the temporary upkeep of the cottage, to Corky. Well, he and Barbara are still homeless, and he's the obvious choice, with his talents for beekeeping and gardening. An agent would cost more and be much less sympathetic."

"She wants to keep her eye on Pedro."

"Of course! She takes a professional interest, but in truth he is her delight! – and then the city is *full* of buskers. Corky can take his one-man-band into Kingsbury and entertain the tourists, all summer. And meanwhile, he can apply to adopt Pedro properly as his son. When, or if ever, the mystery of Mr. Brambling's disappearance is solved, well, I'm sure Mother Constance will ensure that there is a future for him here."

413

Archie joined them, looking for another slice of cake. "That Corky is a genius! Do you know he's worked out the exact vibration ratio that produces a wolf note in a violin? And not only that, he has tuned my radio so that I can analyse astral resonances while listening to Bach! Chocolate is it? Yes, please. Oh, and one of those as well!"

"How did he get out of the asylum?" Hamish mopped up the last of his crumbs with his finger and popped them into his mouth.

Archie knew that: "He *marched* out, the second he recovered his wits, leading all the other inmates to the tune of Men of Harlech!"

"Best of all," added Mrs. Partridge, slipping two lemon-sandwich cookies onto her plate. "I hear that Olaf's old hideout in Bacon Street is to let, together with the shop beneath it and that Barbara has enquired about the lease. Of course it would need lots of renovation. He left the place full of old papers. But imagine what a wonderful rabbit warren of a bookshop she could make there? A new 'Prospero's'!"

"Surely she won't need the flat if she is going to live here."

"No, but *I* shall need somewhere until my house is rebuilt. I can order my academic titles downstairs and sit and weave at that beautiful window all day. Moreover, Barbara has promised to keep me supplied with cake – so you must all come to visit! I've requested maple pecan pie to start with!"

"I suppose poor Sven is out of a job again."

"Oh no," roared Archie. "St. Gregory's have severed their association with Sir Maximus but kept open the offer of the Fellowship. Sven has actually been put up for a University Chair. Of course it means that the whole family will need to move…"

"…and that Kirsten will have to abandon her work for the Tranquillity Centre."

"Ah… well that, I understand, came to a rather unfortunate end. The director of the scheme had to call it all off. Couldn't carry on. The stress was giving him a nervous breakdown!"

As Archie departed, his plate now suitably laden, Scarp sidled up. Conversation had taken on a final note.

"You, Hamish," asked Mrs. Partridge, "what will you do now with your summer?"

"I'm off to the mountains."

"And you, Scarp?"

Scarp grimaced and dug one toe into the flower border. His brow was now adorned with a line of stitches.

"Depends," he sniffed. "Depends what happens here."

"Scarp doesn't think the whole Brambling affair is finished yet," said Sister Bianca.

"I didn't *get* him!" he muttered shaking his head.

"Thank heavens for your soul that you didn't!"

Hamish twitched his eyebrows in a knowing way and turned aside. This mention of the mountains had whisked his heart up into the clouds and he began to regale the captive Mrs. Partridge with an enthusiastic account of his plans. Scarp and Bianca were effectively left alone.

"What do you care about my soul?" Scarp grumbled. "You're going back to that convent, aren't you?"

"Yes."

"You're going back to boiling up old ladies' nighties."

Bianca smiled. *"Yes!"*

"You could come with me…"

Bianca snorted.

"Already married. Sorry." She pointed to her profession ring.

Scarp shrugged. It was unlikely that she would have looked favourably on the likes of him, even if she was not promised to a life of prayer.

She went on, more kindly: "I'm on this adventure, see? I have to find out where it leads."

"I *know* where it leads. It goes to that… that garth thing where you all get buried! In twenty years you'll be like that ancient sister over there and I'll be a corpse. Someone will do for me properly one day."

"Dear man, if I truly thought I could resemble Sister Matilda, I'd be full of hope. *She* is approaching sainthood. If I came with you, I'd almost certainly be damned. *I'd* be the one who murdered you! I'm not the romantic type."

Scarp grinned despite himself. "Nor me." Then he added: "But I'm right about this thing not being finished - you just wait and see - or I'm done with it all."

Her eyes shone back with real affection. "I hope not. You'll come and see us, won't you?"

"Don't worry, I won't walk out on my friends again. I can't trust them not to get into trouble, can I?" When he heard the full story of what had happened to Barbara and Corky and the children, he realized how very much he cared about them all. And now there was Bianca too. Would he have to take tea with the nuns in order to see her? *Him,* passing the buns in a convent? What would that do to his self-esteem? *Ridiculous!* Yet stranger things had been known. That was the whole point about adventures, you never knew *where* they would end up. In that sense he was pleased the affair was unresolved...

Over at another table, Kirsten was arranging little cups of melon and orange. Sophie gazed admiringly at her fingers, and then from her to the gypsy, now busy with that nun.

"Two more for Big Sid please," she asked. She had been in training for a week and already the puffiness had gone out of her face. In a month or two she would be dazzling little Star-Tail again. Sid would take care of her this time.

Kirsten gave her a loving wink and set the glasses on a tray, then called to Jurgen and Pedro who were playing about, stealing the decorations off the cake and feeding them to Bella.

"Hey, boys! Come and take these. And let that poor dog rest. Two sundaes for Big Sid and some raspberry boats for Barbara and Corky. Take them nicely."

The boys giggled and made a detour via the crisps.

"The extraordinary thing," said Barbara, buttonholing Sven, "is that you say this Mincke walked into a police station in Sweden the day the Beedome burnt down, asking to make a telephone call to England. He was as lucid as you or me. But the number he finally rang was Olaf's number. He'd taken it off that villain's business card. It was the only link with the Larssons that he had. And he kept on ringing it till I picked up one day when I was viewing the shop. Quite a talk we had. And the upshot was that I searched all through the papers Olaf had left behind. Much had been shredded, but shredding takes time. I found eight out of ten of Mincke's stories, complete with illustrations, stuffed into a cupboard. Olaf had simply dumped them in bin liners in his hurry to get away... I think we have saved a classic!"

Trudi listened to the voices, letting them wash over her.

The summer sun, the birdsong, the sense of warmth and the delight in being surrounded by so many happy faces, all contributed to her idle sense of pleasure. The Beedome now seemed insubstantial as a dream…

"…To think that the entire BioDawn enterprise has folded!" continued Barbara, balancing a raspberry on her fork. "Well, the second the blueprints for the Honeymeadow products were destroyed, they said the effort of re-programming it all simply wouldn't be cost effective. And if you believe that, you'll believe anything. Laser Wag have coincidentally dropped their 'animus' idea – no more 'personal recognition'… and…" she paused to underline her words: "The Toy Forge has closed too! Isn't *that* curious? In other words, they are covering their tracks as fast as they possibly can, before their dirty dealings come out into daylight."

"But anyone could go to the papers…" mused Sister Emilia.

Barbara popped the raspberry into her mouth and waved the empty fork. "Where's the proof? Nobody knows for sure. No one, except Jurgen here and the other youngsters, who actually saw the Beedome in action. Who is going to believe that what I heard was anything more than the drunken ravings of a man in the last stages of delirium? There has been a most enormous cover up."

"Poor Edmund's death was never reported at all."

"Nor Olaf's…"

"And rumour has it that Sir Maximus Bligh has taken on a new role as Environmental Envoy. Left the country!"

"His so called Institute collapsed when he withdrew the funds…"

"But the truth will out somehow, surely," Corky, having spotted the tartlets on their way, had put down his saxophone and quietly joined the group. "I know no one will believe Sophie or *me. We* were mental cases. But *you'd* tell them, wouldn't you, boys? About what you saw?"

Pedro, holding his tray, grinned self-consciously. "I don't see nothin'. I shut eyes the whole time!"

"Jurgen?"

Jurgen squirmed and looked at Pedro. "Nothing really happened," he dodged. "Trudi made most of it up!"

417

Barbara laughed, but her eyes began to scan the figures lolling and chatting on the lawn, looking for that young minx.

"You and Hamish should do a duet, you know," pronounced Emilia. "There are so many musicians here, we could have a proper jam and perhaps a dance?"

"What a splendid idea! I'll collar him. Sister Emilia, what will happen now to your website?"

"Oh," she clapped her hands. "It's going from strength to strength! I've decided to write a blog, instead of doing the live transmission thing. And it's very popular. People say it makes religion funny and accessible. Now do you understand that? Would you say that I was *funny?* I can't understand it myself, but the donations are rolling in and I think we shall manage to stay open for another year. We've got two new tramps…"

Barbara, peering from one group to another, took a mental snapshot of the scene. Who cared if Sir Maximus got off the hook? Villainy was usually well-rewarded in this world. But courage and loyalty had won out, too. This laughter amongst friends was priceless. Just perfect. From the jasmine-scented cottage, to the golden bee-wall; from the shady orchard trees, to the majestic spires of the garden herbs… that same gentle hum of happy voices… yes, it was perfect. But where was Trudi?

Trudi had wandered apart from the others. She too could hear the hum. She heard Corky and Hamish strike up in concert together and the general cheer that ensued, but her thoughts were far away. Everyone who mattered had a happy ending. Even Mincke would recover his stories in time and Barbara would find him a publisher, she was sure of it. But what about Per? Per remained missing.

Nobody *said,* but everyone had secretly hoped he would turn up. Sometimes she caught a distant, troubled look in her father's eyes. And Kirsten caught it too and put her arms round his neck and kissed his ear to make him forget.

Mr. Brambling had promised, in his final admonition: *"Only you can call him. If you call him he will not be able to resist… Imagine him, lonely and wondering where you are. How pleased he will be to receive even a wish from you. You have only to touch that little amulet at your throat. Just a wish will suffice…"*

Was it true?

She *did* wish him here! She wished he would stomp round the path in his rough reindeer boots and put his hand in hers and she would lead him up to the table and find him some strawberry fizz. She wanted to hear the rumble of his voice amongst those other voices and see the flash of his eyes. *Was* it true?

He had warned her, she knew, that if she followed him, she would turn her back on human belonging – this festive company that was everything she so loved and desired – had *longed* for through the cold months of the spring. If she took his path, there would be worse perils ahead, and darker flights and deeper forests.

Her eyes roamed the garden from face to smiling face. The healing had been in her hands. She had *felt* it. The healing had stitched her own soul back together when it was torn apart with grief, and brought her sweetness like honey. She didn't feel angry any more... But she hadn't finished.

She took the Sami amulet in her hand and gently rubbed the bone.

"I wish Grandfather Larsson would come," she murmured. "I wish he would come and show me that he is alive."

Against the backdrop of the music she heard a sudden commotion, a rustle amongst the leaves, and the excited barking of Bella the dog.

Suddenly, out of a stand of dense bamboo, burst the figure of Mr. Brambling, dishevelled and half-naked. His bare feet hardly touched the ground. His scanty hair stood on end. With outstretched hands he clutched the air before him, eyes wildly fixed ahead, and shot into the herb maze where the stands of hyssop and mullein instantly hid him from view.

One second later, came Mordred, the cockerel, the blood-red webbing between his claws glowing with diabolical intent, his crimson comb a-flame. Mordred was out to kill, and Brambling had no fork for his defence. As the creature thundered by, the very ground trembled. Wings low, his green-black, glossy-black tail held high - a mere blur of beak and spur - he flashed upon the retina like a sun spot and vanished also amidst the herbs. After him dashed Bella, yapping for all she was worth. And Trudi involuntarily joined the chase, brushing past the sage and catmint that straddled the path, all the scents of summer swirling in her head. She must keep Bella's tail in sight or she would lose her

419

way... hyssop, southernwood, fennel and rue... rosemary, tansy, thyme, feverfew... herbs for healing, herbs for eating, herbs for magic and poison too!

She rounded a corner of angelica and stumbled out into the central clearing. Before her, stood the cockerel - Bella playfully snapping at his heels. And behind the cockerel, the arch which Pedro had located on their first visit, where a green-painted door now stood ajar. Trudi did not remember the door. Mr. Brambling must already have gone through.

Mordred let out a stentorian screech and rushed at Bella so fearfully that the little creature whimpered and fled. He then strutted to the threshold, turned, and eyeing Trudi, slowly and deliberately winked. The eye that held her gleamed a moment like a shard of ice, a blue so pale it seemed hardly of this world. And yet she had seen such eyes before and she had seen the snow they dreamt of...

Over there, beyond the door, the white trunks and dark shadows of a birch forest beckoned. It was winter there. Mordred slipped quietly through the opening and was gone. The Elk and the Hunter - the chase must go on. *"Ju have to go through..."* Pedro had said.

Behind her, the garden rang with the sounds of merry-making. They had three instruments playing now - Jurgen had joined in with his cello. And there was to be syllabub for pudding. And her mother had promised to pin up her hair in a chignon like a proper grown-up, and Kirsten was so gentle when she brushed your hair, you could purr like a pussy-cat. Trudi had never seen her so happy. And they were all going to look at Barbara's shop tomorrow and Sister Bianca had given her her very own copy of the Canonical Hours. And tonight, when the nuns went back to the convent, they would crowd into the little cottage parlour and tell stories by lamplight and play with the magic lantern...

For a moment she hesitated, her hand on the handle of the door. Which way should she go? How was a young child to choose?

The birch trunks gleamed, enigmatic and still. The garden glowed in the sun.

Trudi took a deep breath and felt the beating of her heart. Then she bit her lip. Yes, she knew what she must do...

FINIS